The Fall and Rise *of* Landon Harris

A Novel

By

Dirk Wales

ALSO BY DIRK WALES

Shadow Angel

A Lucky Dog: Owney

Abandoned

Twice a Hero:
Polish American Heroes of the American Revolutionary War

The Further Adventures of A Lucky Dog

Love Scenes: Number One to Ten

Jack London's Dog

The Giraffe Who Walked to Paris

TABLE OF CONTENTS

CHAPTER 1

The Eighth Book

1

CHAPTER 2

The Ritual

16

CHAPTER 3

The Yankee Racing Sisters

32

CHAPTER 4

The Ninth Book

40

CHAPTER 5

How To End the Short Story

60

CHAPTER 6

The Book Tour

78

CHAPTER 7

The Three Legged Dog

95

CHAPTER 8
Some Places Along the Way:
Buenos Aires to 72nd Street Harbor
121

CHAPTER 9
Yet Another Book Tour
143

CHAPTER 10
Back to Basics
161

CHAPTER 11
Cross Currents
177

CHAPTER 12
The Crucible
208

CHAPTER 13
Angels
261

CHAPTER 14
The Tenth Book
313

CHAPTER 15
Bridges and Tunnels
323

THE EIGHTH BOOK

*O*n the bright Fall Monday morning when Landon Harris was to give the send off speech for his new book, the sun room of his apartment overlooking New York's Central Park was filled with Landon's Sunday Sprawl. Sections of the *New York Times* covered all the furniture and leaked out into the living room. It would seem that he would start with the Travel Section in his bedroom, the trail then moved to the kitchen where he would have orange juice and the Magazine section. Moving to the writing room provided for a quick email check and a glance through the Books in Review. Splendid. Lawrence Stennam had a new novel called, of all things,

[*Directions for the Use of the Novel.*] Good title.

Landon wondered if mainstream readers would pass it by thinking it was yet another book on how to write, deal with, think about,consider lost, or forget about —"literary fiction". He scanned the review, which was favorable — and, yes, it appeared to be a story quite nicely rendered. He would have to come back to that. No email. Then to the bathroom to brush teeth, brush hair, and scan the front page. Must be a slow news day.

Now, looking in the mirror on Monday morning, getting ready for the luncheon, Landon Harris noticed himself. Not given to extensive self-appraisals, he was surprised for a moment. It's odd, he thought, how people don't look like who they are supposed to be. He recalled a photographic exhibit he had once seen. It was in the form of one of those maddening quizzes. Match column A. with the correct (fill in the blank) from column B. But, it had a clever touch. The Photographer had taken portraits of 25 people dressed non-professionally, and 25 pictures of them at work, but in such a way that you couldn't readily see the person to identify them in their setting. One always guessed wrong, or if right, one was doing just that, guessing. He didn't look like a writer. He didn't have any writer friends who looked like writers. They looked like accountants, engineers, not lawyers, but longshoremen, grocers, dressmakers. Landon leaned into the mirror to look more closely. James Joyce looked like a writer. Hemingway looked like the prizefighter he wanted people to think he was. George Spelvin looked like a wealthy longshoreman. Joyce Carol Oates appeared to be a North Shore Chicago housewife-philanthropist, for God's sake, and she has written more books than any three of us put together. John Updike looks like everyone's favorite college professor.

"And, you, Landon Harris, who the hell do you look like?" He reached down to the water tap and turned it on, lifting up a handful to splash water on his image in the mirror. The light from the small window was just right, it caught the water on edge to show him as a double image with himself behind the water, and another himself reflected ON the water. He needed to stop dawdling and walked into the bedroom, trying to remember what today's speech would be. The first speech for the eighth book — there had been no fancy luncheons at places like the Waldorf for the first two books. Then, at some point in the process, this word always came up: Literature. Lit-er-a-ture.

Production of literary work. Writing, was always the word that ran headlong into it, like some sort of Steinberg cartoon. I am a writer not a literate. He had looked up "literate" one day: *2. A person who can read and write.* Yes. But the first definition was *1. A learned or literary person.* What was that? Better, who was that?

He shook his head. No comment. He picked up his speech for the day, it said "…writing is about surprise…." But, it was really about storytelling in a probing way. Some sort of truth-seeking in a most personal way.

How can you say those things in public? Well, it is about surprise. The presentment of surprise. Surprised that it seems true, real; surprised that it seems meaningful, cogent, concise, not sensible, but seductive. He went to the window and looked out at the Park. His father was right, he spent too much time indoors. He needed to go home. To feel Central California. Feel it not just talk about it. Feel the truth of it, the truth of the San Joaquin Valley.

He looked out the window to the park, to the sun… a mantle of solitude closed in around him. When he last noticed, the shadow of the sun was touching the bedside lamp. When he roused himself, the sun had placed a decorative pattern on the bed beside him. Time danced for Landon Harris, the sun was his emissary, and the world was, well, the world was its own problem. He looked at his watch. If he got himself together quickly now, he would be able to walk down through the Park to Central Park South and catch a cab to the hotel. He grabbed the sheaf of papers that was to be his speech and hurried downstairs, across the street and into the Park.

It always surprised him that he could look at one thing and see another. He would walk downtown through the Park and look off to the East side and see mountains as well as tall buildings. Look to his right and see another set of mountains as well as shorter buildings. He had come to understand that the Park was a special version of his own California. It was his double vision: yet there was another aspect to it. Landon enjoyed being from somewhere vague. A place not fixed in a person's mind. "Whereabouts in Central California—?" The question always had an appendage: "…near L. A.?" or, "…near San Francisco?"

"Maricopa." Landon would say.

"Oh," was always the response.

In truth, the last time he had visited, Maricopa was in the last stages of habitation just before joining the ranks of California's ghost towns, though most of them were in the Gold Country. He had walked along a main street that had been normal and friendly, large enough for the standards of a boy growing up. He went into what seemed to be the most prosperous of shops… Jake's Antiques. He had rooted around among the debris of other lives to find a high school yearbook from the year when his father had graduated. His father had one, now Landon would have his own. He flipped through the pages, May 16th, 1941. What a different world. He would go home and show it to his father. Maybe Landon could entice him to tell more stories, always more stories.

For Landon, that part of the world had not seemed to lose its innocence nor its plain beauty. He looked up suddenly and saw Central Park South looming ahead. Here's a place that has lost its innocence and perhaps all the places downtown from here. Landon didn't feel cynical about New York, but he felt that New York was cynical toward most everything about and around itself. Innocence was not a word that seemed to fit New York.

There were many good earnest things about Central California, right down to the names of the smaller towns in the southern end of the Valley: Derby Acres, Simmer, Colinga, Buttonwillow, Los Olvidos, a Spanish phrase meaning "the forgotten." Every state has these colorful, or plain small towns, villages, wide spots on the road, the poetry of the almost invisible. In this part of the lower San Joaquin Valley the land is undramatic. The majestic Sierra Nevadas are far to the east, not visible from the west side of the valley which nestles into the Sierra Madre range. A person could take a bicycle, ride off into this and be lost to a quiet and golden land. In the Spring, the long rolling hills were green. The remainder of the year they were transformed into gold… warm gold.

Landon looked up and found himself looking back into Central Park and the autumn green of it, the high trees and the marvelous statues of Simon Bolivar and Jose Mateos. They were as Spanish as the Central Valley but seemed to be as out of place here as would the town of Maricopa, set alongside the Zoo in the Park.

…and now finally, the speech for the Eighth Book.

"…and so, to hone it to a fine point, writing novels is about surprise. The ability of the writer to devise and invent continual surprise for the reader is paramount…."

The Ballroom of the Waldorf-Astoria is not actually full. A seasoned staff knows just how to "adjust the room" so that no matter how many come, it looks full. Full enough. Nan Talese was there, tapping a spoon on her napkin. Monte Goldfarb of Random House was there, looking suitably intent. Notables sprinkled about the room like salt and pepper on a plain meal.

Off in a corner, two young unimportant writers listened intently to the coming out speech for Landon Harris' eighth book in hopes that they too might learn enough to write books that would bring them all that money, all that fame, and a room full of notables at the Waldorf to sit at their feet. There must be some trick to this, it must be a learnable trick—can't be all that hard, can it? Each of them had read Mr. Harris' eighth book and had been unimpressed and uninspired. Then they read the acceptable reviews… "Landon Harris has done it again, another insightful book full of…." "The latest from Landon Harris is, once more, proof that this inventive American writer…" The only naysayer, a knowledgeable fellow from the

Boston Globe praised it damply… "…one senses here the force of a story full enough. Had it been written at gale force it would have surely blown us away, however…"

Landon Harris continues for the crowd at the Waldorf "…there is so much of our everyday lives that is devoid of surprise, so full of the stale, that the aware novelist is the perfect magician to transform the reader's life… that's what we hope we do… be Magician Storytellers."

Young Writer One looks across the table at young Writer Two and rolls his eyes. Two slips his fist, balled with thumbs down, above the white tablecloth. One is scribbling a note on the back of the Landon Harris Luncheon Celebration Program and pushes it over to Two:

"This guy is out of gas."

Not so, say the clapping hands of the Ballroom at the Waldorf. Landon Harris gets not a standing ovation from the room, but a resounding acceptance and acknowledgement from his peers. Landon smiles for the room. His eyes catch Celia at the Portman table and she beams at him. Canning Vogel, his editor at Portman, notices this and his lips tighten for a moment before turning back to the business of smiling and clapping for one of his profitable authors. Landon, he notices, is not at ease with this crowd. It's not difficult for the aware person to sense Landon sliding back and forth across an imaginary line of his public self and his private self. Canning thought, where does he go when he does that?

Some of the non-trade guests press forward with copies of the new book for an autograph. The book is thin, but the title hopes to be provocative. *One Woman, Two Men* is the latest offering from Landon Harris. The pre-press is decent. Reporters and stringers for papers all over the country are attentive, asking questions, pressing issues, taking pictures for their Entertainment Sections. Celebrity is everything, catch as many details as possible: which person was it that he winked at during the applause... check on this, get more details.

"Mr. Harris, what's your next book?" one reporter asks. Landon smiles. "Hard to say. To tell the truth, my senses are filled with this one."

He holds up a copy of the book and flash cameras fire. "I am not one of those writers who has half the next book written by the time we are pressing this one into the reader's hands. Sorry, but, I'll find my mind clearer one or two days from" and he waves his hand, "all this—give me a call then." Landon does not offer his phone number but turns to the next question.

"What do you think of the newer young writers like Josh Kimble in Wyoming?" It's Writer One's question. Two stands beside him waiting for what he knows will be a bullshit answer. Landon pauses for just a second to consider the young man and to lean into the question. "I like his work very much, particularly *Laramie Calls*. I thought it was a meaningful story written with a real ear for what I call cross-listening." Landon fumbles. "What I mean is that he has a good ear for the dialogue of the everyday, fused to that inner dialogue that somehow needs to be present on the page without pushing at the reader... You know what I mean..." and without waiting for an answer, "all this combined with a dense sense of what literature is trying to be, which is my opinion, most young writers lack." Landon was surprised at his own use of that word.

Young Writer One nods, impressed. Celia has come up beside the two young men, listening to the interchange, nodding and smiling at the young writers as if to egg them on.

"How do you think your new book compares with Kimble's 'literature'?"

"I wish I could have that dialogue with you this afternoon, but as far as I am concerned, my own jury is out on this book for the next week or so. I need to settle into finished work—perspective is hard to grasp when you are in the thrall of trying honestly to make an introduction of what one hopes is a decent book, and," here Landon nods toward Celia, "as well as keep your publisher and editors happy."

A photographer from a Philadelphia paper edges to get an angle on the two young questioners, but it's a shot at Cecilia Langhorne from Portman Publishes! he wants.

A pause hangs in the air, and then Landon says, "They say that Hawthorne, and I don't mean to compare my work with his, would take a full year before he was willing to venture an opinion about any of his work… and one account I saw suggested that after he wrote *The House of Seven Gables*, he wouldn't speak about the book to anyone for several months." Landon looks down at the faces arrayed around the luncheon dais. "Perhaps hearsay, but it fits my bias about how I feel about my own work just after it's completed." He looks at One and Two, "But, it's a good question, thank you."

"You were good, Landon, very good. I know you hate these things, but they are a necessary evil." Landon looked at Canning, his editor, and shook his hand as they moved through the lobby of the Waldorf,

"Another good title, *Necessary Evil*. Makes me wish I wrote in the mystery genre."

"How about letting me buy you a celebration drink?" offers Canning.

As they approach the waiting car, Landon stops and turns to him. Canning is smiling.

"It's good of you to offer, but I have to do this interview on NPR, and then I think I need to go home and recount my dreams, as Shakespeare might say. OK?"

"OK" said Canning. "Good luck on the air."

Landon moved into the back of the black PR-supplied limo and waved his hand at the driver. After the speech, after the questions, after the inquisition, Landon rested his head and watched Park Avenue slip away behind them. Fall in New York is refreshing. Maybe he would rent a car and go up to see the leaves in the Merritt Parkway. His Western self always considered the notion of changing leaves a miracle of the highest order, even more impressive than the rising of the sun and watching the rays measure out the days by inches on the ground. Then, after the leaves, perhaps dinner at the Griswold Inn... some space from New York would be welcome. Some space away in Connecticut from the "what's next?" questions would be the smallest of pleasures.

Landon looked up from the microphone in front of him to see his companions on NPR.

"I had been interested, you know, as we all must be, with the American notion of *One Man, One Woman*—Brigham Young to the contrary. The notion of one man and two women is an aberration... then, the French 'model' comes easily to mind: the ambitious and powerful man who has a wife to show society, she is a most beautiful and dutiful woman to direct the children and the servants. The opposing force is The Mistress—ravishing, guileless, insatiable, a volcano at best. So, it was my notion to explore a relationship... that is, the possibility of the flip side, we might say, a contemporary relationship of one woman and two men trying to lead normal lives... under one roof...."

He reminded himself how easy this seemed... a mike and some people to talk to, versus a ballroom at the Waldorf full of people gaping at him.

Landon continued, "…and, I didn't say in one bed, nor do I mean some romp as in the French films like *Jules and Jim*… I mean a different emotional configuration. Seems almost un-American and I liked that. *Threezies*. So, I began to look into it, reflect, think about place, persona, a different tone. What kind of men would follow the trivial version of this: the worn wispy guy matched with the sexual sizzler? Sounds like a mainstream movie. No, that's not it, not what I wanted to explore. Lets look at it from the female side. Most women tell us that they want one man who starts out perfect who they could mould into someone more perfect as they trip over his flaws. However, if she could have two—what would suit her? Could she then put all her eggs in two baskets… forgive the pun."

He looked at his audience of three people in a darkish room. "If you don't mind, that's all I really want to say about the book just out today."

"Good, Landon. For you listening in, that was Landon Harris giving you a glimpse, and only that, of his new work, *One Woman, Two Men* from Portman Publishes!. Also with us are two distinguished members of the literary review press… Victor Anderson, currently publisher of the *Journal of Iowa Writers*, say hello, Victor.

"Yes, hello out there…" said Victor Anderson, while the host, Marty Klein, held his breath. Rehearsals with Mr. Anderson had been halting for radio—too many pauses make the listeners wonder if they are having electrical problems. Not so with Mary Anne Lewis,

"And, here with Marty Klein and Victor, I am Mary Anne Lewis, with *Contemporary Book Reviews* here in New York."

"Very nice, Mary Anne," said Marty, "and she was good enough to let me in on her burning question for Landon Harris before the program."

"You are not an often interviewed man, Landon Harris, so my sense is that all the questions have not been asked of you…" Landon nodded to her. Unlike television interviews where one feels he or she is laced into a chair and asked to feel comfortable, one really can be comfortable here. A wooden table, unfinished with a few scattered notes in front of a group of three, and a microphone. Landon leaned back in his chair, he liked the directness of this woman, what was her name again?

"What influence has your Central California upbringing had on your work? And, I won't ask you yet what kinship you feel with your fellow Californian, John Steinbeck. I understand you both went to Stanford."

"That's three questions," said Landon.

The group chuckled and Marty Klein jumped in, "I had not thought of the California beginnings, how 'bout that first."

"You might be interested in knowing, as an aside, that when I first began at Stanford, I had heard that Steinbeck had been there. Then I heard that it had been decided by the English Department, early in his time there, that he wasn't a very good writer, and would probably not grow into a writer. Very simply, he left Stanford, un-graduated, and went back to Salinas—no doubt to take his fill again from that deep well."

Victor Anderson came alive. "That can't be true!" Landon shrugged and remembered that his communications must be oral, "That's what I was told. Perhaps the proof in the pudding is to call the Registrar at Stanford and ask what year John Steinbeck graduated. I think you will learn that he didn't."

"That can't be true!"

Marty Klein leaned back from the mike, this might be good. Mary Anne shook her head.

"Well, Victor, look at it this way, you come from Iowa where there is the well-regarded Iowa Writer's School at the University. Is there a chance that one of the poorest students there, some young person with a will to burn, was considered by his peers and professors as "not very promising"?

"But we are speaking of John Steinbeck!"

"And, he is one of your heroes."

"How did you know that?"

"Just a guess."

Landon was enjoying this pulling the wings off the butterflies. "And, speaking of heroes, what I will tell you now is mere hearsay, but, fits the same idea we have here: I met a fellow who had gone to Drama School at UCLA—we are all Californian—with Jimmy Dean. James Dean, you know, that forever-young fellow you see in the movie posters. This man told me that Dean was not even considered a promising actor in their group… that he was a quiet and private young man. I have never read any of the many Dean bios, so I didn't check this out, but the man seemed credible."

"Landon, I have a feeling you are driving at something." This was Mary Anne.

"To be poetic a moment, I think we have to understand that Promise is not always promising or present, but often hidden in the creative person. It may not be evident. Perhaps it's a subterranean stream: a person may have a burning desire and can train himself or herself. Perhaps something comes along, a thing as simple as a match to set fire to this desire to be burning. It worked for Jimmy Dean… go rent *Rebel Without a Cause*, or better, *East of Eden* by John Steinbeck and see the two misfits together.

They all noticed Marty Klein was quite good at this interviewing business. He didn't linger for a moment. Passing over Victor Anderson's defeat to… "What about facing up to Mary Anne's initial question, Landon… What is it about Central California? …and, if I can add another dimension to your answer, why is it that we have all heard of Southern California and

Northern California, but not this unfamiliar land you came from?"

"A good dimension." Landon took a deep breath. It's so hard to know what to talk about when you can't edit it afterwards. He remembered the advertising woman he met somewhere who seemed to be editing as she went, as if she had a tiny woman inside her mouth, just behind the lips, that would snatch the unsuitable words and place them out of sight, letting only the "right" and "good" ones pass.

"The geography between Bakersfield and the East Bay of San Francisco is mainly empty. If we were to take a look at the population, county by county, I am hoping my thought would be borne out. Yet, there is some of the most splendid scenery to be had… Yosemite Valley, the big trees at Sequoia, the marvelous ocean at Pismo Beach and its adjoining dunes.…"

His studio companions were with him in this, but Landon couldn't help wondering if this rambling on wasn't a sure way to lose the listening audience… he sounded, even to himself, like a travel promoter.…

"And to make a short list, off to the side is the Big Sur. It's the only place in the world I go that seems to be more beautiful than the last time I visited."

Victor Anderson, now a defector, was clearly bored by this. Landon was sure he was waiting for the moment, on a live media, to spear him. Maybe then…

"And, to speak of one of the poet laureates of this space between these two known points, if you want to know about these people, then you must read Steinbeck. He was one of them, could intuit them in prose much the way that Edward Albee does on the stage."

"Did you write stories about these people?" It was Anderson.

"Yes, but not successfully. My first story was spoken to a gentle breeze and never recorded."

Landon took relief in the briefest moment to think about Jane and that gentle moment.

"My second story was called "The Girl From Colinga." Frankly, it was awful. I haven't read it for eons, but I have it...." Just before Victor Anderson could find a point to place his spear, Landon continued, "...I am not John Steinbeck. I think it would have been foolish of me, or anyone, to try to re-write his stories, or to find new stories that attempt to take up where he left off... I needed to find my own way, with talent I considered less than his." A split second of dead air. Klein nods gratefully. Landon has successfully warded off something unwanted. Mary Anne Lewis presses on. "But, aside from your first book, which is autobiographical, what is the name, it slips away...?"

"*I Was a Man Just Before I Became a Boy*" It was Victor. "I thought it a meaningful book, and a very different take on coming of age."

"...aside from this book, Landon, you don't seem to spring from this place that obviously has so much meaning for you. I find that puzzling."

"I think that's a good assessment. Though I have been asked this question before, the answer seems insufficient... and, Marty, I am not trying to hide from you or your audience."

A full second of dead air.

Landon bites down hard on his lip. "I don't want to be glib. Honestly, I don't know. I go back to visit. I write to my father who is still alive... my mother died years ago. I know my hometown Maricopa is dying as well... but, I can't seem to find the words or the feelings."

"Perhaps, we are asking the wrong question." Mary Anne moves closer to her mike, "I think we all know without taking a poll, that the central question to a writer is where do you get your ideas? I am going to spare you that, so… my question is, do you think about Central California often, is it a place you go in your mind?"

"Yes. Often. It's easy to say that here in Manhattan where we are the antithesis of those vast golden and often bare hills. New York is not a lonely place, but it seems to suit my own aloneness. This drives me in and not out. I might be pressed to say also that it keeps me out of balance. I think that's good for a person who writes. No, I don't think a person needs to have some sort of a psychological imbalance to be creative, there are many good normal people writing fluently today. But there has to be a catch, something that 'hooks' you, pulls you out of the mainstream of thinking into an inner stream of unconsciousness… then, the trick is to stay there, almost in stasis, <u>immersed</u>. Then, you are ready."

"That might be a good place for us to take a break. Thanks, Landon Harris, for your thoughts and to you two, Victor Anderson and Mary Anne Lewis for yours…."

THE RITUAL

*D*oes the solitude that is natural to the writer seek and surround him, or is it that a person bent to solitude closes out enough portions of his life to create a wall of quietude around him? For Landon Harris, the answer to both questions was 'yes'. He had been fortunate to have an architect friend, now dead, to whom he could confide his needs, and with that, his quirks and darkness. This man, was clever enough, skillful enough to devise the creation of a room that would be unsuspected, unseen within Landon's apartment. The fact that windows were not a requirement made it easier. Windows to the world seemed unnecessary to Landon, who felt, rightly or wrongly, that he could bring whatever of the world was needed into this room.

Tonight is the ritual. It happens here in this room. This is the eighth book, but not the eighth time in this room. The first ritual, for the first book, happened in a different place. The day that *I Was a Man Just Before I Became a Boy* came out, Landon stayed home with Catherine his then wife now lost to him and waited for his agent to call to say that there had been the smallest fanfare. There was no fanfare, said the agent, it would take time, it's a first book, one must adjust expectations. That night rushed into memory. It had been Catherine's night, too. She lit candles, put them on the cover of the book, and paraded through their apartment in Brooklyn with this lighted shrine as a pagan icon. She danced around him as if to promise a lifetime of dancing, candles, love, and published books. She was a woman for pagan rites... long fingers, slender form, sharp features that would reveal their intelligence one dance at a time. Oh, yes, the greenest eyes a man had ever seen. God, he loved to look into those eyes.

Landon could close his eyes at any moment, and there she was, still dancing for him. Lithe and loose, free as air, light as an angel. My Catherine, oh, my God...

They decided to read this first book together in the candle light. It started as a lark, but it only took pages to "get serious" about what they were doing: really reading the book to see if it held up, had haft, worked. It was Catherine who found a catch in the flow of story. He had missed it, but she was right. This part, this chapter and the character's movement through it did not work, did not track with the meaning around it. It seemed the only major flaw. They finished the book, but went back to talk about the flawed chapter 'till the sun came up. Catherine made breakfast. They talked about the lesson learned, took each others clothes off and made love until late afternoon.

Landon, standing on his own at this moment—now richer, now without her in this world—felt he was in a rainstorm, one you couldn't leave behind a closed door. God, he missed her... a real, live angel. A woman you could stay up with talking all night. A woman with a racing mind, like a throughbred horse: colors, head high and a winning streak. Since Catherine, Landon had not been able to share this evening with another person, though he had once tried. The night after the public offering of a book became sacred in a manner defined by Catherine. She had not intended a ritual, but after she died, it made sense to stop everything and face this thing you had written and were asking the world—all 100,000 copies—to read and admire.

He took a copy of the book out of his case and placed it on the table in the dining room, facing the park. He fetched candles from the flashlight drawer, fumbled with matches and candle bottoms to wax and adhere them to the book. He threw the matchbook away and searched for wooden matches, cursing those people in Ohio for letting the matchbook people get a foothold on fire. Wooden matches made sense! Now, they were lit. How could something this simple and strange be an emotional moment for a grown man? He turned out the lights and walked, book in hand, illuminating his own way around the apartment. Yes.

Yet, even with this high feeling should he continue to do this? Is this really… necessary? Hadn't he learned enough about writing? Was this a lesson to be had? Or was it the best way to be in touch with his own personal blithe spirit. He stopped in the middle of the room and realized that he needed this—a bringing forth of the Candles-on-the-Book Shrine to see if he could conjure her presence once again. If he learned anything about the book, well, that was a plus, if not, it was the best feeling he could possibly have. So, he did more turns around the living room ending face-to-face with his own image in the window hovering over Central Park like a loving Olmsted. And, then it happened—he was filled with her, as if he was a candle in the shrine itself. Warm. Lit from within. God!

Landon walked down the hallway to his writing room. He set the shrine on the desk, empty but for a stack of typed pages half an inch thick. He looked around, candle light flickering and bouncing off the paneled walls, glinting on the brass tabs that identified, drawer by drawer, everything he had ever written. The candles danced a frenzy in the non-existent wind. Can they conjure a gentle breeze in a windowless room? No, it was not time to abandon this practice, as arcane and bizarre as it might seem. This was about Catherine, about the book, and perhaps even wizardry—but it was also about him, self-absorbed as he was.

Landon moved toward what appeared to be a small stage between two wooden columns and pulled the curtains back. A bed chamber worthy of Proust or Nannette d'Fabre, the French woman who managed to sleep with the King and Robespierre on the same night. The chamber had a white fabric ceiling with lights mounted above for a sense of illumination that could be adjusted to your mood. There was a control panel which enabled one to turn on and off the television, start up the computer, double-lock the doors to the room and manage all apartment needs. A guest in the lobby foyer could be heard on the speaker here, be admitted, or turned away as if no one were home. The bed felt large enough for a picnic… and it was here that Landon set the new book in preparation for a good night's read. He turned again to see the room in this light and then reached for his coffee. From a more down to earth vantage point, the results of this night would determine what came next. What book, what idea, where North might be on the new compass. Oh, there were notes for new books, there were files of ideas, languid ideas written on napkins or ticket stubs. All that nonsense. But, Landon knew that what came out of tonight's read would determine what came next. So, will it be sand or stone?

As he settled into the book, he had to remind himself to slow down. The trick was to make himself into a reader—The Reader. After a person has read something so many times—imagine how much of that is necessary when you are a novelist? The need here is to discover, as the reader does, the story, its meaning, and its people, along with all the other subterranean nuances one hopes will be caught in the reader's subconscious net. When he had read with Catherine, and he was going too fast, she would pat him on the arm, and he would slow to her reader-like pace.

Landon was particularly pleased with the beginning of *One Woman, Two Men*. He thought he had caught nicely the metaphor of the central idea.

It was Landon's notion that woman have evolved to the point that they could claim their natural emancipated desires: two people—men—one for each different side of her nature. Men had been doing it for eons.

Now he reads… "if the Ark had been designed by another, other than Noah, perhaps a more playful and, may we say, daring person—then why not one female and two males—as pairs?"

"Against the odds, you say. Well, certainly as good a balance as the adage that one man can satisfy more than one woman. Must have been a powerful person who said that. So, this story is about a powerful woman, Scotty Kendall, who sayeth…"

All this is a huge conceit, I mean, who the hell is this writer to tell women of the world what they want, he doesn't even have a wife *or* a mistress… how could he *know*. By midnight, Landon was at page 57, the candles were still going strong, the rush of the opening continued with gale force. The world was right, he hoped.

It was on page 91 that he had the first stumble. The idea began to thin out in the character of Mathew. Does this guy really have proper dimension? Does he have the weight to… or have I made him into a featherweight and therefore, a cardboard character? Mathew didn't balance right with Scotty Kendall in this scene, or, now he thought about it, in others previously. That was certain. Well, a small lapse. Landon moved on, careful now to read even slower. At page 107, this…

> …oh, how can you be so, so obstinate, Mathew, of course I love you as much as I love Mark, how could I not. You are, I mean, just wizard, you are the perfect man, you are all. Now, stop your face with this. I mean it. How could you question who we are and what we are doing now when we have been through so much together. We made an 'arrangement', yes. We said we would not brook these petty jealousies. If you do this, this thing now, you

who love to change rowboats in midstream, you will upset us all. You don't want to do that do you! You want to continue, you love what we have become, don't you. Don't you?

Landon looked up from the book. Sure, Scotty Kendall might say this, but this was supposed to be the part of the story where it would be fair to question—fair to pay for insurance that this was a right idea, for a woman, as well as the two men. But now she was out of character. Landon had rushed ahead of himself. Not good.

At page 128, Scotty Kendall became as predictable and mundane as possible. As an echo, the candles on the desk guttered out. Landon looked up, he had been so concerned with what he was uncovering, that he forgot to replace them. He dialed up the bed lights and looked down at the book in his lap. It was beginning to resemble a basket of snakes.

…aren't we trying to elevate nature here, Mark? Aren't we try-ing the great loving experiment? We three are doing something that no one has really tried, to fuse ourselves to a new nature, to prove to ourselves that the great Two that everyone has elevated for eons is just, well, foolish. We say, we sing, that a new nature of person can be discovered, unselfishly, and that Three people can merge as, well, I said it, we Three! But now, the end result is that we all feel as One.

"Oh, no," Landon heard someone say. He looked up to confirm that he was alone. He heard it again…"Oh, no…," said Landon Harris, celebrated novelist. "What… what have I done? This is not a real and sensible per-son—the Scotty Kendall I know and have spoken for. This is some sort of a manic New Age no-sense lady trying to convince herself of something she doesn't believe and neither will the reader."

Landon kept still for a moment and then said out loud, "And, neither do I."

He got up to heat the coffee. The book fell on the floor. He settled back for a moment watching the fluttering candles and drifted off before he could move a muscle.

He was in a high tower, round in the sense that it was shaped like a bird cage. No bars but slots, vertical slots that went from the narrow ceiling to the wider floor, which was covered with pencils. Hundreds of #2 yellow pencils rolled on the floor. These were the pencils he had used in school, had written his early stories with. He tried to move to the windows but stumbled on the way there.

Out the high window there were distant clouds, yet he could see clearly below him. It was far to the ground. Perhaps there were stairs and he could walk down. It might be a lovely journey, something like a magical stairway in the movies… was he in some fantasy film with a curving stairway that people were always traipsing up and down? Was he dead? Landon pinched himself… no, blood was still pumping.

What he had not noticed was that underneath the windows and stacked around the tower room, appearing to be an architectural mass, was actually book pages. What was not #2 pencils on the floor was blank pages. He picked one up. See, it was a book page—clean and blank. Well, why not, he thought, I haven't anything else to do. He picked up a pencil and, leaning against the wall which became his desk, he wrote. After each page, he would let it fly out the slotted window. He wrote faster and faster, and the pages flew quicker and quicker. He found that he could write and watch the pages fly away at the same time. Yet, there was something queer about this. He wrote a sheaf of pages, holding each while he wrote the next, and when he had a handful, he pushed them in the slot and let them fly away at the same moment. He watched them catch the wind. They scattered into a cloud of pages, then dispersed and then—disappeared. Poof!

What? He could do all that writing and the pages would disappear? No one would see or read the pages? He reached for one more page, a fresh pencil and wrote three words:

PAGES OF WRATH

Landon let the page catch the wind in the slotted window. He watched it as if it was an odd-shaped bird. This page sheered into the wind stream, and then began slowly floating to earth. It was almost poetic the way it flew this way and that, floated for a moment before descending more and more until he knew it would not disappear, but would find its way to earth. One page. A page of wrath.

Landon roused himself. The candles were dead on the desk beside the bed. The coffee was cold as he picked it up to sip. The book? Where was the damned book? Gone! He got up and looked around the bed for it... it had his notes—oh, there, under the blanket, hiding, hoping not to be found. Landon Harris laughed aloud and walked out of the room into the apartment. Laughing and laughing. What did he think, he could go down to Portman Publishes! in the morning and submit his changes to the "manuscript"? What a joke.

In the middle of the living room he collapsed in tears on the couch. He felt his body shake and twist with an agony that was unfamiliar to him... his skin seemed to be stripped to a bony shell that would be repulsive to see. He would never be able to write again. He would be nobody. People would whisper about him in restaurants. He had to get up, the walls seemed to be shriveling. Get out. Test if others could see him... to be sure he was visible.

As he passed the night doorman, Charlie greeted him. "Oh hi, Charlie... never see you, I must be living a quieter life these days." "Well, here you are Mr. Harris, getting back out. Pretty late start, eh?" Landon nodded and went out into the street and crossed over to the Park.

In the darkness of night, Landon's double vision allowed for Central Park and his Central Valley. On most nights when he walked here, he lifted his view to see the obscurely lit windows in buildings that were dark arrows racing uptown on the east side of the Park, then shifting his view, Central Park West racing uptown to gain momentum to leap the disparate sea to Columbia Presbyterian Hospital. Between these was a calm valley. Trees in the middle of all this cement, ponds for sailboats, even Alice in Wonderland was there, smiling always at her visitors. There were rises, meadows, walks, but old-fashioned streetlights were the only out of character element. Hell, it might not be a calm valley like home, but to his mind, it continued to create a family resemblance that quieted him. On other nights, this was a balm, but tonight it felt like a dark tunnel with hands , instead of trees, reaching out for him. Streetlights began to quiver. Shadows moved alongside... and then it began to rain—he had not noticed the dark and fast moving clouds above him. Could it be that the sky was part of his new enemy? He quickened his pace wondering if maybe this was a good time to go back to the real Central Valley for a visit and some respite.

Maybe.

Everything was 'maybe' now.

Landon Harris rang the buzzer to Celia Langhorne's apartment. Minutes passed and he rang again.

"Hello... hello... who is it?"

"Celia, it's Landon... Landon Harris. I know, ah, it's late, but can you... buzz me up?"

"Landon? Wha... Landon, what are you... you're all wet. Come in. Is it raining?" He stepped into her apartment. It was warm. "It's only just started."

"What are you doing out so late... my God, it's 3:34 ...are you all right?...I don't understand..."

"Sorry." He walked in to stand in the middle of her living room, dripping.

"Can you make me some coffee?" He turned to her, "Listen, I've had the worst night of my life and I was out walking trying to find myself. I, ah, need to have someone to talk to... can you...?"

He had never really looked at her. Not her best moment, dressed in a shapeless, flannel gown, light blond hair awry. But, there was a lightness about her, he thought, a lightness that fitted nicely with her intelligence. She had a fine mind, he knew that.

Celia walked toward the kitchen, glancing at the mirror to regard herself. Her eyes moved to Landon Harris off behind her, standing in her apartment as if he was in the middle of a traffic accident.

"Sure, good idea, some coffee."

Landon dawdled into the kitchen.

Celia said, "You were good at the Luncheon today. Nice light talk."

"I liked those two guys who wanted to talk about Josh Kimble."

"Mm." She dropped a cup, Landon moved to pick it up. "Didn't break," he said.

"Good."

Landon settled at the counter between the kitchen and the dining room and pretended to watch her. He looked out the window and could see a corner of Central Park. He felt her hand on his and it startled him. He turned to see her put a mug of steaming coffee in front of him with her other hand.

"Landon, why don't you tell me what happened tonight?"

She moved to the other side of the counter to sit beside him.

"My book is trash," he said. He felt her tighten.

"Oh, Landon, the book is not trash. But, how dramatic you can be. The book is just fine. It's postpartum jitters, surely you've had them before."

"Never"

"Well, you're lucky... it's genetic with many writers, generic as well. What do you usually do after the book is finally out of the way."

"Well, but it isn't, is it. I have a book tour scheduled and unlike many of my fellows, I hate them. Some one should write a horror story entitled *Book Tour*."

"Have you planned your next book?"

"I can't do that until this is away. I need to focus, there's too much distraction... there should be one person to write the book and another to do everything else... what a waste."

Celia looked at him not knowing what to say next. She moved to the kitchen and more coffee to pour for him.

"You're not having any?" he said.

"Nope, too early, or too late..."

"I'm really sorry."

She shrugged.

"You wrote a book yourself... something about sailing... right?"

"Yes." She said, "*The Yankee Sailing Sisters*. It did very well. Did you read it?"

"No." Landon looked out the window again. "My book is trash... not even insightful trash. Just garbage." He turned to look closely at her, "...not even glittering trash. Just Trash. Another good title. Can we change the title on the second run, if there is one?"

Landon didn't sense the shift in her. "Come in here and sit down. Tell me what happened."

She handed him his cup and guided him, as if he was a child, to the sofa. If Landon had been watching, he would have noticed that Celia Langhorne had made a willful transformation right in front of his eyes. Her mind began to run on two tracks instead of one: on one rail ran the Landon Harris Express, listening carefully to the tale of his dead wife, the Evening of the First Book, the Evening of the Second Book, the candle shrine they created to deify all this, carefully noting his tears and dramatics, his wrath at the Gods of Letters, his fears that he might no longer be a household word if he lost his place on the *Times* list. Celia Langhorne was not a hard-hearted woman, but she had been at Portman four years now and had been treated to such an array of histrionics from writers that this sort of performance lost its edge. It's not that she was unsympathetic, she was, she needed to be—professionally—but there was a...

"I don't want to be dramatic, but I think I have done something serious. I think I have created a horrid book, and that people will laugh at me, and that..."

"...that they won't ask you to speak at Stanford anymore?"

"Yes. That's what I am afraid of."

Something snapped in Celia, and she began to roll on her other track.

"Listen, Landon, the list of authors who have written one so-so book is as long as from here to the Hamptons single spaced. This will pass, believe me, and you will..."

Landon looked deeply into her face. "You know?" Something fell inside his body.

"Yes, Landon I know."

"You aren't even my editor." He felt it hit something else inside his body and bounce up against yet other part. An internal tennis match with spiked balls.

"No, I'm not, but we do have editorial meetings."

"Then Canning knew, too, and he didn't tell me."

"No, he didn't tell you."

"You didn't tell me?"

"No. No, I didn't tell you."

"Who else?"

"Me. Canning. Hobart. We three."

"You didn't tell me, any of you, you didn't try to help me, you couldn't...."

"What you don't realize, Landon, is that you have become prickly to deal with as an author. You have had seven fine successes, and considerable promise, but you have let those seven books make you... now I have to say this—not a pompous ass, not a Richard Clinger, not—not anyone, but someone who doesn't want help with his prose. Someone who isn't interested in another perspective and some frank talk."

"This is not my fault, and I won't take the blame for it. Goddammit, you people are supposed to help me," Landon said, near tears.

"I am not 'your people', Landon, I am not even your fucking editor. You come here to ask me to comfort you, be someone to talk to in the middle of the night, and it is the exact middle of the night. I will be glad to be that, and that only, but there is a real life that begins at 7 or 8 in the morning that we all have to subscribe to like *Time* or *Newsweek*. So, I will help you all I can in the middle of the night, but there is a place here where the ice gets thinner."

By now Celia is up and across the room, shouting at him. Landon has become stiff as a board on the sofa. Dazed.

"Oh, shit, Landon, We're not going to get anywhere with this. You are a man I have never met tonight, and to be honest, you are getting more and more unfamiliar. Get out of here."

As if Landon also could switch tracks, he said, "While I was reading the book, I found passages that were awful, and not true to the book, the story, or the characters. How can this happen? Could I be that unaware?"

"Your Catherine was right, bless her soul, she knew, twice in a row that you had to look deeply into yourself at the end of a creative experience... let the mirror speak to you."

"I miss her."

"It might seem odd to say, but me too. I would have liked Catherine, she seems like a... how to say it and not be trite, a lucky man's find. But, there is a bright side to this."

Celia moved to the chair across from the sofa and leaned on it. "You know, Landon Harris, you are still a lucky man. You will survive this, you have enough credit in the bank with your 'public' that they won't even notice you have written a so-so book..." She paused to let his flinching sink in. She almost enjoyed this. "Yep, that's how we need to think of it, a so-so book, but you are still with us—you have not gone to the top of the Empire State building and jumped—you have found yourself out. That, lucky man, is a blessing... B L E S S I N G. Spell it right and count it dearly."

"So... you mean... this is my fault, right?"

"Right."

"No one will ever tell me that I am about to make a huge mistake."

"Only if you let them. Only if you can hear them. Only if your next lecture at Stanford is titled, *Humility and the Art of Listening in the Writer's Life*."

"You are a cruel woman." Landon paused. "Isn't this the place in the movie where the man and the woman accidentally touch and end up in bed?"

"Absolutely," Celia said reaching over to touch him. "In every single bad movie and wretched book I have ever read. It certainly has been, Mr. Harris, a marvelous and unique experience here tonight. Let me get your coat."

"But what will I write?"

"You will think of something."

THE YANKEE RACING SISTERS

$\mathcal{T}$he Langhorne sisters have a fierce reputation along the Rhode Island coast. Fierce competitors, dogged sailors, with the skills necessary to back them up. The family home on the headlands overlooking the coast has a room, facing the ocean, full of flags and trophies the sisters have won sailing. In the place of honor, in the middle of that room, is a framed certificate from the organization that journals shipbuilding along the Atlantic, as well as the Pacific Coast. The citation was simple:

> To Celia and Nora Langhorne for Excellence in Ship Design:
> THE REPLETE

"Nice blow, today," said Nora.

"We should have been out yesterday too," said Celia. "Would have had a chance to get the boat shaped up more."

"Don't fret."

Celia looked at her sister and to the shore. It was this strip of the world that defined her, she thought. Not just the land, and being from Rhode Island. Not just being at sea, but being at sea along that strip of land, always able to see the joining of the two.

"How's Ned?"

"Passable. Just sliding by."

"That bother you?"

"Yes, and it bothers him."

"And…"

"My hope is that he will give up the company and move on. I'd like that to happen"

"I can imagine."

"No, dear, you can't," she looked at Celia and then away.

"Am I missing something here?"

"Uh huh."

"Care to share?"

"You'll hate it."

"Trim the jib, will you?"

"Dr. Blackstone tells me that I have pancreatic cancer, and that the people at The Brigham last year missed it, so that it's further along."

The sisters were not even a year apart in ages. When they were kids, instead of Nora always chiming in that she was the oldest, they somehow got the idea that they were twins, though they didn't look alike. Nora the thinner and later to become the more attractive; Celia more moon faced, with blue eyes that could be grey at a moment's notice. In all other ways, they were spoon and fork, moon and stars, all but joined at the jib. When the opportunity to work together at Scully's Ships turned up, they both applied for the design job and convinced Scully that he should know a good thing when he sees it, that they would not need double salary, but only 150%. No one was clear about how Celia, an English major from Brown could match the skills of Nora, a design major from the Rhode Island School of

Design and a year and a half at an engineering school. But they were fork and spoon, stars and moon, all but joined at the jib.

In four years they built three ships, the last of which, The Replete, was sold to a banker in Amsterdam, who had the ill fortune to die on the voyage from Bristol, USA, to Holland. Both Celia and Nora were aboard with him. Instinctively, they buried him at sea, after dutifully radioing the news to both sides of the Atlantic. When they arrived in Amsterdam, the banker's three daughters took them to the family home near The Hague. There was a memorial service, followed by a Dutch wake, and it was there that the banker's daughters gave the ship's papers for The Replete to Nora and Celia.

They owned the boat!

"What the hell, Nora, let's just keep going."

"Keep… you mean, go on from here. Not go home?"

Celia hugged Nora and whispered in her ear, "We can sail this treasure around the world, write a book about it, retire to the coast of Rhode Island and dedicate our lives to the search for The Perfect Man."

"I thought you said the one you met Monday was pretty close." Nora looked at the cloudy eyes of her sister. "You didn't… you slept with him, on the first night! Why in the world did you do that…you knew he belonged to Lisabeth, she may not be as welcoming as we need her to be if you keep this up. Surely he told you they were thinking about marriage."

"You said we were leaving soon. We just wanted to say 'good-bye' to each other." Nora grabbed her sister's hand and pulled her out the door, "Let's take a planning walk over to the docks."

It was *The Yankee Sailing Sisters* that landed Celia the starting job of

Assistant Editor at Portman Publishes! First paragraphs of novels are collected in other books, or printed in the Book Review sections of newspapers, but not casual travelers' journals. Yet, *The Washington Record Books Section* quotes from Celia Langhorne's embarking 'paragraphs':

> The oceans, it would seem, are the best teachers. We got to know our professors well. As day sailors, we sought Atlantic tides and succeeded even on rough days.

> That was only kindergarten.

> Sailing against the routes of Magellan and Drake, we met the Indian Ocean. Rounding The Cape of Good Hope, we thought, how could this be any different? Gentle tides, occasional riffs, cloudy days. Like any great teacher, its prologue was pointing and prodding, urging us on. At latitude X and longitude Y, an examination was held: our boat was held in the hands of Titan-sized sea Gods. In a sink-or-swim situation, one doesn't think of these Gods as playful, yet it was as simple as that. We could hear their laughter in the winds as they played catch with our ship… they never tired until the end of the 37th hour, and finally, in a fit of inattention, they tossed us away to drift and bake on a windless sea for yet another day.

> Those moments in life when you seem to have graduated from the rulers of arithmetic to the annals of math philosophy are stunning, exhausting, and yet, the benevolence of this form of instruction is enough to allow you the pleasure of being a Graduate in the oceans that follow.

> It can't be an accident we named our ship The Replete.

Unedited Notes for a lecture at Stanford University
Graduate English Department

by Landon Harris

14 May, Palo Alto—two weeks after the publication of the Sixth Book

There is something comforting about being here, about being asked for the second time to talk to you, the future writers of …America. Sounds odd doesn't it? I'm speaking about you. But, the first time I came, I was too intimidated to say that another comforting part of being here is that this is the English department that told John Steinbeck he would not make it as a writer, or not be a very good writer. So, he packed his stuff and trekked down to the Salinas Valley and began writing stories and later, *Tortilla Flat*, to be followed by *Of Mice and Men*, to be followed by, my goodness, *The Grapes of Wrath*. I got off the Steinbeck boat after *Travels with Charlie*. I got bored with the dog. But, I am proud to be born in the same state and live in the same world where John Steinbeck wrote. I hope, someday, to write my own *Grapes of Wrath*… God help me. (leave time for a laugh here). But I am only on my sixth book now… there is time.

The subject here is *what does it mean to be a writer*?

I would like to walk down into the audience and speak quietly to each of you—ask that question, and record your answer. It would certainly inform me… I say that because until this invitation, I had never considered my writerliness. I never looked at myself in the mirror that way, or if I did, then I must have said to myself that I didn't seem to appear to be a writer. So, you and I start fresh here today.

I recall specifically that I hated the jacket cover design, I loved the typography… they say that, you know, type-og-ra-phy. I hated the jacket copy, and promised myself I would never again let anyone write that for me…But, of course they won't let you write jacket copy. (Shrug here and see if a laugh happens). So, at that moment of feeling myself to be the least worthy and most fortunate writer in the world, or at least in North America, I was already becoming An Author. Let me pause here and say to each of you, no matter what happens to you, how badly you are battered by the commercial forces around you—don't forget that Annie Dillard says in public that your chances of being published are almost nil, and that doesn't have anything to do with the worth of your work.

You must always be making notes, notes for your next story, and the story after that… not to be obsessive about it, but to be realistic about your floatation devices. You need to keep yourself afloat in this writing world. I can tell you from the drawers full of my own unpublished work, that if you don't create your own life preservers and have plenty of spares, you will be sunk by the large and small guns of those who… and I have always wondered about this and them: what is it that they are trying to keep you from? What do they want to preserve for themselves? How are they the (holy) keepers of the flame and the word? On days when the rejection slips come three at a time, this is a difficult thing to remember. What is easier to recall is the number of books you have bought in paperback, borrowed from the library or from friends who make more money than you, that are not worth the paper they are printed on.

So, what is the criteria here? Where do you draw the line between being good and determined? —and being determined but not trivial?

I will share with you a practice that my late wife created for me…us, really. The idea of reading your newly published book, within days of its publication. The simple thought here is, see if it's good. Don't read it as an author or sleepwalker, but read as a reader. See if it works, if you like or hate the characters as you are supposed to, be aware of the story you are putting down. 'Story-Telling.' If you can keep your objectivity and honestly feel that the book works, then you will know if you are meant, not by the Gods, but by you yourself, to keep writing.

The flip side is the hardest part. If you see that what you are writing is …well, there are some words that don't belong here (leave space for laugh here) …words like trivial, drek, unchallenging, old hat, been done—not worthy of <u>your</u> time and sweat or the reader's—give it up! Walk. Find a day job and begin to dedicate yourself to something more, I won't say rewarding, because there is nothing like that, but that will allow you a success experience. Provide a trade for yourself where you can excel, teach at Stanford, (not Berkeley) or Corvallis in Oregon… something, some place where you can make a contribution. Or do something else not related to writing. There is much. Then, for yourself, with no subversive intent, (lower voice here) *write-for-yourself*. No, I don't mean keep a journal, I mean write stories, novels, investigative articles about things you are able to research and have something to say about. Don't trick yourself into thinking that you will, by this misleading diversion, write something you believe has a chance and send to a publisher. It's possible to have true pleasure in writing without being published—to do something for the sheer thrill of doing it and knowing no one will ever read it but your grandchildren.

That's why we write, what and who we write for… ourselves, if to do nothing more than learn how we feel or what we are thinking as we sit and type our fingers bloody. It's really as simple as this. Don't make it into something that can hurt you. Don't let your friends convince you that all your short stories should be sent to *The New Yorker*. If you need to send them to New York, I'll give you my address. Send them to me, I'll read them.

Got any questions? …fire away.

THE NINTH BOOK

$\mathcal{L}$andon felt he was wearing a mask. In fact, as he looked around, he was certain that he was at a masked ball. His sense was that everyone there —dressed for work, dressed for the party, dressed to make out—all were masked. It was a odd feeling for him… since his coming to terms with The Book. Before, he would be approached and be told he had written a fine book… we love it… it's a winner… Landon, you are a talent! Then, he was willing to take these compliments at face value.

But now…

"Landon, Landon, you ol' devil, I have just gotten your new book. I am pages in but not to the heart of it yet. But—here it is—I hear that the deeper you get the better, eh?"

"Well, here's my favorite writer, what an idea! The best twist yet on the triangle… you know, I have always loved John Barth's *Floating Opera* and the marvelous threesome there, but I think you have <u>outdone Barth</u>. Congratulations, Landon…"

"…I have to say I was moved. Positively. I don't see how you do it."

" …it's really different, Landon…"

That was the one that got him. Really Different. Different how? Different better? Different-fucking-awful! Did they know and were just being polite? Or did they not know and just read along as if it was really good, that is, they didn't know the difference.

Halfway through the evening, he felt skewered, a pig at the roast.

"Aren't you Landon Harris?"

He turned to see an attractive woman in her mid-forties. Slender, semi-petite. She seemed familiar, but he knew she was not. She reached out for his hand, and he gave it.

"Yes, I am."

"Good. You won't believe this timing, but I have just read your book and I want to talk about it. Do you mind? I mean, you must be sick and tired of it by now, but I was quite puzzled by it... would you get me some wine?"

No, thought Landon, I won't get you any wine, nor will I talk with you about this. What the hell am I doing here. She smiled at him as if he had just handed her white wine when she had asked for red.

"Of course. Red or white?"

When they were settled in a corner, she said, "I have been confused about this book... oh, I think it's a good idea, and being a woman who has had to choose between partners, I understand the idea, the, ah, concept. But, well, I hope you'll forgive my bluntness, it doesn't feel like you wrote it. You are such a fine writer. I just love to read the flow of your mind... but this is really sort of, well, *stunted* and trashy, don't you think." It was not a question."That's a bit strong, don't you think? Stunted?" Landon replied.

"No, it's tinny, not the real thing, and you have been capable of show-ing real experience."

"But, well, yes, there are some parts that in re-reading, I think are lax... weak... but 'stunted' would seem to compare it to Danielle Steele or..."

"I'm sorry, Landon, really."

She began to back away from him. As she did, he saw that she was not wearing a mask.

"I thought you were a different person, Landon, I have been really rude, and I am most embarrassed. Forgive me."

She turned to go, Landon followed and called after her, "Wait… you haven't told me your name." She looked at him over her shoulder. He looked smaller than she thought he would, and he really needs a haircut.

Landon stood alone while people swirled around him whispering to each other, sloshing their wine. He moved away from the center of the room to a corner that had two chairs and sat. He looked to the other chair and conjured an image of himself. Well, the other chair said, here's the truth of it thus far: dozens of people have lied to you about your stupid book; then, an attractive woman walks up to you, introduces herself, *sin nombre*, tries, at all risk to herself to tell you the simple truth about your precious book, and you, Dumb Ass, get defensive, take umbrage at a word that doesn't suit you. You must be the world's tightest asshole. The other chair paused. Now, what?

The distance between the chairs grew. Landon started to reply to the other chair but it was moving further and further away. Both chairs moved up into smoke drifting through a long open arbor on top of a mountain. There was whispering water. The smoke was now at one end of the arbor. Clear air at the other. On top, bars held the sides of the arbor to each other. A slight breeze came from the side of the arbor nearest the mountain wafting the smoke. Sitting at the end of the arbor, in the tongue of the smoke was Landon, himself, in the chair. The other Landon, himself, was at the clear end of the arbor, sitting in the other corner chair. As the smoke cleared, each recognized himself. As if chess pieces, each took a move forward toward the other and each took a move backward. One more move, no difference. The breeze swirled the smoke continually so that the mirror image was constantly twisted in the smoke. Each thought… I have to do something, I have to… I have… their eyes locked on each other.

"Landon… Landon Harris, what are you doing over here in the corner by yourself? Hey, man, let's join the party."

It was Hally Davis, overdressed as usual, in a three-piece suit and a bold tie. "Come on, now, up and at 'um," Davis' hand gently pulled Landon out of his reverie and into the clarity of the room. They moved into another room. Davis kept asking Landon questions to which he would not wait for an answer before he asked the next question. This was the easiest conversation Landon had all evening. If there is no need to answer the questions, then all is well. They ended up in a smaller room with a knot of people laughing about a joke told by a slender young man with black hair and pale skin in the middle of the knot. Davis asked one more unanswered question as he eased the two of them into the backside of the group.

A small woman in a stunning white gown standing beside the man with black hair said, "OK, Noel, I have always wanted to ask you…" she had a bit more to drink than the rest of the crowd. "Have you ever been gay?" It was as if a rattlesnake had been dropped in the middle of standing horses… some bridled, some just moved away, but the man with the black hair stood his ground and looked at the rattler. He leaned over and kissed it on the cheek.

"Darlene, there isn't another woman in the room that I would rather answer that for than you. Why don't we go out and have some dinner—get something in your stomach, and then go over to your place and get to the truth about that question." His face glistened. Darlene would not be put off, too sloshed to even notice that the other men in the group seemed to have itchy fingers over the very same offer they wished to make to the rattler.

Does every man wish himself this kind of trouble?

"OK, OK. Nice dodge, son-of-a-bitch, but have you ever been a gay guy?"

Noel Chapman looked at each face in the group. Even to Landon and Davis. There was a stage wait until Noel said, "Yes, Darlene, I was gay… for about a year and a half." Darlene touched him, nodding, as if there was an agreement between them and she had just thrown the pen away.

"You going to tell us about it, Noel?"

"Why not."

The women in the small knot seemed to take this with equanimity, but the men seemed divided—half wanted to leave the room, and the other half seemed mesmerized by the rattlesnake and its quarry.

"I had been having a tough time with my writing. No one was reading my short stories, everything was returned unopened. My savings were gone, everything dried up. I was waiting tables at a small dessert place in the Village. On one particular night an older man came in. Well dressed. Soft spoken. Kindly eyes. I waited on him. He tried to draw me into conversation but I was pretty busy. It wasn't that he wasn't an OK guy, he seemed quite civil. He ate, paid the check and gave me a larger tip than the service or the place deserved. When I was clearing away the table I saw he had left a note with the tip. "I'd like to talk with you about something. Can you call me? 686-7733." No signature.

A man in the group whispered, "He's making this up." Noel looked directly at him and said,

"Just like you, I wondered if I should do anything about the note." He looked at Darlene as if to ask her what she would do. He could feel her hot breath three feet away.

"Three days later, I got a letter from my brother asking for money. He was in a jam. I wondered if the note the guy left might be about a job or something that could get cash. I called and he asked me to have dinner with him at his apartment on the East Side." A man off to the side of the group left quietly, brushing Landon as he did. Landon thought this Noel Chapman is either a very brave man, or the best stand-up storyteller in town. Nice pace and delivery. Good hooks.

"The dinner was very gracious, and I'll skip the menu and the décor 'cause I know you want to know why the man wanted to talk to me. He was taking a trip to Italy. He knew a lot of people there and he liked to stay awhile, four to six months, really. He wanted me to go with him. As his companion. All expenses paid. And, as he poured me another glass of wine, ...some new clothes as well."

Noel looked directly into the eyes of each man in the group. He enjoyed seeing the controlled squirm on each face, knowing that man upon man was reaching his own decision about Noel, about the "offer"; and, of course, about himself. At first glance this seemed a no-brainer, but then it became more complex—these men had not worn his shoes, had not traveled his distance, more important, had not faced this crossroad, and Noel's problems that led to it—that seemed to gain common, though silent, acceptance.

"It was pretty plain. No tricks. All the cards right on the table. He never laid a hand on me… then, and when he did, he was very gentle about it."

Even Darlene was intimidated by this urgent frankness, as if the life secrets of a man were an open wound pouring into hands, through fingers, onto the lusty carpet. The hush of the group was deep.

"At first I found that if I kept my eyes closed, it was easier, there was pleasure but it was different, not repulsive, just different, new sensations, some of them quite , well… quite wonderful… he was patient with me. No hurry, plenty of time. He never asked me, for instance, when or if I would ever open my eyes, if I would ever speak to him. When he paid me compliments and said gentle things to me, it was never in bed—until later, when I opened my eyes." Noel paused to take a breath. "He was not a dragon. Just a good man with a taste for something that I had not considered… hell, no, something I was afraid of. I was. Finally, I recognized a feeling that I had with a woman once. A woman I cared for deeply. I had been afraid to look at her for months, and when I did, everything changed. No more making love in the dark. No more Eyes Wide Shut. When I talked to him, finally, I felt better and even safer." Noel looked at the faces.

"Safer, sure. The only one to be afraid of is yourself."

Darlene was shameless, flicking her forked tongue at him. How delicious this was for her—to bring a man down so, and better, in front of such a good crowd.

"How long were you with him? I mean you sound like you came to like it." It was the 'it' that came in at the wrong angle, and the group began to turn away in pairs to talk to themselves. The storm subsided as quickly as it had risen. Noel turned away from Darlene, and took steps toward Davis and Landon.

"You are Landon Harris?"

"Yes, and this is my friend Hally Davis, a literary agent—you might want to ask him to read your writing... I understand short stories are making a deep comeback." Hally looked at Landon with a light bulb over his head. "Don't you have some short stories of your own, Landon?" Landon let that fall on the soiled carpet.

The three men stood looking at each other for what seemed like a long time. Each was deciding if the conversation should continue to be safe, or was there a lingering question. Noel lit a cigarette with an old fashioned Ronson lighter with some engraving on it.

It was Landon who spoke first.

"It was good of you to peel your skin away for these people. You probably didn't have to do that." Chapman nodded. "But, as long as you have, I would like the answer to one more question." Chapman nodded again. Davis was shuffling as if he wanted to run away or get another, stronger drink. Landon turned to him,

"Good idea, Hally, why don't you get us all a refill." Davis, relieved, raced off.

"It's this," Landon continued. "There was a moment, a slight space, where you made your way back to Heterosexuality, something you had been used to, but had not the balm recently. There was a woman who liked you, who you were drawn to... actually, it's two questions if you don't mind." Landon paused to see what the reaction was. No reaction. Was he really going to strip all the skin off his body tonight? "How were you drawn to her? …did it seem familiar, or well—unfamiliar?"

"Is this the 'like riding a bicycle' question?"

Landon shook his head.

"You are more perceptive than I had imagined. No, in fact, it seemed unfamiliar. Not the jarring sensations that I had felt with Noel… yes, his name was just like mine… no, I had to think about it. While I was getting to know her, I… we talked a lot. She knew there was something troubling me, but she let me work with it to a point where she could really help. That was later. In fact, that was the moment you are looking for—why not skip all the lurid details and find 'the moment', your image not mine. One night we were together, I fell asleep in her apartment, in her bed. I had a dream, it was all fuzzy, yet something scared me and I woke up and reached out for the body beside me, which was her. One hand found her face, the other closed around her hair, a lot of it. I screamed. Loud, and she put her hand over my mouth. We lay there for what seemed like… and finally she said to me, 'It's all right now, isn't it?' She pulled me toward her so that all the body points made contact, and hummed a tune in my ear until I went back to sleep."

Over Noel's shoulder, Landon saw Hally returning with drinks, but stopping to chat with someone Landon didn't know. He took Noel's arm gently and moved the two of them off to the side of the room so that it would appear the room was empty and they were gone.

"Would you let me read your short stories?"

"Why?"

"I like the way your mind works. If you can strip your mind in words the way you can in party-storytelling, you may have found a good expression of yourself. I wonder if that carries over into your writing? You are trying to get them published, right?"

"Right."

Noel realized that there was an opportunity here. He was standing with an author who could, perhaps, be helpful. Hally Davis stopped at the threshold, looked into the room, didn't see them, and turned, bewildered, wondering why he was holding, awkwardly, three drinks. He quickly set them on a table, downed one, picked up the other two and raced out of the room.

Landon shifted....

"Sorry to be so seemingly reticent," Chapman said. "It's the skin shredding, I don't do it every day. Stings in the fresh air. Of course, let me drop the stories by your building—that OK? Got an address for me? I'd like to have some feedback." He looked at Landon who now seemed bewildered himself.

"Thanks," Noel stuck out his hand.

Landon took it.

Landon came quickly to the notion that he needed to have some space for a bit of respite. But where to go? For instance, it would be nice, he thought, to have a girlfriend in Connecticut, but nope, there isn't... and, he was looking forward to reading the short stories of Noel Chapman, but he wasn't even certain what that was about.

It seemed like just the right time to BE in his Central Valley, to visit his father. So, he got himself to LAX—Los Angeles... once there, Landon decided to fly directly to Bakersfield rather than drive up from Los Angeles. He liked the drive over the Ridge Route or sometimes up the coast through Malibu and the Ojai Valley, up into Maricopa the back way. Yet now, every fork in the road took forever to decide upon. He had agonized for two days about whether to fly or drive home. Now he was there, at the Bakersfield Airport. He wanted to drive up East along the Kern River just to feel at home, or just to avoid the first words he would have to say to his father. Landon sat at the airport coffee shop for an hour drinking coffee, trying to decide if he should....

"Another cup, mister?"

He finally realized the real agony was facing his father with the news that his new book was nothing special... a blip on the screen, a node on the back, single spaced into oblivion, as Celia Langhorne had said.

"Father?"

"Landon. Great, Son, where are you?"

"In Los Angeles..." he lied, "and I think I'm going to drive up the coast a ways and stay the night. OK with you if I turn up tomorrow afternoon?"

"Fine, fine, Landon, whatever you say, Son.... It sounds like you need some driving and some ocean. Landon nodded at his father on the phone.

"What did you say, boy?"

"I said thanks, Father. Want me to bring you anything from the big city?"

"Just you, Son. Come when you can. I'm here."

It was dark when he got into his rental car. He paused long enough to look at the airport and realize that he had been hanging around the place for more than two hours and had seen no one he knew and no one who recognized him from his jacket covers. He nodded to himself.

The further he got from Bakersfield, the blacker it got. He spelled a-non-y-mous with his finger across the night sky. Must be Greek… name, no name, without a name… yes, he remembered, another word for pseudonym is anonym. Like a pen name. The town limits of McKittrick passed behind him, and then a sign saying 28 miles to Simmler… which he had re-dubbed Simmer. It wasn't in the heart of the Valley, but on the edges, so it would not boil but surely simmer. Now it was really black, yet he could see the outline of the Coastal Range ahead of him, and the halo of what would soon be moonrise.

His mind went back to the party, Noel Chapman and his story of shifting sexes. Good idea for a short story, I wonder if it's in his collection. But, why had Landon been willing to take his book to read? He didn't want to read any goddamn stories. He wasn't interested in short stories any more. He thought back. If he was to count all the books he had written, the collection of his short stories would have been his second book. Trying to sell them in that period had been hopeless, even if some had been published in the Journals. He remembered one about a couple who had been separated by a trip and how she had been able to keep in emotional touch with her man. When his life was at risk in a prairie fire, it was she who reached over thousands of miles to save him. Good images. His first agent, Meredith Casey, had tried hard to sell that book.

He let his mind drift to the stories… 12 or 13 of them, no theme, just a melange of people and places. Meredith had agonized with him about the title and "theme" of them. "How the… how do you expect me to sell these to anybody without an idea of where they are going?" "But, Meredith, they are short stories. One doesn't write them with an overall theme unless you are John Updike for Chrissake." Then she would get stern. "They want a theme. Editors have tidy minds, Landon, they want to focus their readers. Or, to put it another way, we need a theme or a name author. Can you give me one or the other?"

She loved his stories. She said that Landon was a really-really good writer, but even she admitted to being a "star fucker" —she wanted to be in love with famous authors and big money, so that when she finally got one and was having lunch with Michael Korda, Landon Harris had to find a new home. Busted. It was small compensation that, in the end, she had settled on a flash-in-the-pan author, a guy who had great run with one book, and then zero. Busted-busted. Now, Meredith called Landon regularly to ask him to lunch and send him small presents. He hated that.

Perhaps he should have brought Noel Chapman's book with him… good airplane reading. Yes. It would be fun to compare HIS short stories to his own past stories, or maybe even hand the book over to Meredith. Short stories were easier to sell now. A re-discovered genre. What a joke! He would call the housekeeper tomorrow and have her send Noel's book and he would read it here. A diversion. He looked again out to the black sky. He wanted to look anywhere but within himself. Anywhere. Simmer, California. In the summer it would be in the high nineties during July and August. Eyes would be looking west to the higher hills for the smoke of forest fires. The town passed like a firefly and Landon was headed for the Pozo Pass to slip down a back road that would take him by the Mission and onto Pismo Beach. He loved the name Pismo, a small town which was alongside Oceano and the mysterious sand dunes. Who would have looked for a sea of sand along the ocean, stretching inland some five miles. Landon had a school friend who was part girl, part dog. She moved to Oceano with her small dog whom she thought of as her sibling. The two of them roamed the dunes as does the wind from the sea, low and far, kicking white sand up into spirals He wrote a story about her, too… what was it…, yes, The Dune Runners.

The moon was half full and Landon had dreamed his way to Pismo Beach. He was driving on the beach itself, doing 70 miles an hour along that narrow strip enclosed by the dunes on his left and the sea on his right. It was like pavement and he was the silver streak with roaring surf to match. He was not part of this world, but an agent of the moon sent to taste the water and sift the sands. He could live forever here, forgetting everything: the combination of sea and sand had opened a door. There was to be no next book, his wash of jumbled ideas would disappear once he was through that door at the end of the beach. He was a phase of the moon. He was anchored only to the night sky. No need to know that he could not see the end of the beach in the dark, that the hard white sand was not infinite, that somewhere out there was the rock edge of the rising cliffs.

Why had he left this country? He had been happy here. One could write anywhere, people had told him, even before the advent of the fax and the internet. The mails left here and arrived promptly at New York's Grand Central Station. He took his foot off the pedal and let the car coast to a stop. When it did, he got out and walked ahead of the lights to see how far the beach would continue. Twenty yards beyond the headlights was a watery channel with rocks and a lifting headland. The tide was rising. Landon walked to the edge of the stream, found a rock on dry sand to sit and lean against. Finally, peace.

He recalled an American Indian cultural showing in a city he was visiting on a book tour. His hosts had taken him to an exhibit of Navajo weavings and blankets. Compelling designs, close to the heart. Bold colors, rich meanings. One of the young men who made the blankets had spoken to him, making explanations for the art and mystery of the interweavings of thread. "Here," the young Indian had said, and he pointed to a single strand coming from the middle of the blanket to its very edge and then off the blanket, "we leave room for the Spirit to wander from the blanket, to be free and wild." The Indian looked at Landon, "It is the nature of all Spirits to be free." Leaning against a rock pried from his precious golden hills, facing the vast expanse of night ocean, Landon felt free. Tomorrow he would trace his steps back to the middle of the blanket, to his home.

His father still kept ranching hours. They were up an hour before sunrise. As the corona of the sun was tipping the sky to the far east, they were out walking. North, as it happened—the elder Harris, leading the pace, briskly through the open fields.

They looked remarkably alike, this father and son. Ashton Harris had been redheaded in his youth and now had white hair that showed the residue of this redness. They were both about five foot nine. There was a restlessness about Landon's step which fit in nicely with his casual eastern dress. When he was in New York, it was said that he had not accommodated himself to the styles of New York. When he was here, they said the same, that he had not retained his California clothing sensibilities.

As the two approached the Ridge above the town at the edge of Ashton's land, they could see over into the next valley, still in shadow. They followed the spine of the Ridge that reached out in the line of the hills.

Landon, smiled… and thought that everywhere else these might be called mountains, but here they were always hills. Round, shapely, contoured like a woman laying along a fallow field.

"You know, Son, you're not going to be able to put this off forever. You have been with me for a whole day now and not a syllable about the book. I know it exists, because I got the copy you arranged to have sent to me. I know you exist, because you're right here with me. But some way, the book has slipped off the side of something mighty large." Landon looked at his father as this speech was received. His tongue rounded his lips as if the heat of the day was already with them.

"How did the Opening Luncheon go? …you make a good speech."

"Yes, Canning said I did good. Actually, I did better at the radio interviews on NPR."

The older man nodded. "I thought so. But then, I wasn't at the luncheon. I recall the talk for IF… THEN. I believe that was my favorite."

Landon nodded.

They began to move at a slant along the side of the hill into the valley following the dry arroyo. Landon reached over and touched his father on the shoulder. The older man instinctively stopped to look at him.

"Father, the new book is no good. It's… well, it's a seriously so-so book. Flawed. The reviews have been lukewarm, the sort that you get if you have some credit in the bank, and the book isn't just awful."

"How do you know this?"

"I read it," said Landon. He looked up to the Ridge, "Can we walk along the top for awhile?"

Ashton nodded.

"I mean I read it closely after some time away from it, the way that Catherine and I used to do. It's a decent idea for a book and that may carry it. But, it's deeply flawed, and that has thrown me badly off balance."

"How so?"

"I never wrote something bad. Or when I did, I thought I matured away from fuzzy thinking. I hate this." He stopped stone still. A statue on the side of a hill in the middle of nowhere. His east coast cynicism took hold of him before his father looked at him sharply. Then Landon came home again, for the seventh time since he had arrived. He was home and safe. There, he thought, is an idea that has some real meaning.

"I don't know what to write next." Landon laughed and looked away from his father. He felt deeply embarrassed, so to no one in particular, he said, "I have even considered going back to re-read—after all these years — my short stories. Maybe it's time to bring them forward, give them the air they deserve, if they hold up."

"What's good about this is that you know. I would think, in your business, that there are authors who would hide these flaws you speak of behind a façade… you know, mask off the badness, tough it out. I am glad you are not doing that." Landon took a deep breath and let it out slowly. His father did not see him do that, what he saw was his son looking out ahead and catching his breath. Then they looked at each other.

"It's all right Landon. It's a process. There are side trips and blind alleys."

"What do you mean: process?"

"Not the process of doing one thing. The process that informs all the things you do together. What disappoints me is that you have lost your vision, and I know how hard won that was. But, it's as plain as the nose on your face that you have let this stymie you. I am uncomfortable with that," he looked at his son, "and you should be as well."

Landon nodded again. Yes, he thought. That's on the mark.

"What should I do?"

Ashton moved his head quickly as if a fly had buzzed his face, and set off walking again. They walked in silence for almost a mile. Each in his own thoughts. Landon was mainly blank, he knew he didn't know any of the immediate practical steps. His father was right, he was foggy. This must need time, time to process….

"I'm going to get married again."

Landon looked at his father, first in surprise and then in disbelief.

Ashton continued, "It's no disrespect to your mother, she's been gone now 13 years, and if I could marry her again, I would. But, there are things a man can't do without. At my age, companionship gets to be pretty important. Jane Stetson is a good companion." He laughed and looked at Landon, "…thing is, she also makes a very fine cherry pie… no, don't say anything… a man does marry a woman who can make a decent meal no matter what anyone says."

"Then what could I say?"

"Congratulations? Uh, let's see, 'sounds good, Dad' …or, how 'bout… 'when can I meet this nice lady…?' …give you any ideas?"

Landon hugged his father and the two of them held onto each other for several minutes. Landon thought, I will never be too old for this. What a gift, what a gift. This father thought, once a father… and he heard Landon whisper in his ear, "…sounds good, Dad. When can I meet the nice lady? You should have been a writer instead of a ranch manager."

When they had walked further, Ashton Harris said, "We don't have to talk more about it now… but, I want to be straight with you. You and I had a good talk once… forget where we were then, but you had a vision of what a writer means to do. No, not book by book, but a vision of what you wanted to accomplish for yourself as a person who writes for the public. You have slipped away from that in the service of one bad book., Landon, it's not a so-so book, it's just another book, which by my rights is a bad one. That's all right. The path is rocky, we slip, we miss a step. But, it's not all right with me when I see you have thrown your rudder over the side and are land locked." The old man stopped and looked around him to be certain he was the Captain of his ship, here on the high seas of central California. Landon saw the same thing as his father, a matched vision. Ashton looked over at Landon. "Come on, I want to introduce you to my new *fie-an-say*. She is a nice lady."

What Landon felt, over that breakfast, was how happy he had been to know, surely, that his father would be well taken care of, and he could see that they, these two, would be good for each other… right here on the Ranch in his Central Valley.

All Landon remembered about Jane Stetson, as he drove south over the Grapevine down into the caldron glut of Los Angeles, was over dinner that last night, Jane Stetson had said that she liked his last book, that his father had let her read it first. She had, it seemed, failed to discuss her enthusias-tic feelings about the book with Ashton. She turned to him then, as if she wanted to hear Ashton's thoughts about the book, right now, before serving cherry pie for dessert. He looked blankly at her. "In fact, my dear, I'd like another helping of string beans and some of that fine beef juice."

Landon smiled an inner smile, and thought how good it was to be home again.

HOW TO END THE SHORT STORY

By the time Landon returned to New York, he had read Noel Chapman's book of short stories and was satisfied with them. At the moment, he wasn't sure what that meant. He was not surprised no one would publish them. Nothing to do with the quality of the work,—the work was good, solid, with ideas—but, there was a great deal of good, solid work out there—even some ideas, however, if you weren't someone recognized, well, what was the point?

There was one plain wall in Landon's writing room. By contrast, it seemed unfinished, left behind by a designer who had really wanted to create a three-walled room. His revenge, then, was to leave it blank. However, it was part of the scheme. Landon liked to make drawings of characters on this wall. Not real drawings, but interior maps, as if each of his characters was lost in deepest Africa and he was trying to discover the right turning in the jungle for them.

Now the wall was filled with a scatter of paper taped up in what appeared to be a jagged pattern or structure. The top piece of paper said "Stories by Noel Chapman" Then, beside each story was a single page of notes, handwritten, barely legible. Landon moved from the desk to the bed, where he had lain reading the whole book of short stories again through the night. Beside the bed and beside the desk, the floor was littered with coffee cups and spoons.

Well, let's try something. Here we have Noel's stories on this side. Let's put together a wall of Landon's stories… maybe some comparison would be helpful here.

Impulsively, he went to Drawers 11 and 12, and pulled them open. He thumbed through, searching, remembering. As he would find a story that seemed possible, he would turn and toss it on the floor behind him. Then another. A quick thought would move him to a third Drawer, where he would fumble and find a slim folder and then toss it on the floor. He turned at one point to count the number of files on the floor. One, two-three, four, five, six… seven…. Then he turned again to close #11 and #12, and open #10. Two more files hit the floor, a quick return to #12, one more file and then back to—wait! and he moved along the wall to Drawer # 21 and after a moment #29… in each of those he was delighted to find three files which flew to the floor. His fingers were flying and he could feel his pulse rise as if he was back walking the hills with his Father. Perhaps, just perhaps, this was an answer.

In the end, all the drawers were still open, instead of neatly closed. The floor was littered with files, each with a title of one of Landon Harris' short stories, all written years ago… but, then, who's counting? he thought. He was afraid to admit to himself what he was doing, he hated to have to compare his work to that of other writers unless they were dead. But, that was today's assignment, to see if his short stories were better than Noel Chapman's short stories. And, if they were…

But, first, a walk in the Park. He had his hand on the doorknob when the phone rang. It had not rang since he returned. He paused, and then walked to the phone on the desk.

"Landon, you're back. How are the hinterlands, still there?"

It was Sally Dukes, a woman who had dedicated her adult life to climbing: climbing social ladders, climbing men, climbing ivy fearless of pesticides and anything else. She could climb on any-thing.

"How are you, Sally? Good to hear your voice."

"I never got to talk to you after the party. I wanted to hear your version of True Confessions. I am taking for granted that if Noel Chapman doesn't make a novel out of it, and how could he, just another unpublished writer, you will, And, Darling, is that wall in your cute room filled with notes, ideas, provocative ideas... hmmmmm?"

Landon turned to look at the bed between the pillars.

"Sally, you really ought to talk to your whorish friend, Darlene. If you aren't careful, she'll be at one of your parties and instead of taking her prey into a back bedroom, she'll just do him on the glass table in the middle of the living room."

"You are so visual. No wonder you are a *famous-famous*." There was a stage wait on the line. Landon was waiting for her to get to the point, no guessing at what she was after.

"What's your new book going to be about?"

"A rather attractive Manhattan hostess who goes too far one night and is caught in a moral dilemma, whereupon she decides to become a Carmelite Nun."

"You are shameless, which reminds me that I spoke to someone who will be unnamed—she met you at the party and said you were very rude to her. That's not like you, Landon. You may be a self-absorbed bastard, but you are usually civil."

Landon sat down and looked out into the Park. "I was just going out for a walk."

How To End the Short Story / 62

"Whoops," said Sally, "I either hit gold or a nerve. Which?"

Landon shrugged.

"Landon?"

"Sally, do you know what her name is?"

"Of course, I've known her for years. Grace Mathisson."

"Uh-huh. Then you know how to reach her."

"So it might be both a gold mine <u>and</u> a nerve. Hold on here." Landon could hear her shuffle and then, "She lives in Connecticut. 203-778-4412. Westport or Darrien."

"Thanks. So, what are you up to, Sally?"

"I'm glad you asked. I want to do a small party," Sally connived: "with... and then... if we can get them to come...." She went on for what seemed like hours on her latest scheme for a party. She should be a writer, thought Landon, she would be most successful in the Celebrity Genre. He nodded and finally said "Yes," hung up the phone and picked it up again quickly.

2 0 3 - 7 7 8 - 4 4 1 2

"Hi, it's Grace and I'm out and about. Leave you name, and if I don't have it, your number."

"Hello, Grace Mathisson. This is Landon Harris. I wish to apologize for my poor behavior at the party last week. I wonder if I could make amends by taking you to dinner sometime soon? I'm in New York at 641-9060. Landon Harris. Thanks."

Portman Publishes! is located in a historic building on Union Square in Manhattan. Canning Vogel, as one of three senior editors, has a lovely office, demonstrated by his good taste in Edwardian antiques. What's best about it is that not even someone in his position could afford the Prince of Wales desk he keeps off to the side, away from the discussion area, as if it didn't matter, and the surprisingly comfortable chairs. Canning has been wise enough not to speak of his New England ancestor who didn't come over on the Mayflower, but who was friends with a Duke from Suffolk, down-on-his-luck after the first world war. Celia Langhorne walked into the doorway to his office and leaned into her question.

"You have a moment?"

Canning turned to her from his campaign desk to admire her morning look.

"Sure. I am completely rested from a fine weekend with my new friend."

"What's her name?"

"Glorious Gloria."

"Ain't love grand?" said Celia.

"And you, Ms. Langhorne. Off sailing." Celia shook her head, "Nora has been poorly and I am really worried about her. I was in Bristol all week-end. And, despite the strain, it was restful. Makes me wonder why I ever left Rhode Island."

Canning turned to look out his window, as if he could see all the way to Rhode Island from mid-town Manhattan. Celia watched him and said finally, to his back, "I am completely uncertain as to why Landon Harris has been talking to me and not you lately." Canning turned and sat beside Celia in the conference circle of chairs.

"Not that it matters. He has acted a bit aloof from me since the luncheon, and I am not sure of the reason." Celia was sure, but she had decided sometime ago not to share the events of her middle of the night therapy session with Landon. She patted Canning on the arm.

"Well, you're right, it doesn't matter, but I think it better if I tell you what I am hearing. I have been trying to think of how I feel about it. In a word, he is thinking though the idea that his next effort will be the publishing of a collection of his short stories. Canning, I didn't even <u>know</u> he wrote short stories."

"No one does, don't let it bother you. All novelists have collections of short stories. I recall his talking about them from time to time, sort of a reminisce, harmless but lingering there in the back of his mind like a idea waiting to jump out a twelve story window."

"He has no title for them and when I asked if there was a theme, he said he didn't need one."

Canning smiled. "And, of course, darling, he does not"

"Do you mean that?"

"Well, yes and well, no. First of all, he is a "name" author. But," said Canning, "...maybe he's scratching for straws, hmm." He got up and looked again out the window into the Square. "The early reports on *One Woman, Two Men* are not encouraging, but it is not overwhelmingly bad either. It looks, early on, as if it might be a wash. No one will complain about that, but they," and here Canning raised his eyes to look at the ceiling,

"…an idea like that would be a new thrust…."

Celia muffled a giggle and finished his sentence… "Hmmmm."

"Why don't you continue to dialogue with him. Maybe we can do a switch, you edit this one and I'll take over something you are tired of… Reynolds Manning, for instance." Canning turned to look at Celia, "What's that old film line? '…who do you have to fuck to get off this movie?' No, I don't mind dealing with him. He's really harmless, I knew the people who dealt with him when he was with Random House."

Celia thought back to the night with Landon in tears. She was not sure she wanted to sign on for that kind of duty, but on the other hand, if she could get Mr. Harris back on course, that would be good for everyone. And, somewhere, misplaced often, was a respect for him. He was a good writer.

"Are you sure?"

"What have we got to lose. And, with our newest star climbing *The Times* ladder, eyes will be else where and we can do pretty much what we want."

Mrs. Olsen slid the roast out of the oven. Her habit, since she had been Landon's housekeeper, was that she talked to herself. A low mutter, one where the words were not distinguishable, yet there was conversation going on. Landon had worried when she first came that he was supposed to understand what she was saying and respond. As he tried to do that, almost a step at a time, he learned that, unlike the remainder of the world, she required no response. It was an interior dialogue, as if constant communication with the Gods of Kitchen & Broom.

"Damn, Lilly, it looks overdone."

"Not at all, Mister. It's just the way you like it, I did the au jus dark-er today and on purpose, you understand." She threw a dishtowel at him. "You are picky tonight. You have someone special coming?"

Landon waved his hand and rushed out of the kitchen, this time to the writing room. Lilly looked after him muttering something important.

He walked into the room and turned to look at the now jumbled plain wall. On one side were taped Noel Chapman's stories, on the other, his stories, ten of them. There were editing marks over both columns, and if a person had a feeling for cyphers, one might be able to find a pattern or meaning. Landon, intent, moved to the computer and gazed again at the single document on the screen. He read it carefully again, and made three more adjustments to the page. Then, he carefully read it once more and printed it out. He looked at his watch. Landon was not good with quiet moments. He was good at thinking, but not at finding himself in that zone of peace. He closed his eyes and saw himself walking on top of the Ridge with his Father. He dissolved to leaning on the rock with the Dunes at his back, and the Ocean roaring. He opened his eyes and looked over to the bed and saw himself there as the apartment bell rang. He reached to the control panel and pressed a button.

"Yes, yes...."

"Hello... Landon Harris, is that you?"

"It is," he recognized the voice of Noel Chapman and pushed the buzzer. "Third floor, Noel." Just as he was rising, the phone rang. He paused in mid-air and thought to ignore it as his hand reached for the phone.

"Yes, yes."

A woman's voice said, "I am trying to reach Landon Harris."

"You have reached him. Who's speaking?"

"Grace Mathisson, Mr. Harris. How did you get my number?"

"Ah, I spoke to Sally Dukes."

"Oh, of course, Sally. Well, I am not sure why I called back, I am still feeling uneasy about our last meeting, Landon." She paused and he listened to her breathing. "Thanks for saying 'I'm sorry'."

"Grace, I really mean it, and I want very much to talk to you. but I have a dinner meeting here now. Can we meet for dinner soon?"

Another awkward pause. "I suppose so."

"Connecticut or New York?"

"New York is fine."

"How 'bout Shun Lee West near Lincoln Center?"

"I am a married woman, Landon."

"Does that preclude eating?"

No breathing.

"7:30 on Tuesday?"

"All right. Good bye."

Noel Chapman looked just as he did that night at the party. Even his shirt was the same. Landon had not noticed that night how pale was his skin. It gave him a rather etheral look, not common in men.

While Landon puttered at the dining table, he watched Noel saunter around his living room looking at the books. He came to one of the two main wall shelves and pulled out a copy of James Michner's *The Bridge at Andou*. "You have a fine collection of dribs and drabs of almost everything. Are you an eclectic reader, Landon?"

"I try to be. What have you there?"

"Michener, but something I had not realized he wrote. I didn't know he did non-fiction."

"Oh, you have the Andou book, about the Hungarian revolution. It's quite good."

"I don't care much for Michener."

"Can't say I blame you."

"He seems to have taken his talents and turned himself into a soap opera novelist, country-by-country."

"You should be a book reviewer."

"Well, if things keep going the way they are, I might as well." Chapman turned through the pages of the Michener book. "Why don't you cotton to him?"

Landon paused over the napkins. "I liked him at first. He seemed strong, insightful, even original and suddenly, for me anyway, he transformed himself into a formula writer. It was just a disappointment, I think. That old idea, you keep wishing for more, and when it doesn't come... well, you move on. Excuse me for a moment."

Landon went into the kitchen. Lilly Olsen was gone, and all the dishes for dinner were laid out on the serving table. Noel pushed his head in the kitchen door, "Can I help, or do you have help?" He looked at the kitchen and saw no one. "Sure," said Landon, "grab some dishes."

Over dinner, Noel Chapman said, "This is quite good. You are an accomplished cook."

"Thank you."

"Listen, forgive my bluntness," and Landon recalled how blunt Noel could really be, "…but you have read my book? Do you like the stories?"

"In fact, it's quite good. I liked most of them, one or two, maybe three were, I guess what I might call 'filler', but in the main, good. Publishable. Needs editing, but then most things do. Actually, I might help you with that. I have a listing of suggestions, and candidates for removal. Are there other stories you might have as replacements?"

Noel was thoughtful. "Well, to be honest, <u>maybe</u> one."

Spoonfulls of silence. Landon, sensing the quietude, got up and put on music for background. He reached for the Bach, but his fingers searched further and found Chopin, hoping that soothing might be better.

"Have you written short stories, Landon? I have never seen any."

"They are safely locked away."

"You didn't like them?"

"At the time I thought they were quite good. But, when I was doing them, publishers were not interested in collections of short stories… some were printed in small journals. It was just not the time then. It's different now."

"Could I read one or two of yours?"

The question startled Landon, and his fork jerked imperceptibly.

"Well, if it works out, I know you will. More roast?"

"No, but the roasted potatoes are perfect, thanks."

Noel helped himself to the dish still piled high of toast-colored, cut-small potatoes.

"This is a nice place you have here. Lights on the Park make a nice softness."

"I could have been higher up, but I noticed that at this level, I am in the Park, not just observing the Park. I like this better."

Landon was torn between trying to be social and chatty, and getting-to-it. He realized this should not be rushed, but the pressure inside was building, and he was having difficulty playing the smiling host and….

"Do you think Portman would be interested in my book? I met that woman, Celia Langhorne at a party last year. She seems real enough. Not like your average editor."

"A very sensitive woman. I like her, though my editor is Canning Vogel."

"Could you arrange for me to take the book to her?"

Landon surged like Champaign behind the cork. Suddenly, "Noel, I have actually determined a map, if you will, to getting your book some-where, to, ah, a publisher… but, I have what you may consider an odd procedural requirement." Chapman looked at him quizzically.

Landon got half up and reached to the side table for a piece of paper, the same one he pulled out of the computer an hour ago. He listened for his own breathing and set the paper in front of Noel Chapman. "I like to be most frank when I speak to people about their work, and I like that it is just between us. That is, no one knows what we say here, but you and I." He looked inquiringly at Noel. "Do you mind?" Chapman picked up the paper and scanned it.

"What is this?"

"It's a release. That is, it asks only that our confidence in what we say tonight not be breached. Full stop."

Chapman's eyes moved from the paper to Landon and back. Finally, he smiled, as if to say, why not, or what the hell. He pulled a pen out of his pocket and signed it. Landon reached over and carefully folded the paper as if he would not transmit it to the King or the FBI, but to his own safe deposit box.

Landon took a deep breath. "I like your writing very much, Noel. You have a good style and pace. Inventive ideas. Nice visuals. In fact, to be totally candid with you, your book of stories urged me to go back and read my own short stories, written eight to fifteen years ago... there was even one I wrote in college about my father and a ranch. But, what is even more devastating to me is that your stories are much better than mine." Chapman started to say something that would be clearly grateful, but Landon raised his hand. "I re-read fifteen stories of my own and found only three that I liked and two that might be on par with yours. That was a very difficult moment for me. This comes at a time when I am not sure what my own next work should be... those dark moments that should be written about only by famous Russian novelists like Gorki. I find myself in a backwater. So much so that in this event, you and I are brothers. You have a good book you can't get published and I have a bad book that has been published."

"You mean, your latest... you aren't pleased with that?"

"Have you read it."

"Yeah, sure, and…."

"I won't ask you to tell me what you think of it."

Landon stood up, and removed the dinner plates, and replaced them with dessert plates and, under a covered dish, revealed a lemon mouse tart. "Would you like a fresh fork?" Chapman shook his head, no. He had a bewildered look to him, as if his music teacher had told him, finally, that he could truly sing.

"I want to be totally honest and direct with you, Noel," Landon was pleased now, this was one of the lines he had rehearsed. "I want to see that your book is published. I want to do some copy editing, and I want to replace your two stories, *Shoelaces* and *The Crème of Sienna*, with two of my own… and to be totally clear, just those two stories and I'll get them for you after dessert. One will be *An Actor Prepares,* and another one of my favorites, *How to End the Short Story.*"

Landon could see that his plan was beginning to have effect on Chapman, that the tides might be rising. He looked over to the side table to be certain that the lifeboats were ready with oars in locks for the coming storm. Chapman started to speak. Landon continued, overriding Noel's first words. "After the book is complete in the sense that I have outlined, I will submit it to Portman under my own name. They will do the proper and endless procedures they do, and it will be published as Landon Harris' ninth book."

"You are a monster."

"Perhaps."

"You can't be serious. How can you believe I would allow that?"

"I think you will allow it, and willingly when I tell you the terms of the publishing contract. No, not the one with Portman, but the agreement between us… you and me. Would you like to hear it?"

"No." Noel Chapman got up tipping over his chair and took a step toward Landon. "I knew, I felt that there was… was… some THING about you that…"

"Words fail you," said Landon.

Noel nodded his head at Landon. How cool he is, thought Chapman, he is a creation of the Devil of Words. He turned to leave. Landon reached out for Noel's arm and rested his hand there. "Listen, I know this is outrageous, unbelievable, even despicable. But, stop to consider what I am really speaking of. Hold for another paragraph." His face made a pleading statement and Chapman sat down.

"I will have my attorney draw an agreement between us. Six eyes will see it, his, yours, and mine. It will say, this contract, that I will give you upon signing, $20,000 dollars in cash. I will give you a copy of the publishing agreement I will secure for this work with Portman Publishes! That agreement will guarantee me 12% of the retail price of each book. I will give you one-half of that royalty. I won't trouble you with the math of how much that might be, but it will allow you a comfortable living—in Manhattan, not the Bronx—for approximately two years, just enough time to write another book, which I will read and if I like it, show to three publishers. Finally, in exchange for all this, you will give me your book of short stories and your silence."

Landon's speech lay in front of them on the table like a turd alongside the untouched lemon tart. Noel got up again, without overturning his chair and moved to the sitting area in the living room. Landon watched him, step by step. He sat down easily and leaned back in the padded chair. Time passed and Landon picked at the lemon mousse, ignoring the turd, then got up to clear the table without making a sound. He poured coffee into two cups and placed them on a tray. Moving over to Noel Chapman, he placed the entire tray on the low table in front of Noel and lifted a single cup and saucer for himself. He moved, as quickly as he could, away from Chapman's line of sight and sat in a straight backed chair off to the side. He had glimpsed the younger man's eyes and they were half-closed as if he were drugged. They stayed in this configuration for 32 minutes. Noel did not touch his coffee or move during that time.

Noel opened his eyes and looked for Landon. Finding him, he said, "I have to go now." His voice was so quiet that Landon had to lean forward to catch the words. "Fine," said Landon. He went to the closet and found the coat and held it for him at the door. Chapman opened the door and turned to step through the threshold. Landon almost spoke to him, but bit his lip. Chapman, his back to Landon said, "You are the worst person I could imagine. As you wisely say, 'words fail me.'" He is still facing away from Landon Harris, with a foot poised to move to the elevator. "I will sign your agreement, with only one stipulation."

"And…?" asked Landon.

"…that I never have to set eyes on you again."

"Done."

The door closed.

Landon stood by the door listening to his heart beat. The weight of an ocean had flowed away from him. He was clear. Dry. Almost lightheaded. His career would go on. This can work. He would be able to square this. He would, he was certain of it. As he moved into the living room, his attention was caught by the chair Noel had sat in. What was that? He moved closer to the right arm to see the material was torn and shredded, as if an animal had clawed there. He sat in the chair and looked at it from Noel's perspective. He laid his hand on the same arm, his fingers touching the tearing. That must have been it, he had been eyeing Chapman, but on the other side—the left hand, this was the right. He had not seen or heard anything. This then was Chapman's slow, silent, visceral response. He was stunned. How could a man do this and not be aware of it? He tried to put himself in Noel's mind, and he had been careful in his planning not to go too far with that. But his mind slid easily back to the parting at the door minutes earlier. At the time, he was content not to see Noel's face, to be satisfied with the gesture of a turned back. Finally, it hit him that the back was only a mask for hatred on the face. So hateful that he would not, could not show it. I have never been hated. This man hates me. He has allowed an arrangement that is repulsive to him and has walked away, as if leaving his child in a basket on Landon's doorstep in exchange for bread. Isn't it as simple as that? Is it? Yes, the child will be well cared for, better even than the father could on his own. What is the wrong in that? Yet, for saving his child, the man hates me. Perhaps I am the wrong one here. I should have not interceded. I should have not read his book, I should have left it behind as others had done. Noel Chapman would not hate me then. Better for him, he would not even know me. Would he be happier then? —continuing to wait tables, standing on one foot in the middle of the street to be ready when the next man leaves a note for him—this time it surely will be an offer to publish his book, do the hard work of editing the manuscript, throwing out the weak stories to make it into something that only Landon Harris could do with the force of his signature. I don't want to be hated! I knew it would be a difficult choice, but one that would guarantee the book seeing the light of day, money in the pocket, a better lifestyle… isn't that what everyone wants, even Noel Chapman? I don't want, Landon thought, him to be ungrateful after what I have done at considerable expense to myself. And, all of this is not to consider that he, only Landon Harris, has the power to make the book ready for a public, a public that will admire him. Yes. Certainly. Without question!

By the next dawn, Landon was fully into the task, performing the autopsy and resuscitation on the past and future manuscript of his ninth book. His eyes were afire, and his vision was clear, clearer than it had been for some time. He could now see...

HOW TO END THE SHORT STORY
The Collected Short Stories of Landon Harris

THE BOOK TOUR

*T*he double edge that cut Landon on a book tour was that he loved his readers, but he hated their questions after he finished the reading...

"...are your best ideas are drawn from real life or from your imagination...?"

"...do you think writing on a computer makes your work false...?"

"...I guess my long involved questions come down to one thing: how do you gain your inspiration?"

"...do you do much of your research on the internet?"

"...do you read the work of other writers?"

Now, here was a good question. Landon knew from talking to other writers, that opinions varied on this issue. Christopher Siss claimed that to read other people while he was in a piece of work, distracted him. Vinny Carlowe was more honest, he said he read others voraciously to get ideas and technique, but more important, to gain the courage and lessons needed to continue his own work. Landon felt it was good to read the writing of those who are better than you. Not only do you need their inspiration, but you need to find ways, objective and intuitive, to improve your own work, to continue to fill the reservoirs within.

"...thank you, that's so poetic!"

Then there were five questions requesting a reading list.

"...well," Landon said with a hidden sigh, "get out your pencils and paper… I have never done this, but let's give it a try…

one… *West with the Night* by Beryl Markham

two… *The Lady in the Lake* by Raymond Chandler

three… anything by Jack London, but my favorite is *White Fang*

four… *When the World was Lit Only by Fire*… William Manchester

five… these are in no particular order, you know… ah, *The Lost Photographs of Nicholas Kases* by George Spelvin

six… now, you realize that I am ticking off my own personal choices here, and we have yet to list the classics… American and otherwise, *Catcher in the Rye*, *From Here to Eternity*… *Lady Chatterley's Lover*… whatever you like of Roth, Updike, Oates, Heller and Mailer…

seven… *The Tunnel* by Jorge Cantano Suarez

eight… *The Reader* by that German fellow…

nine… don't forget Ken Kesey and Tom Wolfe

ten… *Pitch Dark* by Renata Adler

eleven… *The Body Artist* by Don Delillo

twelve… we could be here all night… how about a novel called *Good Night, You All* by Landon Harris"

He watched them file out of the small hall while fielding yet-one-more question. When they were gone, Landon saw himself standing in the middle of the empty lecture area at Books I Have Loved in Atlanta. Nice small bookstore, the kind he liked best… real books, real place and best of all, the people who worked there actually loved books and could tell you about them. It was a privately owned bookstore, not unlike the one his father had first taken him to in Bakersfield. He sat down in one of the audience chairs. They had, again, asked all the wrong questions about his wasted novel. Not one of them had even suspected the book was not worth their time sitting here, and his time trying to explain it away. His eyes scanned the array of bookshelves surrounding him on three sides. After a few seconds, he blinked to make sure he was seeing what he was seeing… the shelves seemed to be inching toward him. His eyes quickly moved to the corners where the shelves met to see if the corners were disappearing, even in increments. They were indeed. At each breath he took, one book disappeared from each shelf, at each corner, at each breath, at each blink. If he sat there for a few more minutes, would they crush him, these Gods of books, for his temerity? His audaciousness? For the present, he wondered, or the future? Would serve him right, and as he had that thought, he looked at the floor to watch, spellbound, at the rug disappearing under the shelves. It would be right, he thought, for this to happen, and he mentally prepared himself for his obliteration. Then he laughed, "'…those who live by the pen, shall die by the word…' Indeed."

Landon didn't believe in Angels, or angels, nor messengers. But, this might be a good time to revise those feelings, a change of heart. These crushing shelves with their complicit books would be his ticket into Book Heaven. He wondered if he should kneel. Three books disappeared on each shelf at each corner while he meditated on that. How many books would be left to strangle him? Would they stuff their pages down his throat? Or, would there be a drowning rain of letters, hundreds and hundreds of al-phabets, until the room was awash. When it was over, when words had been silenced, the letters would slip back into words, the words back onto their rightful pages, and shelves, adding books to each shelf corner which would then roll back to the walls, and the room would be the same.

"Where has that rueful Author gone?"…they would say, flicking an errant E or A with their toes. "Well, we won't miss him, will we, such an imposter with his Seriously So-So book. The sssss's slipped off their tongues like honest snakes.

"Mr. Harris… ah, Mr. Harris… Sir, the car has come for you. It's just outside…"

"Oh," said Landon, shaking his head… looking desperately at the bookshelves, until Mary Norman said, worried now, "Ah, is there something wrong, Mr. Harris… have you lost something?" Landon looked her square in the eye. "I told you, Mary Norman, to call me Landon." He got up and smiled his most brilliant smile and took her hand, it was very soft.

"Thanks for your generous hospitality, Mary… it was good to be here."

"It was good to have you, Landon. In addition to the fact that you sold 61 books today."

"All mine?" He was still smiling, as if it was a joke.

"Of course yours, you are the marvelous author today. Thanks for coming. See you next book?"

"Definitely."

Next Book? He wanted to ask her if he could come back tomorrow and read again from his next book, and then hold her soft hand again. But, he didn't. That would be bewildering to her, but, who is to say that it wouldn't be a good idea for the next city… what would that be? Atlanta today, Birmingham tomorrow, then loop back to Savannah where the Open Door would welcome him—one of his favorite book places. Yes, The Next Book is a ripe subject.

Canning Vogel slipped into Celia's office without a sound and sat in one of the four meeting chairs. Said not a word. Breathed not a sigh. Looked at the classic yachting photographs. When she turned to reach for something on the table, she was startled. "Oh, you gave me a fright, Canning, what the hell are you doing sitting in my office like the Ghost of Remaindered Past? Son-of-a-bitch… please don't do that." She took a deep breath and grinned at him. Just another guy trying to be cute, she thought. She wished she was out sailing today. She turned away from Canning to look out at the East River. Can't sail there, but it's the right road. Back to Canning. "What can I do for you today, Mr. Vogel?"

"Word from Sav-vannah is that the Book Tour is going well, but that Landon has switched to reading from his forthcoming book—the one you have only begun editing. Better than that, the press has been good…yes, it's only two cities now, but I wonder if that isn't a better idea. "

"Nothing is better than pitching the next thing… and if it's well received… why not?"

"If you believe in the come, as those who play craps do, then it's all right…" Celia had to laugh at this Edwardian-type person who liked to make one think he had been a craps player in the Navy.

"The come?" she said.

"Yes, you need to know that sales of the current book have also dropped a quarter while he has been doing this."

"Two cities, or three?"

"Actually, I said two but it has been three now, and it's an even a quarter across the board."

They both turned and looked at the East River, and almost

simultaneously said, "What would it hurt?"

Celia continued. "We have already admitted that we can survive one so-so book, and the short stories, I believe will be such a turning for everyone—who would have suspected that Landon Harris would... no, could, write a series of arguably good stories, and to put this together so quickly. Maybe what we should do is let him do this as a promotional tour for the next book, and get it out a season earlier."

"Can we do that?"

"I don't know, frankly, but I'll talk with production and marketing. We'll give it a whirl. I'll know soon."

"Are you game for this, old girl?"

"You bet. Now get out of here so I can concentrate."

While this perfectly normal and proper conversation was going on in New York's Union Square, Landon Harris was in his room, three hours earlier on the West Coast, writing to the dawn. Something had struck him last night as he was saying goodbye to his crusty old friend that ran Landon's favorite San Diego bookstore, The Vowel & et. al. The chat had been intellectual yet once in the busy streets of San Diego, Landon had wandering eyes for the passing women. He thought back to the delicious lady sitting off to the side at the reading and recalled his quick-cutting sexual thoughts for her. As he wandered through the streets to the San Diegan Hotel, he wished for her company. The kind of company that an Off-to-the-Side lady might provide—a thrashing through the night. Thinking on East Coast time, he got up in the dark and began to scribble. It went like this...

The Imaginary Interview

Interviewer: Do you sleep with women who offer themselves to you on book tours?

Landon Harris: Yes, I do.

I.   Do you think that is a good and right thing to do?

L.H.   I think it is despicable.

I.   Really. You don't try to justify this behavior to yourself?

L. H.   When it began I did.

I.   ...and...

L. H.   You mean, "later"?

I.   Yes.

L. H.   Like all easy habits, it became something that I did. The women supplied the justification. I think I can honestly say that I did not attempt to seduce a single one. I think it's safe to say that this is a projection that goes on in the mind of someone who needs to attach themselves to an idea that is larger than their own life. A variation of the Rock Groupies, if there could be a literary component. It helps that I am not real, that I drop into a single life like a parachutist, known by previously delivered propaganda. An unknown idea helped enormously by literally falling from the sky.

I   ...like a God?

L.H.   Like a God. But, that's where the analogy ends. A kindly God would behave better—no, that's not right—all that is needed for any successful liaison between two people is for kindness to exist. So, a good god would be kind all right, and that would include keeping his and her clothes on.

I   Have there been exceptions to this sort of—sounds awful —one-night-stand-*ish* behavior?

L.H.   Yes. A woman I met at a reading in Sacramento left her husband—not-a-very-nice man in the best of circumstances—and moved into the Holiday Inn on the upper west side of New York.

I   Can you tell us what happened?

L.H.   I would rather not. It's shameful—shameful all around. It would have been hard to determine which of us behaved worse.

I   Have you thought of writing about this?

L. H.   (pause) No, actually.

I   Why not? Sounds like it has all the ingredients of a good story.

L.H.   Except for one important ingredient for me—a character with a shred of decency.

I   What about the woman? She seems a classic victim.

L.H.   If a predator can be a victim, yes.

I   How do you determine... how do you differentiate between who is the predator and who is the victim?

L.H.   Very good!

I	What?
L.H.	I think you have put your finger on it. <u>You</u>, with little information and much instinct, do see the crux of the matter.
I	What do you mean?
L.H.	Well, you said it yourself.
I	…ah…
L.H.	You presuppose a story in which the predator is the victim. You move quickly into a drama where you insinuate there are three characters all of whom are both victim and predator. You can see this can't you? I am the initial predator, but a sheep really because I am not aggressive in this situation, so you might say that I could be—let it ride for a moment—I could be a victim.
I	…could I…
L.H.	…hold on now. She is really the predator because it is she who comes to the event with claws unsheathed. In bed together—later—we are both interacting parts as victim and predator—often at the same moment… (Landon holds up fingers to illustrate.)
L.H.	One bed
	Two people
	Four characters
I	Oh, I see. But you have forgotten the husband. He is the true victim.

L.H.	No, sorry.
	To be the unadulterated victim, he would have had to be kind—that word again—kind to his wife. He was not, so in his unkindness he has created such a need for affection in his wife that he has turned a good woman into a predator. Do you see that?
I	(waiting)
L.H.	Finally, when he comes to New York and attempts to move into the Holiday Inn with his wife—she denies him. He must, she says, have another room… on another floor.
I	(slightly horrified)…you visit her there?
L.H.	I have to.
I	The predator now, eh?
L. H.	No, it's a reflexive defense. I am the victim again during the time I spend with her there. If I allow her to come to my home, I have an unsolvable problem. If he finds out, then it's even worse.
I	(digging in) How does the husband become the predator?
L.H.	One, he wants his wife back so he can become the victim again in his own home. Two, he wants to damage me be cause I have made him the predator. Finally, because she now sees him in a different light, that is, she thinks I have been kind to her, she acts differently with him and he no- tices that. But, he is not smart enough to realize that the only way to win the game, and for him, it is a game—is to be the victim, but, quite simply, he doesn't know how.

I	How is this resolved?
L.H.	The luck of circumstance intervenes. A young writer friend comes to New York to work with his editor on a manuscript. I create a dinner scene in which he happens upon us —the woman and I. He has been told everything. He is single. He is willing to look in. I introduce them and invite him to stay for the meal. He likes her—he is kind. She responds to him—she needs genuine kindness.
I	You are not saying they fall in love and you are the match maker!
L. H.	I told you that I wanted to be…
I	What happens when the husband finds out there is one more man?
L.H.	When the young writer has completed editing on the manuscript—five weeks later—she returns to California with him and moves from Sacramento to Ukiah, just a bit further north in the state.
I	(impatient) …and the husband?
L.H.	Do you mind turning off the recorder?
I	Why?
L.H.	(silence)
I	Well, all right…
L. H.	In an act of kindness, they kill him.

The phone rang in his room, and Landon revived himself from his trance.

"Yes. Yes?"

"Mr. Harris, your car is here to take you to La Jolla and the Barnes &
Noble store there." La Jolla today meant tomorrow was Los Angeles. After
the relative innocence and beauty of the beach communities of Southern
California, L.A. seemed like Babylon. Not only was it not <u>his</u> California,
but it seemed a place lost to itself. Driving in was better than flying in
because you were not so horrified by the smog. If you avoided Ontario
and East Los Angeles, and stuck to the coastal highway, a person could
convince themselves this would be all right, and that a few days here would
not shorten your life by years. If you could avoid the movie people, so
much the better. Last year he had a good reading at The Book Place on
Sunset Boulevard and the turnout had been fine, the reading splendid, and
the questions tolerable. All except one man. He seemed a kind of grown up
film student, full of furor and fury.

"How is it that your books have never been made into films?"

Landon had noticed that it was possible to detect where Los Angeles
folk were coming from by their word usage about the cinema. Cinema is
European, so it is not local patois. Movies is what they make here. Film is
a higher order of movies and therefore insinuates a higher order of speaker.

"I try to write stories that happen in your mind, and those are usually the most difficult to translate to the screen, don't you agree?" Landon
looked earnestly at the man.

A thoughtful pause. "Well, I suppose so, yet, you have had compelling characters and shouldn't they be able to transcend ideas… I mean films
are about people!" This was a definitive statement.

Landon said, "Books are about ideas and the struggle people have to live out their ideals, much of this inner struggle is difficult to dramatize in car crashes and special effects, don't you agree?" The 'don't you agree' part was something Landon had learned to develop with people who were trying, in their own ways, to attack him... it seemed to give the conversation some distance.

"What about the money?" This was the last resort of a burned out Los Angeles discussion as far as Landon was concerned.

"What about the money?"

"Well, a top novelist gets a lot of it."

"I don't need it."

"You don't need more money?" the man said as if Landon had an incurable disease. The audience that was left in the bookstore chuckled.

"Nope. But, it's nice of you to ask about the book, thanks," Landon said, "and good luck to you."

Landon glazed for a moment. He had hoped for a simple reading, and no more movie students. He reminded himself about the 20-something he met here at a cocktail party who was making fun of the Film Schools at U.C.L.A. and U.S.C. and how many of the kids in screenwriting classes had agents in town. Why don't they call them Movie Preppies, the boy had said, and be done with it. Landon brought his face to mind and smiled.

The crowd at The Book Place was so dense that the reading had to be moved to a larger space, and in the end, there was standing room at the back. Landon couldn't imagine what had occasioned this, he had never had this kind of a crowd in Los Angeles... north of here, yes, but that was for a different reason. The Book Place person, a serious book enthusiast, introduced Landon Harris and made a complete explanation for the crowd. "Mr. Harris decided, some cities ago on this tour, that he was more interested in reading his new short stories than fragments of a novel, his usual genre." The man turned to Landon and said, "We hear that there has been considerably more interest in this forthcoming book—a first for you as short story writer—than the novel currently out, is that correct?" Landon nodded and at this point two hands rose in the audience. Later Landon wished he had understood the portent of the coming line of questioning.

A young woman in the back was acknowledged. "Any chance that you have some advance copies of the short story book here for us to buy and read?" She smiled at Landon and waited for an answer. The Book Place person acknowledged the other hand before turning to Landon. It was another young woman. She shrugged and said, "Same question. We are all looking forward to Mr. Harris' shorter work." Landon was nonplussed. He shook his head at the questioners and Mr. Book Place. "No, sorry. This thought to read the, ah, new stories was an impetuous one on my part… the book is only now going into production." The two young women looked at each other in an aggressive way and nodded to Landon as if to say, 'thanks, later'.

Landon decided to read *The Italian Rope*, a story about two American couples on vacation in Italy who discover a long length of rope in the basement of a villa they have rented. The rope has writing on it, as if a mad poet or an imprisoned mind had found a way to write on rope. The audience was rapt. Landon had not read this story before. He had rehearsed them all —actually this one with Celia two nights before he left. He distracted himself once and stumbled twice while he tried to make marks on the page to remind himself to make some changes in the story. Some of the description of the villa could be improved, and perhaps a character sharpened some.

Rocks in the river, but it flowed along.

This story was one of Noel Chapman's stories. So, as the applause filled the room, Landon, decided to read another story. He asked his audience if they had the time... "...I know time is a valuable commodity here in Paradise...." More applause and he decided to read *An Actor Prepares*, one of his own stories. Same response, same applause. Landon heaved a big sigh. He had not placed his own work side-by-side with that of Noel Chapman's in public, and he was pleased for obvious reasons. No matter how good a talent might be, it's always good to hear the hands clapping. He concentrated his feelings on the goodness of that idea rather than other, meaner thoughts he had while on the tour about this side-by-side-ness. Before he could gather his wits, it seemed that everyone present had picked up his novel, and was in line to get his signature as well as have a word with this eastern star. When the first of the questioning young women appeared for his autograph, she reached to touch his hand and said "I am the only one in the room who grew up here, Landon, a real native Californian"—now her biggest smile— "just like you. I used to collect autographs when I was a kid, so this page gets torn out and put in my A-List autograph book. Any chance that you could spend a few minutes with me after the show?" Of course, Landon nodded, after glancing at The Book Place man. Yes, he could. She stood off to the side to wait to watch the next young woman who had also asked an earlier question.

"Thanks for gracing us with your reading tonight Mr. Harris. I am enthralled with your stories and wonder if it would be possible to get an advanced copy of the book...?" She slid her calling card under his pen. Tracey Gattling of Additional Dialogue Productions and an address in Santa Monica. The waiting woman, leaned forward, trying to hear the conversation. The woman in front of Landon tried not to notice. Landon then realized what all this was about, and froze. "Mr. Harris… ah, Landon, perhaps it would be easier for you if I contacted your editor at Portman Publishes! I am sure they would be happy to help me, after all, isn't it time that your writing makes it to the big screen. What is your editor's name?"

Landon nodded, dumbly. What had he done? His mind raced from Los Angeles to New York and back. While in New York, it made a stop in Brooklyn Heights and watched Noel Chapman's expression when he heard about the possibility of a "movie deal"…and how much of that he could keep for himself. Sitting in front of the autographing crowd, Landon's mind was able to calculate quickly Noel's percentage of the deal and then more contractual difficulties than any of them could manage. He and Greg Bantam, his trusted agent, had not thought about film sales… Landon had never sold a book to the movies so why would they have thought of that? Portman had the kind of contract that would allow them to step in, and as they did, Noel would step out in public. This was not in his agreement. Oh, my God…

"Yes, yes. Sorry to drift off on you." he looked squarely at Tracey Gattling and said, "Of course, I will be back in New York next week to speak to my editor about this… but, I'll get back to you." He waved her nicely designed calling card in the space between them.

Young Woman Number Two, Amy Rosing, was not pleased. She looked at the other woman and realized the scenario was not working somehow. She didn't want to leave with only a signed novel, knowing that no book of Landon Harris' short stories would be forthcoming to her, and that Tracey Gattling now had Landon's ear. When the room cleared, Amy introduced herself asking if Landon would let her buy him a drink. After all, he must need a quiet place after such a good reading, and here they were, in the heart of the Sunset Strip in Hollywood.

She gave him her most sincere smile, and resisted just taking his arm and leading him out of the store as she had done with others. She had a good record with snaring authors with properties unheard of until that moment. She had the instincts of a hummingbird and the technique of an NFL linebacker.

"Yes. Yes. That would be a great pleasure." he said, and that would give him time to think. It finally struck him that if he could steer this woman, and she was clearly someone to be very careful with, toward his stories, and only his, why then this would never come to ashes. He took her arm, and my, she was a lovely thing. "Where should we go?" Landon wondered if he could fit this situation into an "imaginary interview" re-write. Well, probably not... he had an early flight back to New York in the morning. Even thinking this would only make the real or the imagined 'interview' worse.

THE THREE-LEGGED DOG

Landon did not come empty handed. He had a small present for Grace Mathisson when she arrived at Shun Lee West. He had remembered that she wore very simple jewelry when he had seen her at the party. He was at the door when she arrived.

"Oh, Mr. Harris, I thought I should come some early, but you are already early."

"It is very good of you to come." She was more attractive than he recalled, and he railed at her husband at home in Connecticut. Henry Wong showed them to a solitary booth at the head of the enormous white paper dragon that lived on the longest wall of the restaurant. "Oh, isn't that something... the Dragon has red eyes." Grace looked at Landon, and then noticed he was carrying something. As they sat, he placed the silver box with black ribbon at her place with the red-eyed Dragon behind her.

"You really are sorry, aren't you."

Grace touched it with her finger. He nodded with his eyes closed. She wondered what it meant when a man responded to some personal communication with his eyes closed. Landon Harris did not seem that sort of a man.

"Please open it," he said.

It was a sterling silver halo, flat-ish and not evenly round. It hovered, this halo, over a chair. A tiny silver chair. Landon was pleased to see that it just caught her breath. He watched her put it on. It was perfect with what she was wearing, a boat necked black dress with short sleeves and a simple silver bracelet. She took a small mirror out of her purse and examined her green eyes and lipstick, then looked over at him as if seeing him for the first time. Landon was tapping his chopsticks on his left hand.

"What kind of a man are you, Mr. Harris?"

He realized that the Mr. part was her own small game, and didn't do what she expected, which would be to ask her to call him Landon.

"I am trying to be an honest man."

"Trying or pretending?"

"I don't want to fool you Mrs. Mathisson. I am attracted to you, and I am most sorry that there is a Mr. Mathisson. More important, I was a rude fool over your comments to me at the party at Sally's about my latest book. I regret that."

"Sally tells me you two have, ah, been together."

Landon blinked and stammered "Indeed. Well, Sally is a good companion. I have never regretted her company, though she has a tongue like a magpie…"

He realized his gaffe and tried to back out. Grace laughed.

"Are you going to be this honest all evening? I mean, can I say anything and get away with it?"

Landon nodded.

A long pause before she continued.

"I think your book is garbage. I don't understand how or why you have published it."

"Now we are on common ground. I agree completely, and while

I wouldn't want to take up the evening with it, I would like to hear your comments."

"Sally says you are <u>also</u> a good, ah, companion."

"She's a good judge of character. Listen, Grace, we can't go on through the whole of the evening sounding like two people out of someone else's bad novel."

"Won't it be hard to call a truce or backtrack from here? Landon, I have found out more in the last five minutes than I hoped to discover about you in an evening. And, though this restaurant is certainly a good choice for what you had in mind for dinner, I'd like to suggest that we go to a small French place I know over on Eighth Avenue, have some good wine and something provincial, before we decide what to do for the remainder of the evening... I understand that you have a remarkable room in your apartment."

"I thought you were a married woman," Landon said. He pulled his jacket apart and shook himself slightly.

"I was a married woman. Now I am not. I said that, well, I wasn't sure what to expect and even Sally's briefing hasn't helped here." Her hand came across the table for his, and took it at his wrist. "Your pulse is up."

Landon eased his hand away from her and signaled for the waiter.

As they walked from the room of the Red Dragon to the softer place Grace had in mind, Landon thought about the difference between this walk on the west side of New York and the one last week in the heart of San Diego, and his longing for an "imaginary interview" companion. Gone now were the fanciful labels of 'victim' and 'predator'. Gone were the ideas of slipping hands into forbidden places with woman whom he had met an hour ago in a audience of people. He looked over at Grace, who was telling him about a time for her in Buenos Aires, and saw that this 'audience' was asking the right questions, was seeing beyond the notion of celebrity author with all the bad manners he had already displayed. This was different. Different good. Different possible, but in a honest-to-God way. It has been so long since he stood on the shore with one foot in a boat to get to the island, and some one to row with him, that it actually made him shudder on a Spring night.

Well… step into the boat…

Marty Gibbons couldn't wait to sit down at the table before she said in a loud hoarse whisper, "Well, what happened, I want you to tell me everything beginning with desert… did you do it with him?"

Grace leaned over, still taking off her coat and really whispered, "No, we didn't, but either way I don't want everyone in Westport to know about it."

Marty put her hand over her mouth. Whoops. "You look fresh as a daisy," she said, now speaking low, " how do you manage that in the morning without a little wake-me-up?"

"I've been walking around the Harbor mornings. It's refreshing! But, you are also looking fine, you of all people should have no complaints."

"Too true, too true, but…"

"I have to tell you I saw the most remarkable thing this morning. A dog, a three-legged dog was running around one of the boat moorings… there was a circle of boats and not a person in sight. The dog was hopping from deck to deck like he was a bird. A beautiful well-groomed three-legged dog, not a stray or damaged animal."

"That's unusual."

"I thought so. I have never seen him here before. He was so sprightly and quick… how beautiful he was. And, it was odd at first, I thought he was just another dog, but then I began to see that there was something about him that wasn't quite balanced, you know?"

"He made quite an impression on you." Marty looked at Grace, her head cocked slightly, "any reason for that?"

"Only that he was golden and beautiful… and damaged."

"Sounds like a lot of people I know."

Grace reached for the bread. Dipped it in the Italian oil.

Marty continued, " With that description, I might even say that many women I know think men are beautiful three-legged dogs."

"If that's true, then many men must think women are three-legged cats."

Marty shrieked in laughter. "Oh… oh… that's good! Honey, that's really cute! Maybe we should write a story about three-legged dogs and cats together, eh?" Their laughter died down and Grace said, "I hope this is not what we really think, that we have become this cynical…"

"OK, Honey, let's cut to the chase. Is Landon Harris a three-legged dog?"

"Well, I won't say that he is beautiful, but I find him quite attractive. I have known a damaged man or two, but I would say that if he has only three legs, that he has fashioned a peg leg and is getting around nicely. He is smart as a whip and I love that—and he is difficult, but, I have yet to figure out why."

Grace paused and seemed to go to some inner place. Marty watched with a slight smile and asked, "Did you go back to his place?"

"Nope, we had dinner on the Upper West side and a good night drink at some dive near Grand Central. He took me to the train and held my hand. I kissed him on the cheek."

"How chaste," whooped Marty.

"You know, Marty, I am going to have to start taking you to some more inland places for lunch. You are a fog horn."

Marty did a false blush. "Sorry."

"I should hope so."

The waiter appeared and they agonized over which salad to order.

"So, Marty, now that we have discussed everything from chastity to fog horns, what have you to say? Do you want to tell me about your new man, a good eight years your junior? Or the new house you are thinking of buying on the Cape…"

"How did you know about that?"

"I have sources."

"Well, you're not so smart as you think you are, I decided not to buy it. I am going to stay here and flaunt my good fortune."

Marty Gibbons, fancy hat in place, looked like a good catch, as divorcees go in Westport. She is intelligent, a degree in Art History from Rutgers, a good first marriage to a Curator at the Met who turned out to be just a dog: a mutt who loved the table scraps from the marriages of others. Marty didn't act out her faithfulness at cocktail parties or gossiping with friends, One would think she was trying to become the Bonfire of the New Century, yet she was a good woman, faithful to her man and loyal to her friends. It took Grace three years and the need for a good friend to learn this. She sat across the table from Marty in awe that a woman could wear so many masks, while being what so many people wished they could be as they sorted though the shelves and bins at the Mask Store: Marty was a real person.

"And, what, Darling, is your plan?"

"I have invited Landon up to my place here for a weekend soon."

"Do you think it wise to do this on your home turf?"

"I have nothing to hide... well, a pretty long story to tell. But, Landon Harris seems to be a very good listener."

"...and, you want to show him your three-legged cat?"

"Yes, in fact, I do."

"Oh, my, Grace..."

Landon was always surprised at how much had to be done after a Book Tour. Boatloads of needs. Many things to be done: Now! The first was a talk with his agent, Gregg Bantam, about short story movie rights.

"Hey, great! Wined and dined and offered the world, Hollywood-style."

"Not anything I am interested in, Gregg." Landon paused. "Is it 'just strange' to be a person who doesn't want a movie made of his life, his books, his anything?"

"Yep! First rate Strange, Landon. But, I love you for it. Not for my pocket book, which suffers when you say, No, I don't want gold from the Coast, but, I can live with this." One could hear Gregg Bantam get into gear. When the banter was done, he gave Landon a list of things he would do, including a look into the Chapman contract to insure there would be no problem if a Landon Harris short story was contracted for a movie deal or anything else. Finally, a most important item. Landon needed to get with his people at Portman Publishes! and insure that if a call came in to their offices from Hollywood, that it would be automatically turned over to Gregg Bantam and that the Portman people not speak with the Hollywood people. Could Landon guarantee that?

"Certainly, Gregg. Not easy, but do-able. I'll talk to Canning Vogel and see if he can lean on Hobart and the others. What else?"

"I think we can get by this." Gregg was unusually thoughtful, " It helps that you don't feel the need to bend over to the Hollywood people and that you can live without their money or other sinful offerings." It was on the surface of Gregg's face… the question of 'why no money needs?' But, if Agent Bantam had misgivings, he did not share them.

Landon broke into his thought, "Oh, I know, have you double checked the list Chapman gave us—about who might have seen his stories as he was writing them."

"Right… his bad luck was good for us. The two stories you threw out were the ones he chose to send out… his correspondence indicates that few if any read them. Safe here."

Both of them give a sign of relief.

Landon wandered throughout his apartment, looking, as if for the first time, at the place where he lived and worked. Sooner or later, Landon thought, I want to invite Grace up here for dinner. I wonder what she will think of this place. He tried to really see it. The décor was—what, Early Everyday—a place that a man who has been single for a long time lives/works.

And this is what happens: I am on a book tour, someone takes me somewhere in Charleston… that marvelous shop, whatever the name was… they had these pirate maps. I didn't even know I liked pirate maps, but I bought three and here they are in the dining area. He loved the maps, they seemed to speak of a world that couldn't even have existed. Beyond romantic, past cartography, all the way to realms of poetry, like viewing for the first time an N.C. Wyeth illustration of Treasure Island.

He began to pace through the apartment, muttering comments as if he was giving himself a tour. This old bookcase should be given the Salvation Army Heave. Wait, his attention was drawn to a book he hadn't seen in a while… Hmm, this looks fascinating. So why haven't I read it.

STANDING IN THE SUN

The Life of J.M.W. Turner. The British painter.

In the flyleaf,

"Turner was short and stout, and had a sturdy, sailor-like walk. He might be taken for the captain of a river steamboat in France at first glance; but a second would find more in his face than belongs in any ordinary mind. There was a particular keenness of expression in his eye that is only seen in men of constant habits of observation."

Now, he remembered… the publishers are Sinclair-Stevenson in England. He had met—which one was it—and they had given him this book. Nice fellow, and he wanted to read the book. There is even a small Turner watercolor in the bathroom. And, he would order a new bookcase this afternoon. His tour continued and ended up in the bedroom. His bedroom. How do you show a woman you want to sleep with, the bedroom? Clearly one doesn't point at the woman and then the bed and put the two fingers together. No. Not seemly. But, this is a part of the person being visited... and then it hit him. The writing room. Should he show her that room first, or wait until later? He walked around the bedroom. Which room should they spend their first night together? And, why does a man have a grand bed in a writing room? Will she think it odd, as others have, to see a pillared bed in an odd room that is supposed to be about the writing? Hmm, so many questions, and always about the Writing Room... oh, well, what the hell...

Suddenly he wanted to be a regular person with a small apartment on the East Side, or a loft in Soho. He didn't want to have to explain what all this was about. This wasn't a report card on his whole life, it was a visit to his home by someone he cared about. That's it, he thought, and he sat down in the reading chair by the bed. He looked around the bedroom. Night tables on either side of the bed, with overhead reading lights. A picture of his father on one side table, a picture of Catherine on the other. How many women had come to this room to be with him in a special way? Not many, but the ones... he counted on his fingers and it didn't take a whole hand to recall that the reaction of each had been to do a slight freeze when they saw the picture of Catherine in a silver frame. But, then each had known who she was... his late wife, one that was sorely missed, but still present. Norma had thought of Catherine as a competitor. A woman she had to outdo, and she had ruined the relationship by making it a competition when it wasn't a race, wasn't a presence, it was a sweet memory. Does that mean Landon should take the picture away? Put it in a less conspicuous place? Or leave it and hope. He remembered holding Norma close late one night after they had a rousing time and she had turned over, to come face to face with Catherine. He heard her sniffle back a tear and held her tightly not knowing where the tear began.

She whispered to him, "Is this a test?" Landon wasn't sure what "this" was and asked. Norma reached out and lay the picture flat on the table and turned back to him.

"No, of course it isn't…"

She said, "…but, once in a while I feel that way."

Landon took the picture and put it on a high shelf in the closet.

The closet. Long closet. But, not a lot of clothes. Many shoes, some drawers with pictures in frames on top of them. Him graduating from Stanford. His family in England when he was on Fullbright. Bette, the lovely girl he knew in London before he met Catherine. My, she was a plain girl. A plain woman with a heart as large as Big Ben, feet larger than Landon's and perfect breasts. Never before nor since has a woman had such perfect breasts. He had tried writing exercises with himself to see if he could properly, discreetly, subtly, wantonly, deliciously describe Bette's breasts. And, then, even harder, the feeling <u>he</u> got touching them. The tenderness of her skin, the texture of her nipples, and best of all, the look in her eyes when he did touch her there. He set the photograph down and sat on the floor to count his shoes. This "tour" was arousing him, and he needed (desperately) to concentrate on something simpler, perhaps re-visit the idea of inviting Grace over. As he was counting the shoes, he wondered if she would have luscious breasts.

"We're moving fast here, Mr. Harris," said Mrs. Hatch, the PR lady at

Portman Publishes! "and we want to be certain that you are ready to go out on another Book Tour end of August." She paused.

"As Canning and Celia may have told you, I am not wild about Book Tours. In fact I have been considering writing a horror story about an author who is out on book tour…"

"Oh, that's very interesting, Mr. Harris. Could you tell me more about it. I might be able to use this in my Tour Copy… not only are you doing a tour for your book of stories… I keep losing that title… Oh, here… but, that you are also doing research for a new book."

"How do I tell the audience for this tour that they are to be the models for my horrific nightly dreams of suffering at their hands, twisting myself into pretzels over their questions, boring myself to death—my death— over teas at the church, women's league, PTA gatherings, and best of all, local writing clubs… have I missed anything here, Mrs. Hatch? "

Landon paused, smiled to himself and said, "Mrs. Hatch, I love my audiences, I hate to think of myself as some stuffed elitist-writer from New York who cannot love his people—but I sound this way and I am most uncomfortable with my attitude. So, to write a book about, even to think out loud about a horror of Book Tours is not a good thing to even discuss…"

Landon could see Ms. Hatch, the world's most perfect Promotional-PR person pull the phone from her ear and look-at-it as if it was a diseased organ.

"Mrs. Hatch?"

"Yes, Mr. Harris?"

"It's a joke, Ms. Hatch, and not a very good joke at that. I would like to apologize for my gaiety and frivolousness. Entirely inappropriate."

"As you wish Mr. Harris. I try to take my work for your books seriously."

"Yes," said Landon smiling to himself.

"If you have such an idea, I happen to think a book by an author of your stature about Book Tours would be entertaining <u>and</u> instructive. If you are pulling my leg, Sir, well, then…."

"Ms. Hatch, you are the marvelous one here!"

"Why, thank you Mr. Harris. Now, back to my check list…"

How odd they came on the same day: Portman sent a messenger with an pre-production copy of the book, *How To End the Short Story* by Landon Harris. A thin volume with jacket copy written by himself, and a new photograph. Landon was sorry that he had not paid attention to which image of him they would be using. He was leaning against a white wall in the sun, and there beside him on the white wall was a large shadow. Hmmm… a shadow… a large one…

The mail also brought a note card with a printed announcement:

MR. NOEL CHAPMAN

Wishes To Announce His Change Of Address To

347 West 95th Street, New York 10025

Please phone at…

He sat in the sun room and wondered what he had done. Here he was planning to spend a weekend, a first weekend with a woman he was seriously interested in—one who was honest enough to tell him his work was … ah, less than it should be. Now he was thinking of presenting her with a copy of his new book, one which he really didn't write… and, then sit patiently to hear what she has to say about "these stories"? What to do, what to think? Look out the window, the Park was lovely, Spring had come and blessed Central Park with a major wisp of greenery and offered solace, once again, to the city dweller. He should go for a walk. Yet, all he could do was stare out the window and ask unwanted questions:

…how was he to answer questions about the writing of short stories wherein the nucleus was not residing within?

…how was he to smile demurely, accepting compliments for work that he had purchased.

…one thing was certain, he needed to be thinking of *what his own next book would be*… no more of this, oh what was it, this guilt.

And, then it hit him. Broadside. What would he do on the night when the Press Luncheon was over and done, and he was free, as free as he always had been to come home, settle into a ceremony that was indeed sacred to him, to share with his loving and departed wife? Now, he was holding the book with that thought, and he drifted off in a reveille with the image of himself—always himself—riding the book as if it was a flying shrine, candles fluttering in the wind, threatening to blow out. What a ride. Flying low past forests and lakes. It was all so flawlessly beautiful. Finally, ocean, an endless ocean, serene and cobalt, flying so low that he could reach out to touch the tips of the white water. The spray that held the light from the sun fell his way, as if to anoint him: to see him as a Golden Prince.

In the flow of the journey, he had forgotten to look out ahead and when he did... where had this come from? —a mighty pointed mountain on a tiny island... could an island be more like a monster, with smoke and... it was a volcano.

He stood on his invisible shrine to get a sense of how soon he would reach the island, where he would land. The vector veered up, steeply at first and then more dramatically vertical as he came closer to the rim of the volcano. Then a gentle slowing. He held out his hand and there was almost no movement... as if he were floating to the edge of the rim, as if to moor there. How unusual! Finally, directly over the volcano, his raft stopped. Midair. No motion. No breeze. Until he detected a slight sense of dropping. As he looked down, he saw fires leaping up toward the rim, toward him and his book-shrine. No violent motion, only continual gentleness, almost a soft landing, as if this was something he wished to do. The fires leaped up closer now and caught the edges of the book, the jacket with his new picture, some of the loose pages. Yes. This was going to be a—a what... a fiery... shrine. He would be the centerpiece, that part which burns best and last. He watched his book of short stories flame beneath him, as the book opened itself to the fire, as if it wanted to be consumed.

Oh, to be awake... Oh...

Landon couldn't decide how he wanted to travel to Connecticut. Train. Plane. Car. Hmm. He paced anxiously and immediately dismissed a plane, takes longer to get to LaGuardia than to the Connecticut border. He liked the drive up the Merritt Parkway... but this not being the Fall, that might not be so special. The train? Grace said he was to be there by noon and to call her after he had decided yes or no on the train. Suddenly, Landon wanted to go now, tonight, instead of tomorrow morning. He would take the train with the rest of the nightly commuters and spend the night along Long Island Sound. He would call Grace tomorrow and say he would arrive at noon.

He called Wanda at the travel agency and asked her to find him a small place to stay near the water in Westport and to call him back. He went to the library of books on his Number One list and selected a new novel by Guilian Taylor, a thin, new piece he had read about. And, something old... Summerset Maugham... *The Razor's Edge*. Good. Wanda called just as he had the second bag packed and gave him the address of a bed and breakfast near the harbor at Westport.

The train was packed. Landon loved to put himself in other worlds, so this was the perfect world of the Friday night going-home crowd. He looked around delighted at the men and women who did this twice a day, 20 to 23 times a month—he managed to bring out a small piece of paper to do some calculations: 2 x 21, 42 times a month, 12 x 42 is 504 times a year. He was really squeezed. He had gotten the last seat in the car between an overweight woman and an overweight man. Oooffff. 504 times a year. That means that they do this more times a year than they go to the movies, than they go to see the school activities of their kids, than they make love, than they read books—combined. He closed his eyes and thought of Maricopa, and its golden hills... it was May and the green would be just wearing out now, the creeping golden brown, that would mean Summer, was coming.

The woman beside him looked over at his calculations.

"I've never seen you on this train, you miss the earlier one, or did you get lucky and get away early today?"

"I just got lucky today," Landon ventured, "how did you guess? I'm an accountant at Chase and the place cleared out early."

She looked at him curiously. "An accountant, huh… and you are working overtime even on the train." Her eyes looked down at his scribbling.

"I was trying to determine how many times I ride the train every year… I have an idea for a tax break…" What an outrageous lie, he thought, what do I say if she asks me to share it with her?

She shrugged, "It's just death and taxes, can't beat 'em," and with that went back to her magazine. It was a *Health* magazine and she seemed engrossed in an article about how to merge body with mind.

Landon let his eyes rove the other passengers. Finally he settled on a man across from him who was reading his book of short stories. Just as he spied this man, the Conductor cried, "Greenwich is next. Greenwich" and a raft of people got up to get off. How could this man have the book when he had just himself gotten a pre-pub. copy? This man must be part of the publishing trade or, whoops, a reviewer. The seat next to the Reading Man was just empty. Landon nodded to the fat woman and moved across the aisle.

The man was reading *The Untied Knot*, one of Noel's stories about a fishermen in Southern Italy. It was not one of Landon's favorites. He wished the man was reading *The Candid Observer* or *Dipping Water*. He needed to do some research before he left on the gratefully shortened book tour. He began rehearsing opening lines to get the man talking.

"Excuse me, but I couldn't help but notice the book you are reading. I love short stories, but I have never read any of… what's his first name, Lawrence Harris?"

The man looked up. "Lan-don Harris... you're right, it is a funny name, and I haven't read any of his stuff before."

"What do you, ah, think of it?"

The man looked away for a minute, tapping the page.

"Well, you asked at a poor time, this story is a not-so-good-one. I liked the others better... there is one about a man who does nothing with his life but go around the world..." he looked at the book, "...observe people. That is a good one, and another I have liked so far is called..." he flipped the pages of the book, "...*Nancy is My Girl*." I liked that one the best."

Two of Noel's. Landon made a note not to do this any more. He shook his head while the man looked at him...

"...you read a lot?" the man asked.

"...oh, yeah, I do," said Landon. "You think I should invest $21.95 of my hard earned money on this book, or wait for the paperback?"

"I'm reading the new Don Delillo book at home, I think you should get that one."

Landon was about to ask where the man had gotten that copy, when the Conductor walked through the car, "Westport is next. Westport." The man got up and stepped over Landon. "Nice meeting you," he said and moved to the end of the car. Landon watched his back, wondering how he got the book copy and if he was Somebody. Damn.

Wanda did well. This place was perfect, and the sun was still high enough in the sky to take a walk along the shore. He made inquiries about the local pathways and places for dinner, left the room without unpacking. As he found the walking path around the Harbor, Landon wondered if he should have called Grace and asked her to come down for dinner with him.

But, the air was nice and he was pleased to be in it. He was good enough company for now.

There was a cluster of houses along the point across from where he was. Large windows on the Sound. One had a faux-widow's walk and Landon laughed at the modern idea of having a widow's walk on a house today. It didn't take long before he was near the boat moorings. There were row boats tied up to take you out to your slip. As he came through a cluster of trees he saw an old man with a dog, a golden retriever. He settled himself on a log and watched the man row and the dog seem to urge the boat to shore… only a few yards from where Landon sat. The dog made the leap of the last six or seven feet and hit the dock running. The dog saw Landon and ran toward him with a fanning motion of his broom-shaped tail. It wasn't until the dog was within reach that Landon saw he had only three legs. Immediately he nuzzled Landon wanting to be petted and spoken to. Landon was so occupied with the dog and his liveliness that he had not heard the man.

"Howdy, Mister," he hailed.

He had a sailor's hat on, old and battered. A heavy blue sweater that belied May weather, and white pants. He could have stepped out of 1905.

"Hello," said Landon, "what's your dog's name?"

"Rather."

"Rather?"

"Yep… he'd rather be at the shore, or in a boat, or even in the water,"

Landon laughed. "Sounds like you and he have much in common."

"Yep." He sat down on a nearby rock.

Rather was still begging for attention from the stranger.

Landon said, "I could hardly tell that he lost a leg, the way he looks and runs. Sorry to ask the same question over and over... how did it happen?"

"Well, Rather is a good dog and mindful. One day he saw me walking home, he got excited and ran out in front of a car. I blame myself really. But, we got him to the Vet quick-like—the break was high and clean. So the leg came off. Rather wanted to keep coming to the Harbor just like he had all his life, so he learned to be a three-legged dog."

"He is so beautiful, and lucky that—I don't know, it looks like he was born this way... with only three legs."

"Well, he certainly acts that way, Mister, I think it's kind of a tribute to the nature of all animals, you and me included, that we can adapt and still be happy in our lives. This dog has spirit, it pulled him through a bad time. Happens to all of us, but not always the same fine result, eh?

Landon stared a the old man, still petting Rather. He shook his head silently in wonder.

"My name's Horace... Horace Ryan... yours?"

"Landon Harris. I am up from the City to visit a friend."

"She have a boat?"

"I don't think so."

"Well, maybe you and she could come over to the Harbor tomorrow and take a ride with me and Rather. We go out every day...." He gestured to a small sailboat moored at the first circle of boats from the shore.

"Thank you, I'll ask my friend. How do I reach you?"

"Got no phone… but we go out 'bout noon-ish every day. Rather likes to sleep late." He smiled at Landon, "and, I need more sleep now than I used to… it's a bother." He got up and Rather ran to his side. Landon got up as well and nodded to the man.

"Good day, sir," he said.

"Good day to you, Mr. Harris." Rather turned back to Landon as if to say 'Good Bye', and ran off as if he had four legs.

Landon sat back down on the log and closed his eyes. He wondered if it was too late to stop the process of publishing the short stories. Why is he doing this… for what purpose? Wasn't he like Rather? Yes, he would Rather have his writing life back and he would Rather learn to run on three legs. Wouldn't he? Why wasn't he as strong as nature? Why isn't his nature as strong as the dog, and the man, for that matter. They seemed the perfect pair, mated by nature, adversary and love… a man and his dog. Landon set his mind on the sun, and when he came around, the sun was just creeping down past the edge of the world. Landon was always astounded at how fast the sun moved… high in the sky, it seems a motionless orb, but setting, it seems a golden racer. As it curled down to the next dawn, Landon got up and retraced his steps to the B&B and the phone.

"Hello, it's Landon."

"Oh, good. Have you decided when I come to meet you?"

"Yes. Yes, I have."

"Well, …

"Grace, I did something odd… I hope you won't think… ah, me…, but I decided, on the spur of the moment, to come up tonight… I have a small room with a view here in Westport. On the water… it's a bed and breakfast."

"Oh, well, fine… what are your… ah, plans now?"

"I am hoping you would be willing to start our weekend early… to come over here now… don't bother to dress up, we can go to the nearest fish joint and have, ah, something." His voice was imploring, and she noticed that… this was not the same Landon Harris she had dinner with in New York. She listened more carefully now. "Yes, Landon," catching his mood, "of course, I am really delighted to hear from you, I was just bouncing around here aimlessly anyway. I'll throw on a sweater and come…"

"You don't mind…? I mean the impetuousness of it."

"Why is it that I don't think you do impetuous things very often… and that this might be better than your Regular Master Plan?"

"Really? (pause) Great, Grace…"

She thought he was about to ring off. "Ah, Landon, where are you?"

"Oh, yes. I am at…," he reached for a brochure on the small desk. "Here it is, Indian Point Road, number 27. Do you know where that is?"

"Uh huh, I have walked there, not recently, but yes."

Landon is holding the telephone as if he and it had become a wooden statue. Grace is held to his impetuousness so tightly that she is afraid to hang up. What if she gets there, it has melted away, and there is Landon Master Plan Harris again.

"Grace?"

"Yes."

Landon moved slowly to the window to look out at the Sound, and then turned to see there is a fireplace in the room. She says nothing on the phone. She waits. Something will happen, but she hasn't the faintest idea what is going on in his mind... he is a difficult man, but he can't be impenetrable? Can he? It seems the silence has been for hours. Grace stands by her kitchen sink and waits. Saying nothing.

"I saw something today I want to tell you about."

"Do you want to tell me now?"

"Ah, no, I really want to wait."

"Fine." She doesn't offer to get her sweater. No offer to fetch him. Be patient.

"Grace."

"Yes,"

"I'd like you to stay here with me tonight. Would that be all right?"

"Yes, Landon, that would be all right. I'll bring a hair brush for morning."

"Good. See you then." And, he hung up.

After the dinner, during the walk around the Harbor, they chatted idly. They had not talked about anything really. They had laughed about living in New York, California and Buenos Aires. They had not talked about themselves, which was what Grace expected. She had thought, when she had been driving to meet him, that he wanted to tell her some incredibly personal story and then take her to bed having revealed himself. She had never been asked to bed on the phone by a man she was attracted to, whom she had not even kissed. It was all too improbable... yet her skin tingled. She had brought her hair brush. She had pulled over on the road to Westport and brushed her hair then and there. It was fresh and lustrous. She had looked radiant in the rearview mirror before dinner. Now it was later… yet it all felt new to her, as if she hadn't thought about being with him… it was fresh, she was here, he was here… in the room, he had opened all the curtains to the sea. He had carefully looked to see which curtains had to be closed for privacy. He turned out the lights and the moonless night shone in on them. In bed, they held each other, and whispered how crazy this was… that they were in bed together with their bare selves and had yet to kiss. Then they kissed and moved deeper into each other. As the lovemaking became more intense, he began talking to her, in between kisses, before and after stroking, during the melting of selves. He talked about the three-legged dog. How brave it was, how beautiful. Why it represented a nature he longed for. How he loved the three-legged dog and wanted her to see it… to be able to touch it, as he had. They would sail with the dog, Rather, and the old man, Horace Ryan. Grace said only that she would rather be with Landon now than sailing with the dog and the man. She thought how ashamed she was at herself for talking so rudely with Marty about the three-legged dog. It had to be the same one she had seen. She felt dirty for it and the only way she could think to cleanse herself was to kiss him over and over again, as if this could wash away the stain of her ugly thoughts. The waves from the Sound washed over them through the windows—it cleansed them—both of them, as if they were created in this moment, together. She said a small prayer of gratitude for the man with her and his wish to be her talking fool this night—and lost herself in his soft voice and touch.

The sun rises early in May over Long Island Sound. For a short while, it shone directly into Landon and Grace's room, projecting patterns of window and bellowing curtains, window boxes of white flowers. Grace had been sleeping on her side, facing the windows. A chill turned her over toward Landon. They were now holding each other in the bright sunlight—face to face—though neither was awake.

Grace was starting a new dream… one where she was watching a sailboat out in the water. As she watched more closely, she saw there was no one at the helm. It was plowing along completely on its own. Grace watched in wonder. How could it do that? She wondered if someone unseen was in the cabin. Might it be Landon and her…? Does this mean they are in danger? She could feel her muscles tense, and in response, Landon held her tighter.

Then another sailboat came into view. As her eye followed its course, it would crash into the first sailboat. Again she tensed, and Landon held her firm. Would someone come from below and right this sailboat before it ran into the other? Then, there was a streak of golden color along the deck of the second boat. It was the dog, Rather. She smiled at what Landon had said about his name… and here he was doing what a three-legged dog does best. Sailing. His boat followed a sweeping curve until it was alongside the first boat and Rather nimbly jumped from one boat to the other. Both sailed along together until the currents separated them, and Rather sailed on and away in the first boat.

Even as she was dreaming it, she wondered what the dream meant. Who was the first boat? She? Landon? Both of them below? Who was the second boat supposed to be? Was it meant to be she and Landon coming together? Did she have to worry that the boats separated and didn't sail on together? She reached her arm around him and held him tighter. And, then the light began to push its way into her consciousness. She could still feel the sailboats, but now she wondered when she woke up what she would say. She was going to wake up in his arms, she could feel his arms around her, of a man she really didn't know much about. She was not a promiscuous woman. How could she know what to say? And, what about him? What would he say? Will what he says help her to know? What do I want to know? Oh, dear...

Landon opened his eyes. He saw that she was still asleep. He watched her with contentment. She was beautiful to him. He wanted to say something to her, what should it be? —and then he caught himself. What did he feel? that's what should be said.

She opened her eyes to see him very close and looking into her. "Good morning."

"Good morning," came the echo.

SOME PLACES ALONG THE WAY:
BUENOS AIRES TO 72ND STREET HARBOR

*G*race Mathisson had gotten married for all the old-fashioned reasons and was bored for all the old-fashioned reasons. This is to say that she got married because women should get married, and divorced because people grew at such different rates that they actually lost touch with each other. This is not to say that she is not an intelligent woman, or a good companion, that she is or is not the housewife-y sort. Grace Mathisson is a walking contradiction. She is passionate and aloof. She is driven and adrift. She is loyal as the limb to the tree and can blow like a leaf in the wind. The only place where she is truly single minded is in marriage. But, Grace has failed in marriage. She was not the sort to say, '…well, it happens….' What she thinks is '…wonder what I can DO about this…?'

While she was deciding to leave her first husband, Arnold Harper, she had lunch with her friend Sally Dempster, who was mystified: "Grace, what in the world can you be thinking! Leaving Arnold?! You two are the ideal lovebirds. Why, Grace, why?" They were outside of Braxton's in Westport. Sally was wearing one of her hats.

"Darling, I just feel adrift. Listen, do you mind if we take a walk along the Harbor? Are you game?"

"Sure… sure…" Sally gathered up her shopping packages.

As they walked along the Harbor, Hal Minor called to them. "Grace, you look smashing today. You must be in fine spirits." Grace nodded. She did look fine today, she thought, it's the release. It must be good for the skin. "How 'bout some tennis this week, you traveling with Arnie or are you home?"

"I'm home, Hal, I'll give you a call.." She took Sally's arm and walked out toward the Harbor.

"You haven't been sleeping with Hal have you?"

"Nope, I have not."

Sally considered this. "Would you like to sleep with him?"

"No. He's a great tennis player, why would I want to ruin that?"

The Harbor was pleasant. Grace loved it and wanted a sailboat. She smiled at Sally,

"I want to sleep in a sailboat."

When Grace was married to her second husband, Kent Mathisson, she took a trip alone. She wanted to experiment with South America. She would take a cruise. The ship offered seven ports, but by the time she reached Montevideo, she decided to fly home. However, the fares were better from Buenos Aires, so she decided that a day or two more would be all right, and she took the boat across to Buenos Aires.

As she was touring La Recoleta in Buenos Aires, she wandered into the Old Cemetery. It was like a community of small, perfectly designed mausoleums, shoulder to shoulder, yet each one distinct, a masterwork of architecture. Suddenly she found herself confronted with the resting place of the Duarte Family… and Eva Perón. As she was reading the plaque, a voice behind her said, "The English Señora is enchanted with Eva Duarte?" Grace turned.

"Excuse me for speaking, Señora, but I come often and often the English women are not interested in Eva, nor do they understand why Evita Perón is buried in the Duarte family Crypt. She is one of my heroines. I am Juan Carlos Cadiz."

"How nice to meet you, Mr. Cadiz," and Grace extended her hand.

"Yes, Señor Cadiz, an old Spanish family. You are British?"

"No, I am an American, from New York."

"Ah, New York. I have always wished to visit there. But, I have never wanted to go further into the United States…que lástima, eh?"

"You come here often, you said. I can understand why I would come here to tour, but…."

"It is comforting to walk through the serenity here… But, come, can I offer you a coffee? …there is a suitable café nearby."

Grace asked, "Why do you have such affection for Eva Perón?"

They were settled comfortably in the outdoor area of the coffee restaurant. It was a blunted corner facing the largest tree Grace had ever seen. She looked to Juan Carlos to ask about the tree, realizing she should be listening to his explanation of why he was not a Perónist, but an Eva enthusiast. She had never known such a gentle man. Clearly he was well-educated, perhaps even one of the nobility of Buenos Aires… part of the government, a professional, someone of value. Of course! He is a writer. She blurted it out!

"Excuse me, Juan Carlos, but I was wondering if you were a writer, a man of letters?"

"Si, you would know that, you have good instincts, Mrs.Mathisson. You said your husband's name is Kent… we have no Spanish equal to that… it must be a northern European name. He is a good man, yes? You are still married to this man?"

"Oh, yes…."

Juan Carlos was disappointed. He tried not to show it, "Yes, certainly…"

"Are you married, Juan Carlos?"

"No, Señora, I am not. I have lived these 41 years wifeless."

Grace hesitated… "but you like women… yes?"

"Yes, how could one not be constantly in love. I have thought much about this, and have come to a conclusion that I gain love and experience love though my writing. You see, I am a poet."

"A poet."

"A poet, indeed."

Grace jumped ship and moved into the home of Juan Carlos Cadiz. She learned that he was from an old Spanish family, therefore his name, the same as the city Columbus sailed from—or was it Cortez, Grace was never sure of details like this. She was given her own bedroom and did not move into the one occupied by Juan Carlos. She had never been treated like this, it was as if they were above being emotional, beyond being, well, sexual. Juan Carlos seemed to exist on a plane literally above that. She called New York and her husband with excuses of why she could not return yet to New York. Then, there was the dinner with Juan Carlos who was talking about destiny… he had a poem to read to her about destiny…

Destiny is a place where they say I am going.
I attempted to describe it to myself,
this place we speak of,
but no one knows.

Then I realized, I know...
I own Destiny—in my heart.
I have looked at it through my secret windows.
This is how I know my heart is so large.
For it holds all my future, my destiny,
as well as the hope of man.

What then is larger, my heart or destiny?

On another day, she and Juan Carlos would have dinner in a patio café and they would talk about the nearby La Plata River.

"It means *silver*, you know, Grace."

"What a nice image, a silver river. I suppose you have experienced that silver."

"No, in fact. I tried to write a poem about it but failed... I have no poem for you this evening. But, if you wish it, tomorrow we may go on a boat up the La Plata. I have a friend who has a boat."

They had empanadas for dinner. Grace was excited about the food, it seemed so exotic, yet Juan Carlos assured her it was plain for his country.

He had a poem on Wednesday. It was not his poem, but one by Sor Juana Inés de la Cruz. He explained to Grace that Sor Juana had been a poet laureate of Mexico... that she became a Catholic Sister who had written much about life. He read the poem to her... he reads it first in Spanish for the music of the words, then in English, and Grace is taken with a sudden urge to visit the Recoleta Cemetery again.

"Juan Carlos, can we go to the Old Cemetery again tonight? It's warm enough…" Grace had taken some time to acclimate herself to the idea that it was warm in January and chilly in July.

"That is most difficult, but if you will excuse me, I will call a friend."

The friend of Juan Carlos was the Chief of Police of Buenos Aires. Yes, it would be possible to send an officer to open the gates and stand for a few minutes while Señor Cadiz gave La Mujer Americana a turn around the old resting place on this moonlit night. As they were walking through the Recolecta, Grace noticed there were many cats. Cats sitting on crosses, cats walking on the crypts, cats sleeping in the doorways of the small, inspired monuments. Grace thought she had never seen so many cats in one place… but then, why not… no need to ask questions about this. Where could a cat feel safer than this sacred and serene place? She tightened her hold on his arm.

"Juan Carlos," said Grace, "do you think we will find our way to sleep together?"

"You are not happy, Grace." It was not a question. Juan Carlos stopped and faced her, "Don't you believe in the elevation of the spirit, surely you have experienced that here… in this Holy Place, here in Buenos Aires, with me, breathing in poetry as you have been?"

Grace began to cry. She leaned against him and he held her gently. He walked her to a nearby stone bench, which was warm to the touch, and they sat and held each other.

"Will you write a poem about me, Juan Carlos?"

"I have so already."

"Will you read it to me now?"

"Yes…

> *I cannot love you more.*
> *Love, after all, is merely for a person*
> *and we, we love each other*
> 　　　　　　　　　　　*in this way.*
> *But, I cannot love you more than*
> *the stars in the heavens,*
> *more than the birds in the trees of my garden.*
> *I love you as if you were that star, that bird.*
>
> *I cannot love you more.*
> *I cannot love you only.*

On Thursday, Grace stayed in her room the whole day. That night she called her husband in New York and told him she needed a divorce. She told him that she was aware this was a cruel call and that she regretted it. When he asked her why she was doing this, she said only that she was considering taking vows. When this was met with silence at the end of the line, she smiled, knowing that he could not see that, and told him that she loved him. That she had given him all the love she had to give, and that she was emptied. She hoped he would forgive, though she doubted she deserved it. They hung up.

When Juan Carlos knocked on her door for dinner, she declined saying that she had a heartache. He nodded.

The next day, she hugged him goodbye, and his chauffeur took her to the harbor, her way back to New York.

Landon arrived early for his meeting with Celia. He wandered thought fully through the maze of docks and boats, both motor and sail that moored at the 72nd Street Harbor. He was always, no matter if he was in New York or further upriver at Tappan Zee or even at West Point, amazed at the breadth of the Hudson River. So dramatic along Manhattan with the New Jersey Palisades competing with the tall buildings across from them. Landon turned and there was Celia, fifty yards off coming toward him. He had not noticed before that she had a slight roll to her walk. Not all that prominent, and not at all unattractive. He wondered what she might look like at the helm of a sailboat... did she wear a sailor hat with blue piping, or a baseball hat?

"Do you wear a baseball hat, or a sailor hat when you are aboard?"

"Hello, Landon? ...I see you have been tasting the sea air up here at the River Joint. And, I wear a baseball hat with gold leafing on the brim. Nora does too."

"Hmm..."

"That's a disappointment to you?"

"Yes. I am afraid I have a more romantic view of sailing, it comes from being brought up land locked."

"Well, then this may be a new view for you... I did know an older man, Charles Kentfield, who claimed to belong to one of those ancient families off the Gloucester-Marblehead coast. He, you will be pleased to note, wore a blue-billed captain's hat with white piping and an anchor shield—he wore it all his life. His wife complained that he wanted to wear it to bed!"

"That's how I see you."

"Beg-a-pardon?"

"No, not wearing your hat to bed, but wearing a hat like that to sail in." Landon thought for a second of her in her cotton night dress with rumpled hair at 3:00 in the morning. No hat with white piping for her then, for certain.

"You hungry?"

"I am."

"Good."

They turned and walked together back to the café at the Harbor. It seemed that Landon, from the back anyway, had a slight roll to his walk. Something that only a sailor would have noticed. Inside the restaurant, Landon commented on the view.

"Is this the only place on the river where one can get a meal?"

"No, there are others downtown. I must admit I have not investigated. No recommendations to make. Sorry." She put her menu down. "Landon, I don't know how you arrived at the contents for your book of short stories, nor do I know how many stories you have not included. Didn't someone say that the test of a good book is how much good writing you have discarded?"

"Yes, that was Ernest Hemingway."

"Yes. Of course. Hemingway"

"You knew him?"

They both laughed. "Sure, Landon, I was his editor at Scribner's for *The Sun Also Rises*."

"Nicely done, Celia, however I think you will be more remembered for your ability to always look thirty-four years old."

Celia felt at sea with what she considered these off-hand, apparently complimentary thoughts Landon tossed her way. What was he trying to do… say… what…? She recovered and said,

"Anyway, I think your book is good, I even read it again."

"I am complimented." Landon squirmed in his chair. He tensed as if to say to himself, here it comes…

"I have to ask you one question about the stories" she said, "…the technique of what I call triple conversation… three people talking at once: it was quite skillful. I am wondering why you didn't use that same technique for *One Woman, Two Men*?"

She is bright, he thought.

"Good question, and I have to be honest with you, I don't know… and until you mentioned it, I hadn't thought of it. But, as you know, that book is not one of my favorite memories… and…" He picked the napkin out of his lap and wiped his mouth.

"Sorry, I don't mean to be unpleasant, but it would have been effective. Period. Paragraph. On a more positive note, I found the young man in the story *An Actor Prepares* quite touching at the end." Now it was one of <u>his</u> stories. Landon leaned forward into the table, listening carefully. She said, "I thought you had drawn a person who was well-compartmentalized within himself, and yet at the end, he seems honest—for the first time—open…? I don't know… effective and good character growth."

"Thanks." Landon leaned back and seemed to settle. He wished he could be more relaxed with Celia, but she always brought out the edge in him. He needed to settle… just listen.

"Speaking of touching stories, we seem to have a sterling opportunity to touch the readers of *Vanity Fair*. A sex-crazed editor from there has visualized a super cover story."

"Really. Touching?"

She frowns and wrinkles her brow. "No, really Landon, this editor has tapped three prominent authors of short stories, now that includes you, to write just a love scene as if it were a segment of a short story, or even of a novel."

"Was "tapped" the word used?"

"Yes, she said 'tapped'."

"She? I thought all sex-crazed editors were men."

Another wrinkled frown. "We need be serious about this Landon… if "tapped" is the word of the day, works for me. Each of these tapped writers is to write a love scene for this piece in *VF*. Are you in?"

"What does 'a love scene as if it were a segment of a novel' mean?"

"It's a magazine, Landon, and magazines like short stories, better, if they are about celebrities, and if not, then sexy. Thus, a love scene… but not to worry about foundation character development, or hanging loose ends." She leaned back as if to say, *any questions about THAT*? She was surprised to see that Landon nodded thoughtfully and then drifted off into one of his internal séances.

Silence.

Celia shook her head. The waiter arrived and took the order. While Celia decided what to have for lunch Landon looked out the window to New Jersey. The waiter left, Celia looked at Landon. Time passed.

"Two teenagers, perhaps falling together by mistake or accident after the Big Game?"

"Have to be serious here, Landon!"

Landon nodded, and said, "Rest assured that they, in that event, would be most serious… It would be hard to say without knowing the two kids which was the most serious. For him, he's this big kid who isn't really sure of anything but his size and how fast he can run. He's seen enough girly magazines to know where all the parts are, but knows nothing about his own heart which is probably like a bowl of mashed potatoes—unsalted. Her? It could be just an idea to her, mostly in her head with some visceral yearnings—touchy-feely gets you started, but there is a place in the middle, before all the adrenaline kicks in, that is a minefield—a place that is past emotional, 'way past visceral and not emotional: physical and not physical."

Landon leaned forward again and looked Celia in the eye. "I have never believed that love-making is what people do naturally. There are so many instances of the unnatural, the aberrant, the thoughtless, yet found in scenes that are supposed to be about love, that personally I find it, what— frightening and sobering." A pause, "…or just bewildering…."

"…and distressing?"

"That too."

"Did you ever play football, Landon?"

Landon released a big breath. "No, but I made love once. And, Yes, I understand that this must be serious."

"…and perhaps more original, and touching…hmm…"

"Who are the other two prominent writers of short stories?"

"Chelsie Commoner."

"But, she is that formula romance writer… those books where there needs be an obligatory love scene every 25 to 30 pages. Not fair, Celia!"

"What can I say to you, Landon? For Chrissake!" Celia paused, then… "We don't get to make all the choices here… you-are-right-OK. It's a loaded idea which is why the unnamed sex-crazed editor wants to do it."

"The third writer?"

"She hinted that Roth was asked and turned it down."

"As well he should, what if his Ex, Clare Bloom was asked to comment about love scenes with… well, who was next?"

"Well, you'll love this. An unknown they plucked out of a writing competition."

"My…it is a loaded situation. Let me guess." A weighted stage wait while Landon smiles at Celia, "…the unknown has already written his/her love scene for the contest and they are using it as a platform for the other two stories."

"That would be a possibility."

"Loaded, with two barrels."

"Listen, Landon, Roth turned it down, you can too."

Looking directly at Celia, Landon closed his eyes and turned to the River. He was on a round raft drifting down river, but not near Manhattan —upriver, up past the Tappan Zee bridge where the trees crowded down to the River to let their roots drink deeply. On the raft, there were six sex-crazed editors and six short story writers. In the middle, on a high circular platform was a woman in a cloak with a pointed hood. None could see her face as she held her left hand high with a small pistol pointed at the Sun. As she pressured the trigger, each writer and each editor took a deep breath and raised their own pistols. The even match of the circle meant each writer had his editor to aim at, each editor had a writer as an adversary. The sun moved a degree in the sky, the woman's long finger squeezed the trigger firing the shot. At first there was only smoke, enough to obscure all the shooters. It was only when the smoke cleared that Landon realized that each editor, and there were three left, was faceless. Four of the writers remained and Landon's face was on each one of them!

"Where do you go when you do that?" It was Celia's voice speaking very softly as if she was the woman in the cloak on a raft in the river.

He looked over to her and shook his head. "I don't know."

"Or, you won't tell…" She smiled at him and thought, He is really some-thing! It was as if Celia could actually watch, see, Landon return to earth, right here beside the River and at this table with her. She caught his gaze.

"You are right, Celia… and I wish I could be word for word with you here, that is, explanation for question. But, you know," he smiled at her in this moment, "a smart woman like you knows that for every reasonable question, there may not be a "reasonable answer". I am not trying to hide from you, in truth, I would be willing to expose myself to you… barely, in the raw… but, on the other hand, all this, this "writing" that I do for you and Channing and Horace Upstairs… it might be slight-of-hand for all I know… but to put all the—all my—cards on the table, it might be "really true" that even I don't have an answer for all questions, be they creative, reasonable, out-of-the-park or just whatever. It may only be that I am, somehow, against all odds, an instinctive creative person, and that even I cannot answer all questions."

Celia looked at him… wishing to herself, that—what, "that night" he had presented himself to her at 3:32 in the A.M.… that things might have gone differently. Yes…

"…more coffee, Miss? I have just poured some for your friend here."

Landon smiled at her… "…where do you go when you do that?" And they both laughed.

Landon was late coming home. The doorman had a package from Portman. He opened it in the elevator. It was his first printed, finished, copy of the short stories… *How to End the Short Story*. He fumbled the envelope and the book fell on the floor. He stooped to retrieve it. The book felt warm in his hand as if it had been taken out of an oven. As his apartment door swung open, the darkness rushed at him and he hurried to the windows to look at the lighted Park. He held the book in his hand. The Portman people had been as good as their word: they had spared him the press luncheon and the obligatory speech after the meal. But, the book here, in his hands! He wished they had spared him that, or that Celia would have brought it to him, so that he could have walked back over to the reflecting pool in the Park—would he have looked first for Rather, the three-legged dog? —why does a dog in Connecticut come to mind in Central Park in New York?

Yes, the reflecting pond. He would throw the book into the pond, watch calmly while it floated in the gentle wind toward the center of the pond, amid the reflected lights of both sides of the Park. He would look over to where Alice in Wonderland watched his curious actions. He would smile at her and sit on a bench savoring the sinking book and the smiling girl before he went home.

He went to the answering machine and pushed the button. "Hello, darling, it's me. How did it go today? Did you have a good lunch with Celia Langhorne? Was it about the new book? Call me."

The tears had begun to flow down Landon's cheeks as soon as he heard her voice. The 'Call me....' felt like a voice from a great distance.

Landon felt ghostly. A ghost trapped between a dead woman, a living woman and this—this book. The triangular shape felt like a tightening noose. He walked back quickly to the windows and opened one to feel the freshness of the Park, and also to hope he might flow out the window—if he was a ghost, why couldn't he float away—out the windows and into the trees. To be transformed into one of the trees by the reflecting pond. That must be happiness, to be fed by an inner spring and unfailing roots. This is not, he dabbed his eyes as if to put a bandage on his crying. Oh, God, this is ... unbearable.

His hand was over the telephone. 203 (Connecticut) 317 (prefix to help) 7733 (Grace). He couldn't dial the number. He couldn't bring himself to ask her to come to New York for an evening of being-another-woman. The real risk was, Landon knew, that Grace would be able to do it, but Landon would not. He would mess this up and in the bargain damage either Grace or himself further. No, no, no. But, what? He went to the closet and got a jacket and hat and walked out of the apartment and into the Park. Sanctuary. He was either going to have to stop publishing books, and not even a book of his own—don't think of that now—or he was going to have to let Catherine go. As his mind slowed, Landon wondered if she had let him go. Was she the ghost here? Was it her presence that kept her at the edge of his mind, or better, like a shadow leaning against the back of his mind. Always there, always present as she always was. Like a muse. Yes, a muse.

When the Park ended, the barrio was on his right, Harlem was before him, yet he didn't even notice the time or the direction. He was fully with Catherine now. Either she had captured him again… her shining face ready to light candles on the book, this horrible, saving book. Or, he had willed her to walk from the back of his mind into full view. She was lovely in this light. Her fair hair, her oval face with lips that were, well, delicious. A firm chin and slender shoulders framing perfect breasts. Not much of a waist, slender backsides and a runner's legs. When they first met, he had been surprised that her name was Catherine Harris. Later he realized that a woman knew the significance of that. Full of portent. They were meant for each other in some sense of this world and she would always be his, for like family, they shared a name. This was really the essence of their relationship—or maybe better, starts as family, but, being family made it easier to become friends. Was there a Greek writer who said that admiration was the foundation for all marble statues? Maybe. The Greeks clearly understood the role of the muse in the life of an artist or writer. Have muses gone out of fashion because true friendship is so difficult…?

"Hey brother, you help out a person?"

The voice came from nowhere, hollow. Where was he? Without thinking, Landon looked up for the street signs. Fifth Avenue and 121st Street.

"I'm back over her."

Landon looked off to his right, under the elevated tracks. The darkness and shadows combined to make a scary scene and Landon still could not see where the voice came from. Suddenly, it stepped away from an iron column. A black man with a badly scarred face and a bottle in this left hand. His clothes hung from him in shreds.

"You help me?" he said. "I need a bed fur tha night. I get one over near

Drexel Street… you got a dollar, brother?"

Landon pulled a hand out of his pocket with paper money. The first bill in sight was a twenty and then a fifty and a clutch of ones. Landon pulled the fifty away from the others and held it out to the man. "

"What my suppose'd do with that, nigger?"

Landon looked at him without speaking, still lost in his revelry.

"Iff'n I take that, they put me away. Think I stol' it. You, crazy man, wander through her' with green like that in yo pocket. They kill you." The man waved his hands toward downtown. "Get outta here man, they kill you… go… go 'way…" and the man turned back into the shadows and disappeared.

"Wait," Landon called after him.

All he heard was a grunt from the shadows and scuffling feet. He stood there in the street looking around him. It was much later than he realized. No cabs to hail, and he turned to go back downtown, where he belonged. He stopped and looked back. What had happened here… here in the city?

It was 2:13 when he returned to his apartment. He went directly to his bedroom and took the photograph of Catherine from his bedside and went into the writing room and booted up his computer. He placed her picture square in front of him. He typed titles into the file:

The Harris Sisters   My Only Friend   The Perfect Breast
The Muse
A Muse on My Mind   The Muse in the Mist

Landon Harris wrote for twenty one hours intermittently refilling the carafe of coffee and relieving himself. He might have been half way through that when he passed out in the kitchen or napped on the seat of toilet. Past the next nightfall, almost a whole day had passed and his head lowered slowly over the keyboard. At 1:38 in the next morning, Grace came into the room, with the doorman, who saw that she had been right—something had happened to Mr. Harris. He helped her get Landon into bed. As he left, she was standing in the middle of the writing room with a bewildered look. She sat and watched Landon sleep, wondering what had happened, why he had not answered the phone, why this was such a strange room—all drawers and no windows. She noticed the answering machine and pushed the PLAY button:

"Hello, Landon, this is your father. Your last note said the book tour would be soon… when your plans are firm please give me a call. I am looking forward to some time with you."

"Landon, darling, it's Grace. I am wondering why I haven't heard from you? Are you there? Call me."

"Mr. Harris, this is Ralph Callaway at Bowling Green University in Ohio. We are having a writing competition, a national one, and are looking for imaginative writers to help us with judging. I am the chairman of the Creative Writing Program here and would be pleased if someone of your stature would involve yourself in this. I can give you more details if you can call me… oh, yes, the number here is 513-334-7000, extension 702. Thanks for your time."

"Landon… Landon… where ARE you…?" It was Grace again, it was odd to hear her own voice trying to be coaxing to him.

[click]

"Landon, Goddammit, are you there...? is something wrong...? it has been hours now... it is 11:00 at night... the second night. I - am - worried —"

Finally, Grace noticed the thing she should have seen first. The computer. She sat down and began to read the file with all the odd titles. She could tell it was about Catherine, but the rest was... a mystery. This was not a book, nor a story, nor even a history... in truth Grace didn't know what it was beyond a catastrophic flood of the stream of consciousness of a person at the end of—she sat back for a moment and turned to see the man she loved in sleep. Well, if I ever had a chance to look into his naked mind, this is it. She kept digging in the computer, looking for fragments she might understand. In the late middle she came across a section that seemed intelligible—she hoped he wouldn't scold her for reading his raw material. She had no idea what the etiquette was for this, but she read on...

> "...could it be that we have not insistently explored the idea behind the word, friendship. A ship upon which a meeting of friends takes place. The meeting being as long as a journey, a marriage, a life. The extent of the meeting of friends reaches from the bilge pumps where the tough work gets done to the fore deck blown with salty winds forming ideas of where the ship is actually going, to the business at hand in the Captain's cabin, and if of opposite sex, the friends can throw blankets over the cargohold and have as large a bedroom as their love allows. Love is the next to last word here, all the others relate to the shipbuilding specifications of a friend-ship..."

Grace wondered if Landon had been lucky enough to have had a perfect marriage. Like all things that end in death or disaster, a glow is formed that might not last the night if life had lasted longer. But, what an appealing idea, a love based on a friendship. She had known some of her girlfriends referred to their husbands as "best friends", even if that had not been her experience.

She left the dizzying experience of the computer files and began to wander around the apartment. The doorman had seemed to know right off where Mr. Harris would be found, and that room was a puzzle to her so she decided to see what the rest of the place was like… and as she expected, it was pretty much an upper west side apartment lived in by a man alone. Landon had enough money to be comfortable, and this was comfort, but not warmth. A large living room, dining area with some unexpected maps. Nice place for dinner parties, she thought. Be fun to do that with Landon. The kitchen was larger and cleaner than she expected. The three aprons hanging on a hook by the garbage chute answered that question… he had help when needed, therefore he never needed to bother with the dishes. She looked out the kitchen window to the Park and realized that he wouldn't be very good at that anyway. His bedroom was as pleasant and eclectic as the other rooms. The choice of art on the walls was quite unsophisticated… posters from the Metropolitan, Andrew Wyeth, Grant Wood, and one California painter she didn't recognize… Wayne Theibold. Nothing… nothing but the Theibold would be to be said to be contemporary, or risky.

Was Landon a risky man? she wondered. Was he the kind to take risks? She picked up the copy of the new short stories book she found in the sitting room overlooking the Park. For instance, had he taken a risk with these stories… they were all right, good and interesting as just reading, but they were not the best stories she had read, nor could she in her innocence as a reader think of stories in this book she had truly enjoyed, or had made her think—she sat and let her thoughts go… Cal Edwards floated to mind…

she had a book of his stories that she had re-read, that surely meant that she liked them. Who was that woman writer she liked...? Or the stories of a young man in Kentucky who killed himself before his time. She turned her head and caught her reflection in a window. Her brow was wrinkled and she had a stern look on her face. No, I don't think this is a risky book, nor was there risk in its underpinning. Is Landon Harris a man willing to risk everything on his own idea, no matter what? She lay her head back and looked off to the eastern sky. I guess the jury is still out on that one, but maybe there is no hurry, maybe... this is surely a comfortable spot, she thought, as she closed her eyes to rest them for a moment.

It was just two o'clock in the afternoon when she roused herself. She went to check on Landon in that room—she was going to have to find out what this was—he was beginning to be restless in his sleep. Grace took off her clothes, folding them neatly and hanging them over the chairs. She slipped into bed with him as if she had been there all night and all day. As she did, she wondered which might be the most important, to have perfect breasts, or to know how to be a First Mate on The Friend Ship?

YET ANOTHER BOOK TOUR?
OR JUST A MOVIE DEAL?

*T*he first stop on the tour was Memphis. As Landon landed, he was treated to an approach that included a swell aerial view of the Mississippi River. He recalled that the normal sense of a great river from above was as a snake, a large and side-winding snake. Landon thought of it as a ribbon, the north-south part of a ribbon that wraps some incredible package that is too large even for human eyes to see. As he looked closer, he noticed that the ribbon was muddy. Well, so what?

The agenda was slim this trip. The Portman people had reasoned that he had read the short stories in so many of the cities for the last—never say the word—book, that this one needed not to be so expansive. Sales were good, so no need to spend unnecessary monies. The trip would start at the Southern Cross, an independent bookstore, and end at his favorite store in Santa Barbara. From there, he could slip over the pass and be in Maricopa, in the Central Valley… or perhaps slip up the coast for a walk on the beach.

The Southern Cross was fortunate enough to have a large area for folding chairs, and therefore a good sized audience for a reading-signing. Landon was just finishing his last reading section: the ending of *An Actor Prepares*… his favorite story…

> …but, I wasn't on the stage at the Ethel Barrymore Theatre at 49th and Broadway. I was in the apartment of my girlfriend and her roommate, Carole. Just the three of us, all stark naked.

It's not a play, Tom, it's me, your life. Remember that? I remembered only that I wanted to be an actor because I'm a limited person... because I wanted to expand myself to become more than I was. At heart, I felt like I was not very much. When I started acting, my teachers said that I would be drawing for my roles from within. Because I wasn't sure that I had 'a within', I devised this idea of doing 'research'. Watching other people, learning how to be a person, becoming others while watching them play their roles. Watch. Listen Learn. Become a person. Then, Act. Perform. So, tonight I learned how to become the role I play on Thursday on Broadway. I also learned that Sally, my girlfriend, was a switch-hitter and that I get the sweats being in the same space when her roommate, Carole, a lesbian, wears an open bathrobe.

Illusion is gone. We are all naked in front of each other in this very small private apartment on the upper west side. For the first time, this is my real life and I am terrified, wishing desperately that a theatre curtain would fall and save me.

Landon liked signing books for his readers. He liked to ask their names and make a flourishing signature, but he noticed today that he was less chatty with people, and his signature seemed to tremble over Noel Chapman's book. He had taken to referring to it thus. He felt, after his horrific night in New York, that he needed to remind himself who wrote this book, so that he might again be able to be more comfortable sometime in the future when his writing became more familiar—his own. The last one person in line was Millie Anders, an ancient woman with a firm face, clear blue eyes and stark white hair. As she handed the book to Landon, he noticed the knurl of her hands, like it was a tangle of wood—bleached wood.

"We are honored to have you with us, Mr. Harris. Where is it that you live… the book jacket doesn't say?"

"I live in New York City."

"Ah… but you were not raised there."

"No. No, I was raised in California."

"Is that so! Whereabouts?"

"Maricopa." He loved this part of the conversation, and waited for the inevitable question.

"Isn't that a small town near Bakersfield…?"

Landon looked her full in the face and smiled. He waved over the bookstore clerk.

"Yes, Mr. Harris… you are having your most special conversation in Memphis… has Mrs. Anders introduced herself?"

"She has indeed, Cathy, and I would like you to put her book on my tab." Mrs. Anders looked quizzically at the clerk, who only beamed at her.

"Of course, Mr. Harris."

"Mrs. Anders is the only one in recent memory to know exactly where is my home town in California." He turned to the blue-eyed woman, "Congratulations, Mrs. Anders." Landon signed her book while Mrs. Anders chattered away at him about her upbringing in Knoxville in simpler times, the loss of her husband several months ago and her pilgrimage back to the home they had first shared in Knoxville. As Landon watched her tell the story, her face actually seemed to lose age, reduce its wrinkles and become the face of a younger woman. He marveled at the strength of her memory and its ability—the will of her memory to create herself as a different person, one she had been, years ago. When she finished her story, cut short by the lights in the store being turned out around them, she appeared to be 18 or 19 years old, seeing through glistening eyes with an innocence that seemed to offer great hope.

Landon walked Mrs. Anders to her car. She leaned forward, kissed him on the cheek and drove off into the night. He turned around and wondered which way was the River. He needed a walk, a long walk to meditate on the nature of life in Knoxville, Tennessee, in the earlier part of the century... when life had been simpler. My, this is a wide river. He wondered if the Mississippi and the Hudson had been brothers in an earlier world.

The envelope was postmarked Philadelphia. Handwritten from Garrett Gilman. Celia was amused that he had his own stationery, inscribed Garrett Gilman, Critic-at-Large, not including his newspaper affiliation. She could see this overlarge man hovering over pen and paper, as the oldest-fashioned of writers.

Dear Celia,

I must admit to being terribly surprised by the sheaf of papers you sent me comprising Landon Harris' latest efforts. First of all, that he had short stories, then that they fall together so well, and lastly, that there are only two or three that I don't care for, But, that's true with any collection, it only depends on who is the reader, and the disfavored stories will differ. My thought is that Landon has found a new voice. Better? Possibly, but perhaps only different, different enough to intrigue his continuing readers, and bold enough to find some new ones who haven't cared for his prose in the past. I thank you for letting me be the first, one always wants to be first, so that I can continue to raise my stock at cocktail parties with hints here in Philadelphia.

As to your instructions to burn the loose pages you have sent me. Absolutely not! I have a special bookcase for items like this, and there they shall go, along with Barney Thom's *My Own Witness* and Kalia Whitman's *She Rose in Anger*... and let's not forget Celia Langhorne's *The Yankee Racing Sisters*.

Admiringly yours,

Garrett

Note: Yes, I shall be glad to provide suitable quotes for your salvos in the Press.

What a sweetheart! The man from Philly. If he heard her say 'Philly' he would never speak to her again. Celia laid the letter on her desk and placed her hand on top of it. She turned to the window and instinctively her eye was caught by the nearby flags. The wind was perfect. She looked at her watch... 11:42... time for a long pretend lunch. Celia grabbed her racing jacket instead of her summer coat and headed for the door.

Seventy-second Street Harbour was Celia's idea of brilliant city planning. A boat harbor a cab ride away from the office. It was days like this that Celia wished she had a boat here. She recalled dating an account executive from Leo Burnett who maintained a boat here and called it The Client.

So, on a racy afternoon he would tell his secretary he would be out with The Client. She was pleased also to be counted as one of his prized clients, and therefore not to have to have a boat of her own. Also, she learned much about river sailing from him. As she walked into the dining room, she thought of her last lovely lunch with Landon here. She hadn't heard recent news of the book tour—she would have to check with the circulation people later to see about sales. And, "Damn" she said out loud, that story for *Vanity Fair* was due soon, perhaps any day. Oh dear… writers and deadlines, deadlines and writers: two incompatible ideas.

Early the next morning, Celia was at her desk before nine… and there was a FedEx envelope waiting. What and Where in the World…? She pulled out the contents to reveal…

Love in Knoxville, 1915

by

Landon Harris

for *Vanity Fair*, Director of Sex Department (word count 2000)

ShirleeAnn loved to watch Harold sprinkle the lawn. In the late softening light of a muggy summer evening, he began, each night after dinner, with his undershirt on, and within 20 minutes, stripped it off. Then, ShirleeAnn could look fully at the rippling body beneath that undershirt. She could see the broad line of hair that raced down his chest, and often she felt that she could almost touch the thick muscles of his back just under his arms. One evening, she closed her eyes and imagined she felt them, one hand on each side, holding herself to him. ShirleeAnn sensed that their lovemaking was better in the summer when he took off his undershirt to nourish the grass rather than in the colder months when the lawn would have to fend for itself and make due with the rains that came, but then, she had only one winter and one summer of their marriage to compare.

Harold seemed to love the grass, all of it. He watered under the shrubs, he watered the grass alongside the house and even under the stairs. She always asked him why he did that, why under the stairs?

Celia looked out the window of her office. Without looking at Landon's pages, she began slipping forward into his story. She looked down. No matter how many times Canning had told her that... editors read all the way through! ...don't skip ahead—for whatever reason. But she did anyway, flipping through the pages of Landon's story, sexy story, right Landon? Looking for the good parts... yes, here...

She turned the doorknob and felt her way in the dark to the bed. Harold had never questioned the need for this ritual, and its veiled darkness. He assumed all marriages were like this, though no one, not his friends, not his mother, had suggested that this was proper, or that one could make a choice. Choice was something like cement, he thought, once poured, always the same. Yet, there was a deep urge he felt... to see her...

naked… walking toward him. His woman. Coming to him.

Always when he was at this point in his head, she was beside him in the bed. He could feel her hand instinctively reach up to the headboard, sense her fingers grasp one smooth, knurled limb of the headboard. She used that hand to pull herself up so that she would be face to face with him. The other hand went around him tightly and kissed him hard. Harold had only kissed two other women in his life and neither of them had kissed him like this, hard, firm and determinedly. It was as if ShirleeAnn wanted to say something important to him in that first moment that would set their minds for what would follow—active thrashing and kissing and touching. The rule was that either could touch anywhere they wished, but not under her nightdress nor under his pajama bottoms. Harold had not known how to react to this rule. There had only been two other instances and each had been different, without set rules. Bunny Southern had let him undress her to the waist and touch her as he wished. The other girl, one he had met at a carnival, had let him kiss her and then touch her under her dress. Truly, Harold felt uneducated in these touching areas, so when he and ShirleeAnn came together he felt he could not, in honestly, offer his meager experience, or help establish rules.

Following her rules, they arrive at a melting point where they have sculpted themselves into a classic statue, two bodies joined together in a seamless form, one lying, the other sitting, both covered in a Roman way with falling cloth. Tonight, Harold's fingers fumbled for the edges of her nightdress and slipped underneath, finding, touching and warmed by the skin of her thighs. Slowly he slid his hands up her body until he found the golden lode, her small and firm breasts with the pointed buttons. When she felt his hands on her bare skin, she looked down at him in surprise. If only Harold could have seen her expression in that lightening flash, how much it would have told him. Then, equally unseen, she slowly raised her head up and back and he sensed her body through his hands as some marvelous and rare animal caught in a moment of bliss, reaching for the sky beyond their tar paper roof. He too arched and thrust up until....

"Wait," she screamed.

It frightened him so, he almost toppled her off the bed. ShirleeAnn realized as soon as she had screamed what she had done. She reached down to place a single finger over his lips, as if to kiss him. Then, just as quickly, she reached down to where he had found the ends of her nightdress and lifted it slowly over her thighs, her flat belly, her small breasts, her arched neck and finally, her radiant face. It was a sliding sensation that he imprinted in his mind so that wherever he might be, he would have only to close his eyes and feel this revelation of body and soul... and yes, love. For now, at this moment in their marriage, she was giving herself to him, even this small piece—fully, truly—for the first time. Harold closed his eyes and felt the full impact of her gift on his heart. He had not thought about hearts, that had eluded him until now, as he had found one part of the path, and she had shown him another.

Was this how they would be, how things would grow and change?

As ShirleeAnn looked down at her young husband she felt him trembling… as she reached down, she could feel his broad shoulders heaving and then finally know that he was crying softly. His hands had left her breasts and body to tend to his own. She fell forward onto him, held him. He continued to tremble and she thought, though it could not be true, that he might be chilled and she reached in the dark to cover him with the blanket. There it was. She had not seen it before. In the meager light it seemed a golden rod standing out from his body, and as she watched this luminous thing, and felt his body with her hands, heard his sobbing, she watched it unfurl in front of her eyes and seem to disappear within his body. She covered it and his lower body, turned to him and held him tightly.

Harold said through his tears. "I have never loved you more than this night."

I wonder if I have misjudged this man, Celia thought? He doesn't seem, when I am with him, to be a sensitive person. Yet here he is in the middle of a book tour, for God's sake, writing as if he himself had experienced this in, where was he? in Knoxville. Celia shook her head in wonder. I wonder if I have misjudged him, I wonder if I should be in Knoxville with him… In 1915?

I wonder… I wonder…

As he looked out the hotel window, Landon didn't recognize Memphis and the river anymore—he continued to think he was in Knoxville. He was in a daze over Knoxville and his talk with Mrs. Anders, with the story he had written for Celia and also still with the conversation with Grace last night. They had a good talk. What was different for Landon had been that he could concentrate on her, wanted to talk to her, wanted to listen to her.

"Do you think you can make anything out of this, what did you call it, Story Idea you sent to Celia Langhorne?" she tried to gain a foothold on his vocabulary.

"Well, I like the story, but I can't seem to extend the idea… it's as if I wrote the story in a fever dream. Grace, to be honest, I have never done this before. It's all new territory" He could hear her thinking. "How does that feel to you?

A pause. "Just as honestly, I don't know. I proved to myself yesterday that I still could write something, but… hard to say. These pages are short and intended for… oh, I just don't know."

"I wish I was on the tour with you. I want to hear you read, " and before he could object, she said, "and I don't care if you read the Manhattan telephone book, I just want to hear you read. It's that simple."

"Well, let's go somewhere and I'll read you the Manhattan phone book. Maybe at the beach this summer."

"Good, I'll buy a new bathing suit, and hope to come on the next tour as well…"

"Let's hope there will be a reason to have a next tour."

It was also from Memphis that Landon wrote to his father… still in this daze, still trying, hoping to find… what?

Dear Father,

Not that you wouldn't be the perfect help to me on this, but I find myself wishing that I knew Jane Stetson better. It's almost that I need a motherly viewpoint for this urgent itching question. It's not as simple as—in the current saying, 'I have met someone' —it's worse than that, or better than that. A fellow should be happy that he has met a person he can honestly talk to, relate to and better, who relates to him. I am happy in that. She doesn't see me as some sort of a celebrity bug, but as blood and sweat. I am drawn to this woman and I haven't done anything rash, yet I have come to a simple realization: I don't think I know how to love another person anymore… a woman who I can respect and whom I would wish to have grown-up relations with beside a roll in the hay and dinner twice a week.

Could this be possible?

I haven't felt this way since Catherine. And there are parts of this that feel even stronger than they did with Catherine. It has been seven years since she left this world and many of those years have been hard. It has been easy to have companions, but hard to have friends, real friends—oh, I know I am exaggerating but all this is happening at an altitude I am not acclimatized for. Do you suppose that there is some way that Jane could talk to me…? in some way that she would be willing to listen to me and then talk to me? I know it's a great deal to ask, but damn, I have got to get my footing under me before I return to the East, or I am afraid I'm going to make a serious mistake.

Yes, the tour is going fine. Lots to tell you as usual. You

would have gotten a hoot out of this man in Atlanta. Long hair. Distinguished. A good grasp of things. He wanted to know why I was back in Georgia so soon, just after the last book? How could I do a new book so quickly? —he wouldn't accept the notion that every writer has several books in the storage boxes of the mind, as well as the closet. He continued to ask what was the meaning of all this? He actually said that, '…what was the meaning…?' I was stumped and he saw that. He probed me in a kindly way, and then said, "I suppose all of us have done something we have been ashamed of, and you are ashamed of your last novel. So, you created a book you like better… you are not ashamed of it." He actually patted my hand. Then he said, "Well I have only heard the story you read to us here today, but I have completed reading the other book, the novel, and I completely agree with your assessment. Best of luck" he said, and this man waved his way out of the store.

So much for the superficiality of book tours.

Your loving son,

Landon

The El Encanto Hotel in Santa Barbara was a book tour dream. A hotel set away from the town, with dining views of the ocean and Santa Barbara Harbor. Landon was at the dinner table there when the maitre' d approached him with an apprehensive look.

"Mr. Harris, a call for you at the front desk." Landon got up and walked through the rooms to where an attractive Spanish-looking woman held a telephone out to him.

"Yes. Yes. It's Landon Harris here."

"Hi, Landon, I am hoping you will recognize my voice, though there is no reason you should, but the hint is that I am calling you from LA."

Without a shred of dread, Landon said, "Certainly, you are Amy Rosing. How nice to hear from you."

"One might think, Landon, that you are trying to hide from your public, but I finally tracked you down. I was hoping you might let me buy you breakfast tomorrow—I love the drive up along the Malibu Coast early in the morning."

"Do you live in Malibu?" he asked.

"Not yet."

"Well, then, do come up… you already know where I am. The El Encanto Hotel.

"OK, that sounds findable."

"By the way, what is the subject of our breakfast?"

"We want to option one of your short stories for a film."

Does a heart skip a beat?

"Landon?"

"Sorry, I was distracted. Fine, which story?"

"It has been quite an argument among the producers, but we have settled on *The Italian Rope*."

"All right, then, let's talk about it over breakfast."

Damn! One of Noel's stories. Landon went back to his room and got out the book. He thought it odd that he had to have it in front of him to be able to understand how the discussion might have gone with Amy Rosing's producers. As he looked over the Contents page he saw that the logical choice for a film was *The Italian Rope*. It had all the ingredients that could be extended and manipulated into a full length movie. One other of Noel's stories, *The History of Apples According to Abigail and Harry* would be possible but a stretch—and what did he know anyway, he wrote prose, not movies. Who knew how those people thought?

Of his two stories in the book, *How To End The Short Story* was not possible. Too fragmented and too much the short story. *An Actor Prepares* would make a good film but a short one,in his estimation. The character of the Actor was strong and the story had turning points, but much more story would have to be invented. Well, wasn't that what they did? All in all, Landon wished she hadn't called, or that he had known who it was and he would have played Caller I D and pretended she was selling Cable TV dishes. Well, time to face the dragon....

No matter what you might say about Amy Rosing, she was good at her job: she was persistent and attractive. Landon was certain she would have her home in Malibu. She was not glossy, but had taken plain but strong bones and made them up carefully, must have a movie hairdresser to take what might have been over curly, wiry hair and make it lay down and frame her face. These people were image makers all right.

"...so, what do you think of our choice of *The Italian Rope*?" Landon turned his gaze from the harbor below and looked her fully in the eye.

"I worry about it... I know you people are masters of illusion, but there are subtleties of this story I am fond of—that I would be distressed to see, how shall I say it, bent out of shape."

She started to reply and Landon kept on…

"…I personally have known authors who have cried at seeing the first cut of their prose children on the big screen. I don't intend to be one of them."

"What about you writing the screenplay?" She leaned back, wishing she had not had to play that card so early.

"It's a thought, then we all have heard what happens when a movie gets into production. A writer friend who watched the process once called it the Scourge of the Colored Pages…" Amy cocked her head, as if to say… "Don't look at me that way, you know more about this than I."

"I'm not sure what… oh, wait, let's see… script revisions are done during shooting in colors… pink pages, blue pages…"

Landon interrupted, "…and apparently the green pages are the last color… seldom used, but deadly because they are trying to solve, as this fellow said, the unsolvable problems." Landon leaned toward her in his most fatherly manner and put his hand on hers. Amy wondered how this would go… what card would she have to play now?

"Look, Amy, I like you. You seem like a very nice person. I would like to help you get a step up to your new home in Malibu… not in the Colony at first, but somewhere …"

Amy smiled brightly. "So, what will it take to allay your fears of 'green pages', if they indeed exist?"

"Do you think I am trying to negotiate with you?"

Lying she said, "Ah, no, of course not."

Landon smiled, if she only knew. "Doesn't everything exist in our minds and hearts?"

She nodded, waiting.

Landon tightened his hold on her hand. "Amy, look at me, I'm not a bad fellow…" He paused for effect, "…but I am not a screenwriter. I work hard to create decent prose." He looked deeper into her eyes until she was starting to think that she would have to play yet another card too early. Landon squeezed her hand and said, "…but to take you up on your kind offer, would be to put us both in jeopardy. Nope, I think it's a wash… unless, you are willing to take a shot at *An Actor Prepares*, and allow me to approve the story expansion ideas."

It sat on the table between their breakfast dishes like a hill of scrambling ants.

"I would have to take that back to my people, and quite honestly, Landon," and now the positions were reversed, she had her hand on his. "I don't know if they'll go for it, and there is…" —here she paused for effect— "there could be a lot of money on the table, money that would disappear if they gave it a pass. You need to know that."

It pleased Landon to be able to turn what was considered to be the Final Argument: money, against the people offering it. It seemed to mean so much to them, and so little to him. He must have this conversation with Grace sometime, to plumb his safety from money… he would like to know more about it. But, now here was lovely Amy Rosing sitting here, thinking she had left him anxious: he might lose all this money, forget about the fame of being a purchased author or luminous screenwriter.

"Well, then it's in the lap of the Gods, Amy. I'm glad you are the Goddess on my side." As if the ants had reached her mouth, and she might be able to politely spit them out,

"Works for me," she said unconvincingly.

Landon got up and went around to her side of the table to help her get out of the chair and away from the ant hill. He walked her out to the car and received her social kiss on the cheek and watched her drive off, wondering if she would think of stopping in at the Mission of Padre Serra down the road and get an extra blessing.

BACK TO BASICS:
HOME ON THE RANGE

*T*he Harris Ranch, perched on the east of the ridge of the Coastal Mountains, had a "careless" sense about it. Not designed, not planned, it happened the way things did in the West. The ranch house was well cared for, and set at the perfect angle to get a full measure of the sun. The best room in the house, the California kitchen and living room combined, received the sun for most of the day. Ashton Harris favored western artists and had replicas of Remington, Post and Russell—cowboy pictures for a cowboy place. The views out the windows were of a distant Bakersfield. When Landon was a kid, Bakersfield was clearly in view, now it was often muted by the smog in the lower Valley. A native here knows there are mountains beyond Bakersfield, the majestic Sierra Nevadas, but they might as well be a dream now, for they were lost in the modern distance of pollution. Ashton Harris had never visited his son in New York. Their time had always been spent here in Maricopa, or with his son on tours of one sort or another. Ashton had never imagined the vast difference between his son in New York and his son at home in the San Joaquin Valley of California.

Landon arrived from Los Angeles in the late afternoon. The dinner conversation revolved around the tour and all the people Landon had met, the real, the plain, the deranged, the aggressive, the angry, those who adore and those who envy. Ashton was always intrigued with the seeming vast array of people who came to hear another read from a book and go away with a signature. Jane was politely inquisitive.

Jane Stinson was a woman from this area. A no-nonsense sort, attractive not plain, but plain spoken and direct. Ashton liked that in a woman, and clearly these two had grown together on this basis since Landon's last visit. But, Landon was not yet used to a step-mother, nor was Jane like his own mother, who had softer edges and a creme center. Jane had lived most of her life in Modesto, a town further up the Valley, one plainer than Bakersfield, larger than Maricopa, but closer to the eastern mountains. Everything here seemed to relate to geography, and Jane Stinson's topography seemed less generous than had been the rolling hills his mother had comforted him with.

"How can all this trouble your publishers go to be worth it, Landon? It must cost a bushel of money to send you to all these places."

"You're right there, and truth be known, I don't understand it at its roots. But, I do know it's about a large audience being able to lay hands on an author, to be able to 'know' that person in some sense. The publishing industry has always relied on the verisimilitude of a writer and providing channels for his or her continuing work… series is the operative word here. If you build an audience who likes to read your books, then each book's sales effort will not need to be as intense, or as expensive—and more important, a "back list" is created and that will level out to a steady stream of sales. But, as corporate ownership of publishing is a fact of life, more and more publishers have become more interested in sales and not the written word—'backlist' becomes an archaic concept not readily understood by the accountants who serve the corporate owners. To say this is complicated is not even to begin to understand publishing."

Jane Stinson received each word and seemed to turn it over in her mind, and then, perhaps drop it into some deep pit.

"How are your beets? I have discovered your father really likes beets, so I looked back in the family recipes to see if I could find a way to make them better."

"Amazing beets, Jane," said Landon. Ashton laughed. "Tell me, son, you were reading your short stories on the tour, did you bring a copy of them to leave with me? I'd like to see them… seems like it has been a long time since there were short stories."

"Yes. Yes. It has been a long time. I should have sent you this book weeks ago, there has been a whirl in my head that has caused some things —important things like getting the new book to you have dropped away. I'm sorry… I have a copy with me that I can leave with you."

Landon hoped desperately that he would be able to conveniently forget again to give his father this book. He held up his hands, "Now Dad, don't ask me where the ideas for this book came from, or who are the people and do you know any of them… I just don't know if I will be able to answer…".

"Have you ever written about us, here in the San Joaquin?" It was Jane.

"No, and I think that's a very perceptive question… I started years ago a story about a girl and her dog over in Oceano, but never finished it. If I had, it would have been a kids' book." He smiled and dug further into the beets. Jane caught his fleeting thought.

"What is it that makes you laugh?" she asked.

"I can see the dilemma on the faces of my editors, Canning Vogel or Celia Langhorne when confronted with a kids' book by Landon Harris. Particularly if I insisted on publishing it. Can you imagine a book tour that had to reach a different audience... that placed me on a small stool in the Children's Storytelling section reading to them? It's the way those people think... in terms, not of the work, but of the audience and the ease or difficulty of marketing to them..." Landon waved his hand, "Let's not talk about it. Too..."

Jane broke in quietly. "I'd like to read your story about the girl and her dog over in Oceano." Landon looked at her and said, "Fine then, It's called *The Dune Runners*. You shall have a copy." Then Ashton said, "Time for me to retire... no reading for me tonight, good night all..."

It was his way. Years of being out on the ranch at five in the morning had regularized him, even though it had been years since he was a Ranch Manager. Ashton Harris was a man of habit. He wore into his habits as a hand does a glove. Soon a man can't tell his habits from himself. Since he retired, he taught himself to do other things as the dawn broke to the east rather than break his habit of rising.

Landon and Jane settled into the living room as the interchange of their separate versions of California dwindled away.

"Would you like another glass of wine?" she said.

"No. Two is already too many."

"Are you going into Bakersfield tomorrow?" Landon nodded, "There are people who expect me to stop by and say hello." He paused. "Did you read the letter I sent to Dad?"

"Yes, I did."

"Do you think it's possible?"

"Possible? Possible to do what?"

"Forget how to love a… another person?"

"Of course not, don't be silly."

"…like riding a bicycle…"

"What is 'like riding a bicycle'?"

"Loving."

"No, Landon, I am not a writer, so I don't have any colorful ideas like that. Loving is, to me, like a river, I guess. The river is always there, less when it's dry, more when it rains. Pretty simple, I think. But I'm just fine by this Loving River."

"Good metaphor." said Landon and then he really looked at her. She squirmed and finally said, "Thank you."

After each of them had examined the ten year old wallpaper in the room, she said, "Listen Landon, I don't know what you expect me to say to you… I am sorry that I am not your mother, that I don't know enough about you and life to be able to help…" there was an odd ring to the word when she said it, "help you, but I somehow don't feel adequate to it."

"Your husband died, Dad said."

"Yes, he did."

"Long ago?"

"Twelve years ago next month."

"That's hard, you still miss him."

"He was a good man."

"Yes."

"How long have you known Dad."

"Four years."

"Is that how long it takes to learn to love another person?"

The settling darkness outside came to her face. "Pretty smart aleck-y thing to say, Landon."

"Yes. Yes. It is that. I'm sorry. I guess the reason I thought to ask you, beyond the sense I have that Dad thinks the world of you, is that you did have to learn to love again, and my wife died as did your husband. I know that's the last comparison there might be between your emotional life and mine. My sense is that you are a very good and honest woman. The woman I am learning about in New York is like that, given she is younger and has had a different life, one that is not necessarily better, but... different."

The open room became dense. Underbrush seemed to crop up between them, as though windows had been opened by themselves and the evening wind blew through, yet didn't cleanse the air, but thickened it, adding to the internal denseness. They might have been on the coast while fog blew in. They were on different parts of the same pier, yards from each other, unreachable, within clear sight of each other. Landon spoke first. "I'm sorry, Jane. I have no right to ask you how you came to terms with one lost love and the rekindling of yourself for another. It's not fair, and I apologize." He got up and took a step toward her. "I do respect you for the person you are, and the one you have become for my father. " Landon walked to her chair, leaned over and kissed her on the cheek and walked out of the room. Jane Stinson watched him leave. She sat in her chair for some time before she rose to clean the kitchen and retire. When she caught sight of herself in a mirror, her face was pale.

The phone rang in the kitchen at 8:03 A.M. Landon could see his father out by the barn working intently on something by the door. Landon was making himself a cup of coffee and wishing for a bagel with cream cheese. Jane had gone into town.

"Yes. Yes. It's the Harris household."

"Landon?"

She sounded whispery. "Yes, it's me, Landon. You sound as if you had just gotten up."

"Well, I have just gotten up." He looked at his watch… 11:04 in Connecticut.

"The visit with your Dad going well?"

"Very well. He is most happy to see me and spend time with him and Jane." He teetered on alluding to his talk with Jane last night, but realized this was not something to begin on the phone. "…it's always good to be here."

"I'm glad."

"I have thought a lot about you, Grace. I have missed you."

"Not enough to ask me to join you in some city to be one of your admirers?"

"Yes, more than that, but not enough to want to share you with a room full of people."

"How did things go with the studio woman? Did she lure you into bed to offer you the best chance at a contract for a movie of your short story, and if so, which one?"

"No, no, it was very businesslike… we had a simple breakfast and an even simpler difference of opinion. As for an agreement, my guess is that there will be none."

"Does that bother you? —must be a lot of money involved."

"I don't know… we didn't talk about cash, we talked about stories, and I can tell you more when we are together in New York."

Ashton Harris came into the kitchen and saw this was to be a quiet conversation, and walked out again. Landon watched the older man.

"I decided not to wait to find out when you were coming back to New York."

"And…?"

"And, I took a flight from Hartford yesterday noon to Los Angeles and drove up last night to Sequoia Park… it's incredible here… I have never seen trees like this, and it was dark. What must they look like in…"

Landon broke in. "Grace, where are you?"

"In Cabin number 11, in the Sequoia Park Lodge. It's a large room… they said it was large but I would wish it to be larger. It has a suitably large bed, a tub as well as a shower. A view of some stream and these incredible trees. Landon they are SO BIG."

"I don't understand." Landon thought back to the river Jane talked about, but this one seemed to have cross currents. He was feeling both the push and the pull. "How did you get to Sequoia?"

"I just told you."

"Yes. Yes. You did. I mean, why have you come to Sequoia…? I didn't think you even knew where it was."

"I didn't until I went down to the map store. Landon they have maps of every part of the world, I could have gone to Ethiopia, or Lapland, or …"

"Sequoia?"

"Yes, and that's what caught my eye. The map said they have some big trees here, and I love big trees but I never realized they could be this hugely majestic."

"I have been there."

Ashton stuck his head in the doorway to see how the conversation was progressing. He sensed his son's bewilderment, mixed with the amount of tension he applied to pouring a cup of coffee from the pitcher.

"I am sure you have, Landon. And, I am pleased to say you are coming again. My question is how long will I have to stay here alone. I mean, I am comfortable here, I love it and will get up as soon as we hang up and get dressed to go and put my arms around the trees."

"You can't put your arms around the trees."

"That's what you say. And, if you come here, you will see for yourself how well I can hug a tree. Even a big tree."

He was speechless. No one had ever come for him. Across the country. It wasn't the trees she wanted. It couldn't be just the trees.

Those that live here call them the Big Trees. In fact they are the largest trees in the world. The Sequoias. The largest of them is the General Grant tree. The lumber from this tree would been enough, if cut—something hateful to think about—to supply enough wood to build thirty-two houses. How large is a house? How big is a tree?

The next morning, while Landon was saying goodbye to Jane and his father, Grace wandered aimlessly through the grove so carelessly that she got lost.

Landon called to say when he would arrive, then called again and she still wasn't in her room. He was able to marshal the Lodge security people to search for her. He had only wanted to say that he would drive over, this morning, to be with her. A short journey. But, now she was gone. Disappeared. What to do now?

The U.S. Forest people were quick to react to his call. This had happened before. There were dogs, German Shepherds, who went out with the Rangers to find lost people. The dogs were taken quickly to the room of the lost person for the "sniff test". With her scent full with them, she would be found quickly. The Grove was large, but the size of the trees meant that there was a great deal of open space so that it wasn't a dense manhunt through underbrush. The Rangers claimed that a well-trained dog could search for a half an hour an area that would take six men four hours.

It was about the time Landon called that Grace realized she had lost her way. She was deep in the Grove. But, she looked up, as she had a thousand times to see the tallness of the trees and then down to see their invisible roots spread under her, she imagined that she could play tennis in these openings between trees. She danced up and down to feel the mass of tree textures under foot. She could see the sun poking light through the opening in the cathedral-like ceiling above her. Yes, that's what it seemed to be, a vast cathedral. A place where one could be in nature and pray. Grace knelt in the middle of a large space triangulated between three trees. She had a cross around her neck and she yanked it, to break it from her body. She held it tightly in her hand and raised it to the tips of the trees and prayed for serenity and harmony. It seemed to her that the light of the sun penetrated the trees to reach for her tiny soul, to light it from within. She quivered. She had an urge—an undeniable urge to reveal herself to this deity of the trees. She closed her eyes and thought what it would be like to take her clothes off, bit by bit… first her blouse, then the belt, her bra, and then… she raised her face to the sky and the sun, feeling in return this spiky light prickle her skin. She could actually sense this on her body. She lost consciousness for minutes at a time while the sense of her body seemed to fuse with the higher elements. Her eyelids fluttered and then closed. Blackness, beautiful blackness wrapped itself about her and she was warm.

Days, hours or seconds later she heard dogs in the distance. She roused, shook herself and realized, in surprise, that she was naked to the waist. No, she had only imagined that… she felt herself, and they were there, her clothes, where they should be. She reached for her cross on the chain, but it was gone. Yes. She remembered that part. She got up and touched herself as if to assure herself that she was there, in her body. Head up again, she listened for the direction of the dogs yelping and moved toward them. Within minutes, she had her hand out to the lead dog. The Ranger called him Muir.

"Hello, Muir… what a funny name…"

"You gave us quite a scare, Miss Matthison. We worry about folks who stay out in this country. Just—" the Ranger spoke to the dog, "Muir… back home, boy…"

He looked at Grace, "Just follow the dog, Ma'am. What made you think it would be safe to be out here all alone?"

"To be honest with you, I have never in my life felt this safe or sheltered. But, I'm sorry you were worried."

"Good thing Mr. Harris called or we wouldn't have known."

"God! He knows about this?"

"Yes Ma'am... that OK?"

"No," she laughed, "not really." Then... "...is he here?"

They opened Grace Matthison's room to Landon so that he could wait for her there. The Ranger had called—she had been found in Cathedral Grove, and they were walking back now. Landon lay on the bed and thought about how pleased he was that was she was safe. Then, his mind went to the ride up the gorge of the Merced River. The huge boulders at bends of the road where he could see the surface of the white water as it rushed down to the Valley. He thought back to his conversation with Jane Simpson and her analogy of love and the river. Now here was a river, but a different one than he had imagined when Jane spoke. Her river seemed to be larger and more majestic, that helped her analogy, but spoke to him of only one kind of love. Now he looked at the Merced, swifter, more turbulent and demanding. That was yet a different kind of river and love. Maybe this was the love he and Grace felt for each other. He wanted to think of a river that might describe the love he and Catherine had for each other. It felt more like a lake than something that moved... perhaps he misunderstood, or even more, there was his sense that there might be three rivers, or there might be 100 rivers. His yearning would be to trace them, not back to sources, but forward to the branches. To the life that could be possible in a joining of waters. Did that make sense?

She walked in, silhouetted by the outdoor lights. It startled him and for a split second he wasn't sure who she was. "Landon, why are you here in the dark?" He heard steps move toward a light and then he saw Grace's face. He got up and embraced her. He ran his hand along her hair and kissed her ear.

"It's good, very good to see you. "

"Were you worried?"

"Not after they told me they had sent the Ranger and a dog after you."

She stepped back and slapped him with her scarf. "You were supposed to worry." Then, she embraced him, kissed his ear and then his mouth.

"How long does it take to drive up here?"

" 'bout an hour and a half... more if you don't know the road."

He ran his hand over her back, as if to be sure of who she was.

"I have a sense you may be at sixes and sevens.", she said.

"What's that?"

"Haven't you ever heard of sixes and sevens? Not being sure of something, at odds..."

"I don't feel at odds with you."

"...but you are at odds with yourself." She was not asking him a question.

"Yes."

"Want to talk about it?"

"I don't know how to talk about it."

He moved away from her, to the window. Looking out he said, "We haven't talked about this—and I am forever grateful to you for that—but all those pages I gave you about Catherine, I know you read some of them—I would, had I been in your place. Those incomprehensible pages were clear to me. I have carried them with me on this trip and read them often. They make sense to me, and I know I don't know how to translate them for you. If I could for you, then I would be able to do that for the rest of the world. But, I can't. I don't know how. So, this is the long answer to the question, I am at sevens and sixes."

"…sixes and sevens…"

"Yes."

"I thought I lost my bra tonight."

"Ah, how… isn't that unusual? I thought you were alone out there."

"Yes, I was alone, beautifully so."

"How did you lose your bra."

"I thought I took off my blouse and belt and bra… I thought I started to take off my clothes." Landon took steps toward her. His head canted toward her as if to say something.

"I wanted to pray in the Grove. I think I would have made a suitable scene for a new age painting—do they do those? —aren't you taken by the vision of me praying in the Grove, my breasts raised to the stars? Do you think I have beautiful breasts?"

"I am. I do. I will…" Landon turned to her and slipped his hands up under her blouse as if to test the truth of the lost brassiere. His eyes moved from the shape of his hands under her blouse to her eyes. Her eyes were soft blue and rounder than the last time he looked. He had kissed her before , but now her mouth seemed to be softer. He liked that she was a tallish woman and that he could look almost level across to her eyes.

"Your bra is here, on your body."

"Oh dear, it is not lost after all."

"No."

"Well, as long as you're there, you might as well take it off and throw it out the window. Then it will be lost." Landon fumbled with the snap and the bra dropped away from her.

"Do you feel safe with me?"

"Yes."

"Do you wish it was Catherine here with you instead of me?"

His hands fell out from under her blouse and moved to his head, as if he had heard a sound.

Grace said. "I didn't ask you if you loved me. I didn't even ask if you thought you could love me." Landon looked at her, her face in the half light from the window seemed serene.

"I wish you had been with me in the Grove tonight. I want us to go there, not tonight, but another night, to that spot and be with the serenity of that place. I will show you serenity, Landon Harris. I can, you know." She put her hand to his face, "Shhhhhhh, don't answer, I have no need for answers. You are the one who is searching for answers, and I am one of them. Just one… but any port in a storm tonight, right?"

"Right."

Grace pulled the bedding down to the floor and pushed him down on the edge of the bed. She slipped out of her clothes and began to reach up to take his off as well. All the time she did this she whispered to him about her feelings in the Grove. Finally, she had pulled his socks off and pulled him down with her. "We'll do this in the Grove another night, but tonight I want the luxury of softness and the shelter of this place. Some day you will want to write a story about us… after you write the one about Catherine, and you will, you know. You just have to figure it out. My father used to say that all the time… that he needed to figure things out as if he had a pencil and pad built into his head. Landon, this is you and me…" She held him close. "Catherine can be with us, maybe she is anyway, who knows about those things… but, I don't care about anything but you and I and here and now." His hands had been grazing over her body. She could feel him letting go, the tension melting away, leaving a man who was 'way past sevens and sixes, but she knew if she could just hold onto him and keep talking, they would get though it. What he needed was a… and suddenly she felt she was "getting through" it, maybe for the first time. She held him tightly too. He started to talk, she put her finger over his lips…" Shhhhhhhh, not now. I know all I need to know now, Landon, shhhh…"

CROSS CURRENTS

*H*erbert Cohen of Portman Publishes! was a reasonable man, and most certainly when things were going his way. This meeting had not yet come to the base camp of his rage, that place where he felt the need to direct the situation more closely.

"…tells us that you may have passed up some considerable amount of monies, Landon…"

Landon had known it would eventually come to this, and that when it did, the talk would be of Hollywood Money, as if that foolish sign over Hollywood was just across from the windows facing the East River. Landon noticed that Celia had not been listening to the conversation, but was looking out the other windows that faced the convergence of the East and Hudson Rivers, as if she might be awash with the winds there. Landon wondered if she could actually <u>see</u> the winds. Was that a sailing knack?

"…you should feel free to involve us in these matters, Landon, we are here to help you with them… and to find that you have pissed these people off, well, that's just not good."

"Of course, I didn't meant to piss them off, Herbert, of course I meant the best interests of Portman Publishes! for they are my own. But, I have some artistic votes here about which story might be turned into slush on the big screen. That's reasonable isn't it?"

It turned out that in calling Portman, Amy Rosing had not done her homework and had ended up in the Legal Department rather than the

Editorial Department, thus a different focus on money and process.

"I think, actually, that Landon is right in his concern about 'which story'," said Canning, "clearly, *An Actor Prepares* would make a better story for the screen, and I think it's right that we should guide them here."

"You don't guide these people, Canning, you fleece them. What does it matter which story—is there an author in New York who has not learned the 'take the money and run' theory? Really? ...guide them!"

"Is it all right to be offended by your approach here, Herbert?" said Landon.

"What do you mean?"

"Simply, that I do not subscribe to your Theory of 'take the money and run"...why would I want to do that? I have a book that's doing well, as I have had in the past. No one has complained before that the Hollywood people haven't come knocking at the door. Why now?"

"Because they have now, so, why not give them what they want?"

"Did you just hear Canning's opinion?"

"Yes."

"Is he a member of Portman Publishes!?"

"Don't play parliamentary rules with me, Landon," his voice level but his umbrage rising, "...this woman, whatever her name is..."

"Amy Rosing..."

"Yes, Ms Rosing told me that they don't want any story except *The Italian Rope*. In simple negotiating terms, that means that they will walk."

"This could be a good test of your negotiating skills, Herbert, to turn them into our idea."

"We're not getting anywhere here…"

Herbert turned to survey the room and saw that Celia Langhorne had not put her oar in.

"Celia, which story do you think should be offered to them?"

She turned from the window and looked square at Herbert, "I'm so sorry, Herbert, what was the question?"

While Landon Harris was fencing with the Portman people downtown, up in the middle of Central Park, Morris Rubin was waking up from his nap. Lately, he had been napping deeply, so deeply in fact that he was unsure where he had lain down. He had begun to make a game of it, to look up and see how long it might take him to remember or to guess where he had lain down. Were there buildings, and if there were, where were they, West Side or East Side… was he close to any of the sculpture…near Sheepshead Meadow or deep in a glen? When this had been going on for several weeks, he would purposely trick himself and find new unexplored places to lay down for his nap. He was pleased to learn that only once did he frighten himself, rise up quickly and make for the nearest landmark. It's just another old man's game, he thought, as he faced into the sun. It had shifted as always, and though he had lain in the sun, it had shifted to shade. Today there was a slight ground breeze and he was chilled. He rolled over to see the trees, mountainous tops of greenery, bending with the wind. They were so lush and voluminous with high, billowing clouds for a backdrop that they might have been a painting by one of those Western painters. And how extraordinary to be able to wake from your dream to another waking dream. He had become more interested in dreams… more than just the dream-as-measuring-stick that he had used in his therapy practice. He had seen recently a book on how to guide dreams, and he wanted to try that. He idly wondered if he should venture out of Central Park and try his Wake-Up Game in other parts of the city. He wished that there would be a part of New York where he could wake up and feel that he was in one of those paintings by the American painters who covered the West when it was still fresh and clean. Was it Cole or Moran? He was uneducated about all that. But now, a chance to re-learn the world.

Morris Rubin was almost 80, and still felt new in his retirement. He had weathered that time when he had not known what to do in the mornings when his feet touched the floor and could walk wherever they wished, no master nor mistress to serve, no patients to worry about, no late night calls with their inherent desperation. It had taken a full year to shake all that off... and in the middle of that year, as winter was setting in, he had been fearful of never being able to deal with his own freedom. Of looking at his watch, wondering when something might happen. Of keeping the phone with him as he walked from room to room in his apartment. Now he had discovered the wonder of naps in Central Park. Now he had learned that he lived in New York City, where one was offered anything one might desire to distract oneself. Or he could learn to discover. He thought he knew the city. Not a whit. Of course he had known before that there was the grand public library at 42nd Street, but he did not know what was really in there beside books. That there were exhibits, lectures, tours... and so it was for many places he had not thought of completely. 'Completely' became his watchword. Learn what is the completeness of a place. What is there beside the facade? What treasures lie within? Suddenly, he had learned that he might apply his trade to this venture. Could a retirement be like a patient who needed emotional and mental repair? Could free time and enough money be turned into a newly discovered tour of Life? Finally, he realized how fortunate he was to live in New York City, a place where simple inquisitiveness and will might provide a new way of life, better, a new way of thinking and being.

He shifted his head on his knapsack so he could 'see' the 'painting' better. He pulled a bottle of water out of the knapsack and thought of all the times he had made fun of the kids and city travelers who had knapsacks. What, he had thought then, must they do with these sacks they strap over their backs? …he was certain it was some sort of a mass personal identity issue. They needed to feel in touch with something that the knapsack meant to them, therefore, if they had a knapsack, they could be that idea. Could it be that simple? Yes. From the first moment, when he had gone to the North Face store—an identity issue in itself—and bought his first and only knapsack, he understood the real need for the knapsack. It was his nap pillow, it held the things he must have when away from home, a bottle of water, or a book to read; if it might be cold, a windbreaker or sweater. It was a line of preparedness that he had never considered. But, now this whole world of knapsacks opened to him. Younger people had even stopped him in the park to ask if he had something in this sack to loan them. The brotherhood of knapsacks. See, Mr. Psychiatrist, even you can learn a new identity.

"Why are you making such a fuss over this?"

They were walking down the Portman halls, lined with covers of recent and famous books published there. Celia looked refreshed after the meeting. As Landon looked at her, he had to smile. She was a real person, and he liked that. She had the ability to lose herself while seeming to be with others, if their agenda did not fit with hers, they seldom noticed that she was off somewhere.

"Would it surprise you if I said that I thought it would make the better film?" he said.

"Yes."

"No confidence in my ability to "see the movie"?

"No."

"I thought you were on my side."

"Is there a side to be on…? Landon this is such a small issue that I am surprised that you are so involved in it. So, I have had two thoughts, one, I have been thinking about the differences between *The Italian Rope*, the story they want, and *An Actor Prepares*, the story you want them to have. Second, I am wondering why," she looked at him, "why this is so all important to you? Seems somehow out of place for you." She looked at him, her mind was again divided by half. One in sincere admiration of him, the man and the writer and his *Knoxville Story*, and now, what feels like unnecessary attention to a detail that may not or should not matter to him.

She turned to him, "I was attracted to these two, but for reasons that might be alien to Amy Rose and her…"

"Rosing."

"Yes, Amy Rosing… I'll bet she is attractive and young—they are all young aren't they?"

Celia caught herself and looked deeply at Landon as they walked into her office. She waved him to a chair and stood by the windows.

"The style and underlying intent of these two stories is so… divergent, with voices so differently realized, I might think they were written by two different people. Yet, you are sitting right here in front of me and you are the single writer, so I know that can't be. But, I have to say Landon that I didn't really believe you had that range within you."

It lay between them for a moment.

"Am I to believe you have just paid me an enormous compliment?"

"You know Landon, I don't count myself as a great editor. Great ship-builder, yes Sailor, fine. But, I am still trying to find my course here, get the feel of the helm." Landon watched her struggling and had a moment of genuine connection with her. She really was a serious woman, someone to be taken seriously, and he realized in that moment that he had not. She had been just another "publishing" person to him, not one dedicated to writing, to the attempt at literature, but she was on the path… or as she might say, the course, the tack. He wanted to stand close to her small flame, so he stood up and walked to the windows to stand beside her and look out at the rivers of New York.

"I have a problem… for me a serious one, and also unfamiliar."

She looked at him as he spoke. She noticed his proximity and moved toward her desk, away from the windows and standing next to him. She tilted her head slightly as if to be ready to receive something.

"I am trying to work on my next book… it's about my wife, Catherine. I seem to have pages and pages but little focus… yet I am attracted," he smiled at himself, "attracted finally to the idea of her as Muse. In fact she was, but while one is living with a wife and lover and immersed in the everyday, one doesn't think, in close proximity, of people as ideas. Oh, I know that's not even right, there are so many couples in which each is an idea to the other, or a lack of one, that may seem trite. But, though I often surged with her strength, I didn't have the courage to attribute it to her, I needed to think it was I, the writer and Young Turk—my, what an antiquated term—who was the source. The mythology of that alone might make a book, a bad book about how we delude ourselves."

Celia was fascinated. She had the look of the tourist in India mystified by the cross legged man with all the baskets and a snake wrapped around his arm. For a split second she was terrified that he was going to ask in some blinded way that she learn to become his muse... no, he wouldn't do that... but I wonder what that would be like?

"I'd like you to take a look at what I have done and see if you think there is something here of value." Her relief was brief, he didn't want her to be a muse, instead he wanted her to be a great editor, and she was terrified all over again. She sat down at the desk. Landon looked out the window, as if he could intuit the winds, and for a second, felt that he could. He moved back to the chair alongside her desk. They regarded each other across the space before her head began to nod, yes, slightly at first, then accompanied by words...

"Sure, Landon, I might be able to do that, I should also say, I am pleased that you would ask me. Thank you." Celia realized that once again she had two halves of a thought, and she dared not even consider which side of her should be pleased with this new notion of working with Landon Harris. "Could I think about it for a day or so, and then we could get together?"

"Absolutely. Let me know when." A parting glance and then they parted.

Morris Rubin had moved on from his admiration of the paintings in the sky to the steps of the Metropolitan Museum. Today he would not go in, today he would share the steps with those who have gone in and are resting, or who will not go in but have a sense of these steps as a gathering place, as in other worldly cities. Morris had a pretzel from the vendor and from his knapsack, a bottle of water. The steps were crowded today so he was off to the side, facing downtown and the linear fountain. The outer wall of the Museum was close enough to touch. He looked down to see a small bird pecking at a rather large crust of bread. As the bird pecked at the crust, lifting it with his beak, it fell out of his beak. The only sound was that of the crust, stale as time, dropping to the step. Then another peck, another germ of wheat into the gullet and a drop to the step—small clang! This went on in almost poetic harmony until another, larger bird, caught wind of it—do they see this, or smell it—do birds smell things? —and joined the smaller bird in conquest of the crust. First one, then the other, until the larger bird had wrested the crust away from the smaller bird.

Morris sensed a small outrage within. The smaller bird had lost out, and he disapproved of that. As he sat in human judgement, the small bird kept after the larger bird and the crust and for a moment, seized it away. Morris was happy, but the larger bird retaliated. Morris was sad. Back and forth this went until a foreign bird dropped into view and swooped over the crust. The timing of this foreign bird, with different colored feathers, was just right. The crust had been dangling on the edge of the rounded step and his motion carried it down to the next step where he had it to himself. Yes, my crust on my step but… no, first the smaller bird flipping down to advance his cause from yet another interloper… How many would he have to fight to keep this delicious crust he had found? The two smaller birds were pecking it out. But, the bigger bird was not to be denied and joined the Battle of the Crust… three of them, fluttering and flustering for the crust, which was becoming smaller. Just then, the larger bird banged it hard with his beak and the crust broke in two. Now here is justice, the first two birds will each peck a share and the foreign bird will be left out. Morris even noticed that now he was rooting for the larger bird in this new strategy for crust possession, and just as Morris was getting comfortable with that notion, the foreign bird got hold of the smaller of the two pieces and flew off leaving the single, still smaller, crust there between the smaller and larger like-feathered birds. While Morris was most aware of a major piece of crust flying off, the other two paid it no mind. There was still a piece of crust on the lower step. They would have it... justice here was tentative, temporary, entirely satisfactory for these two birds, one smaller than the other, one larger than the other... they continued to peck away until Morris realized that they were not antagonists, they were actually sharing the crust, It was big enough for three, two he could see and one flown away. Why did he need to see it as a struggle? A good thought for a retired psychiatrist to ponder:

The case of the three birds and a lovely crust.

Landon was pleased to be invited again to Celia's apartment, because the invitation assumed she would agree to help on the Muse Pages, as he had come to call them. Not a necessarily good title, but workable for the moment. Their conversation stalled over drinks. He had hoped she would be forthcoming, yet they seemed to talk only about sailing, the coast of Rhode Island, how good a sailor her sister was, apparently Nora was top notch—but no amount of steering, or should he call it helmsmanship, could arrive at the subject he was focused on.

Finally, he said, "I promised myself I would never tell you this, but I think I should."

"What changed your mind? ", she said.

"I need... well, I'm not sure what I need..."

She continued, "You think my feelings for your work and you are not genuine?"

Landon smiled and waved his hand at nothing.

Then, the wind caught his mind, "I had a dream a few weeks ago. It was after I came to your apartment in the rain. I dreamed that you and I were sailing on Long Island Sound. You were teaching me the importance of being able to navigate. Maps and all that. I had spurred this in you by constantly referring to myself as a 'landlubber'. You said that one of the things that sailing has taught you is how to navigate for yourself, by the stars, by the sun, by the tides. In a word, you didn't think I was instinctive enough. I thought you were right and was willing to go 'sailing' with you. I had also never been with you, alone, on anything but an editorial meeting, aside from casual lunches." He paused to look at her closely. "You were tacking around another boat and it was tricky because there was a channel marker there and your freeboard was most narrow."

Celia smiled at his use of the nautical term, somehow it didn't catch the wind right when he said it, yet she was fascinated with him and his story...

"The wind or the water took a sudden shift and the boat did an unexpected lurch against the grain of the water—I am certain that's the wrong phrase, but it happened. You were thrown overboard, and I was standing in the cockpit watching you recede in the water, without a life preserver or anything. I grabbed the helm hoping it would help, that I could turn the boat around, but I wasn't thinking sails—landlubber, remember. You were going back fast behind the boat and I was scared, and I assumed you were too, Indian Ocean or not. I grabbed a rope and tied it around my waist and jumped in.

After I got into the water, I saw double the amount of concern in your face. Now we were both in the soup." Celia was falling into his story, he was the snake charmer of Long Island Sound.

"I went backward in the water fast and you came toward me swimming. I was surprised at how quickly we caught up with each other. We were there together in the water and instinctively we hugged and kissed and held each other for awhile until you and I realized at the same time that all we had to do to get back on the boat was to walk the rope back to where it was tied to the boat. We did that with remarkable collaboration. Suddenly we were safe on the boat. You yelled and shouted at me for doing such a stupid thing. Then you grabbed me in the cockpit and hugged and kissed me for being such a good landlubber. We ended up down in the berth, making love, soaking wet."

Landon paused for effect. "What do you think of that?"

She took a long time to say…"Did you really make that up that long ago?"

"Yes."

More time, then…"And, you are telling me now?"

"Yes."

"Why?"

"Because I think we need to come together to make this happen."

"Make what happen?"

"I don't know. I do know now that I should not make you, or any other woman I come upon, a Muse—so this is my attempt—the Muse Pages, to write a history, if you will, of my experience with Muses. I know that I need to figure out how to tie a rope around my waist and throw myself into the East River and come out with a good, new, original, useful and self-directed book idea and then present it to you in your official offices in Lafayette Square—the only idea I have now is these papers written as a hallucination in the middle of the night—and I need help making them into something."

She looked at him. "You can't mean all that. I mean, you just can't. You are a writer and they are a different species… and I would like to help you, but I don't think we should sleep together."

"Well, if I were an honest man I would agree, but I am not and I don't, but I see your point."

Celia smiled at him, "…Landon, you have done one very important thing. You are an honest man and you have owned up to everything including your wish that we go to bed together. I like that idea and you… so, I will think about it, but I won't edit or work on your Muse Idea."

"Why not?"

"Because you didn't write the short stories."

The electricity in Landon's part of the room went out. He was standing in total darkness. He caught himself and turned on his lights. "How long have you known? …how have you found out?"

Celia shrugged. "Doesn't matter. What I know for certain is that you need to let me throw these papers out the window and you need to come up with your own thought. The wonder of that need and your imagination is that you have just explained how you saved my life in your dream—now, do that with yourself: see yourself falling away from the stern of a boat on Long Island Sound. Stand in the paper boat you create stories in and tie a rope to that and throw yourself overboard. I have supreme confidence in you—that's paying you an enormous compliment—that you will follow the rope back to the paper boat and the idea you need."

Landon came over and sat beside her. Undaunted, she continued,

"When you climb on the boat, you will know how to write it and I will know how to edit and publish it, and if it makes you feel any better, we can revisit the idea of sleeping together."

Landon leaned over and kissed her.

She paused, then pulled away from him enough to look him in the eye, "Now, get out of here… oh, wait…" She got up and walked to the 21st story window of her apartment, opened it and threw out Landon's Muse folder. They both watched how the wind caught the edges of the folder and a second wind blew the papers in a cloud away from Central Park.

It must have been several minutes that they looked out the window of her apartment, watching the papers and folder floating-flying away to the River. In between the minutes, they looked at each other, before Landon turned away from the window. She got his coat and they walked to the door to her apartment. She reached out and took his hand, squeezed it and opened the door for him. All this without words.

"Mr. Harris this is Alec Kelly with Prudential Insurance. I'm sorry to break into your busy day, but we are making a survey of how many of those who make their living from writing would be willing to insure themselves against writer's block."

"Wha…I'm sorry, what company did you say you were with?"

"Prudential Insurance, Mr. Harris. We have been doing some careful research on the vulnerability of writers… income streams, longevity of career, old age preparation… things like that, and we wonder if you would find value in insuring yourself against writer's block?"

"You're kidding, right?"

"Am I to assume that as a writer you have never been blocked?"

"Well, of course… who hasn't? But, how do you intend… is this a joke? It must be… Alec Kelly… oh, sure… you son-of-a-bitch. You really had me there. Writer's Block Premiums. Alec. How are you?"

"Fine, Landon, fine… I just wanted to check your pulse… I see from your new book of short stories, that you are far from blocked. But, you have to admit that it's a decent idea. What would you pay to insure that?"

"You'd be surprised. In the first year of signing people up, you would be a hit on the stock market, in the second year, you would be busted worse than the 2007 crash… I can't think of any writer who wouldn't want to take a ride on that."

"Good to hear your voice, Landon."

"And, you as well. What's the real pitch, Alec?"

"Do you recall getting a call from Ralph Callaway at Bowling Green University? That's in Ohio."

"Vaguely."

"Well, they are… we are—I am with them now, teaching and having a good time—we are having a Fiction Writing Contest… a national one, and we need really fine judges. There are only three categories, it's not one of those all media gang-bangs… only novels, short stories and poems. And, this year we plan to publish the winner in each category in a paperback done by our Press."

"So, guess what, you want me to read 100 novels in four weeks to help you figure out who is the next… who will be the next great hope in writing?"

"Well, you're half right. I would like you to be one of three final judges. We pass the chaff around the University Departments related to writing, and then end up with from 9 to 12 pieces in each category. What we need then is key writers to read the finalists and help us select the winners."

"Have you done this before."

"Yes, twice."

"Has there been good work?"

"Once yes, once so-so."

"So, three's a charm?"

"We can hope… are you in?"

Landon looked across to his file drawers and let his mind go. On a side table rested his original notes and the raw materials from that night when he thought he saw Catherine… Catherine and himself writing a book. A cloud passed quickly over that concept. Was this a fortuitous chance to fish the barrel for some new ideas and ways to think oneself out of the box?

"Landon…?"

"Oh, sorry. I was thinking about…. Alec, I wonder if I could ask something of you?"

"Try."

"I would like to try to work this out as one of your screening judges. I would like to have—these budding writers think they have something to say—whether they do or not, I would like to 'experience' firsthand what they are trying to do… say… the raw material. I assume that those who enter are a mix of writers and would-be writers."

"I think that's fair. But, that means you might have to read fifty novels… or do you favor short stories now that you have a book of them yourself?"

"No, novels, please."

"When are you willing to start?"

"What do you mean?"

"Well, the contest deadline is three months off, but, there are always those who have a file drawer full of material they enter in everything. We call it the 'Persistence Factor'. The theory is that if you keep throwing something at the wall long enough, sooner or later, it will stick."

"Do you believe that?"

"Well, my own experience is limited to our contest here, and it's young. But, if you want to be a screener, I can send you a passel of manuscripts now, and you will have more time to read them… because these are the early birds."

"Fine."

"Send them?"

"Right, Alec… I'm happy to be in if you are the frontispiece for this… it's good to hear from you again… I assume that you will be buying me an air ticket to the final white jacket dinner in Bowling Green?"

"Dinner, yes, White jacket, no… but I am delighted you'll be with us on this. I'll be back in touch soon. All the best…"

"Right, you too. 'Bye…"

Maybe this could help… better than Writer's Block Insurance—what a great joke! If I could see a range of fresh writing, maybe if I could gain some perspective on newer and younger thinking, I could work my way out of this… I need to work my way out of this. I like what Celia said, she's right you know, Landon, he said to himself, you can do this. Yes, we can…" He felt himself nodding over and over.

Landon drifted into the living room and over to the dining table by the windows on the Park. He sat and drank cold coffee. He closed his eyes and saw what appeared to be hundreds of dart boards... though there couldn't have been more than 30 or 35... but many dart boards. As he watched, as if at a dart board regatta, they moved... they had been lined up in rows. As they reconstituted themselves, they gathered, crowded in on each other until they were a huge circle of dart boards, overlapping, bunched up, almost impossible to miss, no matter what direction you threw. If you threw one dart you were throwing at 30 boards... your dart had to hit. He picked up a handful of darts and threw them. Who knows how many darts you can hold in your hand and throw at one time... a flight of darts, a squadron of darts, perhaps... now they were honing in on targets, sure to hit...

Morris Rubin realized he had lived in New York for 27 years and had never been to Grant's Tomb. He was not even certain where Grant's Tomb was. All that came to mind was the stupid joke about "Who is buried in Grant's Tomb?" But suddenly, and unbidden, came to his mind this morning that he would go to Grant's Tomb and see it for himself. He was not a Civil War buff, he knew little about President Grant other than he was supposed to have presided over a corrupt government. Morris dressed, packed his knapsack with all the possible necessities he might need, and commenced to go to Grant's Tomb. Where is it, he wondered? Uptown, and again he grasped the door handle. Uptown where? He turned to his study and called one of his daughters.

"Emily, where is Grant's Tomb?"

"Why, Daddy? You going to go to commune with the spirit of Grant today?"

"In fact, that is my plan. I need to know Grant better in order to plan the rest of my life."

"I see." Slight pause. "Daddy, are you OK?"

Morris Rubin had to smile. He could see Emily sitting in her lawyer's office downtown wondering once again about her father and his sudden turns of interest and activity. A man is blessed with wonderful daughters, he thought... and then into the phone, "A man is blessed with wonderful daughters."

"Thank you, Daddy... I was not fishing for compliments... feel free to use my skills as a New Yorker anytime. Grant's Tomb is off Riverside Drive on the Upper West Side—so, too, is Riverside Church, an old NY landmark, so if you are going to go up to the Tomb, then be sure to walk over to the Park and then to the Church. Sounds like a good day for you."

She was pleased that her father had finally settled into his retirement and seemed at peace.

"When are you going?"

"Right now."

"All right... why don't you take a cab up there and walk back until you get tired. Exercise will do you good."

"All right, Emily... good thought. Good bye, darling."

"'bye, Daddy."

Now Landon noticed that he either woke up with Grace, or he woke up alone. There was a difference now. It took a week or two of feeling some vague difference before he realized that there was a definite difference: he was with her or without her. She was good in the morning, not necessarily a cheery "morning person", but comfortable to wake up with. At first, Landon had to identify that for himself. He felt that he had not much experience waking up with a woman… he thought about that for a few days and then wondered if that was correct. Catherine, as he looked back on rising with her, had seemed to be a part of him and so "getting up with her" was not something that he separated out of the whole experience of being with her. He and Grace were still in that mode where they usually made love the night before, so there was that glow, and sometimes a morning roll, which is always a good way to start the day. But, trying to leave the sexy parts out of the equation, Landon noticed that when he woke up in New York, without Grace, there seemed a presence of her. She was with him even though she was not with him. He found that comfortable. Even better, some mornings she called him, some mornings he called her… and her presence resonated within him. He was comforted. He could go about his morning chores and feel—better than he did before Grace. Hmm… before Grace….

Twelve manuscripts had arrived from Alec Kelly two days before. But he had meetings with Portman, a radio interview and seemingly a million details to take care of that day, but yesterday he sat down with anticipation to read one of them. The thought of that one, and the one he picked up afterward, hoping to save the day, had brought him to a point of dread. Could he do this? Two strikes to begin…. The first manuscript called, what had it been titled? …well, what ever it had been called, that was as far as anyone needed to read. He was surprised that a person would be willing to submit themselves to the thoughts of another person by exposing their shallowness so deeply. There was no idea, no real story and a great deal of violence, as if the writer had been a young person brought up on bad and gristly movies and television. Landon had struggled to gain 17 pages and felt he had to stop. This was against his better nature. He had expected, even committed himself to the idea of reading all that was sent him. He wanted to be fair. But, it seemed at page 15, 16 and 17 that the writer was not being fair with the reader. So, Landon set it down.

He remembered the title of the next book. *Cactus Rising*. That was inventive, and dove into what he guessed would be a modern western. The first pages were trying to be poetic and to be in-the-West. Tumultuous mountains, long reaches of valleys with serpentine rivers glowing in the morning light. Edward Abbey came to mind in the opening pages, and Landon settled himself down for a different read. He was a Westerner, but not that kind... California is hardly the glorious West of Arizona and New Mexico... and then, as if he had been taken to the top of the most incredible ridge to savor the view, he was pushed off into a cow town gathering of shady, dull characters who spoke in clichés. He couldn't believe this was happening, so he bulldozed on, as if he was the Chief Writing Wrangler along with the author, who knew that these "bad meds" and would wear off after a few torpid pages.

Clearly, this was his time to put all the books down and look at something else. How about the Park? So, off he went to clear his head and wonder if it would be easier to take out Writer's Block Insurance.

The next day, he decided to take the walk <u>first</u> and then come back to brace the manuscripts, so, for good luck, he went to the pile and looked through the titles to see which one he might try next... *The Second Madame Bovary, High Country Hi-Jinks, Candy Dan and the Chocolate Witch*—some of the titles were not promising, yet he opened *Candy Dan* to scan a few lines and it seemed light, fun and original. "Original" works, he thought. Couldn't tell if it was for Young Adults or what, but he decided not to worry and grabbed it on the way out the door.

The doorman nodded at Landon as he strode across Central Park West into the Park. Just as he got to the gate, a man slid up beside him, as if he was walking with Landon. It startled him and as he looked, he was startled more. Noel Chapman.

"I'll walk along with you for awhile, Landon." It was not a question or a request.

"Hello, Noel." Landon said quietly. He recalled Noel said he never wanted to see Landon again. In this moment, Landon realized that he felt equally the same. It was as if dark clouds arose in his head to cause pressure and discomfort. He, in fact, wanted to run off.

"How have you been Landon? I see that things are going well with my book."

Landon nodded.

"I see you have a large envelope. Pages of your latest…?"

"No, in fact, I am helping out a friend."

"Have you made the contract with the friend yet?"

Landon stopped. "What's on your mind, Noel? …you haven't come to take a walk with me. If all you want to do is to be unpleasant, do it elsewhere."

Noel kept walking, so that by the time Landon finished the sentence he was talking to Noel's back. Noel turned, "Just walk along with me, I'll make this simple, but I can't guarantee painless, much of that depends on you."

"What do you mean?"

"I have been dating a woman from Portman and…"

"Have you been trying to spy on me! Listen, Noel…"

"Calm down, I met this woman quite by accident, I have no interest in "spying" on you… what might a person learn from that… how to steal other writers' work?" As soon as he said it, Noel put his arm on Landon. "My friend tells me that there is a chance that one of the stories will be sold to the movies."

Landon felt dizzy. "Let's sit over here for a moment," he said. "Listen, Noel…"

"Nope, you listen. If one of my stories is sold to Hollywood, I fully expect to open up the discussions again about "gag money". There was nothing in our agreement that held that condition, and if it happens, I want a share. If I don't get a share, my attorney tells me that I can go public with the whole deal. I know there are a lot of people around town that would be just fascinated with this scandal. So, be warned." Noel made as if to leave, and turned again to Landon, "My resources are good enough that if you try to queer the deal I will know that too. So, don't get cute with this. Play me straight, Landon, and I will continue my clam-like attitude."

Noel looked down at Landon sitting on the park bench and smirked. It was a look of such disdain, of hate that exceeded even the one he had received that night. Noel turned and walked away. Landon watched him go, as his stomach churned. He turned to the end of the bench and wretched, throwing up breakfast. He looked around quickly to see if Noel had turned back or if there were anyone else on the path. He wiped himself off and scuttled toward home. As he did, he looked down and saw that he had stained his shirt.

In another Park, along Riverside Drive, Morris Rubin had savored his visit to U.S. Grant. Now the Tomb was behind him, the Hudson River before him and Morris felt on the brink of a revealed life. It was not that he hadn't a rich life, he had… a good woman for a wife, now passed, three marvelous and successful daughters, and a 36 year blessing as a psychiatrist enabling people. He had left that life tenuously. He had been certain that when he did, the active, participating part of life would be over. He would be driftwood cast up onto the unfriendly beach of Manhattan. In fact, he had wanted to leave New York and find another place where he might be a part of something, now that his past would be dormant and his present tentative. He had even read books—those self-help books for the elderly retired that professed to guide people to the riches of life they never dreamed of. He was unimpressed, and decided he would have to take the plunge on his own, but empowered with two discoveries: a Manhattan he would not have thought existed—how foolish that had been, and resources in himself that were surprising: an ability to create a new life out of the whole cloth of curiosity. Now he found himself on the edge of the limitless horizons that were there all the time, unseen, untested—only because he had been afraid to leave what he believed was the safety of his life as a productive working person tied to a fraction of the world.

The view was spectacular from here, high above the Hudson River. He had placed himself on a park bench where he would turn slightly this way and see the Tomb, that way, he could see New Jersey ahead of him. As he turned around, he noticed a boy, about eight or so, playing with his cat around some low trees. They were quite a pair. The boy, slight and quick, the cat with springs on paws. They would run 'round and 'round three trees that were close together. The cat could actually use a tree to carom off to throw the chasing boy off balance. Then the boy would catch the cat and they would roll around the grass together—giggling and yowling as if they were litter mates. After a moment of quiet, the boy would be lulled and the cat would run up a tree only to jump off the other side, away from the boy, and the chase was on again, punctuated by the boy's screams of delight and calling the cat's name... which, at Morris' distance, was hard to distinguish.

His thoughts went back to the Tomb. Morris was surprised to stand at the railing on top, looking down at the actual tomb of Grant, and find that Grant's wife was there as well. But *why not* was the following thought. Not much was known about Grant's wife... one always thinks of a cigar smoking, hard-drinking man without a family other than his soldiers. But, of course there was a wife. Morris made a note to find at the library a biography of Grant... perhaps there was even a autobiography... where he could learn about the hidden wife and a life that must have been tumultuous. A great war fought with one of the greatest of Americans as president... Morris was ready to leave that moment for the library and more about Grant.

He thought of Grant's life like a bridge spanning American life... one man who could do that and still be reviled as not being the best of Presidents. His gaze drifted to the boy and the cat, still tumbling after one another. Suddenly, the cat ran up to the top of the tree, far enough away from the boy's reach to be able to stop and look down at the boy and laugh like a cat. Morris thought of the lower level of the Tomb where one could walk around the two tombs of husband and wife on an inner circle and then turn to an outer circle where large bronze busts of Grant's generals were placed... from Sherman to Sheridan. Nine of them. All facing Grant, as they had in life, now they did in death. Morris was overcome with... the boy screamed. Morris turned in time to see the boy in the tree with the cat in his arms fall backward onto the ground. A short fall, but not if you land on your head. The cat was thrown off and rolled to the ground on cat feet. Immediately, the cat sprung up and ran to the boy, who had hit hard and didn't move. There was a split second where nothing seemed to move anywhere. The traffic stopped, the people in Grant's Tomb paused on their visit, the breeze in the trees held the leaves firm for just that moment, while the cat and Morris realized what had happened. The first one to move was the cat, who crept to the boy and sniffed at his hair and nudged his ear, urging his friend to get up and play. But, the boy was silent, motionless. Morris was the next to act, along with the gentle breeze which caused, again, the leaves to move. Life was there except for this still form on the grass. Morris touched the boy's carotid artery. He held his finger there, working hope against his physician's knowledge that it would throb if there were life, if it did not, there was not. And, there was not—no throbbing of life. Morris' hand left the boy's throat and reached for the cat whose back spiked and arched and hissed at the interloper. Morris held his hand out for the cat and finally, after long seconds, the cat sniffed his fingers.

Morris sat down beside the boy and listened to his heart. He could almost feel the skin of the boy, for he wore only a thin T-shirt. The boy was about eight, light complexion, blue eyes which were still open but motionless. The boy was smiling as if the play with the cat was continuing behind his eyes and the next thing Morris would hear was the boy's laughter. How he longed to hear that. He touched the boy's throat again and then his chest. All life seemed to be suspended. The cat sat and looked at Morris, as if to say, why are you sitting here? Morris got up and stuffed the cat unwillingly into his knapsack. He picked the boy up with great effort, grateful that he was slender, and looked around him to see where he might find immediate help or a telephone. He saw the Tomb, but shied away from it. He saw a large building which must be the church Emily had spoken of and he rushed, as well as he could, toward it, constantly looking down at the boy's face.

He could feel the fur of the cat at his ear, the cat had crawled up to see the direction they were going, and Morris was afraid that the cat would jump away. For some reason he knew the cat must remain with him. Morris started to jog toward the church, unused as he was to this sort of physical activity, the boy jostled in his arms, and the cat seemed to conspire to keep him off balance. Just as he reached the other side of the street from the Park, and buildings that were on line with the church, now a full block away, Morris slipped. He started to tumble to the sidewalk, but was able to catch his balance and right himself enough to fall against the side of an apartment building. He hit it once and bounced and then hit it again, harder. He had been guiding himself, so as soon as he made the second hit and recovered, he looked down at the boy. The boy blinked. Closed his eyes, and blinked again. The cat had jumped to the sidewalk was now in front of Morris looking up and just as suddenly, jumped up into the lap created by Morris carrying the boy. They were there together, almost face to face: the boy, now blinking regularly, the cat who was reaching over the boy's chin to lick his face, and Morris, who must have looked at that moment like the man on the side of the road when Lazarus rose. The boy was frightened for a moment, as if finding himself where he should not be, wherever that might be. His hand came up and touched the cat and his fright evaporated. If the cat was there then it must be all right.

Morris stopped then. He stood rock still for minutes trying to gather his intellect for what might have happened. His mind went over it minutely... he had slipped, started to fall, had regained his balance, yet hit the side of the building twice, the cat fell and the boy regained life. How could that have happened? The boy was content to watch Morris' face in these minutes, the cat stopped licking the boy's face and reached up to lick Morris' face. It was this that activated Morris again. He moved to a nearby strip of grass and gently laid the boy down. The cat stayed on the boy's stomach until Morris moved him aside and placed his hand again on the carotid artery of the boy. His pulse was there. He felt his heart and it was beating. He closed his eyes to the momentary restfulness of visual silence. Then he heard the boy say, "What is your name, Mister?'

"Morris. Morris Rubin."

"Oh. My name is Alexander."

Morris nodded.

"And my cat. His name is Alex Two." He said the words as if they were one... Alex too.

Morris nodded at the cat, who was washing a dirty spot off his paw.

"What happened?", asked the boy.

"I don't know," said Morris, "I honestly wish I could tell you. But are you all right?"

"Sure, why not?" said the boy, starting to stand up beside Morris.

Landon made himself a drink. He didn't drink this early, but he needed fortification today. He hated to think about continuing reading the raw manuscripts. Too raw. Well, maybe he could find some solace there. By 2:30 that following morning Landon had gone through all the manuscripts but one and it lay on the middle of the desk. One by one, reading deeply into some, skimming others—he hoped that was not cheating, he gave each an honest try. But it is not a surprise to learn, once again, that this thing called "writing the novel", the first or the most recent, is hard, deep work. No one knew that better at this moment than he. He tried not to feel blocked, after all he wasn't in the contest was he?

The most promising had been *A Well-traveled Letter*. Good story, but too thin to be a fulsome novel. Here was the name on the back page, Carrie Sonderburg of Chapel Hill, North Carolina. What to do about this, Landon thought... a good story, nice character touches, but not enough meat for this many pages, for—what to do? Hate to just put a "No" tag on it and let it fall away. I'll bet it's not allowed for judges to write the author suggesting some changes to another category... maybe he could write to Alec and ask to have this moved to the short story group. But then it would be up against short stories that were written differently, as they should be. He in sat the sun, looked past the Park and thought of Carrie Sonderburg in Chapel Hill. He wondered if she was allied in some way with the University. What must she do? He recalled his only visit... well, if he had to live in the South, this would be the place, a real community, not too large, the university atmosphere was lush... Landon got up and booted up the computer.

Dear Ms Sonderburg,

Please don't tell Alec Kelly or anyone else at the Bowling Green U. Writing Contest that I have been in touch with you. It will ruin my credibility with them.

I have read your novel *A Well-Traveled Letter*, and find it engaging. Good, strong story, fine characters. There is definitely some meat here, a hardy meal. But, there is not enough weight to sustain a full-length novel.

My suggestion is this: cut this mercilessly and make it into a short story and re-enter it under another title. There is time. My estimate is that you could have a chance to be a winner in that category if your revision falls right—and I say that not knowing how good are the other stories in your category. But, I urge you to give it a try.

An Unknown Friend   L.

This was his good deed for the day. He hoped that Carrie Sonderburg would be comfortable with his letter and not do anything foolish like call the contest people and query them about a mysterious letter. At least she had some direction, she had been told what to do and it was in front of her. She could turn to the writing machine of her choice and write. Landon felt that need, the deep itch to write, a thirst that was unquenchable, the gambler's urge to play poker, no matter what the odds against were. But now Landon looked down to his hand and the cards were blank. He was in a dream where there were four players, and it was life or death poker. That choking feeling as if the bile was halfway up your throat. Across from him at the table was Noel Chapman, a person who had promised in his anger never to see Landon again. How he wished Noel had kept that promise, and worse, now he faced Noel across the table. That same smirk was on his face as he looked down at his cards and then up at Landon. Next to Landon on the right was Carrie Sonderburg, the writer of the good story, the recipient of good advice. To his left was Celia Langhorne who was smiling at him as if to say, 'Play your cards, don't be afraid…' His waking dream gave way to genuine sleep, the dream of the poker game receding slowly into the arms of darkness, attempting to wall out the other darkest side of his life. He slept for hours sprawled on the bed of the writing room.

In the morning, he called his friend Alec Kelly and told him that he was worn out, that he hoped he had been of some help, but that something had come up—what a lie—he would give anything if SOMETHING WOULD COME UP! But back to the man on the telephone, would Alec let him bow out of the judging, now, please? To his everlasting relief, Alec said, "OK, no problem. Fine, good…."

THE CRUCIBLE

*T*he phone rang at 11:10 A.M. and it was Grace. Landon felt her hand reaching down into the vault of sleep and pulling him out slowly. It is almost a ritual with them now. He picks up the phone and speaks a few words. She understands that he has been under considerable stress, so she does not ask him questions demanding thoughtful answers. She does not ask for intelligent conversation, she talks and tells him about what she has been doing, about going down the Harbor and having a chance meeting with Rather, the three-legged dog. She tells him about her last lunch with Marty Gibbons and how she regaled her with their last lovemaking.

"You don't tell her how we make love!"

"Of course, Darling, why not, she is my best friend, and she has said she wants to learn from us… her own poor love life being what it is."

"You are joking," Landon was fully awake.

Grace laughs, she has played him along, led him to consciousness and then placed the needle carefully in the spot garnered to give the greatest response.

"You are so easy," she says.

Landon rubbed his eyes, now he feels foolish, "You have sandbagged me."

"If that's the phrase, yes, I have. Good morning, Landon Harris."

"What happens next?"

I will be on the 12:15 train and will be at Grand Central thereafter. I'll cab up to your place, trusting you will be fully awake, dressed, ready to take me to a picnic lunch in the Park. Deal?

"Yes… ah, deal!"

When Grace arrived, Landon was reading the *Times* in the lobby. As she stood in front of him, she seemed different. He rose to meet her embrace, and had a lover's urge to take her back upstairs in the elevator. But, that could wait. She looked at the basket on the seat beside Landon.

"My, my, you made all this yourself, in your French kitchen?" Landon nodded. "The basket is from your farm, the one you used to gather French hen eggs?" Landon nodded. "How long have you been French, monsieur?" Landon looked at his watch. "Not long." And, they went arm and arm out into the Park for a picnic.

In the Park, as they passed the statue of Balto, the heroic dog of the North, Landon paused, while Grace read the plaque.

"It says that this dog was very brave, that he risked his life to bring needed medicines to a town that was having an epidemic in the midst of winter storms in Alaska." The statue of the dog was greater than life-sized, bronze and heroic in stance. The dog looked off in the distance as if anticipating the next frozen river or avalanche. There was a harness on his back to carry the supplies needed to save lives. Landon had read the plaque many times so he nodded at her. Grace went around the monument to feel the side of the dog, a place worn to a golden shine by other hands feeling the same emotions. "Courageous dog," she said. Landon nodded. The dog always touched him in a deep and sensitive spot. Grace could see he was affected.

"Have you been here many times?"

"Yes, I have."

She moved to his side, her voice low in his ear..." Isn't odd that we have, you and I, this sense of dogs? ...first Rather, now Balto." She paused to feel him take a breath. "Perhaps we should get a dog of our own. We could share it. It could travel back and forth for the time being... live on the shore, live in the Park. Perhaps even help you in your writing. Who knows what our dog could do?"

Just then, a bunch of school kids were passing, ignoring the statue but whistling at the couple. Grace was giving Landon a deep kiss that startled him so that he almost dropped the basket...and then he did drop it, only to have it caught mid-air by one of the kids, a boy with bad acne who held the basket up to them, eyes full of wonder at the kissing.

"Thank you, young man," Grace said to the boy, and took the basket, "Thank you very much." The boy blushed and his mates jeered at him for being involved with the kissing couple. If a statue of a dog could smile, Balto would have been brave enough to do it.

Landon liked one spot in the Park that was usually less inhabited, and more specifically, one where he would not be able to see the buildings of the city. In this way, he could pretend this was his own Central Valley.

"This is a remarkable spot, Landon. Do you bring all your girlfriends here?" Landon looked at his watch. "We need to hurry this afternoon, we are behind schedule. Alice is due here at four." Grace threw a bunch of napkins at him. As Landon moved to fetch them, he noticed a man, an older man lying in a clump of shadows in a corner of the smallish enclave. His head was on his knapsack, and it seemed like...could it be, a cat was also lying against the odd pillow. A cat? They were the only other inhabitants of this small patch of Park. Grace and Landon thought they had it to themselves. As they worked together to spread out their picnic, Grace kept up a slow chatter, as if throwing the questions away, hoping they would rise to the trees and become inconsequential. "Have you been writing?"

"No, I haven't. I have been acting as a screener—or should I say, I have finished acting as a screener for a writing contest. In all honesty, I agreed to do it hoping I could find an idea, a concept, a fragment of something to hang myself on—no, not that—not hang myself, but an "idea hook".

"Did it work?"

He shook his head, sipped the wine and then cut slices of cheese for them both.

"Could I ask," she was almost whispering now, "why you don't do that yourself?"

"I can't." Landon looked her full in the eyes. "For the first time in my goddamn life I cannot close my eyes and something is there. I don't mean to blame the Ritual Process but that has always worked and now it hasn't so, I guess I am looking for a new pathway." While he was saying that to Grace, his inner vision went to his editing of Noel's book and he shuddered visibly.

"Are you all right? Do you not want to talk about this?"

"I am not all right. I don't want to talk about it. We need desperately to talk about it. I need for you to understand this, if… if we are to move ahead together…" He nodded, not looking at her. Wanting to stab the small keg of cheese.

"How many times in your life have you been asked how you write?"

He looked at her and smiled. His gaze rose to the trees. "Approximately how many leaves would you say were in those three trees?"

"But, faced with this question, this many times, have you come to understand how you, Landon Harris, come to write."

"Do you remember how you learned to tie your shoelaces? …you can certainly recall the mystery of it at some point and trying, against the odds, to get the two pieces of string to come together in a holding knot." Grace looked at him in a dreamy way. "Do you remember how you learned to make love to a man? At first wondering about small mechanical things, and then moving to the more monumental ideas like '…do I do this more and better because I love this man more than the last one, or because I need this <u>now</u>, I feel so lonely, lost, desperate, <u>this moment</u>.'" Grace moved to him, and awkwardly tried to lean into him to kiss him, knocking them both over. Landon continued, "What about just the forming of words? First with a pencil, then with a pen, which was supposed to be different but wasn't. First a typewriter, later a computer. We are talking now about the forming of letters, not ideas. Not dialogue, the way people talk naturally… in half sentences, messed up phrases, in convoluted, almost psychotic ways, depending on the character the person is supposed to be—man or woman, educated? Erudite? Romantic? Hateful? Regional? Racial? Sexual? Dirty?"

She had never seen him like this, so vulnerable, so innocent. From their awkward position, she leaned her body further into him and pressed him down to the grass and lay against him. Landon was looking at her. "It doesn't make any sense to say 'I don't know'. Not only is that not believed, but it's not reasonable. I think I learned to tell stories—he paused, wondering if he should tell Grace about his first story? What would she think of that, and him in the bargain? She touched his lips with the tips of her fingers and the words came rushing as if she had opened a spigot.

"It was Jane, she was my girlfriend when I was seventeen… well, she was seventeen too. We did all the stuff that kids do growing up including going up on the mountain behind the town and necking wildly in the back of her folks car. A green Buick. I noticed when we did this that I needed to talk to her and on the way home she would ask me what all the talking was about because it didn't make any sense to her… and it didn't make any sense to me either. But, I was a talker, I guess.

One night, I was at her house and her folks had gone to Bakers-field—40, 45 miles away to a concert. We weren't in a car and we began necking in the kitchen. Before we knew it we were on the kitchen table. She pulled me up and took me down to the guest room in the basement and we took each other's clothes off and… well, the point of all this is that when we were on the kitchen table, I began telling her a story… when we moved downstairs, she whispered in my ear to tell the rest of the story. I wasn't sure what she meant but I began talking to her, telling her… a story. It was my first story, all of which was buried in my head… and I didn't even know it." Grace had moved to lean against the tree so she could look at him. Her eyes were moist, it was all she could do to keep from crying out loud.

Grace felt something inside take hold of her and she said, "Feels like two stories to me… a story within a story, if you will allow it." Landon smiled and looked down. "What a brave thing to tell me those stories, and how telling me has shown me something about you 'way beyond your 'first story'. Now I really understand what you have been trying to say to me." She paused then said, "Honestly. Landon, this is a treasure, as are you."

She leaned over and kissed him lightly on the lips. Grace saw his eyes roll up into his head. He became quiet and immovable. She watched him, thinking that he could come out of it and make a face at her or say something funny. Minutes went by… where was he? She dared not intrude in what seemed to be some inner dialogue. Suddenly a moving shadow came near and she looked up to see an old man with a knapsack walking by them. He nodded to her, as if to say hello, and looked down, puzzled, at her man. The old man paused. Landon looked up at Grace with a look of disorientation, then over to the old man, who nodded in friendship to him. It was an awkward moment, and the old man was the first to notice. He nodded again and walked off.

"Are you all right, darling?"

"I don't know."

Later, Landon would not remember how they got from the quiet part of the Park to his apartment. It seemed that they had a nice time at the picnic, decided not to go to the afternoon movies, but to come home and have a quiet light snack which Grace would prepare. And then, she wondered, would she have the great fortune to have him take her to bed and tell her a story while he was fully with her—when they were merged as two candles burning brightly, side by side. Eventually, of course, their heat causes them to lean together and they become one flame. As it happened, they did sleep together, lightly, not deeply, and made love. They awoke together as if nothing had transpired, and Landon fixed breakfast for them. Another day, another _____ (please, Lord, fill in the blank.)

Landon insisted on taking her to the train on the way to his appointment. They held hands in the taxi. They kissed on the platform as if they might not see each other for years, and the train left—with all those words unsaid. Grace, looking out the window, decided that it was perfect. It didn't matter what was not said, it mattered what <u>was</u> said. "Isn't the glass always half full?" she said out loud. The woman across from her looked around to see who was speaking.

Landon found himself on time for his appointment at the 92nd St. YMCA. "...I can't tell you, Landon, what it means to us for you to help us out of this spot we are in. It's appreciated beyond what you might expect."

"It's fine. It's fine. This sort of thing is good for us writers who spend too much time alone anyway. As long as you don't mind that I pick the stories to talk about... it will work out well."

"You chose, Landon..." Lettie Barnes fumbled on her desk for the folder on the lecture series. "Oh here. How silly. Did I give you the outline?" She lifted it up and held it out to him to see that he was holding one out to her. It was the same.

"Yes. Yes. I have it and I think I understand. Perhaps I might come an hour early and we could go over my notes to be sure your points are covered."

"Good idea." She was trying hard not to be the precise, controlling Director of Seminars that she was, but she was relieved Landon had made this last offer of security for her. She held out her hand to him and he took it. Lettie's hand was dry, very dry.

As Landon walked out of the building, he glanced at the Announcement Board. He was surprised at the activities, even though he was aware that the 92nd Street YMCA was an active community center in a city where community was not a given. The coming programs were impressive. He noted that even Erik Larson was to come to be part of a lecture series later in the year, and that the Dali Lama was to be in a seminar on

COMPASSION IN THE CITY. What a challenging subject. Landon was thoughtful as he walked out of the building to a lovely day. Up the street there was a hot dog vendor. He would get one and a drink and walk over to the Park… then to his apartment. It would give him a chance to think.

As he looked up to see where he was, finishing the hot dog, he noticed that he was a block from where Celia lived. He thought of his last visit there and smiled. Just another form of Compassion in the City—more immediate, and more encouraging. She was something special, she was. As he entered the sheltering greenery of Central Park, he thought it was a shame that it's working hours now or he would go over and ask her to take a walk in the Park with him.

His instincts in the Park were good, he was roughly aimed at a diagonal for his building. He would come around this path and cross by the sailing pond and then over to… and as he said it, the Pond appeared. The sailing pond is a large one where kids sail toy boats, either by those strange boxes that remotely control the boats, or by setting the boat and its sails on a course, keeping the breeze in mind, and run over to the other side of the pond to wait for your ship to come in. Now, the center of the pond had young bodies roiling around its middle with all the boats. As the scene caught Landon's attention, a boy fell over in the water, apparently pushed by the boy standing in the water beside him. There was another boy in tears trying to rescue his own boat and in the center of this tempest was an older man trying to—trying to do what?

Landon walked quickly over to the edge of the Pond to sort out for himself what this might be about. There was the occasional shout from one of the boys, the voice of the man trying to calm a situation that was clearly out of hand, and there were three boats in the water, crashed together as if this was a busy midtown boat intersection. The old man would first pull one boat apart from the mess to have it taken away by one of the boys who in turn would be pounced on by another boy. That boy would be pushed by a third boy and then they would go 'round and 'round again, churning up the water and attracting more spectators at the edge of the pond.

A woman walked up alongside Landon and yelled at him, "Where are the parents of those boys?" Nearby, two men were laughing at the antics of the older man who was trying to bring order to the tempest, "That guy thinks he is helping, but all he's going to get for his trouble is a dunking." As if this man on the sidelines were writing a script for the scene in the pond, the old man grabbed one of the boys to keep him from pushing another boy who had finally gotten his boat and was trying to leave, the third boy shoved the old man and he went flailing into the pond.

Landon pulled off his shoes and waded into the storm at sea. Quickly upon them, he realized that the fight was over the boats and grabbed two boats and walked away from the three rioting boys and the fallen man. He set the two boats upright and quickly moved to the one boy who was clutching his boat and picked both the boy and the boat up and out of the fight. In a minute, Landon had cleared the space and the remaining two boys were surprised to be fighting each other in the water without their boats. They stopped and looked at Landon.

"Help that man to get up. Now!" Landon said to them. They turned to see the old man, and then back to slosh to their own boats, which Landon shielded with his body.

" I told you to help him… he was trying to help you and now to need to return the favor. Help him."

This stopped their forward motion. The idea of fighting this younger, more agile man for their boats turned them to the old man. One boy on one side of him, the other on the other side of him, they pulled him out of the water and upright... not without difficulty. He had a backpack which had taken much water and he himself was exhausted by the storm in the pond. He was spitting water when he stood up, looking darkly at the two boys who realized it was they who had pushed him into the water. One boy turned to Landon noticing for the first time that the third boy had bolted off and left the pond with his own boat.

He looked at Landon and beyond him, to his boat. "Whot are you goin' ta do now, sur?" He was British.

The old man responded, "Where are your parents?"

"They off to Lost Angeles on business. My nanny is at tha market."

The adults nodded together and turned to the other boy and said almost together, "Where do you live?" The boy ran and swam over to his boat and picked it up... "Over there," he said, pointing toward the west side. He kept on moving as quickly as he could to the edge of the pond. He yelled over his shoulder, "My folks are working, what do you think?"

The boy was off running through the Park as those on the sidelines laughed at the scene. Now only the British boy was left. Landon took steps toward him.

"Wha you goin' ta do?"

Landon looked over to his wet partner, and shrugged.

"We're going to do nothing," said the old man. "Tell your nanny what happened. That will be quite enough." He turned to fish in the water for his backpack, which had slid off his shoulders again.

Landon noticed for the first time how hard it was to walk in the water, that it was taking more of an effort than he would have thought. Must have had a lot of adrenaline going. Then he looked at the old man and wondered how he had stood the onslaught of three nine to ten year old boys. The backpack raised up from the pond like a fish that had put up a good fight.

One of the onlookers at the edge of the pond yelled at them, and they turned to see a young man and his girlfriend standing on the edge of the pond as if to jump in.

"You need some help out there?"

"Where were you when we needed you?" the old man said only loud enough so that Landon could hear. He turned to them and shook his head, no.

Once out of the Pond, "I am Morris Rubin, water adventurer and boat pirate."

"Landon Harris, landlubber."

"Good to meet you, Mr. Landlubber. Thanks for joining the fray. I suspect they would have drowned me if you hadn't come along." They both turned at the same time to see a three foot deep crowd of onlookers at their end of the pond. Landon pointed to the crowd and said,

"Doing what New Yorkers do best, impotent onlooking." He reached for Morris, "Look give me your backpack and let's get out of here, you are drenched and I need a drink. I live just over there on Central Park West. Let's see if I can find you something dry to wear.

When they got to the edge of the pond, three people fought to help Morris Rubin out of the water and threw buckets of questions at him. He had been the central figure so only the ragged edge of the onlookers took notice of Landon. Morris barged through the crowd and joined Landon, answering no one's questions and the two of them moved toward the West Side as the crowd asked more questions to their backs.

Landon said, "I am not even going to ask how all that began, but I am curious as to why you waded into the middle of it." Morris shrugged. "It's been happening to me lately. I don't really know. It's new to me really."

He looked Landon in the eyes. "Did you ever do something you didn't know why you did it?" He took several steps. "Even afterward?"

The two men walked through the Park to Landon's apartment building. As they approached the doorman, he said, "Afternoon, Mr. Harris. You are, ah, Sir, very wet" and then looked at the man he had never seen before and began to speak, but stopped.

"Can I help you, Mr. Harris?"

"Thanks, Donald, but we are beyond help for the moment."

Donald moved quickly to open the doors and slid in behind the two men to produce a Federal Express envelope, "This came an hour ago, Mr. Harris."

"Thanks again, Donald."

Going up in the elevator, Morris said, "You are not someone important, are you, someone I should recognize?"

"Not at all. Don't think about it."

"What do you do? I forgot to ask."

"I am a writer."

"Anything I might have read?"

"What do you like to read?"

"History, biography, science… sometimes stories… not a very broad reach."

"On the contrary." He skipped over saying, as one might, that he had a book of short stories, but he did not. Instead, Landon said, "But, I can loan you a book of mine if you like."

"Why is it that you look so familiar?" Morris said.

"Now that you mention it, you seem familiar as well, as if we have met, but… I don't know…"

"Doesn't matter, now that we are brothers in adventure and boat piracy."

They laughed.

"Nice eastward view. I must say that I envy this sight. I have spent more time in the Park in the last year than I have in the thirty years prior." Morris said. He sat down, now in dry clothes and let Landon hand him a glass of wine. "You didn't open your air envelope… is it not urgent?"

"I forgot… in fact, I didn't even look to see who it was from… will you…?" Morris waved his hand. "Please." Landon walked to the nearby table and picked up the FedEx envelope. From where Morris was sitting, he could see Landon stiffen when he looked at the label. He could see Landon pause over the envelope, then, rip the top off and pull out a single sheet of paper. A letter.

"Landon! Hope you won't forget me or the possibilities. Signed, Amy"

Morris watched Landon read the note, look off into space and put it back into the cardboard envelope. He took a half step and placed the FedEx delivery on the table where he had gotten it. He turned to Morris, "...will wonders will never cease...?"

"I don't know, but if I had to guess, I would say certainly not. Landon, please come and sit down. We have had an exhausting afternoon, don't you think?" Morris took Landon's empty glass and walked to the bar beside the kitchen and poured him another drink. He placed it by Landon's hand in the chair in the alcove.

Landon looked up at him and smiled, " Who are you?"

"No one special. Just a man like you."

"I mean, what do you do?"

"I am now finally retired. I was a psychiatrist. Now I am an angel"

"An angel?"

"Yes," Morris continued his gaze at Landon, "Oh, I know that sounds bizarre, but I have come lately to learn the truth of such a preposterous statement."

Landon nodded. "You seem quite serious."

"It is not something that I created... I should say consciously created. If I can say this without having you wish me to leave you, I would say that this... it... chose me. All the defining events can be described, and are true."

A pause between them. Morris said, "Can you believe me?"

"I don't know. I don't know why I should, and I can't think of why I should not. But, you certainly know that this is not something you can say to people."

Landon sat up in the chair. "You have never said this to anyone else, have you?"

"No, I haven't. I have wanted to tell my daughter. I tell her everything, but she has a very orderly mind and I have been fearful of stretching it unnecessarily. In fact, that is my main focus of late... how to tell Sharon without alarming her, and without having her think her father has... what, gone too far in this stuff about the mind."

"A challenge."

"Yes."

Landon looked at his watch. "Do you like Chinese food?"

"It's all right."

"As it happens, my lady friend is coming to dinner tonight and she will be stopping at the place around the corner, it's quite good, even for those who are 'just all right' with Chinese."

"Are we hungry?"

"I am, and she is certain to be. But more importantly, I would like you to meet her."

"Oh, yes," Morris smiled, "and you would like her to meet an Angel, her first no doubt, excluding you." Landon laughed. "Good, but pause a moment, are you sure you want to... are you certain you want me to stay? Perhaps you would wish to keep your assignation with your lady friend alone?" Morris watched Landon's eyes as he asked, and saw in them that there was no objection, but there was also a secret.

By the time Grace had arrived with two bags of Chinese food from Celestial Delight on Columbus Avenue, the two men had pulled themselves together. Morris noted that Landon had carefully picked up the FedEx envelope and had taken it to another room. They set the dinner table together with real forks and spoons… "I hate plastic eating utensils, don't you?"

"…so, I was faced with accepting that this "Angel thing" had happened three times… the first being the most dramatic with the boy actually coming back to life in my arms. But in truth, I had been accidentally in places in time and space where these things happened—remember, I am a doctor who needs proof of facts as well as from the mental senses. In these three instances, I had acted impulsively to change the course of events for another person and for the better…."

It was Grace who spoke first, as Landon knew she would. She had stopped opening her fortune cookie as Morris got to the part of his amazing story about being "an Angel". "<u>This</u> is how you determined that you are an angel." She didn't believe it.

"No, this is how I determined that something new was happening in my life… based on free time, being in new and different places. I am retired, so my life is different. Then these events happened." Morris looked at Landon, "as I told Landon, I feel strongly that these situations have 'chosen' me. Can you see how that might happen?" Morris was able to speak of this for the first time to someone standing outside his own body. Now, there were to be other judgements, other sensibilities. Perhaps they could help him shed light on this.

Grace pursued. "…you said you have a scientific mind, and, after you examined these events, you determined that you were an angel?"

"No. That is most recent. Something else happened."

"Before we ask what that was, how is it that you see this business, forgive me, I don't mean to sound derogatory, but something must have come to mind to bring up the "idea of Angel".

Grace looked at Landon. Morris looked down to his lap, "Did this just pop into your mind?"

Morris nodded. "A most meaningful question, and all I can say to it is that—" he looked at Grace. "Have you ever done a good deed? Now, I know you have. We all have done small things that have helped others, have stepped in at the right moment to make a difference. A small difference."

Grace nodded, and put her hand on Landon's.

"Of course," Morris continued. "We all have. Now. Have you ever saved a person's life?" Grace shook her head, no. Landon grinned and said, "Well, technically yes, I wanted to kill an editor once but I spared him."

Morris held up his hand, nodding at Landon. "Fine, fine. Now, this incident with the boy and the cat in Riverside Park overwhelmed me, the other two smaller things began to make a pattern… the pattern I have tried to draw for you. But, it was not until after I had—what shall I call it, I know not what."

Grace whispered to Morris. "There is more of this?"

"Yes. And though there was no defining action, it felt like a borderline life/death situation, …well, I had not intended to tell you two this story, but" his eyes crinkled, "you are good therapists… that is you listen well."

He was looking at Landon when he said it.

Turning to Grace, Morris began…

"I was out at night in an unfamiliar area. In fact, I had gone to an event on the Lower East Side and decided to take a walk… I was thoughtful about what I had heard… and without thinking I walked toward the Bowery…"

Grace stiffened, and grasped Landon's hand.

"I had never been to the Bowery, let alone at night. But then I was not really thinking as I walked along. Since I have retired I have learned to let so much of my former ways of thinking fall away. After all, I was forming a new period of my life, and suddenly I was attuned to it. So, the idea of watching where I was going, where I was, was not something I was concerned about. I was lost in a world of new thoughts and unfamiliar places."

Landon watched the expression on Morris' face soften. He was a fleshy man, somewhat overweight, everything about him offering some small portion more than one might expect. He must have been a good therapist, he certainly is demonstrating how an over-sensitive person might be, might act. Landon looked over to Grace who was mesmerized by this performance, and she was not clear yet if it was credible, but she was not missing a word.

"...so, as I walk through the Bowery I am not thinking, as you might, that I should not be in this place. In fact, I now regularly question where is my place? So, though I was on a street where all the businesses had closed, been boarded up... I took no notice of that until afterward. Somewhere ahead of me... it was quite dark, I could hear someone crying. At first I was uncertain if it was a person... there was an animal quality to it and as I looked about to locate the direction of the crying, I saw that in the very bad area I was in, there must be hundreds of animals who have not eaten in days. But, in fact, have preyed on each other. I won't evoke the quality of "jungle", but there was this sense of that nevertheless. I continued to look for the source of the crying. Finally, I looked up to see if I was hearing things... somehow I began to think that I was creating the sounds in my head. But no, they continued. I rounded a corner and was confronted with a dog and a cat who were fighting. I saw no food nor other reason for them to be confronting. As I distracted them for a moment, the cat took a swipe at the dog and then ran off toward an alley right past my leg. The dog yowled and began to chase the cat again, but saw me and thought differently. He stopped short of me and looked up at me in the strangest manner.

Then he sat down in front of me. I swear I sensed his tail wagging at me. Now that the noise had stopped, I began to hear the crying again. The animals had only masked what I had heard at first. I looked out past the dog and saw the East River. It was black as night," Morris laughed self-consciously and noticed that Grace sat enthralled and that Landon seemed to be taking mental notes…. He smiled at her and said, "…well, it was night…"

"Weren't you afraid?" said Grace.

"Two or three years ago, I would certainly have been afraid. In addition, I would never let myself be in such a place. I saw myself then as a civilized man, now I am almost at home in a place where the light of reason has been snuffed out."

"Very poetic," said Landon.

Morris looked at him. At first he thought Landon was joking, but the seriousness of his face told him no. Morris flustered and said, "It was dark. As I approached the railing along the River, I saw in the dark—the form of a person. This was the one that cried. As I came closer, I saw it was a woman, a woman in rags. She had a foot up to the railing—a foot with a sandal hanging from it. I could see from the great effort she was making that her body had already failed her. Initially, I had no sense of what she was trying to do, She was distraught, her words were incomprehensible, her body didn't seem to respond to her instructions. Her affect was nil. I walked right up to her before she noticed me. When she did, she screamed very loud. I was frightened for an instant and then I spoke to her. I kept my voice down, speaking without seeming to intrude on her. I asked her what her name was. Samantha. Samantha something. I asked her if she knew where she was. She looked at me as if I had asked her a complicated question. She shook her head. I had purposely not asked her what she was doing, but now I saw that I must.

> She said she was going into the River.
>
> That the River was beautiful.
>
> That she wanted to rest in the River.
>
> Well, it didn't take long to establish that she was…
>
> was not in possession of her faculties.
>
> I pulled her back off the railing and sat her down on a bench that faced the River."

Morris looked away. Landon said nothing. Grace was beginning to tear.

"What was clear was that she was very sick, that she needed physical care, but more urgently she needed emotional care… therapy. I said I would take her home. She had none. I continued to pursue this, not realizing that there might be many people without a home to go to. Yes, yes, remember where I was. How could I have missed the fact that I lived in a city where a portion of the people have no place but the street to sleep. In fact, I felt that I was awakening myself from some sort of a nostalgic dream. I kept asking her where she lived, or slept, or rested. Finally, she whispered in the most normal of voices, in the most rational of ways, that she had not slept in a bed for months. Then she began crying again and moved to the railing. She was almost over it before I came to my own rational thoughts. Yet I sat there, motionless for several minutes watching. Actually, watching a person, who will not be able to swim, or save themselves, try to get into the softness of the River, as if it were the denied bed. As if, in fact, it was something that offered respite, calmness, and a way to stop her crying and these horrific feelings."

Morris had shifted from looking directly at the two of them, to looking, talking to the walls and the windows to the Park. His voice dropped and looking directly at Landon, said, "It was at that moment that I realized the right thing to do was to let her complete her climb over the railing. In fact, if I really wanted to help her, then I would assist her to fall into the River, as if this was the very best I could do for her." Morris was looking down, as if into the River.

"When I finally came to my senses, and she had two feet over the railing, I got up and pulled her back, laid her on the bench and put my coat over her. I had a towel in my backpack and I took it out and covered her feet with it. I found a small cardboard box in the trash nearby and put that under her head. I stood there over her for the longest time until I pulled some money out of my pocket and stuffed it into her hand—and left—and went home."

Now Morris was looking directly into the Park, as if the woman he was speaking of, speaking to, was there. "I was most grateful to have a home to go to. I realized that, until that moment, I had never given thanks for a simple thing like that."

The room was still. Each of the three people were lost in a thought of their own. One would gaze out the windows, as if to fly away to the Park. Another would retreat inside, as if the walls of self might be safe, though the story told by Morris made it clear that nothing was "safe". When Morris began speaking again, it startled both Grace and Landon. Grace had already moved her chair closer to Landon, and now leaned onto his shoulder.

"That night, that moment, I came as close as I have ever come in my life to saying to myself that I <u>am</u> an angel, an agent of some unknown force that has the power to decide who shall stay and who shall go. I wanted desperately to let her fall asleep and then pick her up in my arms, knock her unconscious on the railing and then let her fall out of my arms into the River. But, somehow I could not do what I thought then, and know now would have been the right thing. The best thing to do for her. My complete sense now is that I failed this woman. I had not allowed some rising power in myself to do this for her. I failed as a person."

Morris looked at his hosts and saw that he had taken a perfectly normal afternoon and evening, and transformed it into a thoughtful morass. "I can't say enough to you, if I may call you this, my new friends. You have allowed me to reveal myself and my own thoughts to you, as if you were the therapist and I the… how shall I name my 'dysfunction'? In any case," he said rising, "this has been a most enjoyable evening, not because of the subject matter, but because you have rained me with your generosity of spirit… something I have needed desperately since all this began."

He walked to the hallway and began putting on his backpack.

Landon was behind him saying, "Morris, there is no need to rush away. This has been the most interesting evening in remembrance… please don't feel…"

Grace carried on, "…like you have to go. We want to talk more about this. Good Lord, these are…" Grace is shaking her head at Morris, "…the most amazing stories I have ever heard." He took her hand and said, "Grace, I hope that you both will join me for a perhaps less dramatic, but equally interesting evening at my home soon. But, it's been a big day for me... and I am an old man."

When Morris had pulled the door closed behind him, Grace turned to Landon and in a whisper, as if Morris was outside the door listening, said, "Could he have meant that? Could he have felt, this generous and sensitive man, that he could be kind to this woman only by ending her life? Oh, Landon, what has happened?"

"I'm not sure. It is distressing. And it goes against everything that we believe about life... but, he was there, we were not, and I don't mean to hide behind that, I just need some time to digest it." He took her hand, and lead her back into the living room,

"...and, so do you."

They cleared the dining table in silence. In clockwork fashion, they got the dinner mess thrown away (thank God for Chinese carry out and only silver to clean) and as if it was a ritual, made ready for bed. Landon absented himself from her to go to The Room and make some notes for the morning. When he came back to the bedroom she already had her cheek to the pillow. Landon took off his clothes, slipping in with her.

Grace moved quickly to him, placing herself within his embrace.

"I am frightened, Landon." There was something different about her in this moment, he thought. What could it be? She continued speaking and her lips brushed against his chest. "He is too intelligent to be affected as he has been. He is not making this up. These things must have happened to him, mustn't they? Yet they seem so… extraordinary. So unreal to happen to such a person. I mean, a man like that could be your own father."

As she talked, she seemed to run down, like a music box that is playing a tune it doesn't care for. "Landon, do you think we should see him again. Do you?"

He waited with his answer, knowing that she was not finished.

"Landon, can we be married? I hope you want to marry me because I want to marry you."

"Grace, darling," he whispered in her ear, "what's happened to you? You are like a runaway horse."

"No, I just have seen a runaway man…. It makes me know how tentative life is… just seeing that a man like that can… Landon, I don't mean to sound crazy. I just want us to be together in the deepest sense before something happens." She could feel him move.

"No, don't ask me what will happen. Morris didn't know what would happen to him and it did. We don't know what will happen to us, but it… …might. Am I glad I was here with you tonight. Now am I glad I am here and you are in my arms. We are lucky."

Landon paused, "Morris is… a miracle. I feel much like you do, but I am not frightened, actually, I think it's sort of exciting. I think we should see him again."

He could feel her fingers tapping on his back.

"You didn't say you hoped you could marry me." She leaned back to look at him. "Or don't you approve of my asking you to…"

"I approve of you and anything you say. I do hope I can marry you. If you want we can have a trial wedding right here. I will go to the bookcase and find my copy of the balcony scene from Romeo and Juliet... no, that has a bad ending...how about some paragraphs from Annie Dillard's *Living like Weasels*... or..."

"*Sonnets from the Portuguese...*" she said, "then we could say we were engaged."

Landon got up, but she pulled at him. "Wait, I was just kidding."

"About getting married or getting engaged, or about what should be read at the ceremony?"

"I wasn't kidding about any of that... you just don't have to do it now. I need you to tell me you love me. I am frightened, Landon."

He got back beside her, she had on her filmy night gown and he could see her breasts through it as he slid into bed. He held her close and said,

> "Though the face of all the world is changed, I think,
> since first I heard the footsteps of thy soul
> move still, beside me, as they came between me
> and the dreadful outer brink of obvious death,
> where I, who thought to sink,
> was caught up into love... with you..."

"What is that?" Grace asked.

"Elizabeth Barrett Browning... with some omissions and additions from me."

"You feel that way about me?"

"Yes, I am coming to... if you will give me enough space and time...

I hope to arrive there... "beside the footsteps of thy soul..."

"Oh, Landon..."

Over breakfast, Landon said, "Grace, I forgot to tell you that my schedule is getting filled with engagements. I had a call from Lettie Barnes at the 92nd Street Y. She needs someone to fill..."

"What is the Y at 92nd Street?"

"Oh, sorry, the YMCA... they do many outreach programs in the literary arts. They can be quite good. She has asked me to fill in on a program of short stories... I am going to use one of mine and something else, not sure...."

"That sounds like fun... do you do a written lecture or do you work from notes."

"Notes, usually, but I find it important to read the stories several times the day before the program and quote from them as I go along. I think it's important to be as fluid as possible."

"Want some more coffee?"

"Yes. I do"

Grace looked at him across the table and said, "Now listen, I have some things to do this morning. Hopefully I can clear away by early afternoon and we can get a slow train to Westport. You can spend some time thinking and let's us spend some days and time not rushing around. What do you say?"

"It's a deal. Anything I can do to help?"

"Nope, I hope I have it covered."

By the third day at Grace's house Landon finally slept late. He reached his hand out for her, but the bed was empty. He put on the robe she had gotten for him and went looking for her. He looked upstairs and then went down, finally to the kitchen, to find a note on the dining table. "Gone to the market, Back soon. G." But, there was warm coffee. Landon poured a cup and wandered around the house.

He realized that he was still a stranger here. In the times he had been here he had not really looked at things beyond the sense of the place and, as was his habit, the bookcase. Grace had many books and they were filled with decent fiction and art... European and American. There was a section of history books of the kind that he wouldn't have expected Grace to be engaged in. Napoleon. MacArthur. Truman. Machiavelli, a book on conducting guerrilla warfare by a Greek named Gravas. It seemed out of character until Landon realized that she had lived in Greece with her second husband. Second husband. What was his name? Hal? Gordon? She doesn't talk much about him, yet she had been married to him for, hmm, about eight years. And, in this looking, he found a group of South American fiction, with some Pablo Neruda poetry books, as well as a book of the poems of Sor Juana Inéz de la Cruz. He flipped that open to see it was in Spanish. Hmm.

Landon walked out to the tiny patio and sat. Pots of flowers everywhere. He wondered if a second husband was imprinted on a woman—Catherine was imprinted on him. He supposed there was a difference in how the partner was lost. Death is a powerful separator. Yet is the death of love any less powerful? You join with a person because you love them, want to be with them, respect them, and feel yourself to be greater for the addition to your life. He had felt that about Catherine. But, did Grace mourn the death of the love for a man, whom for unloving reasons, she must leave? He wondered if he could ask Grace that question.

He walked to the kitchen and refilled the coffee cup and then walked back upstairs. Landon looked up from this reverie to realize he had never been in this room. He stopped to get his directions straight. This was the spare room, obviously. A bed for guests, a desk with a pile of papers that haven't been looked at for months, a shelf with family pictures, but not like those scattered around the house. And yes, here he is, the second husband, with his arm around Grace in some city that had a European feel to it. France, perhaps. His blood rose to this. He sensed envy, jealousness in looking at this man with his arm around Grace. He closed his eyes just long enough to realize she had made love to this man in pleasure and confidence. She had loved him, just as she loves Landon. He quickly walked out of the room. Let's find, he thought, a more neutral place to be.

He walked into the small bathroom and dressing room that Grace went into each morning off her bedroom. It was her bathroom... another was for her partner and that is the one where he had readied himself for the day. He sat on the toilet seat and surveyed the space. A picture of flowers in a garden. A picture of her sister, Danny, who lives in Italy. What is this? He got up to look closer... it was a framed poem, written in Spanish. He looked to the bottom of the piece for the name of the author. Sor Juanna Inéz de la Cruz. I wonder what is the translation... wait, there is a book of her poems in the bookcase. Must ask Grace about this... he was curious that it might be a religious piece and then he noticed that one of the corners of the poem was turned over to reveal a typewritten—on a typewriter, an old one he would judge—piece of paper. But only a corner of it was revealed, not enough to gain any sense of it. How odd. He had an impulse to lift the frame off the wall and turn it around to see the back.

A half page of white paper was taped to the back. It read...

I cannot love you more.

Love, after all, is merely for a person

and we, we love each other

        in this way.

But, I cannot love you more than

the stars in the heavens,

more than the birds in the trees of my garden.

I love you as if you were that star, that bird.

        I cannot love you more.

        I cannot love you only.

"Landon, you up there... you awake, sleepyhead?...helllllllllooooo..."

"Yes, yes, I am up here and awake." He placed the frame back on the wall.

"What are you doing?"

"Nothing... nothing... thinking of getting dressed."

"Well, don't. Come down here so I can open your robe and fix you breakfast."

Landon walked in the kitchen to see her surrounded by bags of groceries. Grace turned to him, walked across the kitchen and opened his robe revealing his naked body and pressed herself into it.

"I just love having you here." She looked into his face. "Do you love it too?”

“Yes, yes I do… in fact I was considering writing a poem for you.”

“Really! Oh, I’d love that.”

“Has anyone ever written a love poem to you?”

Her back was turned to him and he heard her say, “No, no one has. You would be the first.”

“I would like to be the first.”

It was the way he said it. She turned to him and stared silently for a moment.

“That had a sad sound to it. “

“I didn’t mean it to be.” She continued to watch him while pouring a new cup of coffee for him. She walked to the kitchen table and set it down. Landon looked at the coffee.

“Anything on your mind?” she asked.

“I was thinking about love.”

“What part of love moves you this moment?” She looked at his open robe and he closed it.

“The poetry of love… the part that is so elusive and hard to write words about.”

Her eyes widened and her face softened. “What has come over you? Did you have a dream? Have you… ah, made a decision? I have a sure sense there is a sub-dialogue here.”

“Well, if anyone should know about sub-dialogue, it should be me, huh?”

“I suppose, but darling, I didn’t mean it that way. It’s just that you looked different to me just now and…"

"I was wishing I had been the first man… the first… I wish I had been your first husband, I guess. I'm sure, ah, that they were good men and good to you, but I just had this thought while you were at the market that I wish I had been your first man."

She got up and took his hand, pulling him up and walked him into the living room to sit them both down on the sofa, close together.

"I don't think that any man has said any-thing that has meant as much to me as what you have just said. I think that is a beautiful thought. I know at some level of reality that something like that can never be… at least in this lifetime. But in another, it can certainly be so. I think we can make it so, create something between us that will be fresh and new, wholesome and nurturing. I can be a nurturing woman, Landon, and you bring that out in me as no one has ever done." She put her arm around him and kissed his ear, turned his face to her and kissed it.

"I think we can look forward to much hope, I have the will if you will supply the imagination." She kissed him again. "Deal?"

Landon nodded his head. "Yes. Yes." He paused for a moment… "Speaking of imagination, I hope you wouldn't mind if I took myself off to the Harbor for a walk and see if I could sprinkle myself with some 'imagination'… that be all right?"

"Would you like me to go with you?"

"…ah, yes and no, is the real answer, but for the moment, why don't I go by myself now and maybe both of us later."

Grace was clearly puzzled, but nodded, yes…. "Fine."

"See you in awhile…"

At the harbor, Landon looked and stopped, sat and got up, reached his hand up to the sky as if he could pull down a soft cloud to sit on. It is Morris Rubin, he thought, he is the connection to this, us and what will come… And, then Landon remembered… There was a clear path of the sun on the water, as if something was beating a path to him… and riding on this path was his remembrance of the Ashbury poem… what was it…? yes…

> Somewhere someone is traveling furiously toward you.
> At incredible speed, traveling day and night.
> Through blizzards and desert heat, across torrents, through
>   narrow passes.
> But, will he know where to find you.
> Recognize you when he sees you.
> Give you the thing he has for you?

In Landon's mind that translated to mean, 'will he (Landon) recognize the person (Grace) and the gift (vision) the person has for him.' The trick is in recognition, in 'seeing', in wrapping one's mind around the gift, the person, the presentment and making it into something.

It was his sense that Morris Rubin was the man who had traveled to Landon. And now it was his job to recognize Morris and what he had, the gift, if that's what it is. And, Landon was certain it was. There was something in his mind resisting a part of this, something was not quite right yet. The figure in the back of his mind continued to be a shadow, but was still there—essential. How to throw light on this? How to more deeply recognize? This was the task ahead of him. He needed to immerse himself in this.

He needed to… and here he was back at Grace's house..

"You have a nice walk?"

"Yes, I think so…"

The call came in the mid-afternoon. "Yes, this is Grace Mathisson… what…? Oh, no…" She moved her hand over the receiver. "Landon, Landon, come quickly—Yes, I am here. Where is he?" She listens and writes directions and an address. "Yes, Room 214. We'll come right away."

"Grace, what is it?" Landon said.

"It's Horace Ryan. He's had a stroke… he's in the hospital at Stamford. We have to go."

In the car, Landon wondered out loud how the hospital people found Grace. Then his attention was drawn to how fast she could drive in an emergency. He was so impressed he had to close his eyes on three occasions when she did maneuvers that seemed quite dangerous.

The hospital room was the usual array of tubes and machines around him. Horace Ryan was pale and weak. Grace walked alongside the bed and put her hand on his arm. His eyes opened to see Landon at the foot of the bed, then over to Grace. He gave them a weak smile and Grace began crying. She sank in the chair by the bed and began speaking to him so low that Landon only caught a few words and the idea, which had to do with how grateful they—she and Landon were to him and Rather.

"…and, where _is_ Rather?" she asked. Horace patted the air beside his hand and shook his head. He did not know.

Landon walked out to the hall and the nursing station. "Does anyone know where Mr. Ryan's dog is being kept?" The charge nurse didn't know, nor did the other nurse, but they had an idea and walked Landon back to the room and Horace Ryan's chart. Under all the papers were the admitting reports and a notation: Patient appears to live alone. Dog present in house. Left dog in secured house alone. Check on this. (signed) BD.

"Horace, we are going over to get Rather and keep him with us. Is that all right?" said Landon. Horace nods, and Landon goes to the other side of the bed, facing Grace. He takes Horace's hand.

"What else can we do for you… beside pray?" finished Grace. The old man looked from one to the other and gave a weak smile and a salute. His hand looked to be a skeleton, but Landon sensed a strength in it. Landon saluted back and Horace smiled and patted the bed beside him. Landon cocked his head, not understanding. Grace said, "Yes, Horace, we will pet Rather for you. And if we can figure out a way—we'll get him up here to wag his tail at you." The old man smiled and closed his eyes. Landon looked up at Grace. "He seems most weak." She nodded, "but, let's just sit here for awhile. Rather will be all right, he's only been alone since last night."

Landon sat on one side of the bed, Grace on the other. Each was having a three-way silent conversation: they would look at Horace Ryan and wait for him to open his eyes, which he did from time to time. Grace would look at Landon, Landon would look at Grace, and each would look within. The within part was the hardest. There was already a sense of loss, a sense of helplessness. Horace had had a good life, his attitude and his vitality attested to it, and now that was going to end. He was 86 years old and would never be able to sail his boat again, not take long walks with Rather, not settle out at the point of the harbor and watch the other boats break water.

Grace had the address and drove there slowly and carefully. It was as if she didn't want to arrive at the house of Horace Ryan.

"Would you rather put this off, Grace?" She looked steadily at the road. "We can go over and get Rather later."

"He's going to die isn't he?" asked Grace.

"Yes, he is."

"Do you think we could really sneak the dog up to his room?"

"Yes, I think we could. Probably at night, just before they secure the hospital. Do you think that would help Horace?"

She nodded, tearing. "Let's do it then." She turned into a gravel drive-way and toward a small white house.

The house was a miniature. A smaller version of a real house. Grace reminded herself of an area of London where the houses along the streets are diminutive. A normal sized person walks in and though the archway is high enough to walk through, one has a sense to duck, that it will not be high enough. Inside, the place was immaculate, as if two Polish cleaning la-dies had just left. Everywhere were boats, or pictures of boats, or paintings of boats, and over the tiny fireplace there was a painting of a boat, and on the foredeck, a dog. Well, not just a dog, but Rather, who was all over them from the minute they entered. Jumping, tail brushing, tongue wagging, as if he had been imprisoned for centuries. Grace went into the kitchen to see that he still had food and water, so he was all right in that sense. There was an extra sense that was not all right. There was a tension in the animal that both Landon and Grace noticed. They sat in the small living room, win-dows on the Sound, high windows on both sides of the room. Above this room, a loft with a ladder to reach it. At one point, Rather got so excited that he ran up the ladder and stood on the loft looking off as if to see Horace Ryan returning, walking up to the house, opening the door, and then Rather ran down the steps, a feat in itself, and ran to the door and barked. Waiting for his master. Landon got him to come back to the circle at the center of the room and be petted and talked to—and finally coaxed to leave, to get into the back seat of Grace's car and leave his home. Rather was most uncertain about that part. His eyes welled up with questions only a homeless dog can have. It didn't help that a thunderstorm had come up, and though there was no lightening in sight, the thunder was fearsome to the ears of the dog, as if his world was surely—this minute—coming to an end.

Grace fixed two beds out of old pillows and blankets for Rather in her home. He sniffed first the one in the small kitchen dining area, keeping an eye on the storm out the windows, and then followed her upstairs to smell out the sleeping area she prepared in the bedroom. He seemed to favor this one, less noise perhaps, and curled up until she went downstairs. Then he was up and after her. Halfway down the stairs, there was a pounding on the front door that frightened them all.

Tim Dalton is 14 years old as he stands soaking wet at Grace's door. He takes a step back when he sees Landon. *No man lives here*, is written on his face which is already creased with concern. Landon was puzzled, but said, "Well, hello there. Better come in out of the weather."

The boy stepped in asking, "Is Mrs. Mathisson home?"

"Certainly is. Come along," said Landon shutting the rain out the door.

"Oh, hello, Timothy. Please come in. We were just talking to our house guest." She gestured at the dog, but the boy was still confused.

He spoke low to Grace, "I didn't know you had a dog, Mrs. Mathisson."

"We don't, Timothy, he is just visiting for a while. His master is sick in the hospital."

"Oh." The boy turned to Landon and stared.

"I am a friend of Mrs. Mathisson's. My name is Landon Harris."

The boy nodded, but said nothing.

Grace said, "Landon, this is Timothy. He lives with his parents next door. I'll bet your mother sent you over to get an onion or a cup of sugar."

Timothy turned to her and shook his head. "A stick of butter or a pinch of oregano?" Before he could shake his head again Grace said, "I'm just kidding, Timothy."

"My mom isn't home now."

Landon said, "And, your father, he asked you to get something from Mrs. Mathisson?" The boy turned to Landon and shook his head. "My dad isn't home either. The storm. The storm is getting pretty bad and I was checking," he looked at Grace, "you know, to be sure there were flashlights if it gets dark. But, I couldn't find any. So I looked for candles and there are no candles either. So if the lights go out I won't be able to see, you see."

The adults nodded. Landon was beginning to see that this was not about the candles or the flashlights, but then he was not sure what it was about. The boy was timid with him, but seemed all right with Grace. He wondered if he should leave the room to give Timothy some time with Grace.

"Well, when your folks get home I'm sure they will know where all that stuff is, but let me loan you my flashlight until they come." She got up and moved toward the kitchen.

"They aren't coming home tonight. My dad is traveling somewhere and my mom is stuck in the city." Grace came back to stand near Timothy. "Why don't you sit down, Timothy, I was just making some hot chocolate for us, would you like some?"

The boy nodded and moved to a chair away from Landon. Rather followed him and stood close to the boy, nuzzling to be petted. Timothy sat and petted the dog. "I'll finish up with the chocolate, Grace, why don't you talk to Timothy," and he disappeared into the kitchen. As he was leaving, he heard the boy say, "Who is that, Mrs. Mathisson?"

The thoughts in Landon's mind, while searching for a way to make hot chocolate in the kitchen, mirrored Grace's questions to Timothy in the living room. 'How come your folks are both away?' 'Does this happen often?' 'Has your mother left a number for you to call her?' 'Do you know where your father is traveling in case you need to call him?' And finally, "You know, Timothy, I think you need to put a message on your phone machine in case your folks call, saying that you are staying here with me tonight."

She paused, looking deeply into the boy, "Would that be all right with you?"

Timothy thought about that long enough for Landon to come in with a tray of hot chocolate and cookies. Grace nodded approvingly at him, as if to say, not bad, not bad at all. They had cookies and chocolate in silence. Timothy kept looking at Landon.

"I'm a writer, Timothy. Do you know any writers?"

The boy shook his head.

"Well, then I am the first writer you have met. I live in New York and I come up often to visit my friend Mrs. Mathisson. And, Rather is a friend of ours as well. Rather is going to stay here for awhile and maybe you would like to have him stay in the room where you will sleep tonight. What do you say?"

"Oh, that would be good. What did you say his name was?"

Grace stepped in, "Rather, as in I would *rather be sailing*, or *I would rather be by the water*."

Timothy smiled as if he got it, but they knew he didn't. No matter. Grace took the boy and the dog upstairs and settled them into the guest bedroom. Landon stayed with the puzzle of leaving a 13 or 14 year old boy alone at night. The storm is an accident, and he is a young teenager, but he is also clearly afraid of this situation, and of strange men. What is that part about? He would have to ask Grace if she knew, and it was certain that she wouldn't. This looked different than a casual aversion.

The phone rang at 2:38 A.M.. The storm was receding, but there was still a blowing wind to rustle the trees. Grace picked up the phone and it was a woman, Timothy's mother. She was speaking too loud, "Grace, Grace, how nice, and neighborly to take Timothy in and look after him. I got your message…" and she was interrupted here by some laughing in the background and a man's voice. "…sorry, ah, we are just finishing up the meeting here…I'm in Manhattan and won't be able to get home tonight. Do you mind keeping Tim until he has to be off for the school bus?" More noise in the background.

"No, Sharon, not at all. He is settled in the guest bedroom."

"Oooooh, that's sensational, Grace. You are a working mother's savior. Thanks. All very impromptu here tonight and…" Grace thought the line went down for a moment, but no, the background noise at the other end was still there. "…ah, sorry, sorry, I dropped the phone. Well, I owe you one, Grace. See you tomorrow. Bye now." And the line went dead.

Grace lay in bed holding the phone. Landon looked at it and then her. He was groggy but he had a sense of it.

"Is she all right?"

"Yes, she is all right, but Timothy isn't. She's at a drunken party and, unless I miss my guess, there is a man involved as well." She put the receiver down and turned to Landon.

"Poor Timothy."

Timothy was easier with Landon in the morning. Grace made them a nice breakfast and Landon went home with the boy to see that he got a change of clothes and watched him run to the school bus.

Timothy's home was considerably larger—Landon had a sense of enough money but not enough good sense. A huge liquor cabinet in the dining room. But, more important, as Landon walked around the house, waiting for the boy to be ready for school, was the fact that there were so few books, and what there were… a few paperback novels and mysteries… airplane reading, some call them… and some picture books of cities. Nothing to speak of.

Timothy came up to Landon adjusting his backpack. "Thanks, Mr. Harris, for helping me this morning." The boy just stood and looked at him and then turned for the front door. "Say goodbye to Rather."

The next meeting of the day took place in Grace's kitchen.

"I am afraid to call and ask if we can take the dog up, even given the situation."

"You mean, they will say No."

"They will have thirty clinical reasons to say No, and not a humane one, Yes."

"I agree. At least if we get caught, doing it on our own puts us on a better... footing. So, the question is, how to get him upstairs?"

"He's too big to put in one of those bags on wheels, you know for flying trips."

"Right. And, he is too big to carry even if we could pretend he is a load of personal things."

"We need something ingenious."
Some quiet thinking...

"How about a big canvas bag, one of those sports bag things. We could each carry a handle."

"Mmm, that's a good one. I wonder, no matter what we do, will the dog be quiet?"

"I think we can count on that. I was talking to Rather while you were with Timothy. He is fully in control of his barking and all that."

"Good."

"Hey, how 'bout a diversion? You go in and create a fuss or something that will keep the attention on you, while I sneak up the stairs with Rather."

"Oh, fine, I get to make the fuss while you get the easy job up the back stairs."

"OK, I'll make the fuss and you can sneak."

"I suppose it doesn't matter who sneaks, but I think the stairs are a good idea.

"Right, we could go over this afternoon and check out the stairs and see which has the least visibility."

"Good, but a diversion?"

"Let's hope it can be simpler than that... let's check it out after lunch."

Grace had some errands to run and she dropped Landon off at the Harbor. He noticed that a heaviness had dropped away from him. He actually felt lighter, as if he had been dieting or his belt was up a notch. He looked out at the Harbor and saw two sailboats out to catch the wind. Horace wants to be there, right now, he thought. Better, all of us should be there with him... Grace, him, Rather, the whole crew. He looked out at Long Island Sound and because the haze was at the horizon, there was no opposing landfall. He wondered where a sailboat might end up if it just headed east, away from the sun, toward Europe... it must be there somewhere. Then, his mind lapsed into 'that someone coming toward him... at great speed... what does he have for you...?'

In in the final plan, it was decided that Rather should be covered with something, it was then that Landon noticed that the dog was really well trained. If you said, 'sit', Rather sat, no questions. He sat on command. Same with other commands, 'come', 'fetch', 'go to the...', even 'sit up' and he would stop and settle on his haunches and up went the paws.

With that, Grace revised their idea of the bag. If they cut three holes in the bottom, Rather could walk in it when no one was look-ing... and better, could climb the back steps to the rear entrance by himself... big advantage 'cause he was a big dog. Then, if someone came, one of them could whisper "sit" and the bag would hit the floor, as if the person carrying was resting. Perfect. They giggled all the way to the hospital.

The parking lot was empty and there was an "Emergency Parking" section near a side door that was kept locked after 8:00 at night. Landon went into the hospital and opened that door while Grace walked Rather to it. Though they had rehearsed this in an empty parking lot elsewhere, the sight of this huge sports bag with three red legs walking it toward the hospital door toward him was comic. He realized then that a student video crew should be making their next film festival entry of this caper. What a concept! Inside the building, Rather skidded quickly around the closed Gift Shop with Grace hanging on. Who's leading who, she wondered? She aimed the dog to avoid the corridor which lead to the cafeteria (which was still open) and then aimed him toward the stairs. They had a few seconds of exposure until they got to the least used stairs. Someone came out of the cafeteria and down that hall at the perfect wrong moment. Grace automatically whispered "sit" to Rather and he slumped in the bag by the telephones, as if he knew she could make an excuse to rest the bag while she called. She fished in her pocket for coins. Two people chattering passed her without a thought.

"Walk, Rather" and the black bag was up, walking down the hallway and around the corner where Landon was holding the door to the stairs open. Grace and the black bag slipped into the stairwell. They stopped for a moment to catch their breath. Grace's eyes caught Landon's and there was a momentary wordless connection. They were hand and glove, eye of the needle and thread, out walking their sightless dog.

Then, up the stairs. Second floor, no problem, but just as they rounded the steps for Three, an orderly, a small black man, stepped out of the door to Three. He was about to run down the steps when he saw Grace with the bag, behind Landon who was leading the way. "Happy" Hawkins was a gentleman, so his first thought was why is this dude not carrying the woman's bag. He heard the woman whisper something, but didn't catch it. Landon is on a middle stair, the bag and Rather are draped over two steps, and Grace has a silly grin on her face.

"Hey, lady, can I give you a hand? I small, but powerful."

Landon tried to get in his way, but "Happy" slipped right around him.

"That's one big bag. Must be a 'hole week's laundry, huh?"

"Certainly is. It looks heavy, but it's not, thanks anyway." Grace shielded the bag from Hawkins, who tried to reach around her anyway. "No trouble, Miss…" and he was looking up to Landon.

"Hey, mate," said Landon is his best affected English voice, "ah tried to get the lay-dy to let me fetch it, bot, you know, lay-dys… no chance, mate."

The orderly was so stunned with Landon's 'character' that it gave Grace a chance to literally lift Rather to the next step as if she was moving, and moving away from "Happy".

"I am most grateful. I like to, you know," dumb smile, "do things my-self. You are very kind, sir." They both stood staring at "Happy" for the eternity of several seconds when he too smiled, showing off his gold tooth, and ran away down the stairs. They froze until they heard the door below close and then Rather barked. Grace looked upstairs, Landon looked down and around. No response, and they burst out laughing.

Rather made it up the stairs before Grace. Somehow the handles of the bag slipped out of her hands. The black bag stopped and sat upright at the top of the stairs as if it might be golf clubs. Grace grabbed the handle and whispered, "stay" to Rather and she stepped to the door which Landon had gone out of a moment before.

Landon was at the nurses' station. One nurse was bent over her records and endless reports. Landon walked up and greeted her,

"I wonder if you can tell me the way to Room 241?" which he knew was the opposite direction as Horace's.

"You don't have much time, Sir, visiting hours are up soon…"

"Fine. Can you show me the way to the other wing? I have gotten lost here before."

Exasperated, the Nurse came around the desk and lead him away from the stair door, where Grace, peeking out, saw them move off and gave Rather the 'walk' command, and they slid around the corner to the fortunately empty hall where Horace Ryan was. She set the bag down 'sit' and then she leaned and settled herself against the wall 'stay'.

Landon came toward her and the black bag from the other direction. He was hurrying along looking over his shoulder in case the night nurse decided to see exactly where he was going. He kissed Grace and patted the black bag to feel the dog wag his tail in the small space, and then they opened the door to Horace's room.

It took Landon fully ten minutes to understand the simplicity of the scene before him. It was without water, movement of boats or bodies, or even words. Horace and Rather, master and dog, were as they were on the first day that Landon saw them in the Harbor. Rowing, talking, bounding, living. The same as in their miniature house. The same as here in a hospital room. The dog looked at his master, whined some and licked his hand. Horace spoke to the dog low and soft, almost beyond words. The dog, younger and more alive, moved around and within Horace. But, it was limited, as if a whole canvas of active sailing life could be lived in the space of a mattress. No drama here or only the drama supplied by the audience. Here was simplicity, common bonding, friendship. Landon looked over to Grace, tearing. He realized that she would feel the same, yet her description of what she was witnessing would be different. Again, the audience feels the drama. The players live it on their tiny stage as if there were no audience, nothing but their regard and love for each other. It was so peaceful that Grace soon fell asleep and Landon began to worry that a night nurse would appear to do something mechanical like wake Horace up to take his temperature. Landon decided to move his chair near the door, so as to stop the forward motion of anyone entering. They would suffer the consequences of bringing the dog. Willingly, if only to continue to witness this. It was worth a thousand scoldings.

Finally, both Horace and Rather fell asleep. The dog's paw on the arm of his master. Landon easily moved the paw away and let Rather slip to the floor. The dog whimpered a bit, but didn't object as Landon, as carefully as he could, slid the dog under his master's bed. Grace was already asleep, and looked comfortable. Landon went out to find the charge nurse for this area, hoping that it wouldn't be the same woman he had asked directions of an hour ago. No, that woman had been white, this woman was black. She was watching the television monitor of a room labeled ICU. Landon wasn't sure what that meant, but he slipped up to the desk and waited for the woman to be finished. She turned to him with a smile. "You been back with Mr. Ryan, haven't you?"

"Yes, we have and I have a confession to make."

She looked at the clock on the wall behind Landon. "Everyone makes them at this hour. You supposed to be gone home by now. Is Mr. Ryan asleep?"

Landon nodded.

"And, what is this confession you goin' ta make?"

"My friend, sitting alongside his bed, has also fallen asleep. It's been a very emotional day for all of us, and I was hoping we could bend the rules some, and let her and Mr. Ryan sleep 'till they wake."

"What 'bout you?"

"Well, I was thinking of recounting my dreams… no, it's a bad joke. I would be happy just to sit and watch them sleep… if you will permit it."

She looked over at Horace Ryan's chart and flipped though some pages. When she came to the last page, she saw the notes about the dog. "You find the dog all right?"

Landon nodded.

"He's fine and dandy?"

Landon nodded.

"Well, let me go back in with you and take a look at the vitals. If it looks all right, then I'll make this exception."

"Thank you. You are an angel." Landon continued looking at her and she said, "Why you lookin' at me that way?" Landon shrugged. "I was thinking only of angels. I have been thinking of them a great deal lately." He smiled at her.

They went back to the room. She checked the blood pressure monitor, the heart monitor and two other dials that seemed to speak to her. Rather didn't move a muscle. Grace was away in the arms of Morpheus. Horace's breathing was shallow. She shook her head. Touched the old man's hand, and then motioned Landon out of the room.

Her lips tightened as she turned to him in the hallway. "You know, don't you, that he may not last the night? Your woman may wake up, but he may not. Are you prepared for that?" They looked at each other. She reached out an touched his arm.

"You all right now? Don' you be foolin' me." Landon nodded and went back in the room to hold vigil.

There was hell to pay. The nurse had been right, Horace Ryan's heart stopped beating at 4:07 while all around him others slept in a different world. Grace had to be carried out the room sobbing and lain down in an empty room while Landon sorted out the problems with the day shift about the dog and being in the room all night. Finally, Rather was allowed to walk out of the hospital unmasked. Landon donated the black bag to the cause of carrying Horace's things, few as they were, home. In the car, Grace touched Landon's face. "Did you sleep, darling?" Landon nodded. It was a perfect circle he thought. Perfect, I hope I can die with a faithful dog under my bed and a faithful woman beside me. He left himself out of the equation, until he realized that he would be in the bed.

Life finally resumed for Landon and Grace at dinner time. By then, the shock had worn down, naps had been taken. Rather was situated with permanent bedding in the guest room and seemed to be listless, as if he had not understood that as he slept his master's life drained away and there would be no more hands to lick.

"I just don't understand that there was no family at all. Is that reasonable?" she said.

"Hard to know what is reasonable. Remember, we never asked him about a wife, kids, anything. He was absorbed in the life around him, not what was left behind. So, no family."

"What should we do?"

"Begin to think about our own lives, now that we have another mouth to feed."

"Where do you want to start?"

"With Morris Rubin."

She was taken aback, "Morris, why Morris…?"

"I have a sense he is connected to our future… deeply…"

Landon needed to place himself. It was so close, he felt that he might be able to extend his reach to touch it. He reminded himself of the old creative motif, 'if you can see it, you can write it, you can sing it'. He was so close to a vision, something that belonged to him alone. It seemed now so long since he had been so close, that even the proximity of that sense of impending completeness made him feel whole while the sense of yearning drained away.

He looked out to the shining day coming. Bright sky, pillowed clouds, as if he was patient enough the truth would be revealed when the clouds moved west.

They were half way around the Harbor, he and Rather. He hadn't had a dog since he was a kid in Maricopa. He looked down at the dog, moving along briskly on his three strong legs. When he was a kid, dogs were fun.

Now he was grown, this dog was an inspiration. He hoped to learn to fuse his hopes to this dog, to be infused with the dog's courage and spirit. It had always come easily to him, everything up to the point of Catherine's death. Now, with Grace and Rather, that could change. But first, he would have to change himself, shift his shape, face up to his lack of awareness. Face out to the new possibilities. He knew that if a reality could be seen, that he could look over his shoulder and see the rundown machine of the eighth book, the bizarre craziness of all the pages about Catherine as Muse—yet in the back of his mind a shadow stood, nodding at him, as if to say that he was not done here. Yes, yes, that needed to come now. He looked out to sea again. Yes. Always.

"...a good walk, and Rather was fine too. We had to stop and look at his boat... and I had to wonder what we might do about the boat. Family continues not to appear. But, maybe we don't have to worry about that today."

Grace had laid out a luscious breakfast spread, sausages, blueberry pancakes, tasty maple syrup, casaba melon. "This is amazing, Grace" he said as he dug in with relish. "I haven't had a breakfast like this since I was wooed by the Portman people."

"You weren't always with them?"

"Nope, I had to work up to them, but they are the right people I believe."

"What are your plans for a next book?" She said this as if she was asking him to pass the butter.

"I'm glad you brought that up. Rather and I were talking about it on the walk. He thinks I should do a book about him and call it The Sailing Dog. He points out, rightly, that one of my editors, Celia Langhorne, is a sailing woman. She would be perfect to edit this book that Rather and I would write together. And, because Rather is a left pawed dog that would make it even better."

"Works for me. When do you start, and—here's the important question—will Rather need a typewriter, a pad and pencil or a computer?"

They looked over at Rather who was not even interested in begging for table scraps. He was deep in the midst of a morning nap. "So much for my collaborator," Landon said.

When they were done, Grace suggested a morning nap and they lay down on her bed—fully clothed—and continued the conversation. "I am on the right track. I know it now."

"How do you sense that?"

"First of all, I can see what I shouldn't attempt, and there has been much going on in that area that I won't bother you with, but there is a clarity now that I can see."

She settled into the pillow. "What is that? Oh, I know, it's Morris, right?"

His voice dropped even lower. "Yes, yes, certainly, it is Morris and his story. But there are decisions to be made, and it feels so much like there is an important shift to make in how his story is to be told. And, immediately it becomes complex."

"Are you comfortable with this 'theory of angels'?"

"Yes, that is the part I can relate to the strongest. And, I am also aware that I need to be clear about the difference between 'angel' and say, 'saint'."

"Is there a difference?" she put her hand on his face.

"For today, a reader might assume they were one and the same. We are so far away from saints and angels—I must construct something, someone that is immediately credible—we are talking here about a different sort of angel, an angel that can exist reasonably in this world."

"You think people might laugh?"

"Yes. Yes. They have to be cut off from that without even going there."

He brushed the hair that had fallen over her eye to behind her ear.

"Have you ever thought of making this a documentary... I guess books are not—they are non-fiction, but the lines are so blurred, could you write it like that... with blurred lines?"

He looked up to the ceiling, turning his head away from her. She was holding his hand and she concentrated on it to sense him fully.

"The honest answer is that I don't know. I do know I have never tried that, but that doesn't rule it out at all. But it sounds right, the blurring of lines, the presentation of a darker reality that one can not wave away, but is forced to confront."

He looked into her eyes... "But it's a meaningful idea."

ANGELS

"*E*xcuse me, Mr. Harris, but there is a lady here who wants to know if you are accepting, she said, ah, spur of the moment visitors? Her name is Celia Langborne."

Landon looked at his watch. "Certainly, Harold, send Ms. Langborne up right away." Landon whistled as he made his way to the kitchen to see if there were cold drinks. Hmm, he thought, good timing. The bell rang and he dropped the ice tray. "Damn," he said, realizing that his mind at the minute of her arrival had warmer thoughts.

"Celia Langborne, the very person I wanted to see." Celia came in and set her umbrella against a chair. Landon continued, "I'm sorry, Celia, he's a good fellow, but names are a difficult thing for him. They weren't on the Doorman's Test, so he passed." He paused, "Good to see you, Ms. Langhorne."

"Quite all right." She turned to him, "You look different, Landon."

"Well, come in and see. Drink?"

She followed him all the way to the kitchen, doing some subtle rubber-necking as she went. "Diet Coke will do for me… with some ice, please." She turned to the windows. "I have never seen a kitchen along here with windows on the Park."

"I had some extensive remodeling done four years ago."

"Quite nice to be able to wash the dishes and look at the rich folks across the Park."

"<u>You</u> are across the Park, Celia."

"Indeed. Your worst nightmare. A rich woman sailor… and your waiting editor." Landon whistled while he poured the drinks, and turned to hand it to her.

"Want to settle here, or will the living parlour do, where we have a spy glass to peer in on the rich?" She waved her hand and went to the sun area by the living room.

"Hope you don't mind my just blowing in here, I was literally walking by and remembered that I hadn't seen you since you left for Sequoia and somewhere… as well as wondering how your creative juices are simmering. "

They looked at each other for a minute longer than either expected.

Landon turned his head away and then back to her. "A most interesting experience… much like, I might guess, the one I just read about again in this book, *The Yankee Sailing Sisters*… a 37 hour storm in the Indian Ocean. But," and he held up his hand, "I wish I was the courageous writer that you are."

"Oh, and you read it a second time?"

"Yes, I want to compliment you on your book. In my thought, it is the sailing version of Beryl Markham's *West with the Night*."

Her voice lowered. "High praise. Not sure how to take that."

"As it is offered, Ms. Langhorne, don't look at the reverse side of a gift compliment."

"Thank you," she said still low and uncertain.

"I would like to ask a question. I think you did a good job giving us a superlative sense of the storm, but I have a guess that you didn't tell the whole truth, not that you were trying to hide anything." Celia, chin down, looked at him under her eyelids.

"Was there a point where you thought you were lost to the world?"

She clanked her ice, "Let me quantify that. I am a landlocked person, but just over my mountain was another ocean and I would go often and look at it, wishing I could see the other side, the China we hear about. I can't imagine being in the middle of it and realizing that I could sink without a trace."

"Well, you can. And, there was a moment, when my sister and I looked at each other and knew with certainty that we would die. There seemed no other possibility. I don't know about Nora, but I reached for her as if both to hold her—we were tipping—and to be held. In that moment, I actually felt my heart flutter and I was glad for that instant that I would be with Nora and not alone. Then immediately I realized that I had wished her to die too and felt sick. In fact I did retch up, feeling her grab my harness—you wear harnesses in this weather, always tied to something. I turned to her and cried out that it was all right for me to die, but I wanted her to live. I was shouting at my sister who was closer than you are here. We moved to the wheel and just held each other for an hour. Each moment we were certain was the last. We told each other how much we loved, and didn't even try to count the times. At the end of seemingly endless time the storm relented, and we knew we would weather it. Then we laughed at the wind and each other. The biggest 'screw you' two sailors have ever mouthed."

Landon looked at her anew. "You... are a brave woman."

"No, there is no bravery, and we didn't pray. We clung to each other. I like to think there is the smallest lesson in that."

"Thank you for telling me that. I won't ask why you didn't write it into the book."

She nodded as a passing aviator dips her wings.

Celia looked over at the empty chair as if Nora was sitting there. The three of them stayed this way for minutes in silence.

Finally Landon said, "Another Coke?"

"Yes." He returned with clinking ice.

"I believe, with the example of your own courage, and if I may say so, your support and belief in me, I have found my way to a workable concept for a book. I have even begun writing with no sense of continuity or order… but just to feel the thoughts take form. I have several single spaced pages, I am using them as a shield while I try to determine where to commence, ah, how to move forward."

"How exciting. Are you excited?"

"Very excited, and I haven't felt this way for a long time, Celia. I owe you a great debt for your caring encouragement and directions to me that night. Thank you deeply."

A stage wait, and then Landon said, "Can I ask your help on this new project?"

"Yes, absolutely… tell me how I can help you…" She took a step toward him.

"I need some research. It seems to me that this story has two sides to it, like a flipped coin, you keep wondering which side will come up. I need some technical, official types. A social worker, for instance—one who works with kids. I need a couple of cops who have some heart left. I need some people—I don't even know what kinds of titles or work they do. I need to learn about the runaway street kids that are here in New York and who is 'officially' looking into their actions or looking after them when it's too late."

"That's a big order." Landon nodded, and began whispering to her.

"I need to know about his world, because I am creating a creature, a young person, who will—willingly—live in it and thrive."

"Can you tell me a bit more?"

"Soon… yes…. For the moment, it's a large, bright flying tent."

She nodded. "I doubt that's a good metaphor." She smiled at him.

"All I know now is that this is going to go fast. I either have this and can spew it out and hope it is right, or … " He shrugged, "or I will take lessons from you on how to shout into the wind."

Celia came to him and gave him a slight hug, before she moved off to the window. She set her glass down and turned to him. "All I know for certain is that there are a lot… many, many street kids living on the Lower West Side, somewhere like where West Side Drive ends… I hear about it on the news… I guess that's what you are getting at."

"I think so… "

"I will look into your needs and get back to you right away." She smiled, "I understand about shouting into the wind." She put her hand on his arm. "Good luck."

Celia gave him a strong hug. For a moment they were very close.

At the 92nd Street YMCA, the lecture room was large and informal.

Lettie Barnes was pleased with the turnout, and said so to Landon just before she introduced him. Grace wanted to be up close, but realized she might be a distraction so she sat in the third row, but off to the side. She felt a small thrill when Landon stepped to the podium and began to speak. She had wanted to know 'who was Landon Harris' from the first moment she saw him and even through their rough start and the small sense of loss she felt when they fell out so badly at first. However, she had tried to leave doors open around her and concentrated on those openings knowing there was just a chance he would find one of them. Now, finally, she was in his audience and would learn who he was like those who sat out here, hoping to learn something from him that would matter. After all, he had written some decent books, that counted for something, and as she looked around she wasn't the only one to feel that way.

"…common wisdom is that it's easier to write a novel than a short story. As a person who has primarily written novels, I hate that saying…" Small chuckle from the audience here. "I don't understand why it's always easier to do what someone else does than what we do. But, we needn't dwell on the half of the glass that is empty. As I was preparing to talk to you, and I thank you for coming tonight, I realized that it was necessary to adjust all our expectations and get real. You are not going to be able to walk out of here tonight, go home and put your notes beside the keyboard and write an incredible short story…" Landon stopped stock still and looked out at the assembled audience. Then, "…well, who am I to say…? Maybe you will—amazing things happen, don't they?" And there was applause. Grace looked around and saw that he had them… it had taken just moments and he has shown that he is in tune with them—a mixed group of younger, maybe just starting, men and women, and many older people. Did that mean they were more experienced or they had just recently found themselves?

"…we all have stories to tell and some of us can learn to tell them, and I use the word 'learn' advisedly. You don't want to overlearn this craft, you want to try to stick as close as possible to your gut, your intuition, Don't read too many writing books, don't subscribe to *Writer's Digest*. Read the work of writers you admire, work to find what obsesses you. That is my key word tonight: *obsession*. For me, writing short stories is about obsession: something or someone who you are obsessive about. When I realized that was what I wanted to talk to you about I began immediately to search for the story that is the touchstone of that notion… obsession. And, though I pride myself on good filing of stories and notes—I could not find this certain story nor the name of the writer, a Japanese man. But the heart of his obsession is with me still. The man in this story was obsessed with a woman. He wanted to be close to her, he wanted to be in her presence: it was essential to his well-being. After exhausting all reasonable means to fuel his obsession he turned to face his obsession and bend to it. He was a furniture maker. A fine craftsman. He decided that he would make a chair for this woman and he feverishly worked for weeks to create the perfect chair for her, one that would fit her body perfectly, one that could be delivered anonymously and she-would-accept-it-without-question." Landon paused to look over the audience. He looked at Grace and smiled, quickly turning back to the hall of people.

"You can see how this could affect you. You understand obsession… intellectually. Emotionally, you understand your own obsessions. We all have them one way or another, and you may accept the obsession of this man, perhaps one of you may have felt this way about another person—and now the story turns in an unexpected way. Why is he making a chair? How can that help him? How odd, you may think—yet he knows his obsession. He constructs this chair in such a way that there is a vacuum within, if you will, an unexplained space… one that his own body will fit into perfectly.

When he finishes the chair, he instructs his assistant to come in the morning and deliver the chair to the woman, his obsession. The man, our obsessive, arrives just before the assistant in the morning and inserts himself into the chair. The chair is delivered and the woman accepts it simply because it is a work of art. It is taken into her bedroom… then she sits in the chair."

"Now, happiness, total happiness, is delivered to the man. He is surrounding her, he can sense her body, he can inhale her scent, which is a jasmine odor that particularly pleases him. He is as present with her as possible for him. For him. Happiness."

Landon looks up at his audience. "This is the end of this man's story." Landon shifts his papers, walks around in front of the podium. "I need not remind you that the writer is not concerned with any of the practical matters of this… no need to spell them out. This is not about living a life practically, it is about fusing with your obsession."

Landon walks to the side of the lecture area and picks up a book from a chair. He holds it up. It is a copy of his book of short stories. "One of the stories I did not include in this collection is the obsessive one I wrote about a man who wished fervently to own a piece of art by the artist Joseph Cornell. An artist who is well installed in the collection at the Museum of Modern Art here in New York. We are talking about the need to pay a great deal of money for such a piece of art. This man is walking down Madison Avenue—by the way, I like to write stories that are set in New York. Many have wondered why I haven't written about my own home in the Central Valley of California, near Bakersfield—Maricopa, a small community nestled in the western side of the Valley. I have no ready answer for why I do this other than I feel comfortable with this city setting. Unless you have a point about a certain place, a place where you can learn enough about to be credible, write about the place that is comfortable for you."

Grace had been curious about this. She had kept wondering why Landon did not write about Maricopa and his roots. She listened to him talk about this certain story and realized that his naturalness with the New York environment made it easy for him to concentrate on the other elements of the story. Place may be important, but the writer's essential comfort with the patina of the story was, maybe, more important.

"…so finally, as the man walks into the part of the East Side that is the gallery area, he sees a man put a package down beside a pile of trash ready to be picked up by the sanitation people. This package is obviously not trash. It is carefully wrapped. The twine is clean and there is a bow tied. The man leaves the scene. Our hero, without thinking, walks by the package, scoops it up and continues to walk to the corner and then across Madison and wait on the opposing corner to see what happens by the trash. Three minutes after he had passed, a car stopped there, a man got out and looked for the package by the trash. It was certain this is what he was looking for because he up-ended the whole garbage heap on the sidewalk before a cop came by and made him move his car. Our hero stays at the corner and waits longer. The first man reappears and goes to the garbage heap and looks for the package, looks up and down the street, is clearly angry and pulls out his cell phone and calls someone. He has one half of a shouting match with the person at the end of the phone call and becomes so angry that he throws the cell phone on the sidewalk and runs off."

Landon looks out over his audience. "I liked that scene, but I had to put the story away because I felt it too accidental—too impossible—for my protagonist to find a Cornell box wrapped into this "package". Yes, he went to a quiet restaurant, ordered a cup of coffee, opened the package and it was a small Cornell "Pipe set"—one of the series of boxes once made by this artist. Yes, this fit into the obsession mode, but again, I found the circumstances too coincidental, not really credible—even though this matched the obsession of my protagonist. I abandoned the story because it wasn't whole."

A hand raised in the front of the audience. A young woman with black hair and an oval face with intense eyes said, "Are you saying that this story could not have been salvaged, even though it seems to fit your require-ments—is rewriting not an option?"

"Of course it's an option and one that often works. Some like to think that it always works, but that cannot be so. One has to be brutal about one's work in determining if something, a part of a story or the whole of it—works or doesn't. And worse, often there is no one to ask... not every writer is lucky enough to have a mentor," and Landon smiled here, "...or a muse." Grace felt her cheeks burn. He did not look at her but she knew he was talking about her now.

"But," the woman insisted, "how do you know?"

"Knowing is the hardest part. And to judge the tables full of books in the stores now one might think that 'knowing' has gone out of fashion, or beyond the skill set of many publishers... and speaking for them, one has also to think of today's readers." Landon poured a glass of water from the carafe provided and watched the audience as he drank. "We are not here to critique the publishing industry or to take pot shots at our readers. We are here to look inward. For an example of that, let's turn to a story in this book," and again he held up the book of short stories. He turned the pages and found the story in question. "*An Actor Prepares* is a good example of a character in a story who is obsessed… obsessed with being an actor, with preparing his Part, obsessed with his life in the theater to the extent that his apartment is decorated to look like a stage. He can't bring himself to eat with his girlfriend in the early evening because it will spoil his performance. He-is-obsessed." Landon looked at the black haired woman, "… and I think this story is credible—I am proud of it because it mirrors the one I told you about the Japanese writer who creates *The Man in the Chair*—so I judge it to "work".

He walked to the front of the podium again. "How many of you have read this story?" A few more than half the hands went up. Landon nodded, obviously pleased. "Well, so much for homework, clearly you have done yours. Good! Now, do you see this young man as obsessive and how does that help make the story work?"

An older woman waved at Landon from the back. "Yes, Ma'am?" Sitting she said, "I thought he was likeably despicable. I thought the scene of him secretly and invisibly invading that woman's apartment was as outrageously obsessive as I think you want us to be."

Landon nodded. "Memorable helps. We want to stick in the minds of our readers."

A man near to Grace stood up and said,"But, how do we get ideas like that? I have never known anyone like that young fellow. How can I write about someone that I don't know?" Landon smiled and said, "I don't know," and the room dissolved to laughter. The man turned red and Landon walked over closer to where he was. "I am sorry. I am not making fun of you. There are people who are not writers and who can take the background of their life and make it into a story, and there are writers who can imagine things that no one has ever seen and yet not seem to be able to get it on paper. I don't think any of us can explain that."

Landon walked a few steps on the stage. "How many writers have you read about who have suggested that once they are familiar with characters they are writing about the characters begin making story decisions? —I had coffee last week with a writer in such a situation, and he was quite upset because he realized that what the character selected to do was better than what he planned for the character. And that meant the writer had to go back and re-write the beginning of his story to make it fit with the character's most recent decision. These are the facts of writing life."

Another pause and a turn back to the audience. "You are not required to like your characters, but you will have to learn to live with them if you can bring yourself to that level of…" he stopped and looked blankly at the audience… then over to Grace, "…intuitiveness."

Landon looked into his audience. "The whole notion here is not to be mechanical, not to outline stories that seem interesting and then ride them like a rail car down tracks that are supposed, in your view, to lead somewhere. If we want to do that, all we need do is go to movies from Hollywood. They are the best example of 'manufactured entertainment'."

Landon pulled a chair from the side of the area and sat in it. His voice became low and it wasn't clear if he is talking to the audience or to himself. "I am working on a new novel now—after a long drought. It is in the earliest stages. It has an idea that has become an obsession with the protagonist… an older man. In terms of being credible, it strains your mind—the man has come to believe himself to be an Angel. This is not your everyday New Age person, in fact he is the antithesis of that, which is what makes him so appealing. But I am intuitively convinced that the main character of my story should not be an older man. I don't rack my brain and make lists of what kind of a person I want him to be. The mantle of persona needs to fall gently on someone who can also have this obsession but is more fit, in my own estimation, for the part. Beyond that, he, <u>my</u> character, wants to be more interesting than an older person who has found some idea of himself. If I had to chose at this moment, I would say it should be a teenager, say 16 or 17 and that…" Landon stopped talking. Grace, knowing what he was talking about was mesmerized by the thought process and its abrupt ending. It frightened her, for as she looked down at her hand it was trembling.

No one in the hall moved or said a word.

Landon had an inner sense of walking along the West Side, by the ruined piers and seeing a kid. The boy was standing beside a building, so he was actually in the dark and hard to see… except that there was a light behind him that cast a shadow on the rusty planking. The vacuum was opened by Lettie Barnes who moved to the podium and said quietly, "We are very near to the half-time break for those of you who need to get up and stretch. Let's do that now." She looked at her watch, "Let's be seated again, in fifteen minutes. Thank you."

Lettie walked over to Landon and touched his shoulder. Leaning toward his face, she said, "Are you all right, Landon?" He flustered, rose, and smiled foolishly. "I guess so. Just need a whiff of air." Lettie smiled and saw Grace come to his side. The women nodded at each other.

Fortunately, Landon was able to get through the remainder of the lecture without falling into a crevasse. In fact, he got a standing ovation and a strong approval from Lettie, who said he had done very, very well, in fact she liked his talk better than the one that Hal Kantor had given last month, and Kantor was as popular as Landon himself. More good fortune, Grace was there to see him back across the Park at the end of lecture, and get him settled with a glass of his favorite wine. Neither one of them could explain why or how he had gone over the edge at the Y… but then it didn't really matter. Landon was in the grip of The Lost and Found Department these days.

"What I like about angels" said Landon, "and the idea of them in what I want to do is that there are so many kinds of angels who are singular, pure, unique, but always better than the rest of us. Unequivocally. So, I am reaching to create an Angel, a shadowed Angel, a renegade, not from heaven but from the life he has rejected around him. I hate phrases and poses like Rogue Angel and Dark Angel—but I think I can live with Shadowed Angel."

"You are not meaning a title, but a concept," this was Morris Rubin.

"I hate the word 'concept'. Far too intellectual." said Landon

Grace said, "Do I sense you are searching for an essence?"

"Exactly."

"Why not an angel then, a shadowed one, if you favor that?" said Morris.

"What I haven't told you., Morris, is that I intend to use you as the model for the angel."

Morris laughed and sipped some wine. "You are joking!"

Grace tapped her fingers on Morris' lovely inlaid table and wondered if she should tell Morris that at first she suspected that Landon had considered lifting Morris' story about his adventures intact. Landon beat her to it, "Morris, I want to ask something of you. I, ah, I am nervous about this. Things and people and places turn up in the work of a writer—ideas, work, people and things wearing masks, new clothes, different clothes, new tics, and reconditioned ethics... everything comes from somewhere."

"You mean the writer's imagination is not the source of all things? That's shocking!" Morris' acting was excellent. His chest rose, as did his voice, yet his movements were restrained as if he was indeed holding something back, yet he was giving all, and Landon and Grace knew it. Morris was a significant actor.

"No, Morris, the lake of imagination is orange with white trees even in the summer, but everything does not come from this place. Often art must mimic life and I want to do more than that, I want to use all your self described 'angel stories', as well as the idea of being an angel in my new book!" Landon's lips were pursed as he stopped talking.

"I would like to hear more about what you have in mind." Morris saw the expression in Landon's eyes. "Yes, of course, Landon replied, "I will answer all your questions."

Morris said, "I am fascinated by the thrust of all this, and yet I really don't know what you intend."

Landon knew he would say yes, but he wanted to hear it for himself. Then he was willing to pour out an ocean of information and ideas, set in the form of paper boats of possibilities, as if Morris and Grace were a casual couple walking on the boardwalk and looking out to the sea and the idea-boats that Landon floated on it. Landon wanted their feedback, and wanted, they guessed, to pretend that they were onlooking sharks... feeding or feedback?

"Well, here goes," said Landon, leaning into the dining table. "I suppose a teenager in an everyday, middle class family. I am thinking about a nice suburb of Detroit. A father who works in the automobile business. A mother who works in something like market research for a small company.

Both of these people, like most middle management types today, are up against the wall. Too much to do, too committed to their jobs and money needs to create a reasonable home for their family. As we come to their story, their marriage is in trouble... not sure what has precipitated that situation, but they are filing papers against each other. The teenaged boy may have an older sister off at college. But it is explained to him that one of them, his father or his mother will "gain custody" of him—in practical terms, he will live with one of them. A judge will decide this based on what they tell him. The boy learns of all this with distaste and anger. By rifling through his parents papers he learns when the court hearing will be, thinks about what he wants and comes into the courtroom just as things are getting started. He does not call attention to himself but sits in the back and listens to his parents say horrible things about each other. He begins to cry and wonders if he will be able to stay to do what he feels he must do. Doug, that's his name, gets hold of himself just as the lawyers are getting to the "child custody" issues."

Morris is rapt by the story. He has never been present for creativity at this level. He gets up, still listening, and pours more coffee for himself and Landon. Grace shakes her head no, but it seems to Morris that she is listening to the present and the past all at once.

"When the custody battle becomes the most painful for Doug his father is on a witness stand saying bad things about his mother. Doug stands up and walks as close as he can get to the Judge and asks to be heard. There is a momentary fluster in the courtroom until the mother speaks out the boy's name and the father moves to the boy's side to begin to explain why Doug should not be there."

Landon takes a breath and pauses for a moment. He continues, "The boy takes the father's hand off his shoulder and asks the Judge's permission to speak. There is a pointed silence in the courtroom while the Judge, a man about the age of Doug's father, thinks this over. Then he says, speaking to the two attorneys, that he will allow the boy to make a statement. Both lawyers object and the Judge says, 'Overruled.'

"Doug wonders what that means, but the Judge waves the boy to the high chair beside the Judge's bench. Doug settles himself there. His mother is already in tears and the father stands, glaring at her with tight lips."

Breaking out of the story, Landon said, "I have never written dialogue for a teen and I may have to do some research on this… but the thrust of what the boy will say goes like this…

"Mr. Judge, I didn't come to upset what you do here, but my parents tol' me that you were going to decide who gets me and where I have to live. I am not actually sure what 'custody' means, I suppose it is some legal term…"

"Custody means that one parent will have the responsibility to raise the child—I don't mean you are a child, but you are under age… how old are you?"

"Sixteen".

The Judge nods and looks at the parents. "Go on, Doug, this is most interesting."

"… I love my dad and my mother." The looks between the triangle of them will be heartbreaking. "But the truth is that neither of them have taken responsibility for me for 'bout two years now. They are not home much. When they are, they are unhappy because of things that I don't understand.

I thought when you were married for 19 years that you were supposed to be loving the other and really know who they were—and that would mean that you liked the other… but, I have not seen much liking, kissing or holding hands in a while. I had gotten used to that, them being close, you know—but then it stopped. I remember the day that I realized they were not doing that—it was my mother's birthday and Dad had bought her a washing machine. It had a red ribbon on it. He took us all, my sister was living with us then, and we went to the garage and there it was."

Doug paused and looked at his folks.

"My father didn't kiss my mother and say any birthday stuff. My sister and I didn't know what was going on, but we began to sing Happy Birthday, but it was only us singing. When we got to the end of the song, we clapped and then stopped. There were the four of us, quiet as the dead, standing around this dumb washing machine with a red ribbon in a dark garage."

Now, the father begins to tear and the lawyer puts his hand on his shoulder and gently pushes him down. Morris and Grace feel as if this was happening in the same room with them.

"…so, anyway, I don't see much love in my house anymore, or in being responsible for me. I haven't seen that for a long time. I come home after school and do some homework and then go out with my friends… have dinner with one of them and come home late. My buddy Fellner and I have had two scrapes with the police—"Doug looks at the Judge, "I don't have to tell you about them do I?" The Judge nods no and urges the boy to continue. "Look! I don't want this anymore. I don't want to lose my mother or my dad, but I guess you can't lose what you don't have. So, I am hoping," here Doug looks at the Judge, "I am hoping that I won't have to be in anyone's 'custody', you see. I want to live on my own. I think I can do that."

"Unfortunately, Doug, that isn't one of the options. The Court… by my decision, must see that there is a party responsible for you. You are not old enough to be by yourself."

"I have been by myself."

The Judge nods, "Yes… I understand that…" A thought comes to him. "What would you do if, ah, you could 'be by yourself'?"

"One of my friends whose parents travel a lot goes down and stays at the Y… uh, the YMCA. It's not a bad place. Clean. He still goes to school, but I don't want to do that any more. I don't think I should go to school now."

"What do you think you should do?" asked the Judge.

The lawyer of the Mother stands up and objects. "Overruled," says the Judge, and looks at Doug. "What will you do if you don't go to school?"

"I think I can become an angel."

"Ooooh aaaagggg, no, no… " screams the mother.

Doug in a voice that seems to ask for a sandwich says, " I think I can, Mom… really. There are people everywhere… I see them on the news and in the newspaper and hear my friends talk about people who need help. Just someone to do something for them, sometimes just to talk to them, think about their problems, encourage them, stuff like that… "

"No, please, no more… please… " the mother throws herself at the Judge's bench.

"Sergeant, would you help Mrs. Osbourne to a quiet place, please?" The police officer moves quickly to the side of the mother, puts a gentle arm around her and escorts her out of the chamber.

"Do you have any response to this?" the Judge addresses the father.

The father is sitting on the court bench still tearing and tapping the side of his head with his left fist. He looks up at the Judge and tries to stand. "I, uh, your Honor, I am so, so sorry about this… I didn't know, you know, I just didn't have any idea that he felt this way… that he was living this way. I don't want… he should have someone to look after him, but I know that is what you will say to us." The father looks over to where his wife was. "I guess we haven't done a very good job." He grimaces. He shakes his head. "What do, uh, what do you think we should do…?" Now his attorney stands up and asks for a court recess.

"Denied," says the Judge. "I am going to remand Doug Osbourne to the custody of the County Youth Authority for a period of six months. I will have my clerk make out the papers and both parties to this divorce will be given papers to sign. And gentlemen," here the Judge looks at both lawyers, "I advise you to insure that I have the signature of the mother and the father without contest."

"What does that mean?" whispered the father to his lawyer. "Can't you do anything?"

"Not after what happened here, Mr. Osbourne, I am afraid not." the lawyer shakes his head, "I guess I have never seen anything like this. It means that you have lost your son, for the time being, to the Courts."

Morris searches Landon's face and then looks at Grace. "Landon, when did you do this?"

"It's not written down. I have to write it down right away, you see, I might not remember some of the important details."

Grace nods.

Morris asks, "So this is the beginning of your new novel?"

"No, it's not the beginning. This is, the, ah, underpinning. This has to come out in small pieces along the way. The movie people have a good word for this, they call it the Back Story... the story that comes before the story. But that doesn't mean I don't have to write it down so I don't forget."

Grace says, "Don't worry, Landon, neither one of us will forget this story or this night. You have given us a great gift to share this with us."

"What research did you ask of Celia Langton...?" asks Morris.

"Langhorne."

"Yes, Celia... what did you ask her to arrange for you?"

"I need a social worker here in New York. I need to speak to the youth authority people... and I don't even know if that is the right phrase in New York or Michigan. It is in California. They do have a state organization called the California Youth Authority."

"I have some decent connections in this area. Can I come down to your place tomorrow and we can make some calls together. Perhaps I can be helpful. I would like to help you."

"Wonderful, Morris... I need a great deal of help with this portion of it."

Grace smiles, "Looks like you have it in hand, all right... listen, Morris, let me do the dishes before we go, all right?"

"Nonsense," Morris said, "I love to do the dishes… "

"Celia, what does this email mean?" Canning said.

"Come in, don't just stand by the door. Sit. Wag. "

She turned from the window in her office to meet the eyes of Canning Vogel. She was very glad in that moment to be the bearer of the news that meant that she would be fully in charge of Landon Harris' next book. She had meandered her way into the confidence of Mr. Harris. She was supplying him resources and asking the questions that Canning used to. "I am in a good mood today. Doesn't that make you happy, Mr. Vogel?"

"Does it have anything to do with the fact that you have two promising books hitting the streets early this season? And, that you are winnowing out good quotes for them? No wonder you have this smile on your face. I wish my list was out and I have been faced with the impossible truth of that one, the ineffable Mr. Juan Levin… I can't get over that name… may be even later than I guessed. Bastard! I should have known."

"Sorry," she said, not really meaning it.

"So, what is Landon doing?"

"It appears that he is into a racing-mind mode with this new project. I fished out some sources for him in Borough Hall and he emailed me that they were just right, along with what one of the media people gave him. He is making full headway under a following wind."

"Have you been teaching him your sailing lingo?"

"The point is, he may have something quick."

"Will it be good, readable and get us back on the *Times* list??"

She smiled her biggest for him. "Don't know, but I am sticking close to this now. I must say that I am not only impressed with Landon's intentions but also his diligence. I called him this morning and he was at work, tired but cheery after a night on the beat at the Port Authority. Apparently he has arranged to follow the cops and some people that I have never heard of called Shelter Now, or something like that… He wants to find out what is really happening on the streets"

Canning said, "Do you know what the focus of this is?"

"Runaway kids." She dropped it between them as if it was a soggy dishrag. As she suspected, the effete Mr. Vogel found the subject distasteful while she felt it was the key to the new Landon.

"This is a far reach, in your sailing terms, for Landon Harris. First question is, can he pull it off?"

"I honestly don't know. No one knows better than you how hard it is for an author to find a new voice, to re-invent himself in actuality as well as in the minds of his readers." She paused here, "…but Landon Harris has found a new voice."

Canning nodded and got up heavily for such a slight man. Not even looking at Celia he said, "Second. Are you trying to say to me that he might be in time for this current list we are trying to get out the door?"

"It's up in the air."

"And, I suppose, you are willing to blow with the wind."

"As always."

Landon decided to take what information he had into his own hands, and go down to the Lower West side and see what he might be able to see or find for himself.

"Where to, buddy?"

"Take me to the Battery… Battery Park."

"You got it. Hey."

Landon found a place to settle in Battery Park and realized, after a long time sitting, that he was in the same spot he had visualized for the boy of *Shadow Angel*, Doug. That same spot the boy had lifted the wallet of the tourist woman as she and her friends were taking pictures of the Statue of Liberty. There she was, a beam of hope in the night and the day. He needed to walk… that's it, feel, this place.

Landon got up and moved uptown along the River. In a few blocks, he thought, how 'bout a bottle of beer? Sure. He found a liquor store and bought a bottle of Bud Light. The Indian sales clerk put the bottle in a paper bag and handed it to him. Landon walked out to the Piers and swigged some of the bottle and moved along, alternately sitting or moving along, communing with the River. He noticed the wreckage of this part of New York, realizing how far he was, in any kind of calculations, from the 72nd Street Harbor and its secure surroundings. He was in the neighborhood of 16th Street and he noticed that this was the area he had visualized for Doug's first shelter in the basement of one of the abandoned store fronts.

Landon sat down again and didn't realize he was in such a dreamy mood and dozed off. He was with Doug the Shadow Angel… he was wandering the streets with him, watching, always watching and thinking of what might be next… who to help, how to help. Then Landon felt something against his body in the dream. It must have been Grace. She must have not taken the train after all, she must have come back and they are together again. She snuggled against him. But he must have left the window open because the street noise around them was getting louder, and he roused himself to close the window. He was not home in bed with Grace. But there was someone alongside him.

He turned his awake eyes toward her and came face to face with a young woman who was not asleep but was looking wide-eyed at him. It startled him and his body tried to turn away from her. Immediately, he felt her hand come to his arm and pull him back.

"Hey, don't you want some company, sweetheart… I mean, it's nice, huh?" She was young, and as he looked again at her, quite young, and had on a skimpy dress and heavy make up. A great deal of lipstick. Landon finally shook himself up and loose of her.

"Who are you?" he said.

"Lorri. Jus' Lorri. What's yours?"

"My what?"

"Your name, sweetheart." In the mouth of a teenaged girl, the tone and the words seemed incredulous.

"How old are you?"

"Old enough."

Landon nodded, yes, old enough. "Seventeen? Eighteen?"

"Is tha' important?"

He nodded.

"You don't make it with older girls?" He started to speak, but she continued.

"… OK, I'm seventeen, that work for you, sweetie?"

"Yes. Yes. Thank you."

"Actually, I like it with older guys. Something about them, right?"

"Something… " said Landon.

"You pretty well dressed for this neighborhood. You new here? Thinkin' about takin' up the Life?"

"No, no, I'm not… " he paused, "but I am having trouble with the life I have."

"Ooooohhh, baby, I'm sorry. Want to talk about it?" She heard something down the street and turned to see what was coming. Just as quickly, she turned back to him and leaped for his neck and mouth, arms around and mouth on for a big kiss. She pulled back enough to whisper in his mouth, "Jus' make like we are having a good 'un, gettin' ready to have some nice fun." And her mouth went back to his.

Landon heard and he understood that he needed to keep his eyes closed somehow. He heard the steps of two men walk up to them and on by. "Lorri is some fast fucker. I never seen a chick who could find guys so fast."

His buddy agreed, "Ho' many tricks you suppose she do a night?"

Landon opened one eye and saw two young guys, not more than two or three years older than Lorri… in the shadows, walking away from them toward the River. When they were far enough away he gently pushed her back. "You too well suited out for this part o' town, dude… if you and I weren't a trick, they might have rousted you. This way," and suddenly all her artificial years melted away and even her voice changed as she leaned forward with a tissue she seemed to have pulled from nowhere, "…aw, hon', I jus' covered you with my lipstick. I'm sorry." She really looked at him now seeing somehow past her own act into his.

"You look to be a pretty lost dude. And," she looked around them, "You got a problem?"

"Yes, Lorri, I do… " he said as Lorri nodded wisely.

"Listen, can I help you out? I mean, you have been kind to me, ya, know?" Suddenly, he really saw her. She was much like the girls he had been introduced to at Shelter Now, ones who were trying in some way to find their way, back home, a job, to some safety. Unlike Lorri, who had broken Doug's rule about 'no fucking', this was Lorri's way.

"You need money?" he said to her.

"Don' we all?"

"Where you from?"

"Lakeville."

"Where's that?"

"Up in the corner of Connecticut, 'way up. Nearest towns are Miller-ton an' Ashley Falls, an' you never heard of them, neither." She had now reverted to who she had been before she came to New York.

"What's your last name?"

"Naramore… old Connecticut family. Lorri Anne Naramore. Nice sound to it, huh?."

Landon nodded. "How much is a bus ticket home?" wondering if that was the right question.

She shook her head.

"You have any relatives you like?"

She cocked her head as if a new idea was ringing. "Why do you ask that?"

"Just wondering."

"Yeah, I have an aunt in Oklahoma, somewhere near Tulsa. I never been there."

"Would you go?'

"Never thought about it."

"Think about it."

"Who are you anyway. You are real different. Like you know something." She looked hard at Landon, "Do you?" He nodded at her, "Yep, I do." He paused just enough to let the thought sink in.

"Tell you what, Lorri Anne Naramore. What do you say to coming with me to Penn Station and let me put you on a train to Chicago and then onto Oklahoma... uh, Tulsa?"

"You want to do me first?"

"No, Lorri, you need to be playing around with some younger guys in a safer place. I'd like to help you do that. You are a nice girl, I'm sure there are a lot of nice boys in Tulsa who would like you. What do you say?"

Lorri Anne was quiet for several minutes. Landon reached over and held her hand. They sat like that for what seemed like a long time.

"What about my stuff, can I go home?" Landon shrugged. "You want to take anything with you?"

"No."

"Let's go."

They walked from 16th and Twelfth Avenue to Pennsylvania Station. About half way, Lorri asked Landon if she could hold his hand, just until they got to the station. When they did, he bought her a through ticket to Tulsa and gave her enough traveling money to get her there.

"Call your aunt and tell her you're coming. Do me one last favor, will you?" He looked sternly at her. "Tell her the truth… tell her what happened to you at home, what you did here… everything, and then stay there and see if you can find a life…" he tried to pull the word back, "I mean, not The Life, but A Life, right?"

She nodded and hugged him. If he and Catherine had had kids early on, Lorri could have been one of them.

Landon walked Lorri to the train Gate, her good luck was that she was catching the last train to St. Louis where she could change to another train to Tulsa.

She turned to Landon and in front of his eyes became another person. This one was younger than the one downtown. While he had been buying the tickets she had wiped off her lipstick. She stood in front of him now as what seemed to him to be a different person… younger, more attractive, but there was something else… what could it be?

She put her arms around him and her lips to his ear. "I know who I really am, but the, ah, surprise to me is that you knew… right off. You can't know how many guys I have done it with and some other stuff … " She began crying on his shoulder.

"'fore I left home I was a nice Catholic girl… never thought of laying hands on a guy, never let a guy lay hands on me… I was a good girl before it all happened…, I would not be able to even tell you what happened at home." She kissed his ear.

"But you, an' you never even said your name…, you are some Angel, you are. I will never in my life forget you and what you have done for my sorry ass. Thank you, Mr. Angel… thank you…"

The people passing by were puzzled… it didn't seem that they were "a couple", nope, and it didn't seem like she could be his daughter, nope again. So, what was this anyway?

"I love you, Angel."

"…and I love you too, Lorri Anne. It's going to be all right now." And, the train whistle blew…

She smiled and hugged him again, gave him a kiss on the cheek and ran for the train. Landon watched her run off, as if when she got to the train gate she would be in Tulsa. Landon turned and walked out of Penn Station.

The usually empty paneled walls of The Room were covered with squared off note cards, stickie notes with phone numbers, torn bits of paper and the backs of bus schedules. Landon moved easily from the desk to this wall with more sticky information. There was a quickness to his step, and a lightness about his being, as if he could light bulbs with one finger from each hand.

In The Room on the matching wall on the other side of the door were larger sheets of paper with lines and boxes and arrows. He had printed and cut out blocks of copy and taped them onto the wall. It looked like a Bulletin Board at the Center of the World. His walking path was a triangle from one wall to the other to the keyboard of the computer placing lines of dialogue or narration and the intercepting ideas of another world.

He had been astounded at the statistics of it all—
kids on the streets:
In New York City last year, only the five boroughs,
there were between 6,640 and 8,454 kids on the street.
All but a handful of these were runaways.

Then a further breakdown of teens who were alienated from homeless families or who had a "dark" history with their parents and a smattering of other maladies. The demographics—at least in New York City were quite clear... the majority of kids were white and from rural areas around New York State, many from upstate. In addition, there were unfamiliar towns from downstate New Jersey or small places like Jennerstown, Blakeslee, and Cross Fork, Pennsylvania. Not to forget small towns around Danbury, Connecticut.

His sources had pointed out that it was rare to get kids from Chicago or Detroit or other large Midwestern centers. The closer they were to New York in their unhappiness, the easier to get on the bus or a train and come to Pennsylvania Station or the Port Authority... Landon had spent a night there with an NYPD cop, Hanson Knutson. Though Officer Knutson had grown up on Staten Island he certainly could have come from any of the places whose names he reeled off as if he had friends in each. Landon had the clear sense that he did, in fact, have friends there because he told many stories of helping kids get back home, with one large difference. They went home with an official notice from the City of New York that they needed help of one sort or another, to match the differing states of emotional stress each kid was under and it was often the case that the kid him or herself was the problem. Landon came to learn that life for a young person is not simple, even in the small towns of America…

…how could that be?

He sat back in his chair and reflected on his growing up in Maricopa. He had been a compliant teen, but he had known innumerable others who had trouble, either self-imposed or that had fallen onto their shoulders. Fact is, no matter what your situation, it's not easy growing up—and at the Port Authority last night the dark results of that were painful to watch. He thought of the 17 year old girl that Officer Knutson had gently braced last night. First of all, she was lying about her age, second of all, she was scared stiff despite a tough tongue. Officer Knutson could do little but arrest her for loitering, which was useless, so he nodded to Landon, suggesting that he might speak with the girl. Now, what was her name? Landon shuffled through his notes. Oh here, Marie-Louise Anders. Landon had talked with her briefly trying to get her story until a young guy came up to her and offered to see if he could help. Marie-Louise then went off with this young man leaving Landon to look after them, shaking his head in the realization of what had happened. Knutson was not angry but sad. He told Landon that 17 year old Marie-Louise would be spending a lot of time in cars circling The Corridor, taking on men who paid more for younger girls.

Landon shuddered.

Into the middle of this, in his developing New York story, Landon was going to place an out-of-state kid from an upper middle class family. A seemingly well-adjusted boy who has honorable motives, who makes personal decisions on a very different basis than his street peers. Landon stopped himself in mid-sentence… street peers. How, he thought, does any kid learn to survive in this environment? There is nothing in any of these lives growing up until you are 13 to 18 years old—no matter where that "growing up" had happened, to prepare them for this kind of New York street life. Landon had been told by those who interact at many levels with the kids that prostitution was almost always involved—Marie-Louse Anders was a case in point—these kids were forced to—by the simple arithmetic of street survival to become objects in a game that we all used to think involved only adults. Growing up on the street is quick and often deadly. Landon's 16 year old hero was going to have to become adept at not only his own survival but the survival of others he chose to help. Landon had forcefully changed his model from Morris Rubin and his "angel antics" to those of the boy, whose name would be Doug Osbourne Greene, who would be forced to change his name should his parents try to find him. The true impact of this would be that there is a 63 year old age and experience difference between the model and Landon's character who hits the streets. When he realized this it had a sobering effect on Landon. This, plus the fact that Landon had no first person experience of this. Research is one thing, but the need to have visceral sense was essential.

A writer is curious, a writer is a tightrope walker, a writer is a man or woman who wants to be other people, all this plus the adrenalin rush of putting your book out there and wanting to see it float away, not sink like a rock. The challenge of this is exhilarating and terrifying.

This triangular path in the room settled into hours at the keyboard. First, learn and study. Then, immersion. It was as if there were invisible strings between him and the walls where he had placed his notes. Occasionally he would rush to one wall or the other to check a detail and then back to the immersion tank for an outpouring into the keyboard, the pages flying by, only to be… His eyes drilled into what he was writing and a thought of the boy, Doug, his new hero and the challenges he is facing, that Landon is arraying in front of him! Responsibility would be an interesting struggle for him, a runaway kid in the worst of cities—to be responsible for your own actions... yes, Doug would come to New York as a runaway for his own reasons and then add on to that: help people, as a younger version of Morris Rubin. But... but... how could he be tested in a wider sense? How could he face something that the rest of us might have to face and come up with a different answer? An answer that may work, but has terrible edges of rightness and wrongness to it? Landon leaned into the keyboard as if it was a racing car at Monte Carlo with all the marvelous curves ahead.

Morris was the first to arrive. "In deference to your palate, Grace decided not to inflict Chinese on you a second time and has located a good Italian take out place." Before Morris could say anything, Landon continued, "...no, not pizza."

"Good," then Morris gave him a second look, "how did you know?'

Landon shrugged.

By the time Morris was taking off his jacket and looking out the windows the doorbell rang again. As Landon passed Morris, he wished it was possible to give Morris a view of the Park to take home with him. He seems to love it so.

"Hello, darling." Grace hugs Landon intensely. They kiss deeply. Morris interrupts his rubbernecking to look at them and smile. "When are you two going to move in together?"

Grace winks at Morris over Landon's shoulder and makes a mouth gesture suggesting silence and caution... SSSShhhhhhhhhhh. Landon turns, aware, and smiles dumbly at Morris. The Italian take out is conveyed to the kitchen where Morris detects more silence than activity.

Then came the after dinner storytelling.

"…you can't mean that… you just can't mean that!" said Morris.

Grace decided it was better to listen for the moment, and perhaps be even more circumspect to air her views later in bed. Landon was on a steady course. She had not seen him like this before. He listened better, he thought before he said things and now he had laid before them the very sobering idea of the book and he expressed it softly…

"I want to confront the idea of individual responsibility, nothing more."

Morris replied, "You want to wade in the religious pool of playing God!"

Landon smiled. "Well, philosophy aside, I am glad to see that this gets such a rise out of you. And, by the way, Morris, my angel, you are the one that brought this idea to the table. You were the one who stood holding the old woman over the East River and had strong feelings… strong urges to knock her unconscious and drop her in."

"But, I didn't… "

Landon broke in, "…you didn't have the courage to do so, and "courage" is not the word. I am not calling you anything but moral. No sin. And, in a way, sin is an issue here… we don't talk about it any more and I won't in what I am doing, but you didn't drop her in for purely moral reasons, right?"

Morris looked from one to the other for a long time. He took a sip of water. He did everything but get up and leave the room to think this over. Finally, "I was torn. You're right, but what I am trying to determine here, and my process works slower than yours, is what I was feeling, and **why**

I didn't save her that night, you know?" Grace and Landon knew that by "saving her", he had meant the very thing he avoided… he could have 'saved her' by letting her join the River that night.

Morris looked again from Grace, whose face showed great sympathy for him, to Landon who was more impatient, hoping for an answer. He was gaining confidence in noting that Morris had said, 'saving her that night'… meaning that saving her was not saving her, but that to really save her he would have had to do something that everything in his long life railed against. Landon was feeling better and better about his decision to make his character in the new book a teenager with few moral preconceptions—a cleaner slate to work with, he thought.

"…let's put this aside, shall we?" said Landon, "I will work it out."

Morris smiled, but had another thought. "…just for the sake of argument, what about that other decision? How will this episode with his friend, Bonnie, end? Will it be like the movies of my childhood and end with the 'do the right thing'… recall that you said that Doug, the teen boy who was trying only to be honest for and with his young friend, the one who is with him in that basement—it's a boy, I assume?"

"No, it's a girl and I don't know yet how it will end… there's a long way to go."

Grace took in a deep breath and at the same time had a small smile.

Morris licked his lips and continued, "Or, will your ending for her have a newer more contemporary moral… something out of a Arnold Schwartzenegger film where he kills everyone but does something in the last 40 seconds to make it OK…?"

Landon said, "I don't know. Honestly, Morris, I don't know. I haven't gotten that far in the book or my thinking. I just have a sense that this is moving in a right direction. Who is responsible? If we are responsible, then does that extend to the responsibly for another life?"

It lay there on the table between them. Grace got up to clear the debris. Morris got up to look out the windows. Landon went to a pad and made some notes—he smiled to himself and thought, well, you'll have to read the book to find out... yes... and, he added to himself, I have to work this out too... but they have given me an idea about Doug and his girlfriend, Bonnie.

They were preoccupied, each with their own thoughts, as they readied for bed. Grace gazed over to Landon and his ritual of taking off his watch and his ring to place them carefully on the dresser. He looked at the time, it was early for them to go to bed. She slipped into the bathroom and put on a negligée out of his sight, as if not to distract him with the radiance of her body—did she have marvelous breasts?—and came back into the bedroom to find him in bed reading.

"What are you reading?"

"The people at the Shelter Now gave me a booklet about them and their activities. It's quite interesting. And worse, I have lived in Manhattan all this time and have never heard of them. Doesn't show a very good level of awareness."

"No," she slipped in beside him.

He continued to read, while putting out his hand to take hers. She loved to hold hands in bed, and he knew that. Altogether, she thought, he has been good about being aware and sensitive to what she liked. She had no sense of a power play in bed with him.

In fact, she thought, it was as if when he took off his watch and ring that he took something else off and laid it on the dresser that she did not notice. She had thought of the discussions with so many girlfriends about men in bed... Marty was the worst of them, but the best about sharing activities, she was searingly honest about her love life. She had said once that she was most interested in finding a man who was willing to become a woman in bed. Who would let the woman lead as if it was dancing, which both Grace and Marty agreed it was. Some sort of a fantastic dance when it was true and good, and the rest of the time, like your first Tea Dance in high school. But that was all right too, they agreed. They fell out over the nature of what it actually meant to have "the man lead". Grace said she did not want to be the aggressor all the time, that she DID want to be 'taken'... and Marty, drinking a martini at the time, waved in the air, sloshing the clear liquid almost out of the glass, saying, "Well, I want to screw _him_."

Grace looked over at Landon.

"What's your thought?" he said.

"What's _your_ thought?" she responded.

"I asked first."

"How far are you going to go with your idea of letting the boy in the book play God?"

"All the way."

"Will that be all right?"

"What do you mean?"

"Will that hinder the book in getting people interested in it?"

"Do you mean am I trying to write a controversial book? No, I am not.

I am on my hands and knees here. I am most attracted to Morris' idea of angel. So I have created my own Angel, but one who won't have any preconceived notions about the deeper sense of morality… the kid is moral to my way of thinking, but he has a new twist on it. I hope to be able to make that instinctive within him. That is, he will instinctively do what Morris will not… and that is the interesting part of it for me. Past that, I have to make it real."

"Is that hard to do?"

"Yes. Very hard, and a challenge that I have not had up to now. But I have found two or three people who are helping me with that. The advantage is that I can also bounce the morals of this against them."

"And… "

"… so far so good. But you slid out from under the discussion tonight. I need to know where you stand on this."

"Do I have to tell you now? I mean, tonight. Can I think about it?"

"It's better if you don't think about it. If you can kick it out of your mind as it stands."

"Oh yes, I see what you mean… "

"Grace," he switched off his light and turned to her. She was silhouetted by the light behind her. He spoke softly again as he had earlier tonight. He leaned into her. "…you can't know—and it is difficult for me to realize this as well—but this book is racing out of my mind. As if my fingers were thoroughbred race horses rounding the three-quarter pole and the pages were spinning out of me. It's exciting in a most internal way to know that I am onto something, that I will be an author again, that I can keep lecturing at Stanford and that I will be making enough money to be able to keep you in the manner in which you are most comfortable…"

"Is this a marriage proposal?" she said, remembering that other night. "Do you want to marry me?"

"You know I do," he said.

She was thrown off for a moment, and then slapped him on the shoulder. "… and as you have said about other, equally important matters, I don't have to say now. I can think about it, even if I have already. You won't take 'yes' for an answer now?"

"Nope." His arms circled her body and held her tight, reaching up to turn off the light behind her knowing that the light from the Park would be enough to see her, and it didn't matter anyway, he was going to close his eyes and let her make the first move.

It seemed like minutes from the time that Grace shook Landon awake about her dream—to their racing up the Henry Hudson Parkway toward Connecticut and her home which had been the site of her dream. The tunnel of darkness at 4:48 in the morning provided a comfortable idyll for private thoughts… yet Grace kept coming back to the fact that she knew— k n e w—that Rather was in some imminent danger. Landon listened carefully to her words and the images behind them and they were out of his apartment in the time it took them to throw on clothes. She drove, and relentlessly. There was no traffic at this hour so they flew up and over the Parkways and Turnpikes to home. Landon wondered if this was a characteristic Grace shared with Catherine, or if he was trying too hard to duplicate persona. It would be all right to have a different woman, he kept saying to himself.

The let down was at home. The house was not on fire. The water still ran in the sinks. The house next door was still dark, but then it was still too early to get up. In the house they looked around for Rather. But he wasn't running out to greet them… Landon wondered if Rather wasn't smarter than they were. Why get up when there is no place to go? But, then, do dogs dream? And, if Rather dreamed, Landon would expect him to be with Horace Ryan and his sailboat instead of…

Curled up with Rather in the second bedroom was Timothy. Certainly they were sharing a dream, a dog-boy combo. Grace and Landon stood over them and wondered what had happened to create this ball of boy and fur, arms and paws overlapping as if they were litter mates. Landon suspected that this touching sight had a darker underbelly and he walked out of the room and downstairs. Grace found him with a glass of orange juice looking out the kitchen window at the house next door.

"What's your thought?" she asked.

"That no one is home next door."

"Oh… yes… of course." She walked to her own front door and out.

Landon watched her cross her own lawn and turn 'round the country fencing onto the driveway and path to Timothy's front door. She moved out of his sight then.

What is to become of Timothy? Landon thought, what indeed? He was amazed and horrified that he had seen the other end of Timothy's bad dream in Manhattan only days before. For kids who had been mistreated in a variety of ways, neglect is only one of the punishments for the sins of the fathers.

Grace retraced her steps from next door until she was standing in front of Landon.

"No one is home."

"Do you still have the mother's cell phone number?"

"Hmm… I wonder if I do…?" She began rummaging through scraps of paper in the kitchen. She turned abruptly and moved toward the stairs. He could hear her opening and closing things until her step was racing down toward him again. She had a notebook sheet in her hand with many scribbles. "Here it is." She looked at him. "What should we do?"

"Based on the experiences I have seen and heard this past week about the difficulties of kids, we can call the police… there is a network of social worker and state departments who deal with these problems—he paused for a moment and Grace said, "…or we can wake Timothy and ask him what he would like us to do."

"Or we can call his mom."

She looked at her watch. "That's my vote," and she reached for the phone. Dialed. Waited. Grace walked over to Landon and stood beside him as if he could hear the phone too.

"Hello, Mrs. Dalton…? It's your neighbor, Grace Mathisson."

"Yes, actually, something is wrong, but the danger is not that your house is burning—" then Landon mouthed… "or that your husband came home unexpectedly."

Grace repeated, "…that your husband came home unexpectedly and wondered where you are. Where are you by the way? Oh, yes, certainly… the meetings ran late and you decided to… oh, it's too pathetic. Your meetings may have run late, but not too late to get home to your child instead of falling into bed with someone closer… I can't tell you how upset I am about Timothy…" and she dropped the phone to her side. Landon reached over and took it out of her hand.

"Mrs. Dalton, this is Grace's friend, Landon Harris. We have Timothy here in Grace's house. We were in the city and came home late ourselves only to find that Timothy had needed some comfort—Grace had given him a key to her house to be able to visit our dog. When we came home we found Timothy curled up with the dog instead of home in his own bed with a parent in the room next door."

Landon got, for his clear explanation, a mouthful of anger and righteous, lying excuses. "All that may be true, Mrs. Dalton, but I would be happy to call the Connecticut State Department of Family Services and see if this falls into their jurisdiction or whether they think it's a matter for the police… or even better, I can call your husband—

Grace mouthed, "I think he goes to Atlanta…"

"…in Atlanta, and see if he would like to come home to see Timothy dressed and given breakfast before going off to school… it's your choice, really."

Landon listened and nodded. Nodded also to Grace as if to say, now the voice of reason is at the other end of the line. Hello, this is the Voice of Reason calling.

"Yes. Yes, Mrs. Dalton… you can? That would be wonderful. I know that Timothy will be glad to see you. In fact, I'll ask Grace if she will be willing to come down to the station to pick you up. Yes. No. No, we won't call Aaron in Atlanta… we'll just wait here for you, with Timothy.

"Bye, Mrs. Dalton."

He hung up. "Sleazy bitch."

"Worse, really." Grace moved toward the stairs and let her eyes look up. Landon looked at his watch. "How long will it take her to get here?"

"Couple of hours…" she looked at her own watch, turning to him. "Time enough to make you something to eat." She walked toward the stove. Landon put himself between her and where she was going. She walked into his arms. They stood together like that for minutes, each with their own thought. The boy slept unknowing upstairs with Rather.

"None of this would have happened without your dream and your willingness to live it, you know that don't you?" She nodded into his chest. "I admire you, Grace."

There is something soothing about eggs and potatoes and toast in the early morning while the sun streams through the windows. Buffeted by the problems that are past, present and coming, the act of eating breakfast is respite, holy respite. A man on one side of the table, a woman on the other. The child, no matter whose, upstairs with a head on a dog's side rather than a pillow. This is the equation of a moment of peace.

Landon and Grace shared it in silence. A look up occasionally. A gesture to pass the salt, understood in any language. The gentle touching of forks to plates, of food to lips, counterpointed by the rasp of butter to toast. Finally, a deep sigh that the world must be faced again in all its obtuse meanness and possibility for…

…what? Landon thought. Perhaps just a 'possibility' was enough. He grabbed his jacket for the ride to the train station with Grace.

In the car coming home Timothy's mother, was a trainwreck. She had not had time to apply make up and her face was a litany of the wine and song, gone sour. She was almost a poster child for the dark end of that... a life in distress, a home in disarray, an errant wife of—and we don't even know his side of the story. On the way back from the station, Landon sat in the back and told Sharon Dalton about the research he was doing for a book he was writing—and that it would be largely the street life of runaway kids. When she started to object, he told her about the social workers he had spoken to who described home lives that were more onerous than Timothy's but just as vacant... and that was really the point here, Timothy was feeling more of an absence than a presence.

When Sharon Dalton finally was confronted with the sight of her son hugging the dog Rather on Grace's made up bed on the floor, rather than his pillow in his own bed, she seemed to come to, as if she had been in a deranged sleep, which of course she had. But she felt it now. Landon pointed out, that even technically, Timothy had run away from home... maybe this time only next door, the demon that is more familiar is the one in 'another place', but a demon to the boy at least.

"Guess what he wants, Sharon?" said Grace. Sharon looked at Grace as if she had kicked her. Sharon kneeled on the floor and reached over to touch the cheek of the boy. She held her hand there to let him feel its warmth. Finally, he stirred. His eyes opened and he saw her, his mother, there with him. A soundless response. The boy disentangled his arms from Rather and put them around his mother, as she did to him. As Landon and Grace looked on, even if you didn't know what had brought each one to this time and place, you would feel a sense of fulfillment, of grace, of motherly love, of... home.

Sharon hugged Grace and Landon in turn, begged off the offer of breakfast saying that <u>she</u> would make breakfast for Timothy and herself even if that would make Timothy late for... and the doorbell rang. Grace was surprised and looked out the window to the front door. Not recognizing the person there, she shrugged and went to answer the door while Sharon and Timothy prepared for the journey home.

As they all converged on the front door, Grace was there with an attractive blond woman in her mid-forties. She was talking fast, as if to announce that she had limited time for this. Landon noted that Grace had not asked her in. The woman was saying, "...didn't have a lot of time to prep this visit, Mrs. Mathisson, but they told me at the hospital that you had Dad's dog and I need to take him with me."

Grace was in shock. When Landon appeared at the door she grasped his arm.

"I have been told that the dog is valuable and so I need to take him... sorry you were bothered with him... dogs are a nuisance, aren't they? But I'll take him off your hands."

Landon moved to Grace's side and said, "Sorry, I didn't get your name."

"Oh, sorry, Maddie Ryan. I am Mr. Ryan's daughter."

Landon smiled, "Good to meet you, Maddie. I'll bet you don't live around here."

"Nope, down from Manchester, on the way to Philly and I wanted to get the dog… I can't ever hold onto that crazy name… "

"Rather." Grace enunciated.

"Right. Well, if you can get him, I'll put him in the back of the car and be off."

No one moved.

Timothy pushed his way through the adults and said, "You can't take him. I need him."

"Well, son, I can take him and I will. Get your Daddy to give a hand here and I'll be out of your hair."

"Maddie, I wonder if I could get you to come in and have a cup of coffee and talk to us some about your plans for Rather?" said Landon.

The woman's head moved to the side and then back to Landon. "Sure," she said. They parted to let her pass and Grace ushered her into the living room. Timothy was right at the woman's side. "Why are you going to take Rather?" as if Rather was <u>his</u> dog.

"Well, I think your Mommy or Daddy could explain that to you," she said sitting.

The others arrayed themselves around her and sat.

"I think it might be helpful for you, Maddie, to know that Timothy lives next door and this is his mom, Sharon. He comes here to visit Rather all the time. Rather is," he looked at Sharon here, "very important to Timothy."

"Uh huh. I see," she said, not seeing.

Skipping to an easy explanation, "…and, Grace and I live here and knew your father very well. Marvelous old gentleman."

Finally, a softening in her face. "Yes, he was. I miss him. I'm the only family, you know."

"No, we didn't know that. We spent some time looking for family. But Horace made it clear before he died that he was very comfortable with us having Rather. We had made a good relationship with the dog as well as his Master."

"Uh huh."

Grace came in with coffee for Maddie and gave a cup to Sharon. "How 'bout an apple or banana, Timothy?" The boy shook his head, and finally sat next to the woman.

"Do you have a good home for Rather?" he said.

"Yes, of course I do."

"What are you going to do with him?" Landon was surprised at the boy's acuity, he had picked up the fact that the woman was doing this for procedural reasons, not out of love.

The boy continued, "I don't want you to take Rather. I…" he looked around him to Grace and Landon, "we really need him here."

"Where is Rather anyway?"

"He has a home upstairs," said Timothy, "a good home."

Maddie put her cup down suddenly and stood. "I'd like to see the dog now."

Grace stood as quickly. Instead of saying she would bring him down, she went to Maddie and took her arm. "Let me take you up to him." A forced budge, then movement toward the stairs.

The two women led the way to the room where Rather was. He was at the door, seeing Grace and wagging his broom tail. When Maddie walked up to him he backed up a step and his tail came to a halt. Maddie reached down carefully to pet him. Rather allowed it.

"Do you have a leash for him?"

Suddenly, no one had an answer. Finally Timothy piped up, "He just comes with us."

"Uh huh. Fine. Come on Rather." She started down the stairs and Rather sat down in place. Landon stepped up to her. "Maddie, I wish there was some arrangement we could make with you to allow us to take care of Rather for you. Perhaps until you come back from Philadelphia... make an easier car trip for you and for him."

"Nope, he has to come to Philly with me."

It was a rope with no slack. Worse, no knife at hand. Landon moved to the table in the hallway and picked up a sheet of paper. "Do us one courtesy, Maddie, write down here where we can reach you in Philly and Manchester. Just in case..."

"In case of what?" she said.

"In case we find something of your father's that we need to send to you."

"Uh huh. Well, do you have anything?"

"Some snapshots and a few letters, but not sure where to lay hands on them now." He handed her the paper. She went to the table and wrote a telephone number in Philadelphia and an address in Manchester, Maine.

"That work for you?" she said.

"Thank you." said Landon.

Now the problem came in getting Rather to go with her. Everyone but

Maddie sensed that, and she asked again, "You got a leash for him?"

"I have one at home... just wait, will you... " and Timothy raced down the steps.

Landon patted his leg and said, "Come on, Rather, let's go down for some breakfast."

The entourage moved from the upstairs hall to the kitchen to watch Rather have a dish of wet dog food. Timothy came back and handed Landon a dog leash. He looked at his mother to be sure he had done the right thing. Sharon put her hand on his shoulder and smiled down at him. I am here, she thought. I am not getting up in New York with a hangover, I am here with my son. She looked over to Grace and smiled shyly, as if to say something that was impossible to say. Grace nodded and looked at the boy.

"I hope you will bring Rather back," Timothy said.

The woman looked first at him, then at the adults and decided not to speak.

"I think what Timothy is trying to say is that we have all grown fond of Rather, as we were of your father. We had known Rather for some time before your father's death. It is the most difficult thing for us to part with him. We hope you understand that and if there is anything we could do to..." Landon implored her, "...to get him back, anything, why we would do it."

"Well, I'll think about it. Such a valuable dog, you know." She took the leash with Rather on it and pulled the dog toward her car. Timothy began crying, Grace was on the edges of tears herself. Sharon didn't know what to say or do. Only Landon saw that this would be even worse if Rather fought the idea of leaving with this woman.

"Let me help you," as he took the leash and released the strain on the dog's neck. Rather looked up at Landon and waited. "Come on, Rather, you get to have a nice ride today." He opened the back door to the car and urged Rather to jump in. Even with Landon's steady hand and voice, he hesitated. "Come on, Rather." Grace ran forward to hug Rather. Maddie stood by as if watching awkward children do something dumb simple. While Grace was hugging Rather, Landon leaned over to the dog's ear and said softly, "We'll see you, Rather, be patient with this woman. You'll see all of us again." In a loud voice he said, "OK. Rather, here we go…" and he urged the dog into the car and shut the door. Timothy's crying as the door closed intensified. Maddie looked over and shook her head, quietly she said to Landon, "Never saw so much fuss over a dog." Landon gave her a glazed stare back, hoping it wouldn't show the unbridled distaste he had for this woman.

"Have a good trip," he said. Sharon was right behind him with a dish of water. Landon took the dish and opened the door long enough to put the dish inside on the floor.

"Water," he said to the woman, now in the front seat. "He needs water, too."

As the car pulled away Rather looked out of the back window to a group of unhappy people and didn't know what happened, except that he was in a strange car with a strange woman. Animals know this.

Grace turned to Landon. "What are we going to do?"

"I'm going to the phone and call Gregg Bantam."

"Who's that?" asked Timothy.

"My lawyer."

"What can he do?" she said.

"I haven't the faintest idea, but fortunately he is a very resourceful person… and I believe he can find a way to get Rather back to us."

Timothy nodded, vacantly. Sharon brushed his cheeks with her tissue and lead him home. Grace and Landon stood on the front steps watching the empty driveway.

THE TENTH BOOK

from SHADOW ANGEL / Landon Harris Manuscript pps.

Section Eight

I teach survival school now. Word has gotten around and kids find me. Everything about this is stealth and scramble, but the words don't really have the right meaning. >teach< is just an idea of passing tricks that are nothing more than experience and observation. >survival< is real, but holding a class in survival is like asking bullets to hold in midair, while one teaches another how to dodge them. Sud and Shana were with me yesterday and I noticed that I am beginning to sound more together all the time. The words and the ideas stay the same but I am better at telling than when I started.

Now, there are rules.

Rule #1—no drugs. Don't sell drugs for anyone no matter how good or safe it sounds. It's neither.

Rule #2—no screwing for money, anyone. If you need to do it, find someone who is safe and who likes you. To be safer, you might like them. Use rubbers. Think how many needles there are out there and carry rubbers with you. Either sex. No excepts.

Rule #3A—Find yourself. Figure out why you are here and think about changing something.

Rule #3B—Think about the future. This is no time to think about the past. Get an idea. Talk to people. Go over to Shelter Now and find someone to talk to. These are good people.

Rule #4—It's okay to steal, but do it in pairs. One watches while the other sneaks. If you are one of a pair, be honest with your bud.

There are other rules, but I keep to the basic four food groups. I have learned that on the street, people have no patience for long stories. Short and sweet, like that was really possible out here. Sud and Shana have started doing it... I can tell now. I asked them if they are using rubbers and he says no. So, I give her a handful and tell her to make him use them. I don't tell her that he has been doing the gay thing for some extra cash. He cleans up fine so the money for him is good. We talk about how to get cash, and I suggest that one of them look for a job. His eyes glaze and I stop talking.

NYPD Houston West / Friday June 12 / Officer S. Hunts

Two white female, age 15 and 17 taken in custody to
Prct. 14 for prostitution in car parked at 261 Mott St.
Marie Windom, 17, has ID from Cherry Hill NJ. Other
girl has no ID and won't talk. Windom released to NY
Probation Div. South for action. No Name printed and
held pending. hearing.

We get over to 42nd St. and I ask Sud and Shana to look at the people here. They are all tourists. I point out to them that the Port Authority is just down the block. We go all the way to Times Square and I show them you can still see the P.A. Then I tell them a story. We sit in a coffee place and I get them to really listen to me. This is the story... >>> excuse me, but we have a personal problem... wonder if you can help. Me and my girl... Shana say hello to the folks... we been saving to get home and got just enough for bus tickets, we go to Ohio... do you know Youngstown? But they raised the fare and we need eight dollars more to buy the ticket. Do you see, there is the Port Authority >>>point to the P.A.<<< where we get the bus and it leaves in 25 minutes. We got just enough time to finally get home if you could give us the eight dollars.<<<

I get them to say it over to me. First Sud, then Shana. Then I get them to say it together, each one says part of it. Then I get them to say it in a rush, like time is running out. Then we hit the street and pick out a tourist couple to work it. First man waves them away... don't talk to them, he tells his wife. Second couple listens, looks at each other and pulls out a ten, gives it to Shana... the woman hugs her. Now, they have some confidence. I am always near enough to hear. I give them talk back so they can improve. Shana needs to look like she is there. One of them needs to keep looking at the P.A. as if it might leave 42nd and Eighth. We wait a half hour and move to the other end of the street and do it again. This time they get an even eight. So, eighteen dollars is enough. Don't hang around. Leave. Don't blow your ID. Work somewhere else. Get some new ideas. Think about where you want to be next month. Not here.

Port Auth. Manhattan West / June 12 /
Officers Kelly, DeLotto, Canfield
Three perps. grab and run at lover level P.A. 2120 hours.
In custody, Adam Massey, 16, Dawn Kentfield, 16
and Shawn Carwell, 17. Five victims assert that
they lost wallets, two purses and laptop computer.
Have names address of victims.
Holding three perps at Prct. 24 for hearing.

"Did you read this… all of it?"

"Yes, Canning, I did. Isn't it incredible?"

"But Celia, I don't understand. This has to be written by someone other than Landon Harris. He has stolen this, right?"

"Landon Harris has found a new voice. What's wrong with that, not only has he done something that every writer would like to do once in a while, but in addition, it's really good."

"Well, it's stunning, I'll say that for it, and him. Have you talked to him about this?"

"It arrived while I was down in Philadelphia Monday, and I have been reading it since I got back. I have read it twice now. The note says that he believes he can have the complete manuscript in our hands by next week. He wants to know what I think. I called him this morning and congratulated him on his—I still don't know what to call it—amazing concept. And, how real it seems. It feels very credible to me and I think that will be one of its selling points. Canning, I want to run with this. I want to call design and production and put this on the List we are hurtling out the door now. I want to get a freelancer to work on some extra publicity. I want to start sending out pieces of this, those that I have, to get some quotes. I think we have something very special here, a different animal, and I want to paper the walls with it."

"We should take it upstairs. Just for some backing, you know."

"Fine. Fine. But I have a plan in place now that I want to put into the works. It will take some time to go through the motions, and if I start to work now, by the time everyone gets through their shock of seeing something really different, God save us from "different and original", there will be no way this can get put off because there is not enough time. I will have used that time to make us ready to launch. What do you say?"

Canning looked at the pages in his hand and read some more. "Has he been talking to you about this. Has there been any indication this is in his mind?"

"No. Only that he asked me to find him some police and probation sources in Manhattan. That was weeks ago."

"He has done all of this since then?"

"It seems to be burning a hole in his... heart."

Canning looked up at her as if she had been quoting poetry. He got up and went to her side table where the manuscript was stacked. He lifted it and seemed to be measuring it.

He nodded to the heft of it and returned to sit. "How does this end?"

"It's a cliffhanger!"

Celia stopped and gazed out the window to the River. "He says he is re-writing and doing some 'touch up' on other parts."

Canning moved his mouth as if telling himself what to think. "I just can't get over the feel of this. It is not Landon Harris."

"Did you think that about the short stories?" she said, holding back.

"No, they are bound to be different, especially if you don't know their vintage. As we see here," he gestured to the portion of the manuscript in his lap, "time makes a difference to a writer. You and I have talked about how the writing can either slip away in one book or exceed its own promise in another."

Celia said, "You were the one who said he has a burning hole in his heart. On target. The short stories were a holding pattern, buying time after the severely limited 'eighth book'."

"…and he was trying out an idea about his lost wife and couldn't make sense of that…" she said.

"…did we talk about that?"

"Only briefly." Canning looked at her. She was a hard one to get to know, in addition, he sensed that there was a part of Celia that was drawn in visceral ways to Landon.

Canning thought back to the evening when he and Celia had drinks with Grace and Landon. He had a sense of Celia for Landon and against his girlfriend. That Celia wanted more than just to be Landon's editor, but in the same breath not to get too close to the… he wished he knew her sailing terms, one of them might do now, something to do with the ropes and the sails… or was it the helm? But no matter what, she was enjoying the sail itself and now it seemed there would be some gusting winds and, oh yes, he had heard her say, following winds. Go faster. He handed her the pages she had shared with him.

"Yes. Fine. Let's go with this. Get all the balls rolling and I will begin to set up a situation upstairs where we can be assured of the right answer. The List this season is strong, we can only win. If Landon hits big we'll do even better. If he doesn't it won't hurt. Get to your quotes people soon. We'll need that… what was it you said…? Landon Harris has found a new voice. Good line, only the folks at Barnes and Noble will think it's about singing."

They laughed. Just as he was getting to the door he heard her say,

"Thanks, Canning, you are a good Skipper."

Landon had fallen asleep on the bed in The Room. At 7:38 the phone rang. At first he thought it was a part of his dream, and he was somewhere in Lower Manhattan. Finally, a hand found the phone. "Morning, Landon, it's Greg Bantam."

"'morning, Greg. I thought lawyers didn't come to work until late morning."

"... ah, sorry Landon... want me to call back?"

"What time is it?"

"I can make this quick. I missed finding the woman in Philly, the woman with the dog, Rather. But she will be back in Maine later in the week. I spoke to her daughter who sounds more reasonable than the woman you described to me. She says I can call back on Thursday. Okay with you?"

"Fine, Greg, thanks..."

"Have a good day."

Grace thought of how much her life had changed in the past few months. She looked across the harbor to the point, around which she had spent her first night with Landon. Between the point and where she was walking now was where she first saw Rather. Life was so unexpected. She wondered if people who had better lives than others learned to search for the unexpected as if that was what to prize. You are living your life and suddenly there is a curve in the road, or better, a fork in the road, but one is the main road and the other is the unexpected—and you take that. It would be nice if there were road signs to help...

She had never seen a person so immersed in a creative project. Yet, even as she had the thought it gave her a tingle of pleasure to be with the man who was so immersed. How differently she sensed him since he met Morris Rubin in the Sailing Pond in the Park. He was, what is it... more

alive, yet more absent or distracted, more interesting, and finally, she realized, more intense with her. Yet when he was with her, there were moments
of the pure loss of him. But even that is different now. She remembered that
he would seem to go away for several seconds, just blank. But now that
seems to be gone… somewhere…. Now there is a sense of more continual
immersion—that word again—and a more vibrant awareness of her and the
details and people around him. In bed,   more marvelous, as if she and he
become some instrument that in itself creates. Even as it dissolves between
their bodies, she has a sense of it being there for that faction of an instant,
as if he is trying to tell her something and his body is the instrument.

Grace stops at the railing and looks out to the Sound. Three gulls circle
around her, yacking at each other. She knows that when this book is done
they will walk here in the morning, and if they are blessed, the dog Rather
will be with them. Her mind drifts to the love making and she is more aware
of the times when he <u>does</u> tell her things. He speaks in her ear and tells her
how much she means to him and he tells her small stories, stories that seem
unrelated to their lives, yet seem to be fantasies to share. One of them was
at a beach. She had been walking along, much as she is now, only there was
surf, rolling surf, and sand… was the sand a different color? Not sure. A
man was walking toward her with a dog. Was it Landon and Rather? No, it
was another man and another dog. Then, behind the first man and dog was
another, and she was thrilled that it was him, but again it was not. And then
again, and another disappointment. This seemed to go on for hours and then
suddenly, just as she had gotten used to the pattern of disappointment, it
<u>was</u> Rather. It <u>was</u> Landon. They greeted each other. The dog was excited
as usual, his tail brushing the sand all around them. Landon took off her
clothes and then his own and they both walked out into the surf, holding
hands… with the dog running after them.

Celia had written six letters since arriving at her computer this morning. She had a call from Nora about sailing this weekend. Nora had something to tell her, and No, she would not tell her now. The six letters all had the same message:

> I would love it if you would read this portion of a new book we are just getting out this season and give me your thoughts. Yes, know I am supposed to send you the whole book, but I can't and yet I think you may find these pages even more provocative. Think of it as a literary strip-tease. If you will do this for me, I will send you the completed book and buy you cocktails at your favorite watering place.

The idea of a "watering place" varied depending on the recipient. For one it might be 'joint', for another it would be 'expensive place', and then it might be 'high tea at Wonder Haus... or for Harold Spenski, it would be The Oak Bar at the Plaza. Appeal to the best and worst instincts of your colleagues, her mentor had said. So she did.

And, then Jennings Cormus came to mind. Jennings, Jennings, she thought, what a delightful scoundrel, a word that is not in common use, though there are several around, but particularly a literary scoundrel. One who can put himself in the mind of some of the writing greats of the past, but who can't get his own work published, even if he is sleeping with editors of both sexes in high places. But, he can write as if he is thinking like Upton Sinclair, a younger and lucid Hunter Thompson, an acid Gloria Steinem, a journalistic Tom Wolfe. Now Celia begins pacing in her office. Several people walk by and notice this in a glaring way, so she walks to the window and looks out to the Harbor.

What if she persuaded Jennings to write about the new style and penetrating idea behind Landon Harris' new book in the style and persona of those people or others like them that he may be more comfortable with. Yes! I'll call him now. She paused midway to her phone. Hmm, that means he will have to be fended off with promises, promises. Oh, well...

BRIDGES AND TUNNELS

*E*merging from the narrow tunnel of recent events, all taken together, Landon didn't like to dwell on them. The inner feeling of dishonor of using Noel Chapman's book, the confused attempts to make literary hay of his relationship with Catherine... all this fell away as he held in his hands a first copy of his tenth book... the New Book. That's the way he liked to think of it, as his-new-book. Finally, thank God and the Muses that he was back on track. His track as an author, as a creator of words as well as surprise for his readers, and his hope for the future—not to forget the miracle of Grace.

As he stood along the Hudson River, book in hand, soaking up the night and the River, he realized that she had been the bridge, his bridge over his sense of loss, both of Catherine and his profession. He had not realized, until Grace, that one person could be a bridge to another person, carrying them over the tumult and turbulent waters of life. As he approached the 72nd Street Harbor, Celia's favorite lunch hangout, he looked up to see the night lights of the George Washington Bridge hovering over the Hudson. Grace was like that, he thought, this marvelous lighted graceful structure. She was Landon's Bridge. At the same time, he realized that perhaps he had not met some of her unknown needs, that he may yet need to be a bridge to her. Had he been selfish? She seemed so even, so sensible, so present that it had not occurred to him that she might need a form of the same lift she had performed for him. As his gaze turned down river, he saw what was not to be seen.

One couldn't tell by looking at the Jersey shore where the Lincoln Tunnel arrived and departed. But, it was there, obscured by all that water… and further down river, its mate, the Holland Tunnel.

Landon smiled, thinking of a Steinberg cartoon in the New Yorker. It was a map he had drawn detailing the New Jersey "Invasion" of Manhattan with battle lines along Eighth Avenue moving uptown to the incursion along Central Park. The gifted man's crazy quilt map of New York. Crazy quilt might describe more than Steinberg's art, he thought, as he mused over his own good fortune at navigating through his own narrow tunnels and great escapes to the wide end, where the light was full. Full of light on this balmy night, his hand, a firm grasp on *Shadow Angel* and his new life. Along the docks, his eye fell on a loose plank, slightly bigger than his book, slightly thicker too. Landon picked it up. He stood there, book in one hand and wood plank in the other, and he thought it's time for a new ritual. He should not subject himself or Grace to a time that has past meanings. He would not think of her and say that they needed to put candles on <u>this</u> <u>book</u> and read it all night long. That belongs to another part of the *tunnel* and now we are at *bridges*. He patted his pocket to see if he had a book of matches to go with this new book of his. Yes, in the dark he placed the book of matches on the plank, tucked the flap of the matches inside the pages of the book and set alight the live matches sticking out of the pages. Quickly, he set the book shrine onto the water and watched it catch the current out to the middle of the River. A small recognition of the past, a small hope for the future, and a flashing light moving out, out into the river current. He was surprised how long the matches held, almost until he couldn't see them, before blackness took the vanguard of his new crossing—no more inside the river tunnel, but now always approaching the next bridge.

At his feet, on the decking, he saw the note from Celia that had come with the book, and then, unnoticed, the ripped out newspaper review that had come attached to it.

Another Side of Landon Harris by Genevieve Cates

A new book, *Shadow Angel*

Landon Harris has shown us a multitude of great favors in his new book, *Shadow Angel*, by showing us another side of himself and his writing style. In the language of the authorial, he is allowing us to hear another voice of style and point-of-view. In the patois of his leading character, all the above applies as well. Doug Osbourne Green is the Shadow Angel of the novel, and by the way, that is his real name, yet we never learn the "street name" he assumes as he becomes one of New York's thousands of runaway kids. This is his other side as he runs away from an upper middle class life in another city because his parents are those we hear so much about these days—they are too involved with their own lives. They have abandoned their son to give primary attention to their workaholic lifestyles, leaving him on his own. A familiar situation, but as this family falls apart, Doug decides he is not going to follow the norm. He will opt out not realizing that Landon Harris will describe a new life for him as Shadow Angel.

It's not clear at the outset that the boy, whatever his street name is, has decided to give himself a new role to live up to at age 17. But, he grows into it as we look on helplessly. We do so with pride as the boy helps the lost kids of New York learn to live on the streets with a modicum of morals, a tablespoon of savvy, and always with his helping hand in the mix. What we are not ready for is <u>his</u> instinctive ethic. He proves to himself that a girl younger than he, more lost and more troubled, that he wants desperately to help, but he can't. The quandary is: should she be put out of her pain? Now, Harris and Shadow Angel must prove to us that this other side of life they have wandered into is safe and right moral ground.

It's a hard sell, yet what we cannot deny is the force of the mirror that Harris and the boy are showing us. The underside of our own city in the face of the children we have allowed to be lost, and it's most clear that we do bear this responsibility for we have failed them. The scenes, for instance, in New York's Shelter Now are most revealing. This is a place most of us have not been. It is dedicated to the idea that all kids can be saved and they do save hundreds. It is a devastating picture that holds out promise.

The image we see through Harris eyes and new voice is a stylistic one. This is not the Landon Harris of his recent collection of short stories, the lukewarm novel that preceded it, nor even of the seven books that led him and us down this path. This book is pungent and direct, a no holds barred use of first person narrative and official reports from the battlefield as Doug and his alter ego move through the new life they have found in the streets using their new found morals, picked from these streets like black concrete flowers. To make it better, or for those readers who are inured of pat answers: to make it worse, in the end, Harris and the boy leave us to determine where is the right and wrong of this. It is as if they are say- ing to us, "Well, if you want to be appalled by this, then tell us what your solution is. It worked on me. I sat for a half hour after this strong read trying to determine for myself what the right of this was, and where they might have gone wrong. It's a raw edge, a horrific new-old world where the dogs are still eating the dogs. The single message: take better care of your kids before they decide to take things into their own hands, and I for one am willing to let Doug, as Shadow Angel, make the choices.

As you will see, from Harris' breakthrough novel, the Doug of *Shadow Angel* has some remarkable solutions to show us older folks with little imagination.

Nice review, thought Landon. He mused for a moment, and then thought, it's nice to have a character one can respect... particularly these days, a teenager. He smiled to himself... and particularly not to forget the older person who has lived and learned and shown us another way to be and think. He was glad that he had dedicated his book to Morris Rubin. Well, he thought, maybe there's only one more thing to do… go down there and look around and say 'thank you' and 'goodbye'…if a place could wish us well, maybe this place can do it.

"Oh, Landon… really… no, you're kidding me… the National Book Award." Grace was not certain with him about this, his face seemed to belie what he was saying, as if he was kidding her. But, he nodded and had a deadpan smile.

"Yes. Yes. The National Book Award nomination."

"But, isn't that one of the big deals?"

"It is indeed one of 'the big deals'."

She felt happy, even though she was straining to believe it, but there seemed something else in motion here. "I am very happy for you," she moved to him and put her arms around him and held him tight. What incredible good fortune and how lucky she was to have found such a gifted man. Not only that, but she loved the new book, so intent, so serious and such a fine new thought in it. She would not have believed it.

"I am happy, Grace, and I am also pleased that I can share this with you. That's important to me as well."

He paused. "I think you know that I am not a very spontaneous person, that we have had some time together that must have been puzzling or bewildering or well, whatever."

He paused to look at her.

"I would like to say that 'we' have been talking about getting married, but I know you are the heart and thought leader here—if you weren't..." He smiled at her, "...it would be easy to see that we wouldn't do anything but roll in the hay. You are a very good roll in the hay..." Grace smiled her biggest, but was still tense waiting to see where, indeed, this was going....

"Let's get married." He got down on one knee and said, "Grace, will you marry me?" She threw herself at him... yelling "...are you kidding?"

PORTMAN PUBLISHES!

Is Pleased To Present The First Chapter Of

A New Novel By

Landon Harris

Shadow Angel

Edited By Celia Langhorne

NOW IN BOOKSTORES

SHADOW ANGEL

by Landon Harris

My real name is Doug Osborne Greene. When I was in grade school, the teacher used initials in class one day and everyone learned that mine were D.O.G.—so I was called Doggie for years. When I was in high school and divorce crunch time came with my parents, I decided I needed a new name and changed it when I left home. I drifted around Detroit for awhile and learned that I couldn't do much there. I met a social worker there, Jane Wynant, and she told me I would end up in the lock-up. Michigan laws say that runaway kids can be put in jail. She said there were more runaway kids in New York City than in any other place in the country. So, I asked around and found a ride to New York. Jane gave me enough money to get me a start here.

I am living in the basement of a deserted storefront on 15th Street near 12th Ave. I can walk to the river. I am trying to find a way to move my space upstairs, but it's not really safe. I am trying to find a way to get a computer. I need to get onto the net.

Detroit Metro/Dept. Social Services/
Wynant, Jane (off the record). April 12.

Gave D. O. Greene, aged 16, $350 out of the Fund. Needs to get out of town. Says he is going to New York on a mission, my phrase not his. Not certain what is going to happen to this kid. He's a ringer, very different, very determined. Semi-unskilled on the street. I gave him numbers to call here in Detroit if he needs back-up. God help him.

When I first came to the city, I walked for a week, maybe more. Just walked. I wanted to see it, feel it and have it feel me. It's like one of my puzzles at home, what I had noticed was that I would get a puzzle box and I would pour it on a table and begin to fit it together. One day when my folks were screaming at each other upstairs I was finishing a puzzle picture. I put the last handful of easy pieces in. At the end, it's always easy, like I could drop the pieces on the puzzle and they would almost fit themselves. Then, I thought, hey, all the pieces always fit. I never had a puzzle where there was one piece left over, or one short. All the years, since I was small, I did jigsaw puzzles, everything fit. What a lie!

I stood in the middle of the East Village and thought, what a lie! In the puzzles for kids, all the pieces fit neat and easy. I looked around me at the mess of this place and how nothing fit, how no one was looking to put the pieces together and make them into this cool picture. All there are here are pieces from hundreds and hundreds of puzzles, one, two pieces from this one, one piece from that one, like a blind mother was scattering them all 'round, and we all landed here in New York City. Right after that, I met Sardo, maybe a year older than me. All these kids have crazy names. He had a crazy face. He was two or three misfit jigsaw pieces glued together. Street rags, white shoes that hadn't been white for years, green paint smeared on them, and a hat that looked foreign, but no bill so he couldn't wear it backwards. But, it was his face. More tattoo than white skin, as if he was going to hide who he was. All the shapes had pointed edges, and the pointed edges fit into his face so it looked like he had some crazy shaped mask. Then everywhere on his face is rings, tiny silver rings, must have had ten or fifteen rings on his face. Everything he said was pointed too, angry, wants to hit you. I had thought before that if you were a dealer, you had to be invisible, see, so no one would notice you. He was the flip side of that. He would stand at a street corner and pass dope like he was giving away balloons. Later I found out that he had a "shield". That he had a woman looking out for him, and she would signal him if it was goin' down. He saw me watching him. After awhile, he walked away from me, turned around and came toward me and stopped close beside me, and whispered, "Hey, Mother, want to lick me rings, I got 'em on my ditty too, kiddo. If'in you don't want a hurt, git. Jus' git."

> *For Immediate Release, Shelter Now, May 5*
> *Andrew Will, Executive Director of Shelter Now, New York—*
> *a large shelter for runaway and homeless children and*
> *teenagers is announcing its Annual Fund Drive to serve*
> *its shelters in the United States and in Canada.*
>
> *Mr. Will is quoted as saying, "I am sorry to say that*
> *our business has been better than ever. Despite advanced*
> *funding last year, we have been hard put to keep our own*
> *books in the black. The number of runaway kids in New York*
> *alone last year reached 8,763 in the five boroughs. This is*
> *up from 8,454 last year. I don't like to point fingers, but more*
> *time and care spent at home would certainly reduce our*
> *funding needs and increase the number of safe children...*
> *which is our goal."*

I had been over to La Guardia again. I had been watching dressed up street folks work the tourists. I took a walk and then I saw this bridge that goes over to Riker's. I didn't know what Riker's was, fact, I got it mixed up with Ellis and all that tourist baggage. No one was on the bridge but this woman. I watched her, wondering where she came from and what was on the Island. Then, I noticed she was a Nun. Short grey skirt, white blouse and grey sweater and a headpiece, but simpler than the regular Nun ones. It takes four or more minutes to walk the bridge and I kept watching her 'cause she was the only one walking. I supposed there was a church on the Island, but I couldn't see one. Then I saw her look at me. But she was looking at everything, like she did this five times a day, and she was looking for something new or different. She kept looking at me, so I decided to move away and I walked from the bridge and sat further away, behind a tree along the strip way. When she got over the bridge, she turned and walked to where I had been, and then on past that to where I had moved to. She sat down beside me and began to read a small book she pulled out of her pocket. She wasn't carrying anything. She didn't look at me. She read in her book. I guessed it was a Bible. I saw later it wasn't. We sat there together for half hour, not noticing each other. Truth was I was scared to leave, but I wanted to. Finally, she turned to me and said, "You want to tell me now?"

I must have looked really stupid. I had been watching her all the time over the bridge, now we had sat together for a half hour or longer, and suddenly it's like we are buds. Definitely not like she is an older woman and I am a kid. Definitely not like we are strangers and this is New York City where no one makes eye contact unless you are trying to get a John. I knew I was not her John. I wanted to say that I wish she had asked me that question before Bonnie died.

Journal entry, St. Mathew's, September 17

I met this most unusual young man... I asked him how old he was, 17 now, he said. He asked me why I spoke to him, and I told him we try to speak to everyone young, we believe that all the young people in New York have something to say to us, so we listen. He asked me why I was a Nun, and I told him that I believed in Jesus and the ideas of the Bible and the Saints. He asked me about angels, but did not continue that idea with me. What is unusual about this young person is he is not of the street like the others. He is better educated than the others who come from rural areas. He was different, almost an aura about him, but what it was I could not determine. He asked me if I was safe to talk to, and I said I was. He asked me if I could help him with a problem he had. We made an appointment to meet next week.

Sister S.

It was Marty who took over the plan for the wedding at the Westport Harbor. That the identity of the best man was either unknown or a secret was the intriguing idea and she jumped at the chance to make this happen. Landon had made it known that he would like to be IN the harbor for the ceremony, and Grace had insisted only on a lovely day. Pretty easy. As the participants would be few, Marty had a clear field. This was going to be fun! Even better, Marty was to be the Maid of Honor. First thing she did was to engage one of the men from the Harbormaster's office in her scheme, which was to get a raft set up with a bridging walkway from the docks on the far end of the harbor near the point. The man said it was do-able, but complicated and why didn't Marty decide to have the whole thing on the shore, where there was already a place to put everyone. Marty zoned in on him with the attendance list: seven people and a teenaged ring bearer.

"So," said Henry Camper, "it don't need to be a very big raft, eh?"

"No, but already I miscounted, there will be a preacher and he makes eight."

"Makes no difference. I can do that 'un."

"Fine… and the little bridge, too?"

"Yeah, that too."

"Good," and she gave him the dates.

The Maypole was Marty's idea. That there would be a tallish pole, that it would have ribbons coming down from the top, that each ribbon would have a name of the person who would attach themselves to that ribbon, that Grace and Landon would be on opposite sides of the Maypole. She stopped for a moment and considered this outrageous idea, and then stopped to consider Landon's description of his stepmother as a fairly stern, no nonsense western woman. Marty tried to see Jane Simpson holding her ribbon going 'round and 'round. It didn't work very well, but she went ahead with the plan anyway. What a fun idea, she thought. And, she began to determine how many ribbons she would need. One for the minister, who would be the local Lutheran preacher, one for Timothy who would be the ring bearer, one for Marty herself, one for Morris Rubin, two for Landon's parents, one for Canning Vogel who would be the Portman representative… Marty wondered about this. Did an editor from a writer's publishing house come to an author's wedding? And, what about the woman editor Marty had heard about, Celia Langhorne? Why wasn't she coming too, or instead? Marty shook her head, things are always complicated, even at a wedding. Or is it especially at a wedding? She recalled the recent wedding of a friend, and noticed that one woman was trailing three ex-husbands… well, maybe 'trailing' was not the word, but they were there.

As the week wore on, Marty would come down each day to watch another piece of her "ceremony idea" come together. The walkway/bridge from the landing to the space where the raft would go, then the raft, then the Maypole—and then regrets that the Maypole was not on the raft. And, then the handrails on the raft, just in case anyone had final last thoughts. Marty smiled and tried to picture either Grace or Landon diving and swimming off toward the Harbormaster's tiny house when asked the final marital question: Do you, Landon Harris…? Do you, Grace Mathisson…? Finally, Marty realized she was projecting. It was not either of them that would swim away, it was her. The next thought that came rushing at her was about the Maypole and why she had it put up. Another projection of her own fears of flying… marriage… commitment. Well, she was glad Grace was getting married and to Landon. Grace was more sensible than she was, more able to bring stability to the table. Marty sat down on the bench at the landing and considered her own love life and what everyone would say when they saw the Maypole. What the hell, she thought. It's just for fun.

SHADOW ANGEL

by Landon Harris
(from a later Chapter)

Metro North Security   Internal Report

*All officers need to be more vigilant about
soliciting of passengers in Grand Central. Complaints
are increasing by 9% of incidents involving panhandling,
theft of articles, and WCFR on the trains.*

*NYPD will be instituting new procedures to deal
with these infractions without need for arrest or booking.*

Back at Grand Central with Sid and Crissy and a new kid we just took into Our Shelter, he says his name is Brandt. Funny how after awhile you can tell it's a ringer. Not a real name, not a real person, just another new kid in town trying to create a life for himself. He's 17 like me. Says he's from California, some small town with a funny name. Tularary or something in a big valley. No one believes him 'cause they can't say the name. I laugh out loud at Hillary when she says " if I can't say the name, he must have made it up." Hillary wants everyone to be from someplace she can spell or at least heard of. Like L.A. or San Francisco. Kenny asked her if she knew the names of any other towns in California and she walked away from him.

Now, we are showing her how to brace women. It seems like we have found out that women will give girls money. Easier than men. Hillary is attractive and looks older, like Molly with smaller tits is the main diff. I let her drift off and try out her line. She is getting 2 to 10. Well, that's a living. I am tired tonight so I go to the wooden benches and sit and wait for Hillary to come back. The benches are crowded at rush hour and I squeeze in between a girl and a big black guy with this huge briefcase.

I eye the case and wonder if he will ask me to watch it while he goes to get a ticket or something. It looks like it has gear in it, valuable gear. He keeps looking at his watch and then this white woman comes up to him and he gets up to go with her taking the case. I look at the girl on the other side of me. She is pretty and about my age. She is wearing a blue dress and nice shoes. She notices me looking at her and I look away. She says something to me, but I don't hear it right and turn to her. She smiles, and says that she thought she recognized me, from the way I was looking at her. Did I live in Port Chester? Nope, I say, dumb. Near Port Chester, she says. She thinks she has seen me on the train she takes. Nope, I say, dumb. I don't know what to say to her I realize. It's been so long since I—since I what, talked to a real girl, one that I might have gone to school with. I realize then that it feels like years since then. I wonder if I am a different person.

My name is Meredith, she says, Meredith Hope. She got me there. Nice name I say. Got *hope* in it. She smiles. That's nice, she says. Most kids rhyme it with dope not hope. I shrug at her. Dumb kids, I say.

We talk for awhile. She tells me she lives at Port Chester and is surprised that I don't know where that is. She goes to East High School there and is a Junior and is trying to decide where to apply for college. She asks me where I want to go to college, and I realize I need to get away from her. I start to get up and she holds my arm. Where am I going, she wants to know. Am I going on the same train as her? I can't go on any train, I gave all the money I had to Molly. I shrug and say I lost my train pass. I look up quick at the board that has the train towns on it and say I am going to Bridgeport. Oh, she says, as if we were neighbors, I have some friends there. And she rattles off some names, now I know I need to leave, but she is such a nice person I don't want to. I start to leave anyway and she grabs me again. I'll pay for your fare to get home tonight. She takes my hand and takes me to the ticket booth and buys me a ticket to Bridgeport. When we leave the booth, she smiles and says, secret like someone will hear us, that I can get off in Port Chester if I want.

Suddenly, I realize, and one of the Metro cops gives me the thought. I say to her that she really shouldn't be talking to strange kids. She could get into trouble, I say and start to leave. She looks right at me and says that she knows I am not that sort of person.

This hasn't happened to me since I left home. A nice girl talks to me and I am not a criminal threat to her or her family. I don't have to worry that the Metro cop will come back and jug me for talking to a nice girl. A nice girl tries to help a person, and I am that person. Does this mean I am real? Does this mean that I am home in Detroit again, and around nice girls all the time? So, when her train is called, she gets me up and takes me to the right track. I have never been on a train but I don't say that. I just go with her and we are talking as if we had the same home room. She tells me about her family. She has a mother. She has a father. They like each other. She has no brothers or sisters and she is sad about that, but they are a good family. We are on the train and I watch her to do the right thing. I see now that I am scruffy. All the people on the train are business commuters and dressed. We are the only kids, and she looks better than I do. She tells me the schools she is considering for college, she tells me she had a boyfriend but he was more interested in football and she thought that was dumb. She tells me her boyfriend kissed her. I asked if she liked that—I was thinking of Bonnie. I kissed Bonnie and she liked that and so did I, but I haven't kissed any girls here, though Molly offered to do me for free, and some other girls have made a play for me. Meredith doesn't lay a hand on me or try to kiss me and I am relieved. I don't know if I will be able to do that again. When it is two stops from Port Chester, Meredith asks me if I will come home to have dinner with her and her family. She thinks I will like them, they will like me, she says. I don't know what to say. I don't even know how to get back to Grand Central tonight. Well, if I can teach the other kids how to get money to "get home" I guess I can too.

The man in the uniform on the train yells Port Chester, and Meredith looks at me as if I am twisting her arm. Please, she says. I nod. Sure, all kids like me get invited to have dinner with nice girls in blue dresses. Happens every day in midtown. It's boring it happens so much.

We get off the train and she is looking around until she sees a car and she grabs my hand and we run to the car. She opens the back door and shoves me in. She gets in the front and the driver, her mother, looks at her and gives Meredith a kiss and then looks at me. I smile and say I am Terry Masters. Meredith jumps in and answers all her mother's questions as if I wasn't there. Her mother nods and smiles and looks at me. I know she is trying to scope this out, that Meredith doesn't bring a strange friend home very often. I wonder if this can turn out badly. I hope not, well, I am with the Hope family.

(To be Continued)

Grace got her wish. It was a lovely day for the ceremony. A gentle warm breeze off the Sound.

Earlier, Landon had walked around the point from the B&B where they had spent their first night together, and unknown by the others, except Marty, where they would spend this night together.

Now, he stood at the center of the raft, flanked by Morris Rubin in a business suit and Ashley and Jane Harris. Landon's eyes continually made the trip from the place where Grace would be brought, along the walkway, across the bridge to the raft and alongside him, guided by Marty. He thought again about the symbolism of the raft, that tenuous collection of wooden planks that can weather the storm though somewhat wobbly. A portable floor that is often adrift but is always wishing to be moored in safe harbor.

Ashley Harris watched his son closely. This was a different man who stood here now, not the young, impetuous person who had married Catherine in a civil ceremony in Manhattan and then repeated the ceremony again, at his father's request, in the patio of the ranch house in Maricopa. That person, that Landon had been restless, but had a steady gaze. This Landon, dressed in a light beige business suit with a yellow tie, was steady but had a restless gaze. He watched Landon look out to Long Island Sound and wondered what he was thinking.

Landon wondered if Celia was out there making a long reach along the Connecticut coast in her marvelous sailboat. He owed so much to her, yet she declined the invitation to the ceremony, saying that she had commitments to her sister, Nora. Landon asked Celia if she would come and bring Nora with her. 'Nope, sorry, but it's Nora's day out.' In the end, Canning asked if he might be invited. Yes, but in this minute, with Canning standing beside him, Landon wondered about Celia, her boat, long reaches and how grateful he was to her for the many miles she had stood by him through the tunnel, into the sunlight.

This is the end of the tunnel and the real beginning of the sunlight. A horse neighed and Landon shifted his gaze to the place where Grace was stepping lightly to the ground. She took his breath away. A pale yellow dress with light, breezy tulle, holding a large bunch of white flowers. It was the feeling of her that hit him, the sense that he would be joined with her and in that special moment was the strongest feeling he must have had in his whole life. The electricity of love, the poets might say, coursing through his body. He must have moved, for he felt his father's hand at his shoulder, as if to steady him.

The whole sense was as if Marty became a guiding spirit down the walkways of the dock and landing, across the bridge—across one of the many bridges Grace had walked across for him—to the raft and beside him.

Ashley and Jane nodded to her and Jane whispered something to Grace that Landon didn't hear. Timothy moved close to Grace and leaned up to kiss her cheek and opened his jacket to show that he had the ring. Grace clung to Marty's arm until Landon took it himself. Just then a waft of wind caught the ribbons on the Maypole and everyone on the raft looked again and wondered what in the world that thing was, and if it was to be some final marital wish that they all walk around it and be joined. It was the Lutheran minister who had the deepest look of wonder, and turned it into a beaming smile at the bride and groom. More wonder yet.

"Dearly beloved, we are gathered here in the presence of God…"

Morris interjected softly, a whisper, but a stage one meant to be heard by everyone, "Excuse me, but, there is one more participant to our group," and he lifted his eyes toward where Grace had come with the buggy.

It was Rather, the three-legged dog, who was leaping ahead of a short bulky man, Greg Bantam. Rather had a white bow tied to his golden neck, and a red vest with one front leg running along the wooden decks toward the ceremony.

Rather seemed to be smiling, and Landon knew the dog had a view of the world that usually made him seem to smile. What a view of the world! Marty braced herself in case the dog should jump on Grace, who was completely off balance turning to Landon. Grace's look to him was aged with the events of the past few months, spiced with the sparkle of the day—their wedding day, and now with this lovely… this wonderful surprise. Just as Rather hit the bridge to the raft, Grace kissed Landon, while the minister tried to say, 'not yet, please, we have to conform to the ritual here.'

They turned together, Landon and Grace, to receive the leaps of joy from Rather. Marty was taking pictures with her cardboard camera as fast as she could. Jane looked at Ashley and squeezed his arm.

Morris, the clearest head on the raft, looked the minister in the eye and said, "Now we can proceed with the wedding ceremony, Sir. The Best Dog has arrived."

www.ingramcontent.com/pod-product-compliance
Lightning Source LLC
Chambersburg PA
CBHW022151260626
47155CB00017B/274